MUSIC THEORY TRANSLATION SERIES, 3

Claude V. Palisca, *Editor*

The assistance of the Martha Baird Rockefeller Fund for Music, Inc., is gratefully acknowledged.

PREVIOUSLY PUBLISHED VOLUMES IN THE MUSIC THEORY TRANSLATION SERIES:

1. *The Practical Harmonist at the Harpsichord*, 1708, by Francesco Gasparini, translated by Frank S. Stillings, edited by David L. Burrows.

2. *The Art of Counterpoint*, Part Three of *Le Istitutioni harmoniche*, 1558, by Gioseffo Zarlino, translated by Guy A. Marco and Claude V. Palisca.

HUCBALD, GUIDO, AND JOHN ON MUSIC

THREE MEDIEVAL TREATISES

Translated by Warren Babb

Edited, with Introductions, by Claude V. Palisca

Index of Chants by Alejandro Enrique Planchart

New Haven and London, Yale University Press

1978

Designed by John O. C. McCrillis
and set in Baskerville type by
Asco Trade Typesetting Limited, Hong Kong
Printed in the United States of America by
The Murray Printing Co., Westford, Massachusetts.

Published in Great Britain, Europe, Africa, and Asia (except Japan) by Yale University Press, Ltd., London. Distributed in Australia and New Zealand by Book & Film Services, Artarmon, N.S.W., Australia; and in Japan by Harper & Row, Publishers, Tokyo Office.

Library of Congress Cataloging in Publication Data
Main entry under title:

Hucbald, Guido, and John on music.

(Music theory translation series; 3)
Includes bibliographical references and indexes.
1. Music—Theory—Medieval, 400–1500. I. Hucbald of Saint Amand, d. 930. De harmonica institutione. English. 1978. II. Guido Aretinus, d. 1050? Micrologus. English. 1978. III. Cotton, Joannes, 11th–12th cent. De musica. English. 1978. IV. Babb, Warren. V. Palisca, Claude V. VI. Series.
ML170.H82 781 77–1331
ISBN 0-300-02040-6

Contents

Preface

The fields in which this volume aspires to make a contribution—the history of theory and that of plainchant and early polyphony—have enjoyed a remarkable growth in English-speaking universities and scholarly circles. Yet very few of the fundamental documents are adequately translated into English, or for that matter into any modern language. Names such as Hucbald of St. Amand, Guido of Arezzo, and John "Cotton" are dropped frequently enough, but their treatises are known directly only to handfuls of scholars practiced in the musically technical Latin of the Middle Ages.

Syntactically the ancient prose of these treatises presents few problems; indeed, it is often primitive. The real difficulties for a modern reader stem from the authors' lack of a theoretical tradition and a consistent vocabulary and our uncertainties about the contemporary musical practices they describe. At every step of the way documents of this sort demand, before and beyond translation, interpretation.

To render the authors' ideas into the normal language of music theory while preserving as faithfully as possible the literary form of the original has been the goal in these three translations. They are intended for reading quite apart from the original by those mainly interested in the content of the texts, but they can also serve to make the Latin accessible, and this is encouraged by page numbers of the standard edition in brackets.

Although historical and philological considerations and theoretical positions underlay the multitude of decisions made by the translator and editor, we have not claimed space to defend these in elaborate annotations. This series has aimed to present texts as free of costly encumbrances and accretions as possible so that they may appeal to and reach a wide variety of students and scholars both within and outside the music field. Footnotes have been kept to a minimum: to mark emendations in the Latin text, to identify authors cited, to indicate the most important debts to earlier authors (though not exhaustively), to clarify obscure terms and references, and to illustrate music cited. A glossary of equivalent terms was prepared but is not here published, because medieval terminology cannot be dismissed in a few succinct definitions. The proper approach is happily being pursued by the ongoing *Handwörterbuch der musikalischen Terminologie* under the direction of Hans Heinrich Eggebrecht and the editorship of Fritz Reckow and published by Franz Steiner of Wiesbaden. Unfortunately, the earliest installments of the *Handwörterbuch*, of 1972, 1973, and 1974, arrived after the translations and annotations were nearly in their final form, so no references are made to this exhaustive lexicon, but readers are encouraged to consult the entries *clavis*, *diaphonia*, *organum*, and *tenor*, already published, and others to come.

My predecessors as general editors of this series, David Kraehenbuehl and Richard Crocker, decided upon the policy to submit each translation to an editor expert in its field who would carefully check it against the original word for word. I have continued this policy, but usually found it easier to assume the role of editor than to assign it to someone else. John's treatise, which was first prepared under Professor Crocker's custody, received this kind of vetting at two stages of its evolution. Upon Professor Crocker's bidding, Janet Knapp verified the translation's fidelity to the original before it was submitted to this series in 1968. For Professor Knapp's advice and consultations Professor Warren Babb and I are enormously grateful. After some regrettable delay during which I edited the Guido translation, my own comparison of the English with John's Latin confirmed Professor Knapp's opinion, though I felt that numerous details needed to be reconsidered in the light of our aim to make the translations transparent to non-specialists and to remove unwanted Latinisms. The revised translation of John that ensued was read during the fall of 1974 by students in my seminar on the history of theory in the Middle Ages, and each student wrote a commentary upon and illustrated with music one or two chapters. This review resulted in still further revisions. The class agreed that John's comments on specific chants would be more illuminating if the chants themselves were immediately available, even if the version John knew could not be identified. A very able member of the seminar, Mrs. Maria Fowler, selected and transcribed the chants that are given in the footnotes, for which she has earned our sincere thanks.

Guido's ideas and his expression of them are subtler than John's, demanding even more intensive consultation and collaboration. Mr. Babb's draft reached me in November 1968. Although the revisions I thought necessary were minor, they were numerous enough to require a new draft, in which the letter notation of the examples was converted to staff notation. I acknowledge with thanks the help of Ms. Ellen Beebe in the preparation of the final copy. In this form *Micrologus* was submitted in the fall of 1969 to my seminar in the history of theory, whose members contributed critiques of the translation and commentaries on individual chapters. These led to numerous additional changes in the translation and notes.

Meanwhile we became convinced that Hucbald's treatise, published by Gerbert as *De harmonica institutione*, although unrelated and probably unread by either Guido or John, would add an independent perspective on the subject and content of the other two treatises. Mr. Babb's translation of Hucbald reached me in August 1971. Because Gerbert's edition of this treatise was the only one available, Mr. Babb found it necessary to produce a corrected Latin edition with the help of the text in Brussels, Bibliothèque royale, MS 10078/95, fols. 84v–92r, dating from the eleventh to the twelfth century.

Gerbert's text was based on a paper manuscript once in the municipal library of Strassburg but no longer extant and on a manuscript copied in the fifteenth century for Malatesta Novello Malatesti, Signore di Cesena (1418–65), preserved in Cesena, Biblioteca Malatestiana, S. XXVI. 1. Of the other manuscripts of the treatise, only one is complete, Oxford, Bodleian Library, Canon. misc. 212, probably from the fourteenth century. The oldest text, in Einsiedeln, Klosterbibliothek MS 169, from the tenth to the eleventh century stops at Gerbert's page 117b.

Mr. Babb's text represents a correction of Gerbert's by means only of the Brussels text. Where the Brussels text differed from Gerbert's, the Brussels was usually preferred. The most important such choices are listed at the end of the Hucbald translation. The charts, where not given in facsimile from the Brussels manuscript, follow that source. Originally we intended to provide an exhaustive list of emendations to Gerbert's text, but news of a critical text in preparation by Yves Chartier has led us to omit it in the expectation that students will soon be able to refer to the more complete *apparatus criticus* in that forthcoming edition.

So as not to delay its publication, the Hucbald translation was not submitted to student readers. The most notable editorial problem encountered was to decide upon a format for the musical examples that would not falsify the old sources. The neumatic notation of the Brussels manuscript, though it may not stem directly from the author, is so clearly copied that we decided to provide facsimile cutouts from that source over our transcriptions. The facsimiles are reproduced in the examples and charts with the consent of the Bibliothèque royale Albert 1er of Brussels. I am indebted to my research assistants Ellen Beebe and Maria Fowler for preparing the final draft incorporating these and many other revisions.

The textual problems encountered in the Hucbald treatise highlighted the advantage enjoyed by the translator in possessing Joseph Smits van Waesberghe's punctilious critical editions of Guido and John. Without these it is doubtful that he would have embarked on this project. To Father van Waesberghe and to the copyright owner and publisher, Dr. Armen Carapetyan, who generously gave his blessing to this volume of translations, we owe profuse thanks.

The three treatises share as their main subject the study of melody and sacred chant. Only a small proportion of the chants mentioned were left in one kind of notation or other by the authors. We have added a few in footnotes. But for most of the cited chants, the studious reader will need to consult the standard chantbooks and facsimile editions. To facilitate this Mr. Babb provided an index of chants from a limited number of published sources.

This was augmented by Alejandro Planchart to include references to a larger repertory of sources, including some with staffless neumes and one unedited manuscript, Zagreb, University Library, MS MR 8. Professor Planchart also added an appendix of transcriptions of chants, mainly based on this same Zagreb Antiphoner, that appear in print only in undecipherable neumes. The final draft of the chant index we owe to Susan Cox, to whom we are grateful also for the General Index.

The introductions were not conceived as studies of the three documents so much as aids to their reading. As such, each of the three serves a somewhat different set of purposes. In the case of Hucbald, Rembert Weakland's analysis of the contents of the treatise and a forthcoming study by Yves Chartier counseled brevity except concerning certain applications of older theoretical traditions that a reader not immersed in these matters might find perplexing. Because of Guido's fame and the number of achievements and theoretical formulations wrongly attributed to him, to recognize what is new in *Micrologus* a reader must place it in the context of Guido's surviving work and in that of the theory of his age, with particular reference to Pseudo-Odo's *Dialogus*. An introduction to John's treatise, on the other hand, had to come to terms with the author's identity, which after years of debate remains unresolved. It was desirable to locate the author's activity, since he deals with a chant repertory that is partly regional. John's dependence on Guido needed less comment, since the documents are here for the reader's own investigation. More interesting was to point out where he blundered and where he was inventive. An appreciation of the man and his work as they emerge from the treatise was called for, since this is not available anywhere else.

A grant from the Martha Baird Rockefeller Fund for Music Inc., received in 1966, for which we are ever thankful, remains an indispensable base for the preparation of manuscripts for this series and contributed to pricing this book within the budgets of students and scholars.

CLAUDE V. PALISCA

New Haven, January 1976

Abbreviations

Aix	*Le prosaire d'Aix-la-Chapelle: manuscrit 13 du chapitre d'Aix-la-Chapelle (XIIIe siècle, début).* Collection de manuscrits et d'études publiée sous la direction de Dom Hesbert, 3. Rouen, 1961.
AM	*Antiphonale monasticum pro diurnis horis* (no. 818). Tournai, 1934.
AR	*Antiphonale sacrosanctae Romanae ecclesiae pro diurnis horis* (no. 820). Tournai, 1924 (reprint, 1949).
AS	*Antiphonale Sarisburiense*, ed. W. H. Frere. London, 1901–25.
B	Brussels, Bibliothèque royale, MS 10078/95.
CA	*Codex Albensis: Ein Antiphonar aus den 12. Jahrhundert* (Graz, Universitätsbibliothek, MS NR. 211), ed. Z. Falvy and L. Mezey. Graz, 1963.
Collins	A. Jefferies Collins, ed., *The Bridgettine Breviary of Syon Abbey*. Henry Bradshaw Society, 96. Worcester, 1969.
CS	Edmond de Coussemaker. *Scriptorum de musica medii aevi novam seriem a Gerbertina alteram.* 4 vols. Paris, 1864–76; reprint, Hildesheim, 1963.
CSM	*Corpus scriptorum de musica.* Rome: American Institute of Musicology, 1950–.
Drinkwelder	*Ein deutsches Sequentiar aus dem Ende des 12. Jahrhunderts*, ed. O. Drinkwelder. Veröffentlichungen der Gregorianischen Akademie zu Freiburg in der Schweiz, 7. Graz and Vienna, 1914.
GB	*Le codex VI. 34 de la Bibliothèque Capitulaire de Bénévent (XIe–XIIe siècle): Graduel de Bénévent avec prosaire et tropaire.* Paléographie musicale, 15. Tournai, 1937–53.
Goede	*The Utrecht Prosarium: Liber sequentiarium ecclesiae capitulis Sanctae Mariae Ultraiectensis, saeeuli XIII, codex Ultraiectensis Bibliotheca 417*, ed. N. de Goede. Monumenta musica Neerlandica, 6. Amsterdam, 1965.
GR	*Graduale sacrosanctae Romanae ecclesiae de tempore et de sanctis* (no. 696). Tournai, 1938; reprint, 1956.
GS	*Graduale Sarisburiense*, ed. W. H. Frere. London, 1894.
GS 1, 2, 3	Martin Gerbert. *Scriptores ecclesiastici de musica sacra potissimum.* 3 vols. St. Blasien, 1784; reprint, Milan, 1931.
HA	*Antiphonale officii monastici écri par le B. Hartker, No. 390–391 de la Bibliothèque de Saint-Gall.* Paléographie musicale, ser. 2, vol. 1. Solesmes, 1900.

Hesbert — *Corpus antiphonalium officii*, 4 vols., ed. René-Jean Hesbert. Rome, 1963–70.

Huglo — Michel Huglo. *Les tonaires, inventaire, analyse, comparaison*. Paris, 1971.

LA — *Antiphonaire monastique (XIIe siècle): Le codex 601 de la Bibliothèque Capitulaire de Lucques*. Paléographie musicale, 9. Tournai, 1906–09.

LR — *Liber responsorialis pro festis I. classis et communi sanctorum juxta ritum monasticum*. Solesmes, 1895; reprint, 1950.

LU (#780) — *Liber usualis missae et officii pro dominicis et festis* (no. 780). Tournai, 1896; reprint, 1937.

LU (#801) — *The Liber Usualis, with Introduction and Rubrics in English* (no. 801). Tournai, 1934; reprint, 1958.

Ott — *Offertoriale sive versus offertoriorum*, ed. Karl Ott. Tournai, 1935.

PrM — *Processionale monasticum ad usum congregatione Gallicae ordinis Sancti Benedicti*. Solesmes, 1893; reprint, 1949.

Rajeczky — *Himnuszok és Sequetiak*, ed. B. Rajeczky. Melodiarium Hungariae medii aevi, 1. Budapest, 1956.

RISM — *The Theory of Music from the Carolingian Era up to 1400*, ed. Joseph Smits van Waesberghe. 2 vols. Répertoire international des sources musicales (International Inventory of Musical Sources). Munich and Duisburg, 1961–68.

Schlager A — *Alleluia-melodien I, bis 1100*, ed. Karlheinz Schlager. Monumenta monodica medii aevi, 7. Kassel and Basel, 1968.

Schlager T — Karlheinz Schlager, *Thematisches Katalog der ältesten Alleluia-melodien*. Erlanger Arbeiten zur Musikwissenschaft, 2. Munich, 1965.

Stäblein — *Hymnen (I): Die mittelalterlichen Hymnenmelodien des Abendlandes*, ed. Bruno Stäblein. Monumenta monodica medii aevi, 1. Kassel and Basel, 1956.

SYG — *Le Codex 903 de la Bibliothèque Nationale de Paris (XIe siècle): Graduel de Saint-Yrieix*. Paléographie musicale, 13. Tournai, 1925–30.

Vecchi — *Troparium sequentiarium nonantulanum: cod. Casanat. 1741*, ed. Giuseppe Vecchi. Monumenta lyrica medii aevi italica, 1. Latina. Modena, 1955.

VP — *Variae preces ex liturgia tum hodierna tum antiqua collectae aut usu receptae* (no. 808). Tournai, 1901; reprint, 1939.

VR — *Vesperale romanum* (no. 840). Tournai, 1924; reprint, 1955.

WA — *Antiphonaire monastique (XIIIe siècle): Le codex F. 160 de la bibliothèque de la cathédrale de Worcester*. Paléographie musicale, 12. Tournai, 1922–25.

Wagner — *Das Graduale des St. Thomaskirche zu Leipzig*, 2 vols., ed. Peter Wagner. Publikationen älterer Musik, 5. Leipzig, 1930.

ZA — Zagreb, University Library, MS MR 8 (14th–15th-century Pauline Antiphoner).

HUCBALD

MELODIC INSTRUCTION

(*DE HARMONICA INSTITUTIONE*)

retro speculatur. Nam prima consonantia est musicae artis sesquitertia hoc est diatessaron
inde pervenitur ad sesqualteram hoc est diapente inde ad duplam quae est diapason [illegible]

INCIPIT MUSICA HUCBALDI

Ad musicae initiamenta quilibet ingredi cupientem qui aliquam scilicet interim cantilenarum percipere intellegentiam quaerit qualitatem sive positionem diligenter advertere oportebit. Et primo quae sint aequales voces atque uniformiter sibi consimiles, quae deinde inaequales et quibusdam spatiis a se discrepantes, ipsorumque denique spatiorum quanta habeantur discrimina, quotque etiam varietatibus ea moderari contingat. Post et praeterea quot vel quibus sonis qui vicem habentur elementorum tota regatur cantilena. Iam vero his non parvi temporis exercitiis tamquam pro foribus assuetum ad ipsius demum penetralia disciplinae acie quodammodo visus obtunsi paulatim summota caligine radiata admitti forte donabitur, quomodo scilicet haec omnia vel vis de quibus ea tractat consonantiarum rationabilitate congruentissima disponantur numerorum atque ad eorundem sint exemplar universa composita atque compacta. Et de aequalibus quidem vocibus quoniam ipsae per se patent nihil aliud dicendum nisi quod continuo vocis impetu proferuntur in modum soluta oratione legentis et quod una tantum vox est quotienscumque repetantur velut si unam quamlibet litteram saepius scribas aut proferas ut a a a a et quod nulla inter eas consonantia est. Sunt enim aequisonae non consonae. Nam in consonantia duae voces a se omnino distantes simul concorditer sonant. In his autem vocibus etiam si a pluribus eadem promantur nullo tamen a se spatio distant ut est in hac antiphona Astiterunt reges: et Dum sacrificaret. Sebastianus dixit ad Nicostratum usque ad id dignatus est suam exhibere. Et in huiusmodi quidem locis ubi tot syllabae continuatim sub una voce nectuntur nulla eminentiori aut pressiori intercedente quasi linea in directum deducta facile aequalitas potest adverti. In quolibet autem diversisono cantu si quaeratur quae vox alii in eodem melo similis vel aequa habeatur, id non nisi assuetiori tam ultro se ingerit, quod tamen studiosum quemlibet nullatenus morabitur, ut in hoc: Puer natus est nobis; si quaeras quae vox eiusdem introitus cum prima coaequetur, apparet in prima et tertia huius syllabae: datus est nobis, cum et angelus. Hoc nomen vocatur circus vel circulus, cum in eundem quo coeptum est [illegible] revertitur. [illegible] quae [illegible] hac puer. [illegible] nobis. et filius. [illegible]. Sic et de aliis. Inter consimilia quoque partium sive neumarum huiusmodi creberrimus observationis est usus, ut in hoc: Ave Maria.
Item Benedicta. Agnes in medio flammarum [illegible].

Inaequalitatem vero sonorum qui distantes dicuntur diversa spatia efferunt. Inaequales autem

Brussels, Bibliothèque royale, MS 10078/95, fol. 84v (11th–12th century)

INTRODUCTION

by Claude V. Palisca

The choice of Hucbald's treatise to open this volume rather than that of Aurelian, which preceded it in time, or of Regino of Prüm, or Remi of Auxerre, can be justified on several grounds. Hucbald was more theoretically inclined than Aurelian and more in touch with the music of his time than either Regino or Remi. Aurelian was concerned essentially with the performance of plainchant; the theoretical chapters are perfunctory recapitulations of traditional doctrine, without attempting to adapt it to modern needs or, for that matter, to comprehend it. The treatises of Regino and Remi, on the other hand, were addressed to students of liberal arts rather than to musicians. Another candidate for inclusion in this volume would have been the anonymous *Musica enchiriadis*, once attributed to Hucbald. This is a more original and substantial treatise than Hucbald's, but a critical text has not yet been established from the very large number of sources,[1] and its emphasis on polyphony harmonizes less with the other two treatises selected for this volume, which are concerned predominantly with the theory of plainchant.

Unlike the treatises of Guido and John, Hucbald's *De harmonica institutione* did not enjoy wide diffusion in its time, nor was it much read in subsequent years. Its importance lies in the solutions it proposed for contemporary problems and the authority with which the author, a composer and performer, wrote about the tonal system underlying plainchant.

More is known about Hucbald's life than about most medieval musical writers, thanks to his having narrated the lives of a number of saints.[2] He was born around 840[3] and died, it is said, at the age of ninety on 20 June 930. While quite young he went to the Benedictine Monastery of Saint Amand in

1. According to *Huglo*, p. 61, the *Enchiriadis* treatise is preserved in 50 MSS. A critical text of chapters XIII–XVIII is in Ernst L. Waeltner, *Die Lehre vom Organum bis zur Mitte des II. Jahrhunderts* (Tutzing: H. Schneider, 1975), pp. 2–37.

2. This short sketch is based on Rembert Weakland. "Hucbald as Musician and Theorist," *Musical Quarterly* 42 (1956): 66–84; Weakland, "Hucbald," *Die Musik in Geschichte und Gegenwart*, (1957), 821–27; Hans Müller, *Hucbalds echte und unechte Schriften über Musik* (Leipzig, 1884); Jacques Paul Migne, ed., *Patrologiae cursus completus: Series latina* (Paris, 1957–66), vol. 132, cols. 815–24: "Hucbaldus Monachus S. Amandi: Notitia historica et bibliographica." Hucbald's lives of saints are in ibid., cols. 825–906.

3. Yves Chartier, Abstract of Ph.D. dissertation "La *Musica* d'Hucbald de Saint-Amand (traité de musique du IXe siècle). Introduction, établissement du texte, traduction et commentaire," Paris-Sorbonne,

the diocese of Tournay in Flanders. He was educated there, in Nevers, and under Heiric in Saint Germain d'Auxerre. The school at Saint Amand was directed by his uncle Milo, whom Hucbald eventually succeeded.

Hucbald's reputation as a teacher traveled widely, for around 872 he was invited by Abbot Rudolf of Saint Bertin to found a school there. Around 893 Archbishop Fulco of Rheims requested him and Remi of Auxerre, who had been fellow students at Auxerre, to set up a school in Rheims. His musical treatise may have been written for that school.[4] Aside from these occasional absences, Hucbald evidently spent most of his life at Saint Amand, to which he had returned by 905 at latest.

Hucbald was probably a more prolific composer than the surviving evidence and chants give him credit for. Literary sources ascribe to him offices for Saint Andrew, Saint Theodoric, and Saint Peter. The Office for Saint Peter, which begins *In plateis ponebantur infirmi*, is found in the Worcester and Sarum antiphoners.[5] Also believed to be by him is the famous Gloria trope *Quem vere pia laus*[6] and two introit tropes in honor of Saint Vincent, *Tripudians martyr* and *Culminibus coeli*,[7] and the prosa *Pangat simul eia*.[8]

Hucbald is remembered also for a song, "Carmina clarisonae calvis cantate Camenae," in honor of Charles the Bold, in which each word of the 146 verses begins with the letter C (for Carolus Calvus).[9] *De harmonica institutione* is his only theoretical work.

Hucbald's treatise has many marks of a school text, not so much for beginners as for monks who already know a large repertory of chants. From the known —the intervals and the notes of the scale as experienced in musical practice, both vocal and instrumental—he proceeded to the unknown, the Greek theory of tetrachords and system of notation transmitted by Boethius. It has been observed that the treatise breaks off suddenly, suggesting that we may not possess the complete text.[10] But since the main goal of the treatise appears to

---

1973, in *Répertoire international de littérature musicale*, 7/1 (1973), 218dd, p. 18. Chartier's dissertation, as revised for publication, became available to this editor only after our manuscript had been consigned to the press. Otherwise we would have gladly profited by the critical text and the rich and profound interpretation of the commentary and notes. I am greatly indebted to Professor Chartier for generously providing a copy of his draft, for his careful reading of the Hucbald section of this book, and for his acute comments upon it. I only regret that the printer's production schedule did not permit us to act but on a few of his good suggestions.

4. Ibid.

5. *Paléographie musicale* 12, facs. 325ff. (see Jacques Handschin, "Etwas Griefbares über Hucbald," *Acta musicologica* 7 (1935): 158–59); *AS* 2, facs. 441.

6. *Analecta hymnica* 47, 248, no. 185.

7. Joseph Smits van Waesberghe, "Neue Kompositionen des Johannes von Metz (um 975), Hucbalds von St. Amand und Sigeberts von Gembloux?" in *Speculum musicae artis: Festgabe für Heinrich Husmann zum 60. Geburtstag*, ed. Heinz Becher and Reinhard Gerlach (Munich, 1970), pp. 285–303 (a facsimile of *Tripudians martyr* is included, from the Hague, Museum Mermann, MS 10.b.12, fol. 55v).

8. Yves Chartier, Abstract (see n. 3 above).

9. It was published numerous times, the first apparently in Basel, 1516. See *Patrologia . . . latina*, 132:818.

10. Lawrence Gushee, "Questions of Genre in Medieval Treatises on Music" in *Gattungen der Musik in Einzeldarstellungen: Gedenkschrift Leo Schrade*, ed. Wulf Arlt et al. (Bern, 1973), p. 573.

be the reform of musical practice by improving the precision of pitch notation while retaining the subtle nuances of neumatic notation, and this is accomplished at the end of the extant text, we may well have all of it. The book has another interesting pedagogic feature, which may not have been intentional; it conforms to what is sometimes termed the cyclical curriculum. Essentially the same topics are treated three times, first without musical notation (*GS* 1: 104a to 109a—the paging of Gerbert's *editio princeps* will be used for reference) then with conventional neumatic notation but using tetrachordal theory (109a to 114b); finally using the Greek fifteen-note system and Greek letter notation (114b to 121a).

Rembert Weakland's perceptive and detailed analysis and evaluation of the treatise in "Hucbald as Musician and Theorist" in *The Musical Quarterly* of 1956 and Yves Chartier's forthcoming study[11] render it unnecessary to present here a guide to its contents. There are a number of points, nevertheless, that ought to be flagged and clarified, and this is more effectively accomplished discursively than through footnotes.

At the outset Hucbald makes several distinctions among intervals. First he uses the terms *aequisonae* and *consonae*, which are here translated "equisones" and "consones" (104a). These are terms derived from Boethius,[12] who in turn got them from Ptolemy,[13] but Hucbald, whether deliberately or through misunderstanding, altered their meaning. For Boethius two notes of the same pitch are *unisonae*; two notes which sound almost identical, such as the octave and double octave, are *equisonae*; whereas the diapente and diatessaron are *consonae*. All these together comprise the genus *consonantia* or consonance. For Hucbald *aequisonae* are unisons, *consonae* are simply consonances, and he transfers the condition of agreeably sounding simultaneously (*simul pulsae*), which Boethius ascribed to the octaves, from these to all consonances. For this Hucbald had good reason, as he shows when he later refers to the practice of *organizatio*, in which boys and men sing together, making organum.

Hucbald distinguishes consonance, which is a calculated blending of simultaneous sounds, from melodic interval (107a). Among the consonances, only the diatessaron and diapente are allowed as melodic intervals; the diapason, diapason-plus-diapente, diapason-plus-diatessaron, and double diapason are exclusively simultaneous consonances. Ancient theory is thus adjusted to the budding practice of polyphony.

The Ptolemaic-Boethian concepts are distorted in the process, to be sure, but they are ingeniously fitted to modern use. In the Greek tradition all consonances were essentially melodic intervals; intervals that joined consonances in melody but were not themselves consonances were called emmelic.

11. See n. 3 above.

12. *De institutione musica libri quinque*, ed. Gottfried Friedlein (Leipzig, 1867) 5. 11. 361.

13. *Harmonics*. 1. 4, 10.

In Hucbald's category of melodic intervals, which he calls *spatia* (he employs the word *emmeles* [108a] but not as a category), Hucbald adds two consonances to the ancient emmelic intervals.

Hucbald derived his fifteen-step vocal gamut from the Greek system set forth by Boethius, but the first time he presents it (110a) he avoids the Greek string names. He also notes that it may not coincide in range or arrangement of tones and semitones with water organs and other instruments of his time. He specifically points out that instruments with a large number of strings or pipes normally begin on the third note of the vocal gamut and extend to sixteen or twenty-one and more notes. Thus three types of gamut are recognized: a fifteen-note vocal span, a sixteen-keyed organ, and an extended instrumental gamut (Fig. 1).

Figure 1

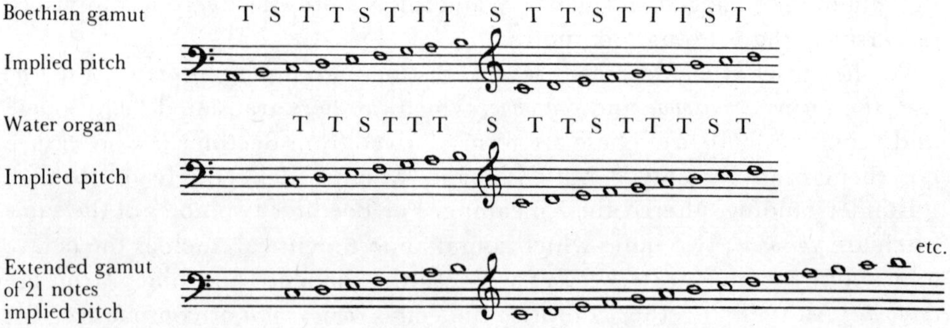

The offertory Hucbald cites as illustration, *Angelus Domini descendit*, assures us that Hucbald did, indeed, locate the water organ gamut on the basis of the C octave, for this chant has the range C–c.

The vocal scale is made explicit by reference to the *Noeane* syllables (111b), a system of solmization derived from the Byzantine intonations or *enechemata*.[14] They were earlier mentioned by Regino of Prüm[15] and Aurelian of Réôme,[16] who explained that each mode had a pattern of these syllables associated with a melodic formula. A treatise once incorrectly attributed to Hucbald but probably of the tenth century, *Commemoratio brevis*, presented the formulas for each of the eight modes in daseian notation.[17] Its author said of them, "*Noane* are not words signifying anything but syllables suitable for studying melody

14. See Gustave Reese, *Music in the Middle Ages* (New York, 1940), pp. 87ff. Regarding the introduction of the intonations in the West see Huglo, "Introduction of Byzantine Intonation Formulae into Western Practice" in *Studies in Eastern Chant* 3 (Oxford, 1971); and Huglo, *Les tonaires*, pp. 383–90. See also Guido, *Micrologus*, chap. 13.

15. *De harmonica institutione*, *GS* 1 : 247.

16. *Musica disciplina*, *GS* 1 : 41b–42b; ed. L. Gushee, CMM 21 (1975), cap. viii, p. 82.

17. *GS* 1 : 229. They are transcribed in Antoine Auda, *Les modes et les tons de la musique et spécialement de la musique médiévale* (Brussels, 1930), pp. 171–76.

[*investigandam melodiam*]."[18] Hucbald's tetrachord solmization, *no-ne-no-o*, does not correspond with any of the intonations in *Commemoratio brevis*, though the opening of its formula for the authentic protus does have the descending tone-tone-semitone pattern with the syllables *no-a-no* (Ex. 1).

Example 1

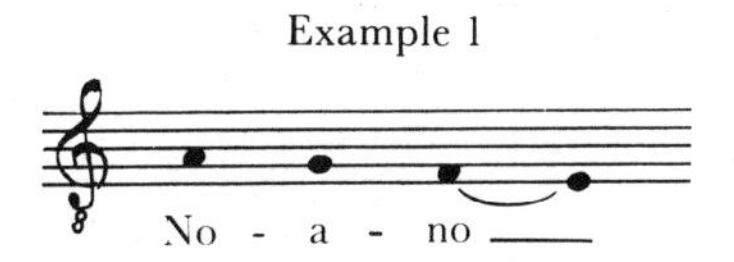

If the beginning of the formula of the first mode illustrated later in the treatise is compared to that of *Commemoratio brevis*, it is evident that the two authors were working with slightly different versions of the system (Ex. 2).

Example 2

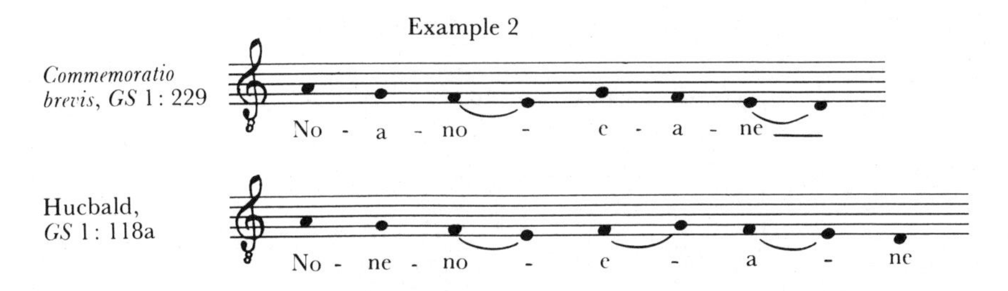

Hucbald's vocalization *no-ne-no-o* stood for the same descending Greek tetrachord pattern that the later standard syllables *no-a-no-o* were supposed to recall. The arrangement of two descending pairs of conjunct tone-tone-semitone tetrachords separated by a tone of disjunction, with an added note below the bottommost tetrachord, is the standard Greek system. One detail of the diagram is puzzling: why is the added note below the lowest tetrachord sung *ne*, when it does not have a potential tone-semitone *no-o* pattern below it?

Hucbald also demonstrates an alternate arrangement, utilizing a tetrachord of the ascending pattern tone-semitone-tone. Again two pairs of conjunct tetrachords are separated by a tone of disjunction in the middle, but the added tone is moved to the top. This produces the pre-Pseudo-Odonian gamut with the tetrachordal arrangement later canonized by Hermannus Contractus. Throughout this demonstration Hucbald uses chant models rather than *noeane* syllables. Then, in imitation of Greek theory, he tacks on a conjunct "synemmenon" tetrachord, also ascending tone-semitone-tone, to the lowest pair. The result is a deliberate distortion of the Greek system, for the latter system is faithfully set forth in the following pages (114b–17a), complete with the string names, now given for the first time, and explanations of the names.

18. *GS* 1 : 216.

Figure 2

Tetrachordal Systems Described by Hucbald

	ne a ne No ne a ne No
	ne ne a ne No ne a ne No
Hucbald's modified Greek (descending)	[A B C D E F G a b c d e f g $\frac{a}{a}$]
	T S T T S T T T S T T S T T
Hucbald's modern (ascending)	[A B C D E F G a b c d e f g $\frac{a}{a}$]
	T S T T S T T T S T T S T T
Ancient Greek (descending)	[A B C D E F G a b c d e f g $\frac{a}{a}$]
	T S T T S T T T S T T S T T
Hucbald's modern synemmenon (ascending)	[A B C D E F G a b♭ c]
	T S T T S T T S T
Ancient Greek synemmenon (descending)	[A B C D E F G a b♭ c d]
	T S T T S T T S T T

The different systems are compared in Figure 2, with Pseudo-Odonian pitch letters supplied.

Hucbald's reason for demonstrating the Greek greater and lesser perfect systems, which up to now were avoided in this treatise, is apparent in the final section. Neumatic notation was an aid to memory, but it did not permit reading new chants at sight. Borrowing the Greek letter notation transmitted by Boethius made it possible to pinpoint the exact height of the notes in relation to each other. As Henri Potiron has noted, Hucbald did not adopt the signs that Boethius identified as the vocal notation but selected for each note of the gamut one from the pair of Greek signs, sometimes the vocal, sometimes the instrumental.[19] His choice was probably based on the legibility and familiarity of the symbol. Since Boethius described in detail the shapes only of the signs for the Lydian tonos—or "mode," as he calls it—while for the other tonoi the signs are not described but simply included in a chart,[20] Hucbald chose the signs from the Lydian. Figure 3 shows the signs as given by Boethius, with a circle around those chosen by Hucbald.

19. "La notation grecque dans *L'Institution harmonique* d'Hucbald," *Etudes grégoriennes* 2 (1957): 37–50.
20. The descriptions are in *De inst. mus.* 4. 3–4; the chart in 4. 15.

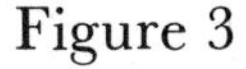

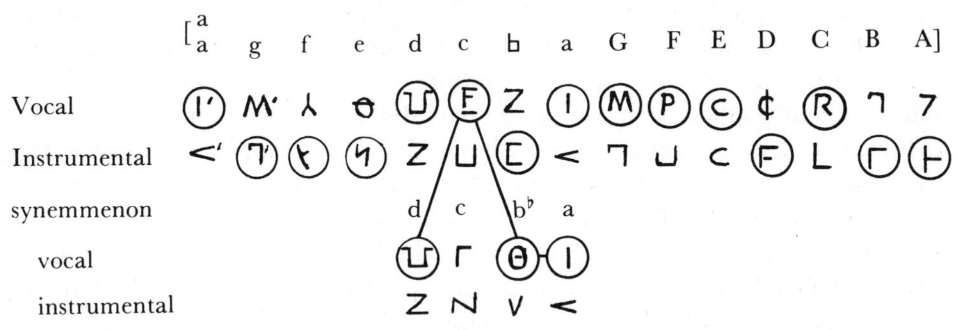

If Hucbald, as is reasonable to believe, derived his knowledge of the Greek notational signs from Boethius, then he must have had a copy in which they were not clearly drawn, for he changed several of the signs and with them their descriptions. Figure 4 shows Hucbald's deviations from Alypius[21] and Boethius.[22]

From this chart it is apparent that Alypius and Boethius were in substantial agreement, with two exceptions. The sign for trite hyperbolaeon was described by Boethius as a supine right half of an alpha, but by Alypius as a left half of an alpha bent upside down. Meibom amended Alypius's "right half" to "left half" to agree with the description of the sign for the nete diezeugmenon of

Figure 4

	Alypius	*Boethius*	*Hucbald*
nete hyperbolaeon	I′ "iota with an acute accent above"	I′ "iota habens acutam"	Ɨ "iota extensum"
paranete hyperbolaeon	Π′ "Prolonged pi with an acute accent above"	Π′ "pi deductum habens acutam"	ΠƗ "pi graecum extensum"
trite hyperbolaeon	⅄ "left half of alpha bent upside down"	⅄ "semialpha dextrum supinum habens retro lineam"	Y "Y simplex"
nete diezeugmenon	կ "eta made carelessly and prolonged"	կ "ny inversum deductum"	N "N contractum"
parhypate hypaton	B "incomplete beta	B "beta non integrum"	B "beta simplex"
Proslambanomenos	⊢ "tau lying down"	⊢ "tau iacens"	⊦ "dasian rectum"

21. Karl von Jan, *Musici scriptores graeci* (Leipzig, 1895; reprinted Hildesheim, 1962), p. 369.
22. *De inst. mus.* 4. 3–4.

the Hypodorian, which is the same pitch, thus agreeing with Boethius.[23] The other discrepancy between Alypius and Boethius is at nete diezeugmenon, where Boethius called a "stretched nu" the sign that Alypius had qualified as a careless eta with prolongation. In both cases Hucbald's copy must have had divergent symbols, so he described what he saw. In the remaining symbols of Figure 4 Hucbald departed from both Alypius and Boethius. In nete and paranete hyperbolaeon, the accent mark, which signified the upper octave in Greek notation, probably appeared in his copy to grow out of the letter, therefore "iota extended" and "pi extended." In parhypate hypaton he must have read a capital beta instead of an incomplete beta, while for proslambanomenos it was easier to describe the sign as "an upright dasia" than as an inclined tau.

The purpose of presenting the Greek notation was to apply it to the problem of fixing the pitch of neumes. The next paragraphs of the treatise (119a–19b) show how this may be done. The only example that follows with neumes, however, is one showing the tetrachord of the "finals" descending from lichanos meson to lichanos hypaton [G to D]. Previously, though (117b–18a), Hucbald presented the opening of an *Alleluia*, with the range of a fifth [a down to D], and the beginning of the *Noanoeane* formula for the first mode, using the same range. In these few musical examples with neumes and letters the manuscripts have a confusion of lower case and capital Greek letters, the capital letters written as if they were uncial Latin letters, namely i, m, p, c, f for I (iota), M (mu), P (rho), C (sigma), F (digamma).

It was apparently Hucbald's intention that Greek and not Latin letters be used, and that neumes always accompany them, because then the subtle instructions to the performer embodied in neumes, intimating duration, tempo, tremulant or normal voice, grouping or separation of notes, and certain intonation of cadences (118a), are preserved. The final table of initial notes of each mode and the examples accompanying them (120–21) lack neumes except for the melisma of *Ve* in *Veni et ostende* illustrating the proslambanomenos *initium* in the protus modes. For the examples in authentic and plagal deuterus (120) neither Greek letters nor neumes were found over the texts in the manuscripts available to the translator and editor.

Besides neumatic and letter notation there is another kind used in the treatise that has occasioned comment but which Hucbald introduced without fanfare. It is a staff notation in which the textual syllables are written in the spaces, and the distances between the spaces are indicated in the margin by T and S for Tone and Semitone (109b). This was probably meant by Hucbald, if indeed he designed it, as a visual aid rather than a demonstration of notation.

23. Marcus Meibom, *Antiquae musicae auctores septem*, 2 vols. (Amsterdam, 1652), vol. 1, pt. 4, pp. 4, 72. The problems of transmission of this sign are considered by Ubaldo Pizzani in "Studi sulle fonti del 'De Institutione Musica' di Boezio," *Sacris erudiri* 16 (1965): 103–04.

However this layout became the basis of the daseian notation of the treatises *Musica enchiriadis*, *Scolica enchiriadis* and *Commemoratio brevis*. The daseia sign itself is a further link to these, for the letter for the bottom note of the Greek gamut is called by Hucbald *dasia*. By adding a flag to it and rotating and distorting the resultant symbol in various ways, the daseian notation achieved a representation of pitch height that in most sources was then also accompanied in the margin by T and S for the interval distances between staff lines.

Although it lacks chapter headings, Hucbald's treatise gives every indication of having been thoughtfully organized and carefully composed. It is didactic without giving the impression of a primer. Unlike the other two treatises of this volume, its object was not to instruct in either performance or composition. Rather it sets forth a system that was intended to make discourse possible about the practice of sacred chant. It was the treatise first freely rather than dogmatically to apply Greek theoretical concepts and methods as transmitted by Boethius to contemporary problems.

HUCBALD, MELODIC INSTRUCTION (*DE HARMONICA INSTITUTIONE*)

Translated by Warren Babb
Edited by Claude V. Palisca

[104a][1] Anyone eager to be initiated into music, who seeks to attain to some—albeit preliminary—understanding of melody, should give careful attention to the quality, or position, of all the tones.

[104a/7] Let him note first which tones are equal and consistently alike; next, which are unequal and are sundry intervals apart; and lastly, how many different sizes of these intervals there are judged to be, and in how many different ways they may be measured off. Let him note, furthermore, from how many sounds, and which ones, all melody is composed; for these are held to be its elements.

[104a/16] One trained for no short time in these, as it were, preliminary exercises may at length be granted entry to the inner regions of this discipline, the darkness being gradually withdrawn from his dull eyes and their vision made keen. He may understand, that is, how all these materials and whichever of the consonances this discipline deals with are ordered with the utmost fitness by the logic of numbers, and how according to their pattern everything is brought together and connected.

[104a/27] Since equal tones are self-explanatory, one need say only that they are performed by articulating a continued tone in the manner of one speaking prose. Moreover, they are but one tone, however many times repeated, as if one wrote or pronounced any single letter over and over, thus, a a a. Further, they do not constitute a consonance; they are, to be sure, equisones [*aequisonae*], not consones [*consonae*]. In a consonance two tones

Example 1

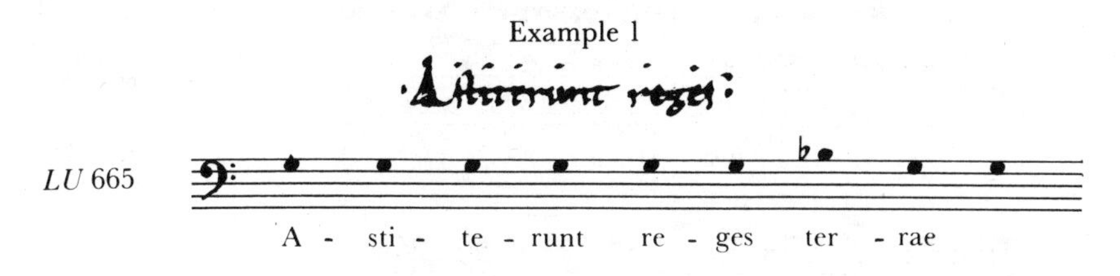

1. Numbers in brackets before each paragraph indicate the column in *GS* 1, followed by the line number.

clearly distant from each other in pitch sound at once, concordantly. In the case of equal tones, even if they are performed by several persons, still they are no distance apart; thus in the antiphon *Astiterunt reges terrae* [Ex. 1], [in the introit] *Dum sanctificatus fuero* [Ex. 2],

Example 2

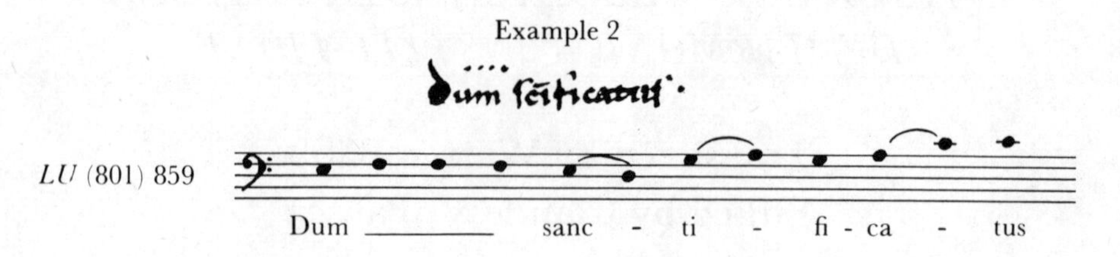

and [in the antiphon] *Sebastianus dixit ad Nicostratum* at (*usque ad id*) *dignatus est suam exhibere* [Ex. 3].

Example 3

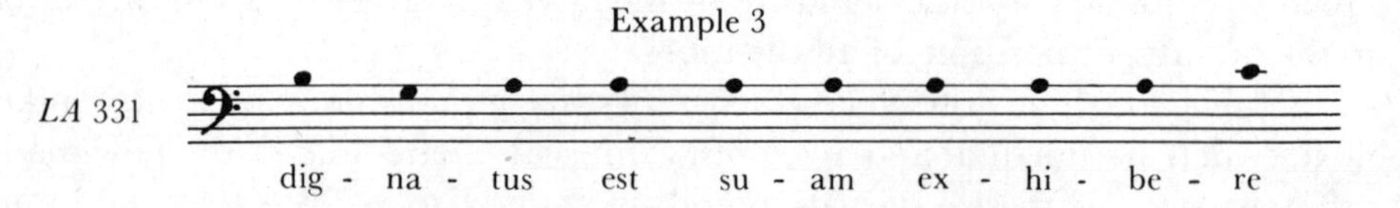

In such passages, where so many syllables in succession are strung together on one tone with none higher or lower intervening, like a line drawn straight, this equality can easily be perceived. If in any chant with various pitches it be asked what tone is deemed like or equal to another elsewhere in the same melody, the answer occurs readily only to the more experienced, but it will give no pause to the learned. Thus in [the introit] *Puer natus est nobis* [Ex. 4], if you look for a tone the same as the first one, it appears [both elsewhere and] as the first and third of the syllable[s *-bis* and *-ge-*] [Ex. 5].

Example 4

Example 5

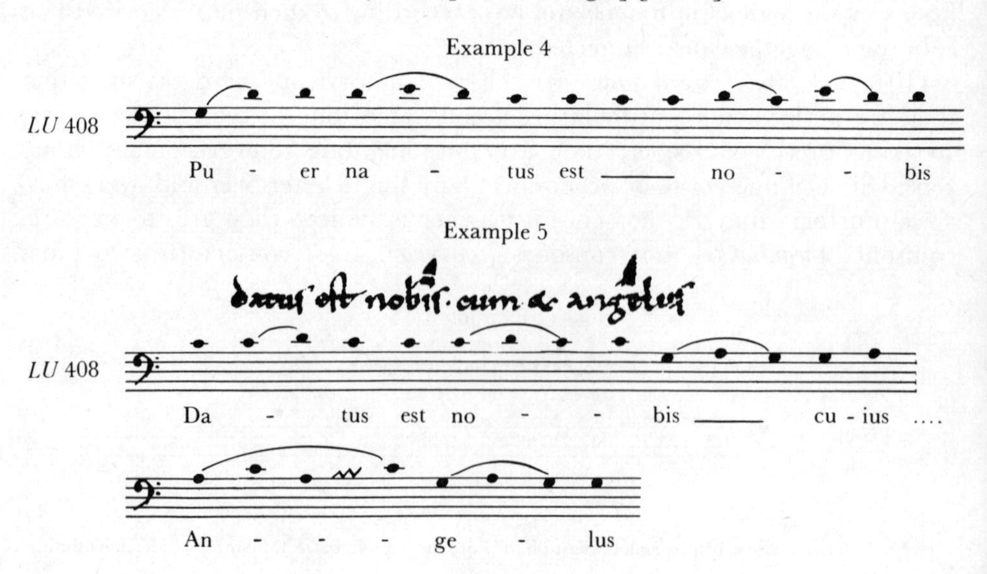

This [neume] is called a "circle" or "ring," as it returns to the same point where it began. Again, if you ask which [syllables have a circle or ring on the pitch of the *second* syllable of] *Puer* [Ex. 6] they are these [Ex. 7].

Example 6

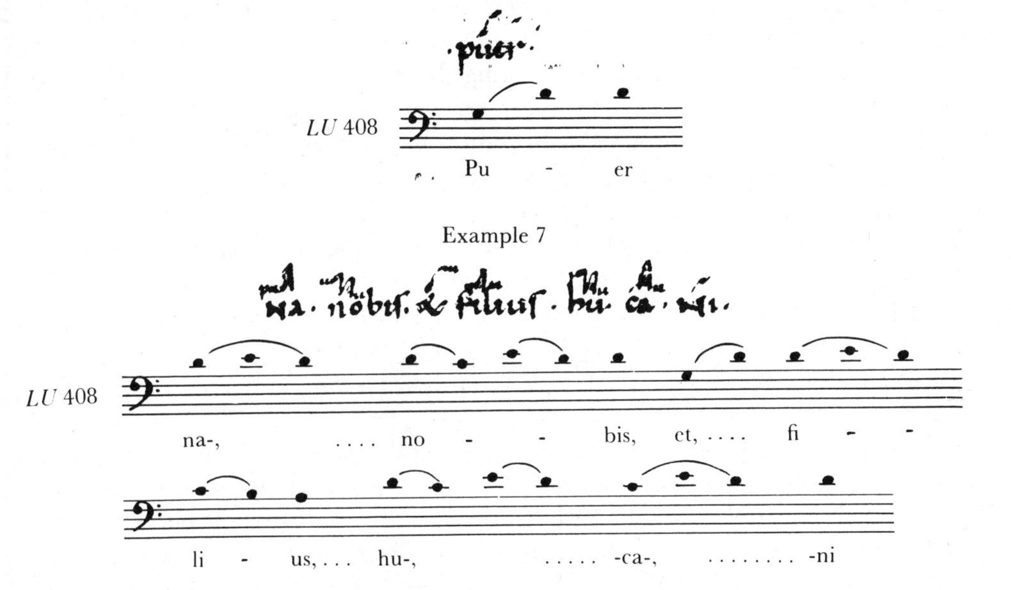

And so too in other cases. Within "parts" or neumes, too, such imitation is used very frequently, as in [Ex. 8].

Example 8

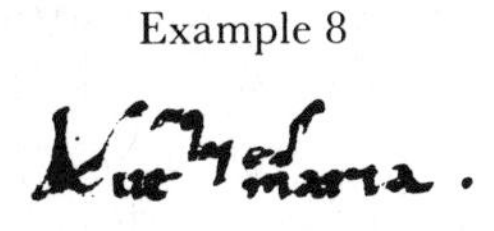

Likewise [Ex. 9].

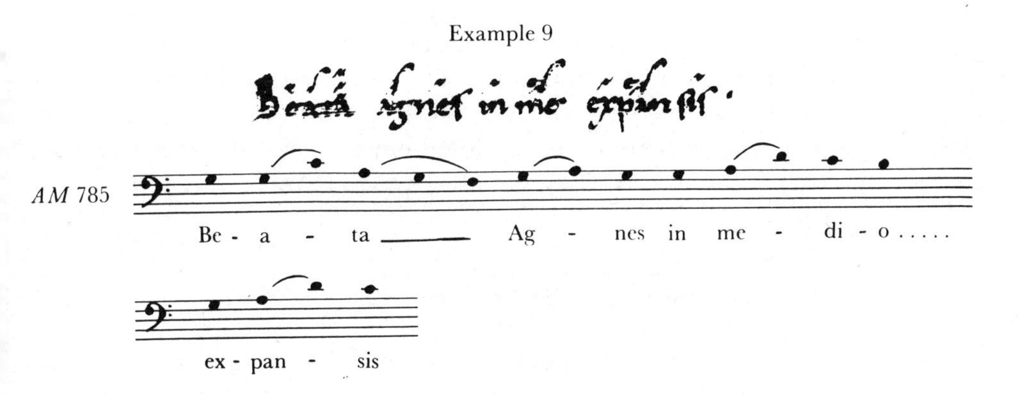

[105a/6] Of unequal sounds, which are called disjunct, various types appear. Those tones are called unequal of which two occur in juxtaposition, one sounding higher, the other lower, at any interval apart; and these intervals are sometimes smaller, sometimes larger. Beginning with the very smallest and increasing stepwise one after the other, they mount up to nine successively larger intervals. They can never be perfectly understood until the series of all fifteen tones is learned completely. This will be discussed later. For the present, let them be mentioned briefly, each being illustrated, ascending and descending, with a pair of examples.

[105a/24] The first interval[, the semitone,] occurs when two tones are separated by the smallest distance, so that the space between them is scarcely perceived, as in the antiphon *Missus est Gabriel* at *Mariam* and *Virginem* [Ex. 10a]. The second[, the whole tone,] is a more perceptible interval, as at *Missus est* and *Angelus* [Ex. 10b]. The third [interval, the semiditone or minor third,] is a little larger, as in *Missus est* at *ad Mariam Virginem* [Ex. 10c]. The fourth [interval, the ditone or major third,] extends farther than this, as in the antiphon *Beati qui ambulant.*[2] The fifth [interval, the diatessaron or perfect fourth,] is even greater, as in *Ne timeas, Maria* [Ex. 10d] and *In illa die* at *fluent* [Ex. 10e]. The sixth [interval, the tritone,] is still ampler, as in the responsories *Iam corpus eius* at *cuius pater feminam* [Ex. 10f] and *Isti sunt dies quos* at *debetis temporibus* [Ex. 10g]. The seventh [interval, the diapente or perfect fifth,] too, surpasses these by the due amount, as in the antiphon *Beata Agnes in medio . . . minas* [Ex. 10h]. The eighth [interval, the semitone-plus-diapente or minor sixth,] you will find in *Tu vir Symphoriane suspende in tormentis.*[3] The ninth [interval, the whole-tone-plus-diapente or major sixth,] extending over the widest space of all, has the last place among these intervals [*divisionum* (i.e. *monochordi*)], for you will never find one larger than it or smaller than the first. It occurs in the introit *Ad te levavi animam meam: Deus meus in te* [Ex. 10i] and the responsory *Inter natos mulierum non* [Ex. 10j].

[105b/16] Among these kinds of intervals any clever person can see how, from equality of pitch as a starting-point and with the material proposed, this whole system of intervals between unidentical notes unfolds, so that at first equality is departed from by the smallest distance possible, and thereafter the increase is made step by step until it reaches the point where man's mind would itself naturally set the boundary. For beyond this farthest limit of musical intervals [*divisionis*], if you seek tones spanning a greater distance, you will not come upon them in any rational music, nor will any practicable possibility exist of a human's coping with them so as to traverse readily at one

2. The nearest found is *WA* 99/8:

3. *B* alone cites also *F*[*uit?*] *in heremo*, not listed by John R. Bryden and David G. Hughes, *An Index of Gregorian Chant* (Cambridge, Mass., 1969). *Fuit in deserto* is listed, but has no such skip in *WA* 323/3.

Example 10

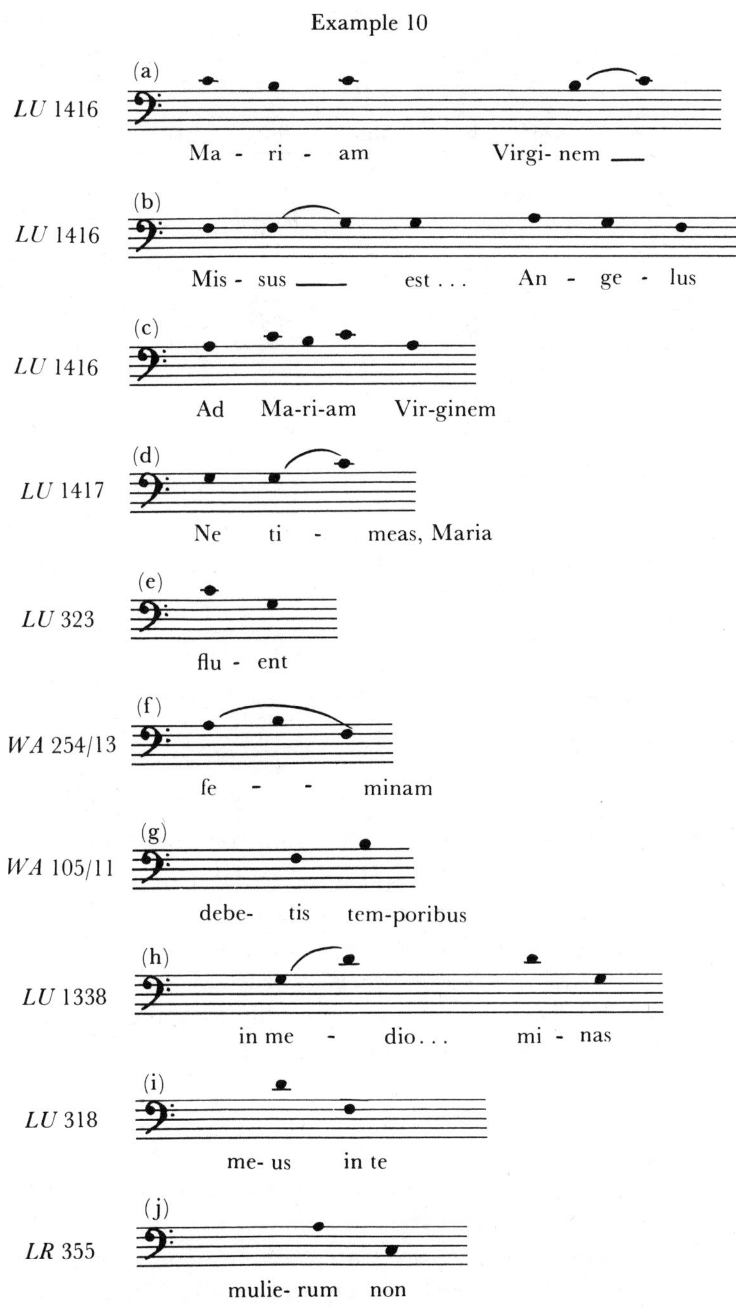

bound such widely separated tones, from the heights to the depths, for even a leap in pitch up to the ninth tone[4] [a major sixth away] is made with strain.[5] The following diagram may set forth these intervals, provided their distances are scrupulously observed by the copyist [Fig. 1].

4. Reading *nonam* for the *novam* of *GS* 1 : 105b/33 and *B* 85/26.
5. Or "is rarely [*paene*] made."

Figure 1

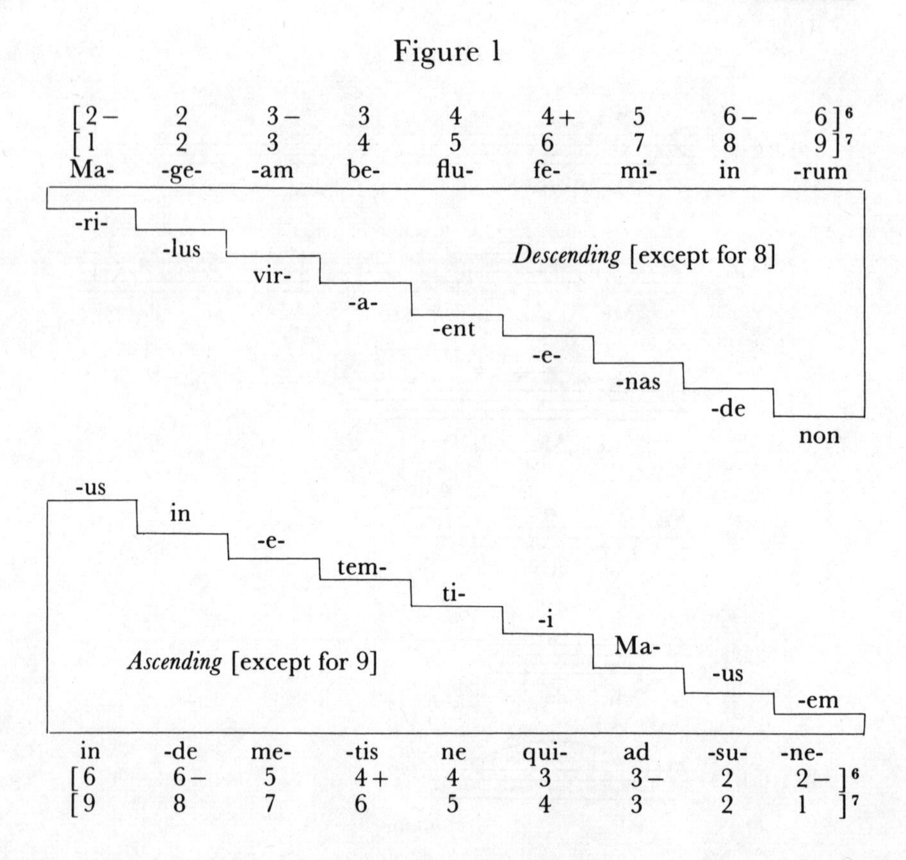

[106a/1] Concerning these intervals it should be noted how what follows always grows out of what precedes and how the later items are based on the earlier. Thus, whereas the first interval is adjacent to equality itself, which it succeeds in the order of musical intervals, it appears when doubled to produce the second interval. But this is not precisely true, as will be discussed later. Therefore this second interval is regarded simply as being a certain amount more than the first one. The third interval consists of the first plus the second, that is, it has in itself as great a span as these together; the fourth interval consists of two of the second; the fifth, of the first plus two of the second; the sixth, of three of the second; the seventh, of the first and three of the second; the eighth, of four of the second; and the ninth, of the first and four of the second. To a close observer it is clear, moreover, that the amount of the first interval is added on to each successive interval in a regular progression. Thus to the first interval you add another such and produce the second—though here something of a discrepancy appears, as was said above. Again, to the second interval the first is added and the third is created, and the fourth

6. Modern name of the interval: 2– is minor second; 2, major second; 4, perfect fourth; 4+, augmented fourth, etc.

7. Hucbald's number for the interval; number of semitones therein.

likewise by the addition of the first to the third; and the same rate of increase is equally maintained for the fifth and the rest. Of the first two intervals, the first is designated according to musical theory as the semitone, the second as the tone. From these the size of all the others is established. Thus the third consists of a semitone and a tone; the fourth embraces two tones; the fifth combines a semitone with two tones; the sixth in a like manner comprises three tones; the seventh, three tones and a semitone; the eighth spans the distance of four tones; and the ninth, of four tones and a semitone. If to this last you add a tone and a semitone, the sound now transfers itself [*prosiliet*] to a new voice [octave].

[107a/3] Do not assume that these intervals between tones are to be equated with the "consonances" with which musical theorizing deals. For a "consonance" is one thing, an "interval" another. "Consonance" is the calculated and concordant blending of two sounds, which will come about only when two simultaneous sounds from different sources combine into a single musical whole [*modulatio*], as happens when a man's and a boy's voices sound at once [*pariter*], and [*vel*] indeed in what is usually called "making organum" [*organizatio*].

[107a/15] There are six of these "consonances," three simple and three composite; they are designated by specific names: diapason, diapente, diatessaron, diapason-plus-diapente, diapason-plus-diatessaron, and double diapason. The distances of only two of these "consonances" can be found among the melodic intervals [*spatia*] discussed above, namely of the diatessaron and the diapente, as the fifth and seventh kinds; and the two tones of either of these make a "consonance" provided that they are performed simultaneously. Otherwise there is no "consonance" in either these six or in any other intervals between notes, only sundry differences between tones, these being confined to the aforementioned particular intervals [*spatia*] between successive notes [*termini*]. These we shall not discuss at present, especially since profit can rarely be had from knowledge of them until the regular arrangement of the sounds has been systematically set forth. When this has come to be understood, the consideration of all these matters, and of certain others as well, may bring no small accrual of both profit and pleasure.

[107b/1] Only this need be added concerning the aforesaid nine intervals, that they are contained within precisely seven tones, of which you have specimens in the antiphon of the authentic tetrardus *Undecim discipuli in Galilea videntes Dominum adoraverunt* [Ex. 11], where these seven tones occur by the end of the syllable *-ve-*. If [the note to] the last of these syllables, *-runt*, which is an octave [*octavus locus*] below the first, is compared with this, it will sound the same, although the one is in men's range, the other in boys'. This is the "consonance of the diapason," and this is why it is excluded from the category of intervals [between different notes]. Let these same notes be ranged in their proper stations, their intervals being spaced by the due amounts; let the tones

Example 11

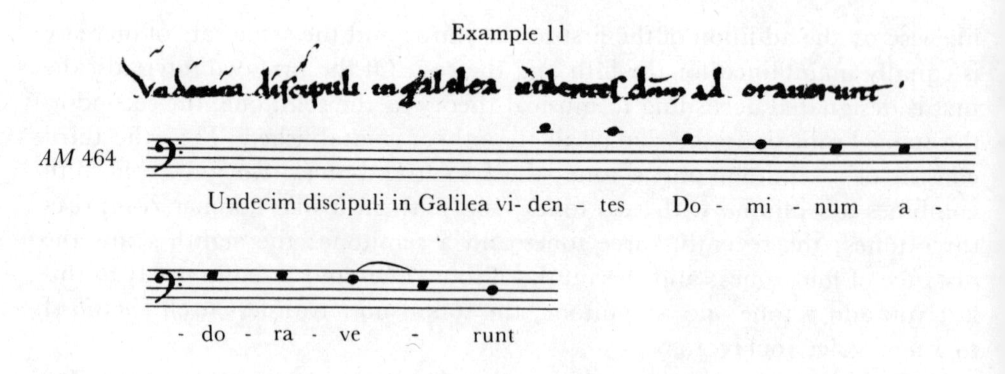

and semitones be labeled; and let these small intervals be marked off by lines drawn between the notes [Fig. 2].

Figure 2

T	s	T	T	T	s	T
-DEN-	-TES	DO-	-MI-	-NUM	VE-	-E-

[d c ♮ a G F E D]

[107b/19] This illustration is set forth here since [it shows those notes] from the middle of the gamut of musical sounds that are relevant to [the beginnings of melodies in] the authentic [*sic*][8] tetrardus and its plagal. We shall find these same sounds in the same way, with the very same intervals between them, in other series or modes [*toni*] as well. We must defer their exposition for the present and proceed now to the gamut of musical sounds.

[107b/28] Those sounds through which, as elements, the ancients deemed that one should approach music, they chose to designate by the Greek word *phthongi*. These were not just any sounds, as for instance those of inanimate objects, or even the cries of animals lacking reason. Only those sounds which they thought were distinguished and determined by calculable quantities and were serviceable for melody—only these did they set as the sure foundation for all song. These, then, they called "elements" or "*phthongi*." Just as all the diversity of language is contained in its elements, the letters, and whatever can be said is expressed through them, so through expert activity the ancients brought about that the immense sum total of melodies have only certain beginnings, these being subject to a definite rule. So whatever is sung proceeds without going astray and nothing is included that does not enjoy complete

8. Compare below, 121/1–12. Hucbald gives no limits of range for the modes.

rationality. They are called "phthongi" from φθέγγεσθαι [*phthengesthai*, to utter a sound], by analogy with speaking, because just as words are communicated by speaking, so sounds enter the mind by means of these phthongi. Moreover the trained intelligence of the experts discriminates even among some unanalyzable sounds.

[108a/19] Therefore they have chosen to define such sound—not, of course, sound in general—as follows: sound is the particular melodious [ἐμμελές] category [*casus*] of tone that is suitable for song, maintaining a steady pitch [*una intensione*], as when the voice produces any [vowel] sound, such as *a*, or sounds in unison with a stretched string.

[108a/26] Few of these calculable phthongi existed originally; at first, indeed, only four of them were distinguished; hence these few have been in use by singers so much the longer. Thereafter, for various subsequent and not unreasonable causes, the number of phthongi gradually increased, and the total came progressively to at first seven or eight, then nine, eleven, and at length up to fifteen. These phthongi have usually been designated by the names of the strings, since they could be illustrated most readily by the instruments with which they were associated. Their invention and arrangement and individual names have been sufficiently expounded by many other writers in this discipline, Greek and Latin, and especially by that wondrous teacher and most discerning investigator in all the liberal arts, Boethius, in the first book of his harmonic instruction.[9] One must realize that among these phthongi or sounds none is identical with another, but that they proceed like a ladder from the lowest to the highest or from the highest to the lowest, each being the proper degree of distance away from the other. However, the same distance does not separate them all. But by the use of the first two intervals set forth in the foregoing outline of intervals, those called the tone and the semitone, and provided that each of them stands in the right place, each series of phthongi proceeds at measured pace.

[108b/23] First it must be said what a tone is, and what a semitone. Once these, which are judged to serve as elements, are understood, all the rest are easily comprehended. It is a "tone" when a note is lowered or raised from another note, either low or high, by a moderately small interval, a displacement, as it were, by one degree [*punctum*], so that the hearing notices the discreteness of the notes quite easily. The "tone," then, is the distance between the two notes so connected—not the notes themselves, observe, for they are simply sounds, but the interval between them. On any musical instrument you have an example of this between the first two strings, if properly tuned, or on water organs between the first two pipes. And you can examine it also in the antiphon *Ite dicite* [Ex. 12].

9. *De inst. mus.* 1. 20.

Example 12

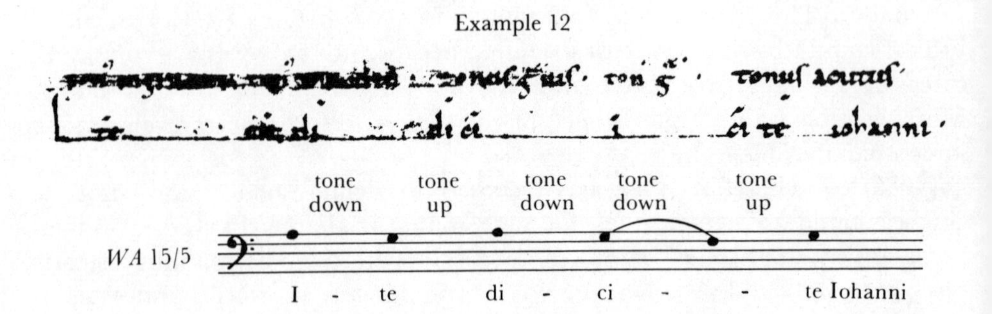

[109a/7] A semitone appears to be so called from its containing approximately half a tone. But if this were so, a tone could be divided into two equal parts, whereas proof has been furnished by some of the most careful analysts that this is utterly impossible. A tone is divided in two only in such a way that either part either exceeds or is less than a half. Both of these parts are called semitones: the one, a major; the other, a minor; as though you made this division [Fig. 3]. When these combine into one, they make a whole tone.

Figure 3

tone — semitones: major | minor

Furthermore, if two major semitones are combined, they exceed a tone; if two minor, they by no means attain to its extent. A semitone is so designated, not because it is half of a tone, but because "semi-" is customarily said of either part of anything divided into two parts, even unequal ones, as when you divide three into one and two. It is a semitone if two notes are linked by the very shortest space, so that scarcely any distance can be descried between them. Sometimes, however, this is said only of the minor semitone; for although the major, too, has its notes extremely close together, still the interval between them is a little more clearly perceptible. Let it here be noted yet again that not the notes themselves but the space between them is the semitone. There are, then, two kinds of semitone but only one kind of tone, for at however high or low a pitch a tone is performed, it will contain no more or less distance and will thus remain one and the same. An example of a semitone can be seen on the cithara of six strings between the third string and the fourth, either ascending or descending. Its scale ascending is as in the antiphon *Cum audisset populus* at *acceperunt ramos* [Ex. 13]; descending, as in the antiphon *Hodie completi sunt dies Pentecostes* [Ex. 14]. And likewise on water organs. Let specimens also be written down of both tone and semitone from any chant, distinguishing the six strings, whose place is taken by the lines, and always

Example 13

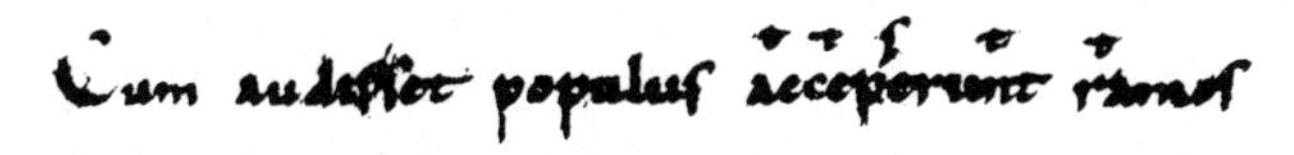

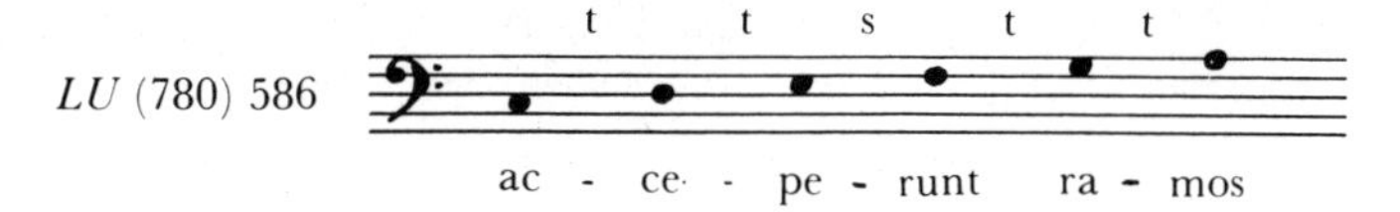

Example 14

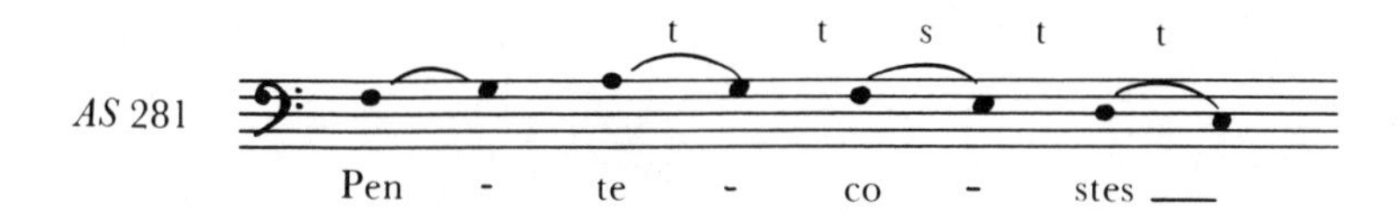

with a notation between the strings as to where there is a tone and where a semitone [Fig. 4].

Figure 4

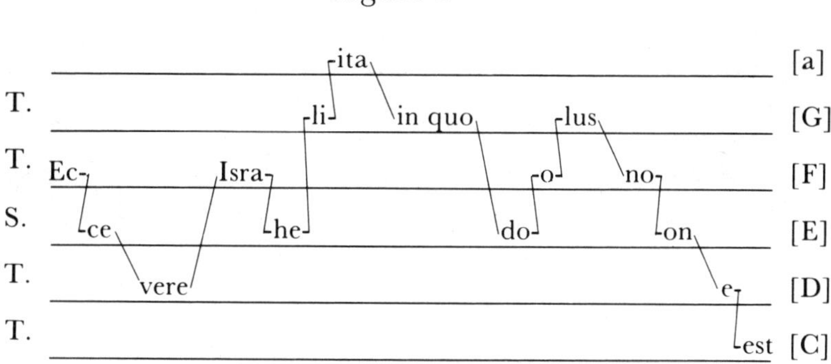

[109b/27] Wherever, then, you find in any melody an interval such as here between the syllables *ec-* and *-ce*, or *-ra-* and *-he-*, or *do-* and *-o-*, or *no-* and *-on*, do not doubt that it is a semitone. But where you find notes differing in sound as do *-li-* and *-ita*, or *-ta* and *in*, or *-lus* and *no-*, or *-ce* and *ve-*, or the end of *non* and the beginning of *est*, [or the beginning] and end of *est*, there, indubitably, is a tone. From *-re* to *Is-*, *-he-* to *-li-*, and *quo* to *do-* is the interval of a semitone plus a tone. Others are performed without change of pitch or level: thus *vere* and *Isra-* and *in quo*.

[110a/5] In accordance, then, with these two kinds of interval, the tone and the semitone, they being set in due place and order, are ranged all the others, as fixed by calculation. A sum total of fifteen phthongi are arrayed thus, one above the other. In ascending order, after you first place one extra note, as it were, separating it by a tone from the next one, you then go up through [the pattern] semitone, tone, tone for seven notes. Thereupon, after again inserting a gap [*disiunctio*] of a tone, you proceed through the next seven notes higher in just the same way. In descending, if you begin at the top, you go down [through the pattern] tone, tone, semitone, likewise for seven notes, and after a gap of a tone you arrange the lower seven notes in the same way. Then add the last one, which had first place when you were ascending, at the distance of a tone away. The whole series of notes may be indicated by this diagram [Fig. 5].

Figure 5

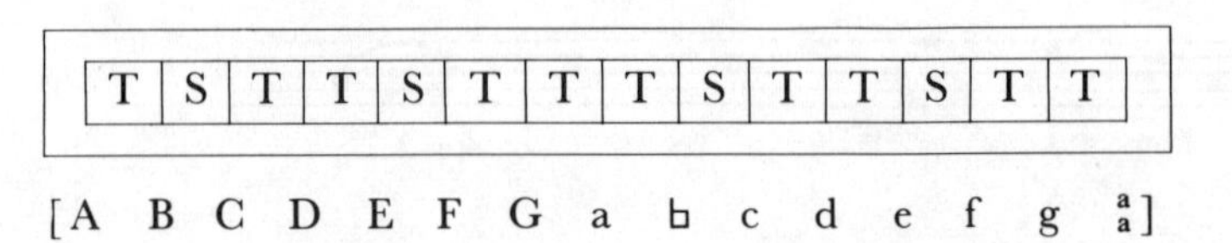

Figure 6

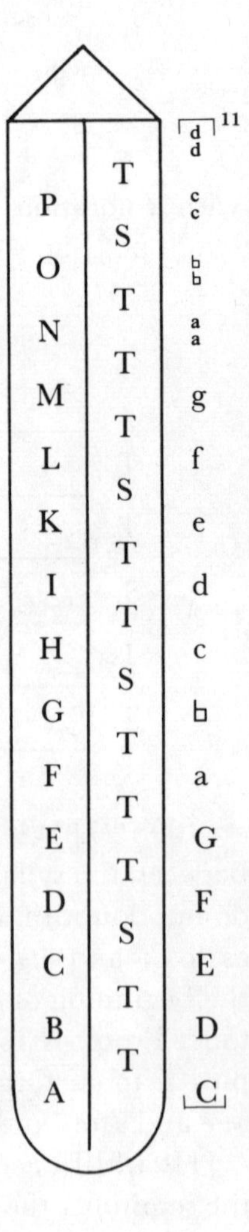

[110a/17] Let it cause you no misgiving if perchance when inspecting a water organ or any other kind of musical instrument you find that its notes are not arranged in this pattern or that they clearly exceed this number of strings. For this arrangement is based on the plan of that most sagacious man, Boethius, who weighs all this with careful judgment in the light of the harmony of commensurable numbers.

[110a/27] But such musical instruments should not for this reason be thought at variance with the understanding, since during long ages they have been handled[10] by so many intelligent men that they now stand tested and approved by the greatest intellects, and since, too, one observes that the pattern of the above arrangement of the notes appertains fully to these musical instruments. For the latter are planned in all respects duly according to those same two kinds [of interval, the tone and the semitone,] and one may rest assured that they differ in no other respect than that their starting points are not calculated in the way here set forth, for they begin with the third note of the above arrangement. Moreover the large number of strings or pipes—as for instance twenty-one or more—is not caused by extending the sounds beyond

10. Reading *pertractata* for the *pertracta* of *GS* 1 : 110a/30 and *B* 87v/4.

11. The letters in the left-hand column, from Boethius, *De inst. mus.* 4. 17, are neither explained nor used hereinafter and thus seem a scribal addition.

fifteen or perhaps sixteen, but by repeating the same ones as below [in a higher octave]. This large number derives from the variety of modes, which are nowadays called "tones," such as the authentic protus and the others. Since, obviously, they cannot all begin with the same bottom notes, the [larger number of notes permits] a mode sufficient scope for its range, whatever note it starts from.

[110b/32] Water organs etc. are, then, so planned as to ascend by a tone, a tone, and a semitone, and again three adjacent tones and a semitone for eight notes; and, beginning again from this eighth note, a higher series is measured off by the same steps, in this manner [Fig. 6]. An example of this from the offertory *Angelus Domini descendit* is supplied by the following passage, which has all the [eight] notes together [*pro* (*bis* in B) *totis vocibus super se positis*] [Ex. 15].

Example 15

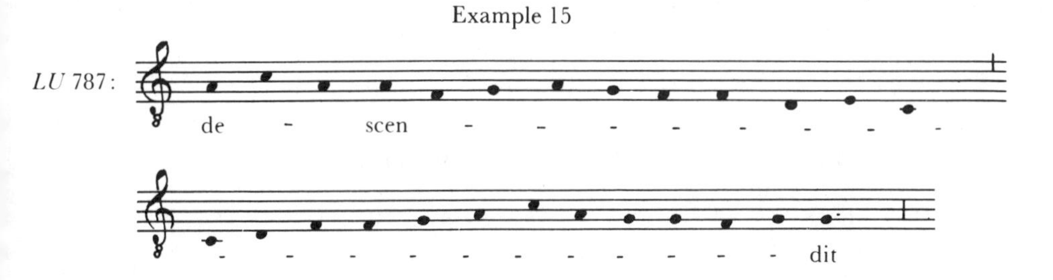

[111a/7] Both in this arrangement [C—$\overset{c}{c}$] and in the prior one [A—$\overset{a}{a}$] it is to be noted that the upper eight notes are the same as the lower, except that the former are like boys' voices, the latter, on the other hand, like men's. Therefore as soon as you have produced the seventh sound you will proceed straight to the eighth as if it were a new [*sic*] note. Thus if the first note is sounded together with the eighth, the second with the ninth, the third with the tenth, and so, throughout the range, individual lower notes are sounded with the corresponding [*singulis*] upper notes, they will blend with an altogether pleasant and harmonious sweetness, as though the sound were one and single. This sort of concord is termed "the consonance of the diapason."

[111a/21] Boethius,[12] dividing the prior arrangement of notes into four tetrachords, so distributes them as to link two tetrachords together by a shared string and to disjoin from them two more tetrachords similarly linked to each other.

[111a/27] A tetrachord is a group of four strings. These strings we call "notes," and we interchangeably call notes "strings." These four notes or strings of which every tetrachord consists are so arranged that they always cluster side by side, so that no other sound can properly be inserted between them, and they are only a tone or a semitone apart—these intervals being set

12. Boethius, *De inst. mus.* 1. 20.

at the right places. Nor does equality of sound claim [*defendet*] anything for itself here, but all notes will mount progressively upwards according to the rule for ascent, or else move downwards correspondingly. The structure of all tetrachords follows a single pattern. Boethius arranges the tetrachords beginning from the highest notes, placing the tetrachords one below the other, adding at the bottom in fifteenth place one note by itself. He sets out the tetrachords by tone, tone, and semitone, so spacing them that while the top two are interlinked by a common tone, they are separated by the space of a tone from the lower two, which are similarly interlinked by a shared tone. In this way there are only fourteen notes, but, to round out the full number of consonant [diapasons], a fifteenth note, as we have said, is set in the lowest region beyond the series of tetrachords. The first four notes of the [*Noeane*]-melody of the authentic protus[13] will offer an example of such a tetrachord. The tetrachords may succeed each other without a break as in the following formula [Fig. 7].

Figure 7

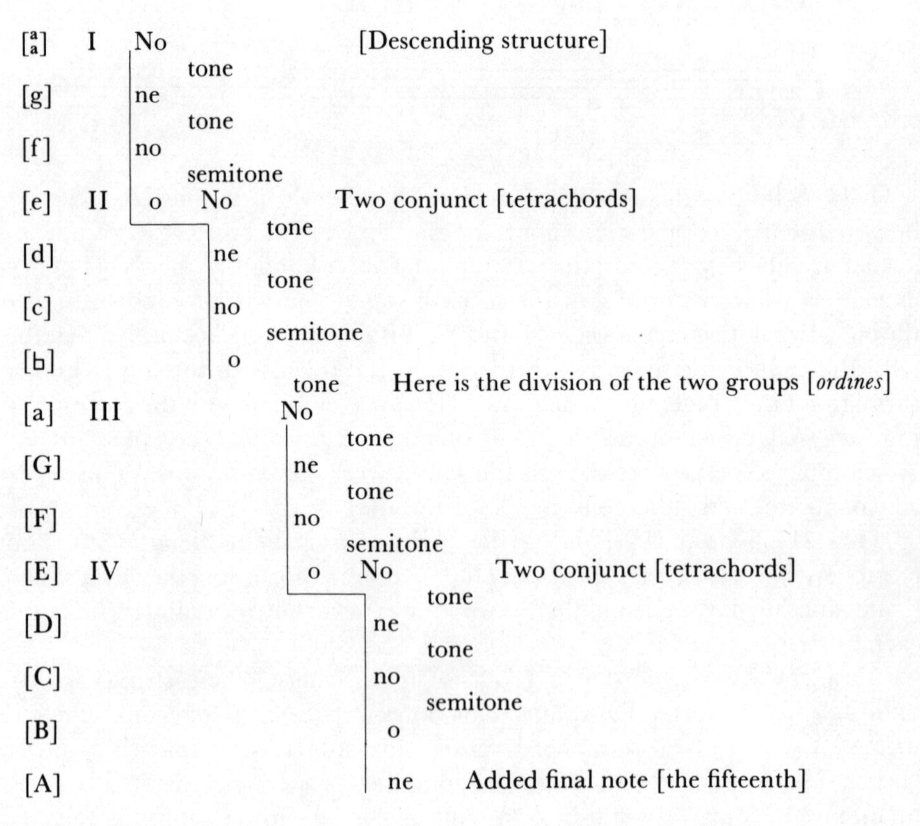

13. Compare below, pp. 27, 35, 36; and in the *Commemoratio brevis de tonis et psalmis modulandis*, *GS* 1 : 214/5, 229/1.

[112a/1] If you wish to begin this same series from the bottom, again leave the first note outside the series and proceed with the rest by a semitone, a tone, and a tone, the opposite of before, while carefully keeping the same places as before for conjunction and disjunction of the tetrachords. As a model for the first four notes you may take the first syllable of the responsory *Redimet dominus populus suum* [Ex. 16a] or of *et liberavit eos* [Ex. 16b] later therein; they are written

Example 16

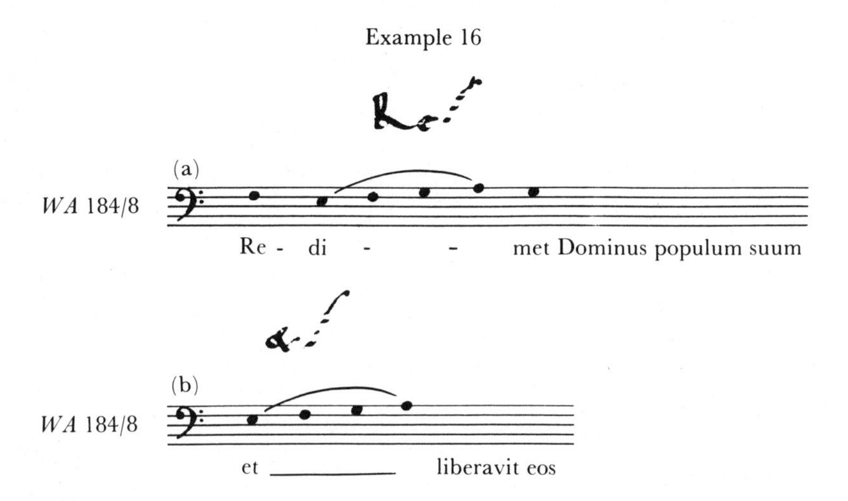

[as in Ex. 16]. These notes you place in four tetrachords one above the other, in due order [Fig. 8].[14]

Figure 8

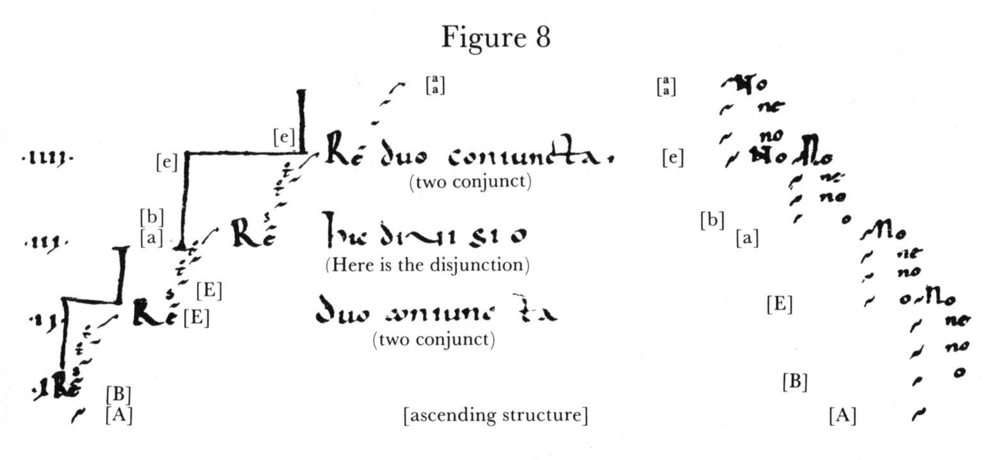

[112b/2] If you wish to build up the whole series of tetrachords from the very first note [of the gamut, the "extra" bottom note, A], you take your

14. This chart and the next three do not correct the frequent places where the scribe of *B*, disregarding the conjunction and disjunction, writes on a different level neumes for the same pitch, or on the same level neumes for different pitches.

model from the invitatorium *Christus natus est nobis* at *Venite* [Ex. 17] and proceed through [the pattern] tone, semitone, tone to the seventh note, whereupon, locating a note above this by disjunction, you order the remaining

Example 17

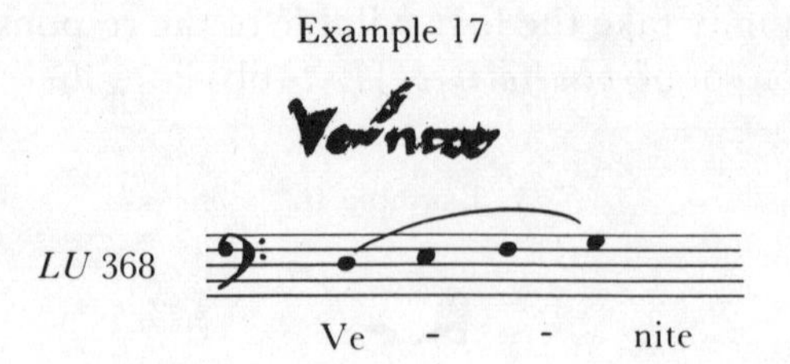

two tetrachords in the same manner, placing [the "extra" fifteenth] note on top, as in the diagram [Fig. 9].

Figure 9

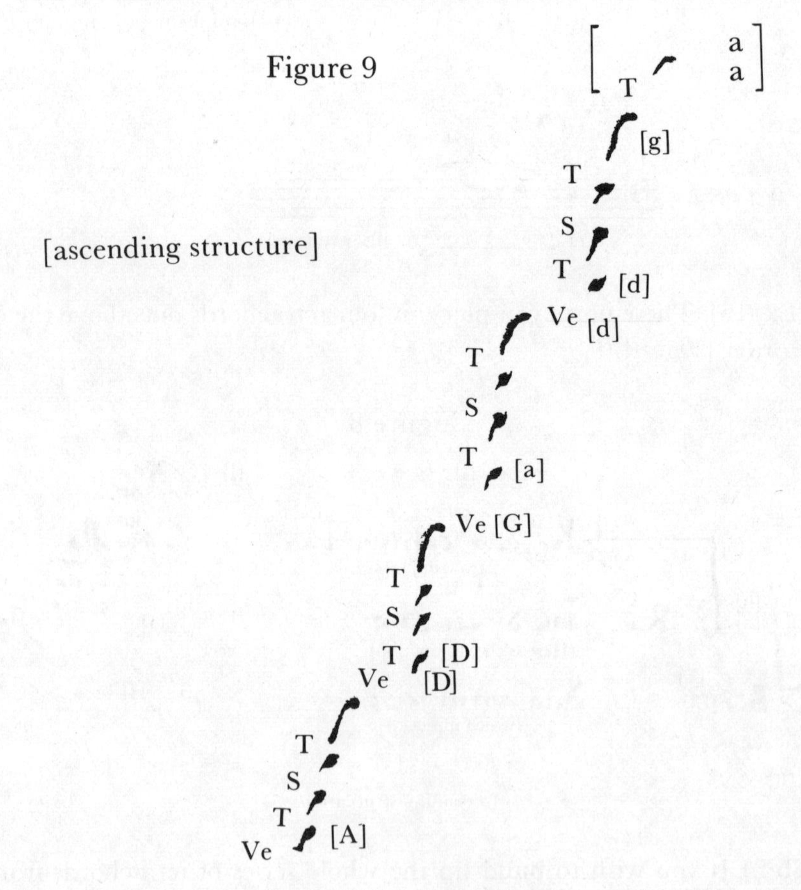

[113/1] If you wish to set down this diagram from the top to the bottom, you will leave the top note outside the pattern and lay out the descending path by tone, semitone, and tone. An example of this is offered [just after] the beginning of the sequence *Stans a longe*[15] [at *Qui plurima/atque sua*], notated thus in neumes [Fig. 10].[16]

Figure 10

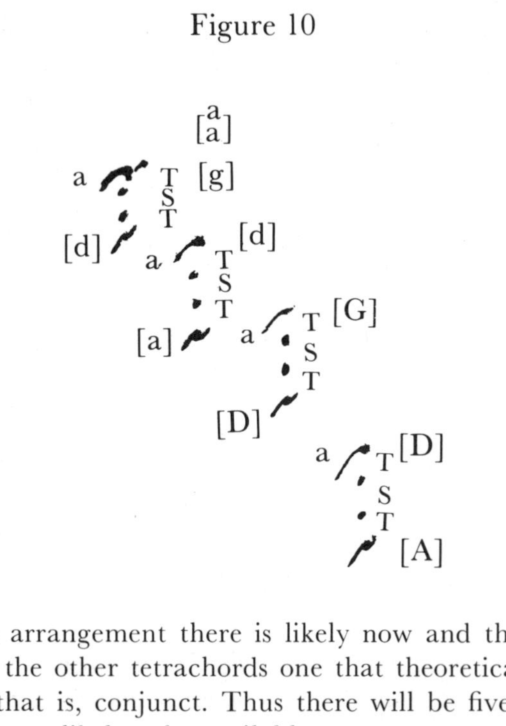

[113/6] In this arrangement there is likely now and then to be inserted midway between the other tetrachords one that theoretical writers call the "synemmenon," that is, conjunct. Thus there will be five tetrachords. But since this one is very unlikely to be available on water organs and other organs, there are a great many melodies (*cantibus*) that many of them lack the means to perform. This tetrachord of the synemmenon is located after the seventh note [from the bottom] of the above arrangement, so that this seventh note [G] is the first of the synemmenon,[17] and by this arrangement three adjacent tetrachords will be linked together. Thus the semitone will come after the eighth note, where a whole tone came in the preceding arrangements. These three tetrachords will be set out as shown [Fig. 11].

[113a/19] But if the tetrachord of the synemmenon is not inserted, then the tetrachord which in the above arrangements was placed third [from the

15. No. 66, p. 115 in *Goede*:

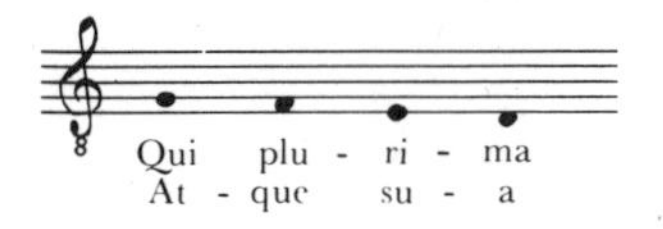

16. In this chart and the next, the unbracketed a's stand for *atque sua*, from *Stans a longe*.

17. This, of course, does not agree with the Greek system, in which the eighth note, counting up from proslambanomenos, is the first of the synemmenon tetrachord.

Figure 11

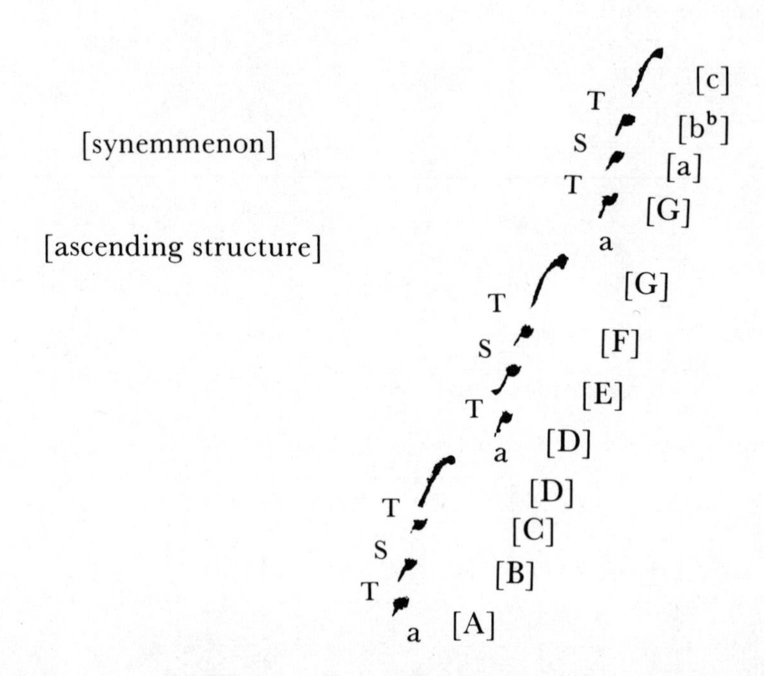

bottom], after the seventh note, is called the tetrachord of the diezeugmenon, that is disjunct. You will find on every hand melodies in the various melodic modes proceeding with now one, now the other of these two tetrachords: sometimes with either one of them persisting throughout the melody, sometimes with the melody shifting from one to the other, as perhaps when it is first among the synemmenon and then soon slips into the diezeugmenon, or from the diezeugmenon into the synemmenon. An example of this is afforded by the responsory *Nativitas gloriosae Virginis Mariae*, which proceeds wholly according to the diezeugmenon up to the music for *ex stirpe*. But at the third note of the syllable *-pe*, notated thus [Ex. 18a] it is taken down into the synemmenon, and the whole neume for the word *David* [Ex. 18b] is sung with the synemmenon.

Example 18

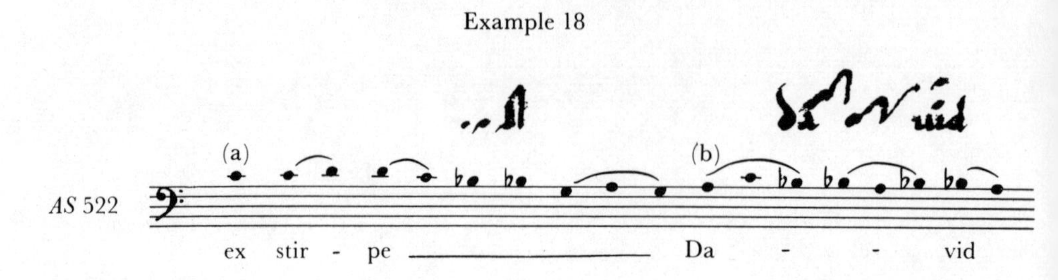

[113b/25] In the introit *Statuit ei dominus* [Ex. 19] the second note [a] for the syllable *Sta* [Ex. 19a], which is a fifth away from the first [D], ascends to the third note [b♭] via the synemmenon, and there is a semitone between these second [a] and third [b♭] notes. And whereas the syllable *Do* [Ex. 19b] rises to the diezeugmenon, the syllable *mi* [Ex. 19c] subsides again to the synemmenon. Moreover the syllables *tes*- [Ex. 19d] and *fe*- [Ex. 19e] call for the synemmenon; *sit* [Ex. 19f] and *sa*- [Ex. 19g], the diezeugmenon; -*ni*- [Ex. 19h] again the synemmenon, back and forth.

Example 19

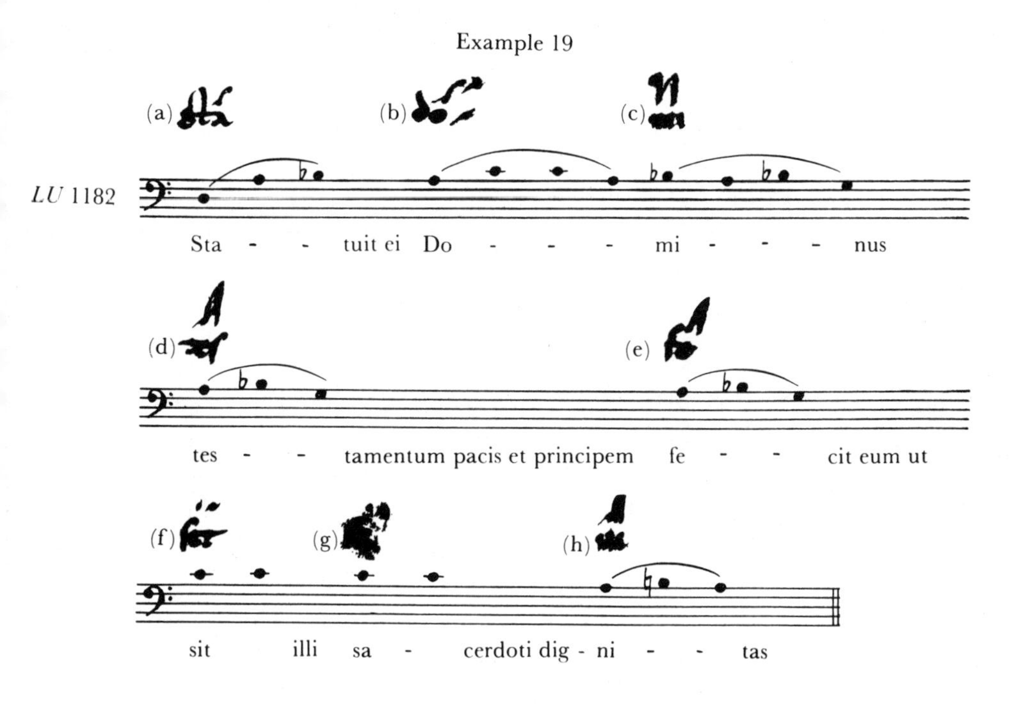

[114a/10] While examples of the tetrachord of the synemmenon are often encountered in all the modes, or tones, they can be seen especially in the authentic and plagal tritus so ubiquitously that in these scarcely any melody is found without a mixture of the tetrachords of the synemmenon and the diezeugmenon. Any attentive person will be able to perceive this in the melody of the authentic tritus which is notated thus:

Example 20

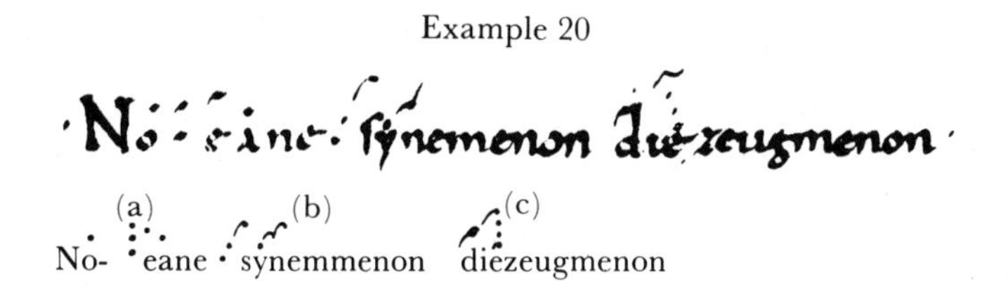

Noeane [Ex. 20a], [in the] synemmenon [Ex. 20b], [in the] diezeugmenon [Ex. 20c]. Also in the antiphon *Ecce iam venit* [in the] diezeugmenon [Ex. 21a], with *plenitudo* [in the] synemmenon [Ex. 21b]. Also in the antiphon *Paganorum multitudo* [Ex. 22] where with only the beginning up to the syllable *-tu-* setting out in the diezeugmenon, the rest up to the end is regulated by the inflections of the synemmenon.

[114a/last] These, then, are the five tetrachords, to each of which the writers on this art have given a particular name, designating the first of them, since it is the lowest or deepest, that of the *hypaton*; the second, of the *meson*; the third, of the *synemmenon*; the fourth, of the *diezeugmenon*; and the fifth, of the *hyperbolaeon*. The first gets its name from the principal note of this tetrachord, which is called the *hypate*; the second, from the *mese*, the middle of the whole series; the third, fourth, and fifth, from the word describing their position. For synemmenon means "of conjunct"; diezeugmenon, "of disjunct"; and hyperbolaeon, "of preeminent."

[114b/14] To make the whole series easier to understand, the names of all the strings will here be set down in order. It is acknowledged beyond question that the notes already ranged clearly in the diagrams above represent the sounds of these strings absolutely. The first arrangement, which proceeds by semitone, tone, and tone, will be particularly suited to this scheme. For thus a rational plan for the notes was constructed by that most illustrious man, Boethius. Here, then, are the names of all the fifteen tones, the tetrachord of the synemmenon excepted, for with this included they total eighteen [Fig. 12].

[116a/7] If the tetrachord of the synemmenon is inserted, whose place[18] is

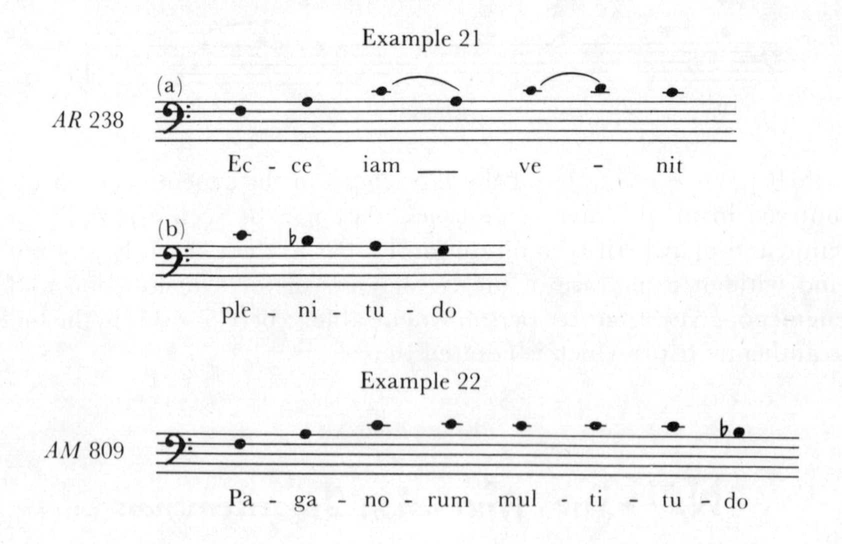

18. That is, whose characteristic note and raison d'être is the ♭-flat between the mese and the paramese, whether produced in a tetrachord G a b ♭ c, as above, or in a tetrachord a b ♭ c d, as below and in the Greek system.

Figure 12

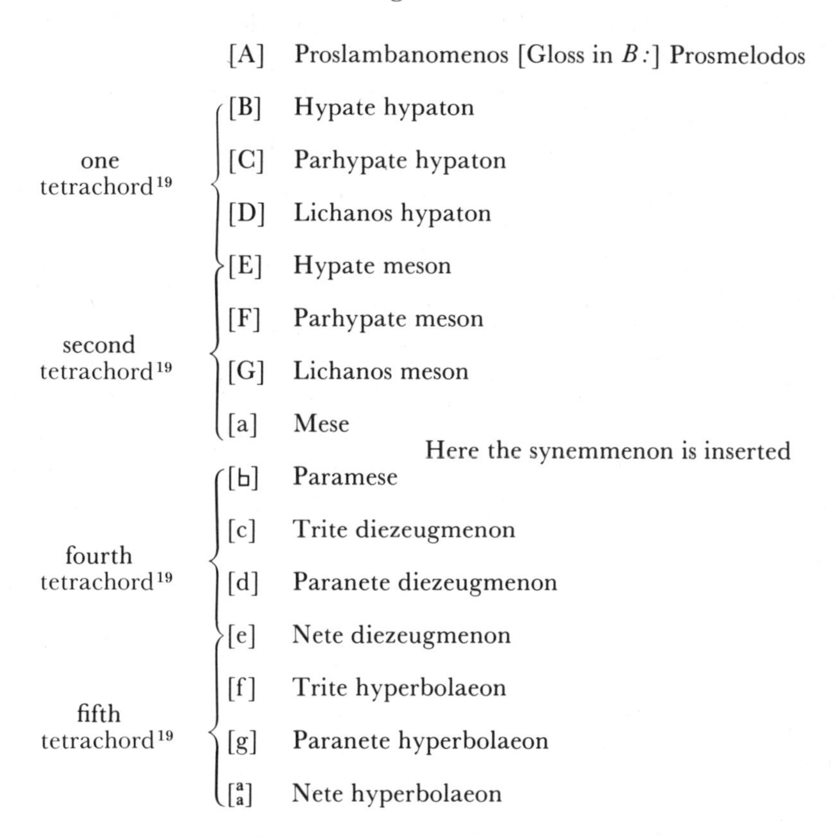

Figure 13

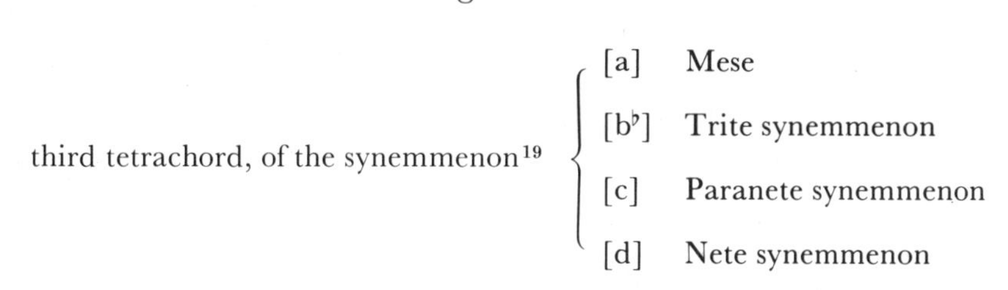

between the mese [a] and the paramese [♮], then these three notes will be inserted after the mese in this order [Fig. 13].

[116a/12] Of these, only one, that is the trite synemmenon [b♭], has a sound not among those previously given. For the paranete synemmenon [c] is the same in sound as the trite diezeugmenon [c], and the nete synemmenon [d] the same as the paranete diezeugmenon [d]; they differ only in name. The names will be assigned on the basis that whenever any melody is so composed

19. *GS*, not in *B* 89v.

that after the mese [a] there is a semitone, a tone, and a tone upwards and it returns by the same route of a tone, a tone, and a semitone to the mese [a], it must be said to proceed by a tetrachord correctly identified as of the synemmenon, that is, conjunct, because it makes a semitone above the mese [a] [*cum mese per semitonium iungitur*].

[116a/27] But whenever a tetrachord parts by the interval of a tone from the mese [a] and proceeds from the paramese [♮] up to the nete diezeugmenon [e], this tetrachord ought to be called by the other name, that is "of the diezeugmenon," which means disjunct, because there is the distance of a tone between the mese [a] and the paramese [♮].

[116a/35] Beginning the arrangement from above, there is one tetrachord from the nete hyperbolaeon [$\overset{a}{a}$] through the nete diezeugmenon [e] and another from the nete diezeugmenon [e] through the paramese [♮], and these two are conjunct with each other. For in the nete diezeugmenon [e] are merged the last and lowest of the upper tetrachord and the first and highest of the lower. Each consists of a tone, a tone, and a semitone; their order is shown [Fig. 14].

Figure 14

[$\overset{a}{a}$]	Nete hyperbolaeon	
		Tone[20]
[g]	Paranete hyperbolaeon	
		Tone
[f]	Trite hyperbolaeon	
		Semitone
[e]	Nete diezeugmenon	This is common to both.
		Tone
[d]	Paranete diezeugmenon	
		Tone
[c]	Trite diezeugmenon	
		Semitone
[♮]	Paramese	

[116b/15] Separate from these, moreover, there are two lower tetrachords, spaced out by the same intervals of tones and semitones: one, the third, from the mese [a] to the hypate meson [E]; the other, the fourth, from the hypate meson [E] down [*rursus*] to the hypate hypaton [B]. These likewise are conjunct with each other, as shown [Fig. 15].

[116b/30] There remains the proslambanomenos [A], which, as Boethius affirms,[21] is added for the sake of the interval of the double octave. If we desire three conjunct tetrachords, the synemmenon [b♭] is placed between the mese [a] and the paramese [♮], concerning which we have spoken copiously above.

20. The interval distances in this column are from *GS*; not in *B*, 89v.

21. Boethius, *De inst. mus.* 1. 20.

Figure 15

[a]	Mese	
		Tone
[G]	Lichanos meson	
		Tone
[F]	Parhypate meson	
		Semitone
[E]	Hypate meson	This is common to both.
		Tone
[D]	Lichanos hypaton	
		Tone
[C]	Parhypate hypaton	
		Semitone
[B]	Hypate hypaton	

The sounds of these notes have been abundantly explicated already, where we set down as a pattern the first four notes from the melody for the authentic protus, that is [Ex. 23].[22]

Example 23

[117a/4] The meaning of these names is briefly touched upon by Boethius;[23] Martianus Capella[24] expounds it more intelligibly. Proslambanomenos means "obtained in addition," for this string was added after all the others. Hypate means "low" or "first"; parhypate, "next to the hypate." As for lichanos, in Greek the index finger is so called, and if on the cithara you touch with the little finger the first string, which is the proslambanomenos, the index finger falls on the fourth string, which also, therefore, has acquired this name. Mese means "middle," and it is located midway in the whole array, for it is the eighth from either end. Paramese [means] "next to the mese"; trite, "third" from the mese or from the nete; nete, "high"; and paranete, "next to the nete." At first there were only eight strings, with these names: hypate [E], parhypate [F], lichanos [G], mese [a], paramese [♮], trite [c], paranete [d], and nete [e]. Subsequently, when the number of strings increased from this, the names given them above were devised. If someone wishes to know more about their invention and proliferation, Book 1 of the harmonic discipline of Boethius will instruct him more thoroughly.[25]

[117a/30] Let our course turn next to the written musical signs, which,

22. See above, Figs. 7–8, and below, Ex. 26.
23. Ibid., 1. 22.
24. *De nuptiis* 9, in Meibom, *musicae auctores*, 2 : 179–80.
25. *De inst. mus.* 1. 20.

placed by each of the string names, bring no slight profit to students of music.

As the sounds and differences of words are recognized by letters in writing in such a way that the reader is not led into doubt, musical signs were devised so that every melody notated by their means, once these signs have been learned, can be sung even without a teacher. But this can scarcely happen using the signs which custom has handed down to us and which in various regions are given no less various shapes, although they are of some help as an aid to one's memory, for the markings by which they guide the reader are always indefinite, as, for instance, if you consider the illustration [Ex. 24]. Looking

Example 24

at the first mark, which appears to be rather high, you may easily sing it at any pitch in your range. But when you try to connect to it the second note, which you observe is lower, and you inquire by what interval you should do so—whether the second should be one or two or even three steps [*puncta*] away from the first—you cannot even vaguely detect how this was prescribed by the composer unless you get it by ear from someone. The same is the case with the other notes. But if you see this same illustration written down in the string notation, which a subsequent chart will set forth, you will soon perceive with no uncertainty how it goes [Ex. 25].[26] Here "i" is the mese [a], and "m" the

Example 25

lichanos meson [G], between which there is the distance of a tone; "p" is the parhypate meson [F], which is likewise a tone away from the lichanos meson [G]; a second "m," the lichanos meson [G], sounding above the parhypate meson "p" [F], descends again to the parhypate meson [F]; "c" thereupon is the hypate meson [E], a semitone away from the parhypate meson [F]; and the concluding "f" is the lichanos hypaton [D], making a tone with the hypate meson [E].

26. Throughout the examples *B* uses Latin letters instead of the Greek capitals of Fig. 16. Thus I is rendered i, M as m, P (rho) as p, C (sigma) as c, and F (digamma) as f. See the Introduction.

[118a/1] From the following familiar melody of the authentic protus, above which we have written these signs [Ex. 26], it will be clearer what sounds are in the preceding illustration.[27] For whichever of these little signs or letters you

Example 26

see in the next-to-last illustration you will not hesitate to perform [there] in the same way. Yet the customary notes are not considered wholly unnecessary, since they are deemed quite serviceable in showing the slowness or speed of the melody, and where the sound demands a tremulous voice, or how the sounds are grouped together or separated from each other, also where a cadence is made upon them, lower or higher, according to the sense of certain letters—things of which these more scientific signs can show nothing whatsoever. Therefore if these little letters which we accept as a musical notation are placed above or near the customary notes, sound by sound, there will clearly be on view a full and flawless record [*indago*] of the truth, the one set of signs indicating how much higher or lower each tone is placed, the other informing one about the afore-mentioned varieties of performance, without which valid melody is not created.

[118b/6] There are many signs for the strings, suited to the use of the ancients, two of which were set by Boethius to each string throughout each of the eight modes, to the total of 288.[28] These are written in Greek letters, some of them normal, some of them altered in various ways; they clearly take up a great deal of page space. So, for the present, we shall employ only those of the Lydian mode, some lying above [the Lydian final, or even the notes on which a chant in the Lydian mode may begin, and] some below. And these, as closely curtailed as possible, that is as briefly and concisely as they can be set down, we think will suffice for contemporary use [Fig. 16].

[119a/1] Now that the point has been reached to which from the outset everything looked forward, it should be more clearly shown what may be made out of these materials and how great a harvest may arise from the seeds already sown. Since the distances between the tones have been clearly established—first by the differences between notes, next by those between tetrachords, then by the names of the strings themselves, and lastly by the signs for

27. I.e., Ex. 25. See also Fig. 7 and Ex. 23.

28. Boethius, *De inst. mus.* 4. 3, 15, 16. See Friedlein ed., *descriptiones* 1 and 2, p. 343. Note that Hucbald's signs do not always agree with Boethius's.

Figure 16

Nete hyperbolaeon: it has an amplified iota, thus:	[aa]
Paranete hyperbolaeon: [has] an amplified Greek Π	[g]
Trite hyperbolaeon: a simple y	[f]
Nete diezeugmenon: a small N	[e]
Paranete diezeugmenon: a square *ω*	[d]
Trite diezeugmenon: a simple e	[c]
Paramese: a Greek Π lying on its side	[♮]
Nete synemmenon: the same as the paranete diezeugmenon	[d]
Paranete synemmenon: the same as the trite diezeugmenon	[c]
Trite synemmenon: a Greek theta	[b♭]
Mese: a simple iota	[a]
Lichanos meson: a simple M	[G]
Parhypate meson: a simple Greek P [Rho]	[F]
Hypate meson: a simple Greek sigma	[E]
Lichanos hypaton: a simple digamma	[D]
Parhypate hypaton: a simple beta	[C]
Hypate hypaton: a simple gamma	[B]
Proslambanomenos: an upright daseia	[A]

them—it is now time to show how these elements may be combined with each other, that is, how they proceed in the various modes.

[119a/12] Passing over the first three notes, the next four, namely the lichanos hypaton [D], the hypate meson [E], the parhypate meson [F], and the lichanos meson [G] are used in constructing the four modes or tropes. These are nowadays called "tones" and are the protus, deuterus, tritus, and tetrardus. This is done in such a way that each of these four notes reigns over a pair of tropes subject to it, namely, a principal one, which is called the "authentic," and a collateral one, which is called the "plagal." Thus the lichanos hypaton [D] rules over the authentic protus and its plagal, that is the first and second modes; the hypate meson [E] over the authentic deuterus and its plagal, that is the third and fourth; the parhypate meson [F] over the

Figure 17

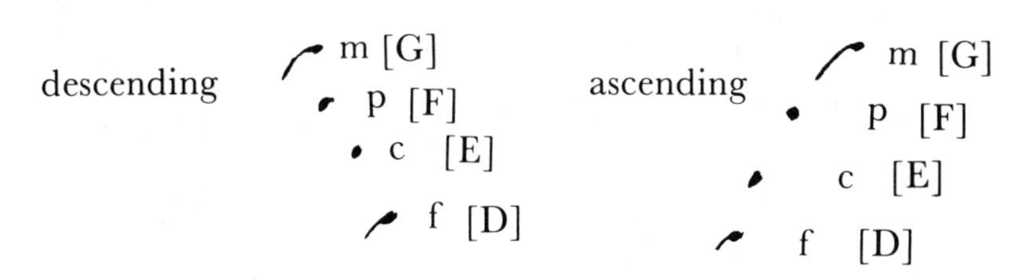

authentic tritus and its plagal, that is the fifth and sixth; and the lichanos meson [G] over the authentic tetrardus and its plagal, that is the seventh and eighth. Consequently any melody whatsoever is perforce classified under some one of these four pairs of modes, however variously it ranges about, whether far afield or close to the final. These four notes are called "finals" since everything that is sung ends among them. We write them as shown [Fig. 17] in the notation just presented.

[119b/1] The other tetrachords—one stationed below, three above—arrange their intervals and characteristics of sound after the model of these [four notes, D, E, F, and G]. The earlier examples make all this sufficiently clear. In them it is to be observed that, leaving out the tetrachord of the synemmenon, the notes a fifth above each of these four finals respectively are joined with them in such a bond of similarity that one will generally find that melodies can close on these notes a fifth above without offending either one's judgment or ear. They remain entirely within the same mode or trope, as though according to some principle. In this relationship are linked the lichanos hypaton [D] with the mese [a], the hypate meson [E] with the paramese [♮], the parhypate meson [F] with the trite diezeugmenon [c], and the lichanos meson [G] with the paranete diezeugmenon [d], they being respectively a fifth apart. The four finals also possess somewhat of a like relationship to the notes a fourth below, and in certain cases a fifth below, but such notes are used for beginnings, not endings. For the limit for beginnings extends down to these notes. Thus related are: the proslambanomenos [A] to the lichanos hypaton [D]; the hypate hypaton [B] to the hypate meson [E], but this only rarely; the parhypate hypaton [C] with the parhypate meson [F]; and the lichanos hypaton [D] with the lichanos meson [G]. Moreover, when the lichanos meson [G] is the final, the beginning is sometimes placed as low as the parhypate hypaton [C], a fifth away, but this is very rare with other finals.

[119b/32] No mode or trope at all can ever begin more than a fifth above or below its final. Rather, the endings and beginnings are confined within these series of eight—or sometimes nine—notes, be the mode authentic or plagal. This may be made clear by examples successively in each mode. The following eight notes are connected to the authentic protus and its plagal. You will see that melodies begin with them as shown [Fig. 18].

Figure 18

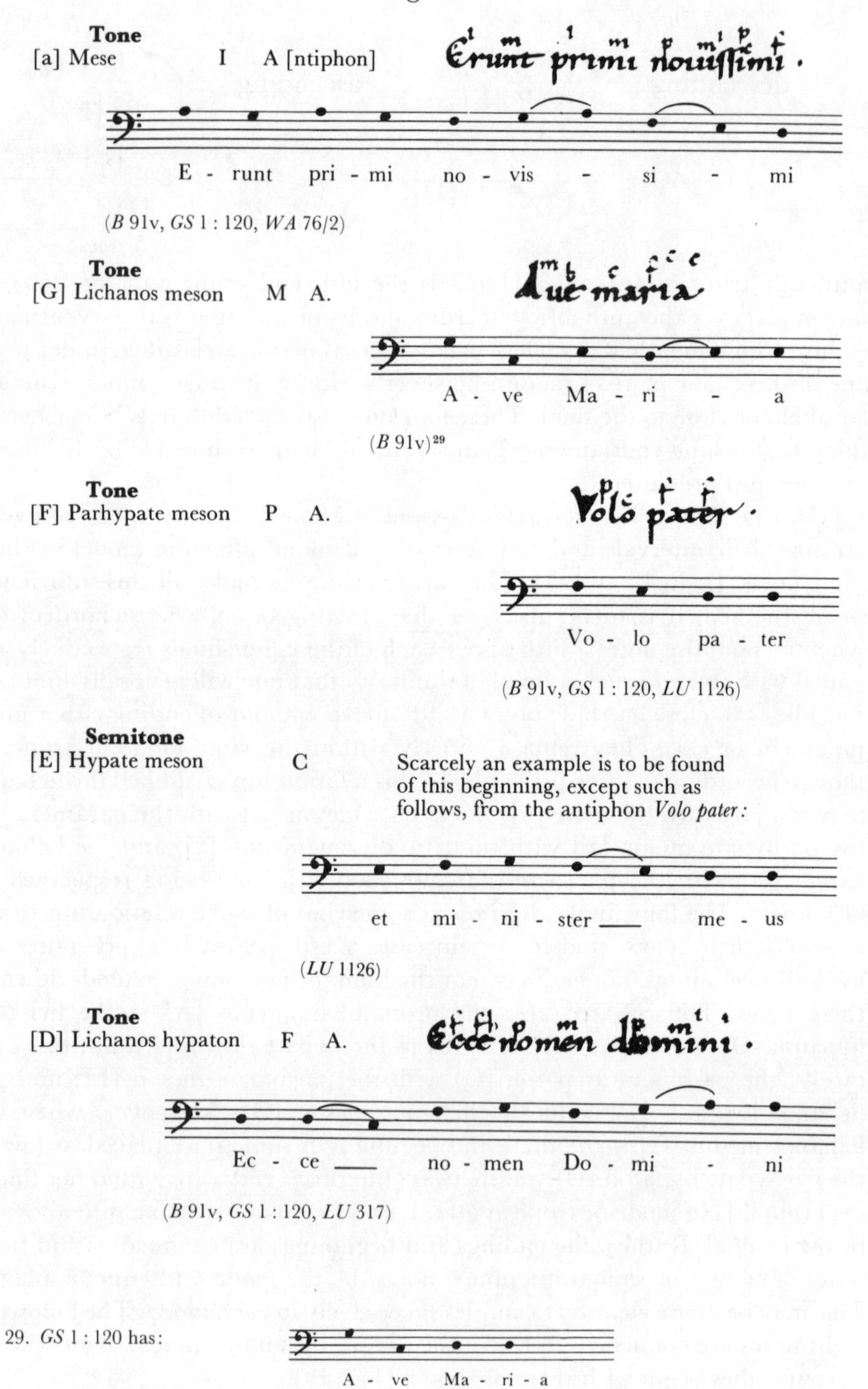
Tone
[a] Mese I A [ntiphon]
E - runt pri - mi no - vis - si - mi
(*B* 91v, *GS* 1 : 120, *WA* 76/2)
Tone
[G] Lichanos meson M A.
A - ve Ma - ri - a
(*B* 91v)[29]
Tone
[F] Parhypate meson P A.
Vo - lo pa - ter
(*B* 91v, *GS* 1 : 120, *LU* 1126)
Semitone
[E] Hypate meson C
Scarcely an example is to be found of this beginning, except such as follows, from the antiphon *Volo pater*:
et mi - ni - ster me - us
(*LU* 1126)
Tone
[D] Lichanos hypaton F A.
Ec - ce no - men Do - mi - ni
(*B* 91v, *GS* 1 : 120, *LU* 317)
29. *GS* 1 : 120 has:
A - ve Ma - ri - a

Tone
[C] Parhypate hypaton B A.

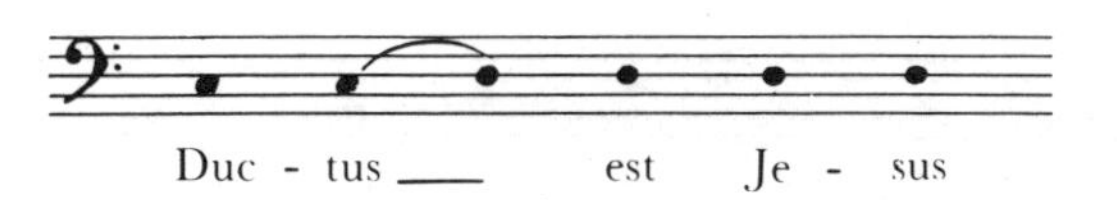

(*B* 91v, *AM* 342)[30]

Semitone
[B] Hypate hypaton Γ Here, too [there is] almost never [a beginning], so [*et*] it is like [the note E a fourth] above. In the antiphon:

(*B* 91v, *GS* 1 : 120, *AM* 400)

[occurs]:

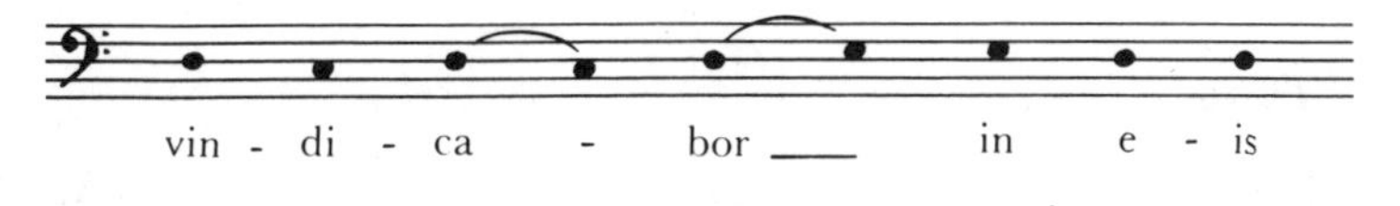

(*B* 91v)[31]

30. *GS* 1 : 120 has:

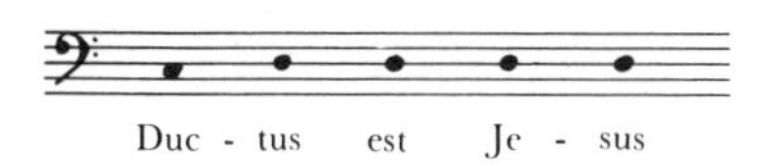

31. *GS* 1 : 120 has Ex. a. More recent sources show the following readings: (b) *AM* 400, (c) *WA* 113. They suggest that *B*'s second f and *GS* 1's a should be emended to the Γ for which Hucbald quotes this chant. Potiron in "La notation grecque," p. 47, agrees.

Tone
[A] Proslambanomenos ⊢ [introit]

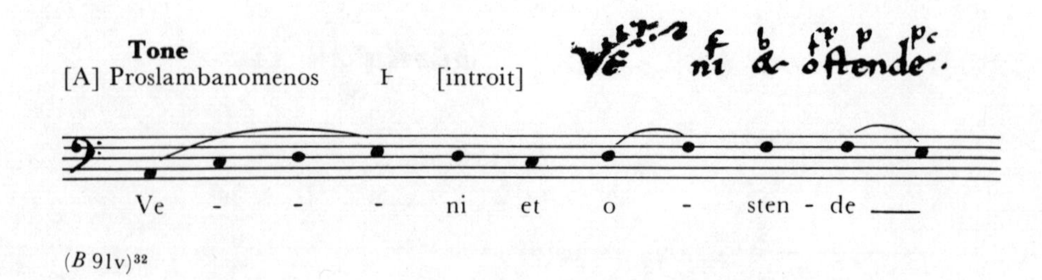

(*B* 91v)[32]

[120/14] Likewise, these eight begin [*regunt*] the authentic deuterus and its plagal:

Semitone

[♮] Paramese ⊏ A. [*B*:] *Vivo ego* [responsory verse] [*GS* 1:] *Notam fecisti*

Tone

[a] Mese I A. [*B*:] *Reddet Deus*

Tone

[G] Lichanos meson M A. *Orietur in diebus domini* [A.] *Iusti autem*

Tone

[F] Parhypate meson P A. *Maria et flumina* [A.] *Qui de terra est* [A.][*GS* 1:] *Sinite me inquit*

Semitone

[E] Hypate meson C A. *Haec est quae nescivit* [A.][*B*:] *Vigilate animo*

Tone

[D] Lichanos hypaton F A. [*B*:] *Rubum quem viderat*

32. *LU* 343 (a) has a slightly variant reading: *GS* 1:120 (b) differs appreciably. Gerbert's initial f (i.e. D) is no doubt an error for ⊢ (i.e. A):

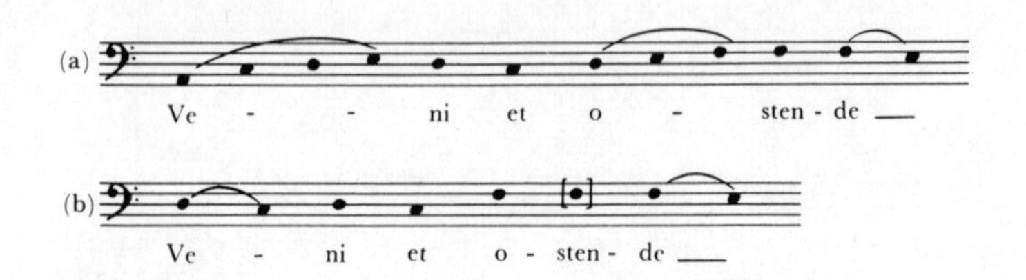

	Tone		
[C]	Parhypate hypaton	B	A. [*B*:] *Iste cognovit*
	Semitone		
[B]	Hypate hypaton	Γ	A.

[120/23] The authentic tritus and its plagal commence among the following notes:

	Tone		
[c]	Trite diezeugmenon	E	A. *Ecce dominus veniet et omnes sancti*
	Semitone		
[♮]	Paramese	⊏	A. *Aspice in me, domine*
	Tone		
[a]	Mese	I	A. *Solvite templum hoc*
	Tone		
[G]	Lichanos meson	M	A.
	Tone		
[F]	Parhypate meson	P	A. *Haurietis aquas* A. *Puer Iesus*
	Semitone		
[E]	Hypate meson	C	A.
	Tone		
[D]	Lichanos hypaton	F	[introit] *Hodie scietis*
	Tone		
[C]	Parhypate hypaton	B	[*B*:] A.

[121/1] The confines of the authentic tetrardus and its plagal require consideration of the following nine notes:

	Tone		
[d]	Paranete diezeugmenon	ʊ	A. *Ecce sacerdos*
	Tone		
[c]	Trite diezeugmenon	E	A. *Beatus venter* A. *Quomodo fiet*
	Semitone		
[♮]	Paramese	⊏	A. *Dixit dominus domino meo*
	Tone		
[a]	Mese	I	A. *Erumpant montes* [A.] *Beati quos elegisti*
	Tone		
[G]	Lichanos meson	M	A. *Dirupisti domine* A. *In illa die*
	Tone		
[F]	Parhypate meson	P	A. *Vitam petiit*
	Semitone		
[E]	Hypate meson	C	[*B*:] A.
	Tone		
[D]	Lichanos hypaton	F	A. *Spiritus domini replevit*
	Tone		
[C]	Parhypate hypaton	B	A. *Stabunt iusti* [*B*:][A.] *Cum venerit paraclitus*[33]

[121a/13] In the tetrardus the beginning may be taken precisely as far as a ninth below the topmost admissible beginning note, and the range of these beginnings extends a fifth in either direction from the final, which is the lichanos meson [G].

[FINIS]

33. *GS* 1 : 121 reads "Ant. *Dum venerit filius hominis putas.*"

CORRECTIONS AND EMENDATIONS OF THE GERBERT TEXT

A partial list of the chief readings of *B* (Brussels, Bibliothèque Royale, MS 10078/95) fols. 84v–92 for Hucbald, *De harmonica institutione* differing from and preferred to those of *GS* 1:104–21. This list does not deal with plainchant notation, charts, spelling, word order, and punctuation.

To the left of the / are the page numbers in *GS* 1; following the / are the line numbers. Gerbert's reading precedes the colon; that of the Brussels MS follows it. // separates entries.

104a/last communis : continuo // 104b/22 cantus : cantu // 104b/31 Haec : Hoc // 104b/32 eandem : eundem // 104b/34 hanc : quae cum hac // 105a/1 Interfinia : Inter confinia // 105a/22 monstrabo : monstrato // 105a/29 est, ut : est intervalli ut // 105a/32 diductiori : diductior // 105b/17 quique : quisque // 105b/19–20 ratione : ratio // 105b/26 novissimum divisionis : novissimum modu[m] divisionis // 106a/up 15 semper bisfactum : secundum bis factum // 106b/up 15 additur primus : addito primo // 106b/last semitonio. Quod : semitonio. Octavus spatio iiii clauditur tonorum. Nonus iiii tonis & semitonio. Quod // 107a/1–2 in nonam vocem prosiliet. : in novam vocem mox sonus prosiliet. // 107a/12 sonuerit : sonuerint // 107a/15 ut : (omits) // 107b/3–4 exempla hac : exempla in hac // 107b/5 Dum : dominum // 107b/16 direpta : dirempta // 107b/17 annotentur : adnotetur // 107b/17–18 modi : moduli // 107b/24 scilicet : similiter // 108a/7 ipsam : ipsa // 108a/16 subintellecto decidant : sub intellectum decidunt // 108a/22 mensione : intensione // 108a/23 qualibet voce : quilibet sonus voce // 108b/3–4 mentione : inventione // 108b/17 semper : secundum // 108b/30 direptione : diremptione // 109a/3 habet simul, & : habes. Simul et // 109b/last ultima *non* & *est*, tonus : ultimam non et primam est et eius ultimam, tonus // 110a/10–11 uno fuerit : fuerit uno // 110b/7 eiusdemque : eisdemque // 110b/7 direptis : diremptis // 110a/17 affert : afferat // 110a/28 intellectualis : intellectualitatis // 110a/33 advertat : advertatur // 110b/17 aliis : aliud // 111a/1–2 incipiendo superior : incipiendo ordo superior // 111a/13–14 et nonam : quasi in novam // 111a/last Haec : Hae // 111b/1 sive: voces sive // 111b/5 sono: solo // 111b/7 . Haec : ; nec // 111b/19 diductae : diducit // 111b/21 superioribus : inferioribus // 119b/21–22 similiter sibi sunt (per) vocem : similiter per unam sibi sunt vocem // 112a/1 intus : imis // 112a/11 submitto : sumito // 112b/2 superat : superpones // 112b/3 serie : seriem // 112b/8 vocis : voce // 112b/9 exposita duo : exposita reliqua duo // 113/11 facilitate : facultate // 113a/20 item : idest // 113a/24 melo : mela // 113a/last synemmenon, relabatur : synemenon, mox ab ipso in diezeugmenon, vel cum hic diezeugmenon in synemenon relabatur. // 114b/19–20 redire : reddere // 116a/15–16 diezeugmenon, resonabit : diezeugmenon et nete sinemenon ipsa qua paranete diezeugmenon resonabit // 116a/20 totius & totius : tonus et tonus // 117a/5 attracta : attacta // 117a/25–26 substituta : sunt composita // 117b/1 iudicio: indicio // 117b/7 remunerationis: rememorationis // 117b/10 adiectam : ad subiectam // 117b/31–32 parhypatemeson inclinatur : paripatemeson sonans p item ad paripatemeson inclinatur // 118a/9 et tarditatem cantilenae : et ad tarditatem seu celeritatem cantilenae // 118b/17 decursatas : decurtatas // 119a/3 quod : quid // 119a/3 quodque : quoque // 119a/6–7 tetrachordum : tetrachordorum // 119a/29 aliquam : aliquem // 119a/30 ipsarum : ipsorum // 119a/30 quantavis : quamvis // 119b/6 nihil : in his // 119b/8–9 his quatuor : his singulis quatuor // 119b/18–19 "quae . . . disparantur" are put by the Brussels MS between 119b/20 "diezeugmenon" and "cum", a new sentence beginning with "Cum inferioribus." // 119b/36 novem : octo // 119b/37 octo : novem // 120/7 aliquid (f. solet) afferunt enim : aliquod offertur exemplum; est tamen // 121/2 coërcentur examine : cohercent examen //

GUIDO OF AREZZO

MICROLOGUS

Vienna, Nationalbibliothek, MS Cpv. 51, fol. 35v, figure showing Guido with monochord and Bishop Theodaldus, to whom the *Micrologus* is dedicated (12th century).

INTRODUCTION

by Claude V. Palisca

Guido's reputation as a theorist and pedagogue has rested as much on legend as on the works he left behind. John, in the treatise translated in this volume, credited him with introducing neumatic notation.[1] Sigebert de Gembloux around 1105–10 hailed him as inventor of the "Guidonian" hand,[2] and by tradition he is thought responsible for the system of hexachords and mutations.[3] Yet none of these innovations can be securely attributed to him, although he surely laid the ground for the hand and the hexachord system. During several centuries after his death his accomplishments were progressively inflated, such was the reverence for his name. Only by returning to those writings that can be established as his can we know his thought and appreciate its impact.

His surviving writings, all of uncertain date, are four: *Micrologus*; a prologue to an antiphoner, which begins "Temporibus nostris" and is often referred to as *Aliae regulae;*[4] a verse-introduction to the same antiphoner,[5] known as *Regulae rhythmicae;* and *Epistola de ignoto cantu*, a letter to his friend, Brother Michael.[6] Of these, *Aliae regulae* has been available in a translation published by Oliver Strunk;[7] *Epistola de ignoto cantu* is also there but with a lengthy omission.[8] *Regulae rhythmicae* has not been translated into English. The present English version of *Micrologus* is the first to be published.[9]

Micrologus is Guido's most important and wide-ranging work. But it does not contain the two brilliant proposals that launched the Guido legend, the device of staff notation, described in the Prologue, and the application in the

1. Chap. 21, p. 148.

2. *De viris illustribus*, in Jacques Paul Migne, *Patrologia cursus completus: Series latina*, 160 : 204, under year 1028. For the early history of the hand see Joseph Smits van Waesberghe, *Musikerziehung, Lehre und Theorie der Musik im Mittelalter*, Musikgeschichte in Bildern vol. 3, fasc. 3 (Leipzig, 1969), pp. 120ff.

3. The exposition of the hexachord system in Engelbert of Admont, *De musica*, tractatus 3, cap. 6–8, *GS* 2 : 323a–28b, is believed to be the first.

4. GS 2 : 34–37a.

5. *GS* 2 : 25–33.

6. *GS* 2 : 43–50.

7. *Source Readings in Music History* (New York, 1950), pp. 117–20.

8. Ibid., pp. 121–25. The passage omitted is *GS* 2 : 46a/10 to 50b/11.

9. There are two German translations: Raymund Schlecht, *Micrologus Guidonis de disciplina artis musicae*, in *Monatshefte für Musikwissenschaft* 5 (1873) : 135–65, 167–77; and Michael Hermesdorff, *Micrologus Guidonis de disciplina artis musicae, d. i. Kurze Abhandlung Guidos über die Regeln der musikalischen Kunst* (Trier, 1876).

Epistola of the syllables *ut-re-mi-fa-sol-la* in the hymn *Ut queant laxis* as an aid to sight-singing. Whereas *Micrologus* was addressed to boys learning the elements of music, the other two prose works seem to have been directed at seasoned singers ultimately to improve the state of musical practice at the highest level.

Although what can be said about the chronology of his writings is not conclusive, the reader of *Micrologus* will want to consider the relationship of this treatise to his others, and that in the context of the few facts known of the author's life.

Guido's own words are the best witness to the events of his life.[10] In the dedicatory letter to *Micrologus* addressed to Bishop Theodaldus of Arezzo, who held that post from 1023 to 1036, Guido praises the bishop for his plan of the cathedral church of St. Donatus, which from a contemporary document is known to have been commissioned of the architect Adalbertus Maginardo in 1026 and finished in 1032.[11] Since he refers to a plan rather than a finished cathedral, it is possible that *Micrologus* was completed around this time. The explicit of a manuscript no longer extant states that the treatise was completed in the author's thirty-fourth year during the pontificate of John XX (*recte* XIX), who reigned between 1024 and 1033.[12]

From the letter to Brother Michael we learn that the addressee and Guido had been at the Benedictine monastery of Pomposa under Abbot Guido,[13] and a reference there to "our Antiphoner" suggests that Michael and Guido had collaborated in this project "by means of which boys could learn chants that they had never heard."[14] These remarks imply that the Antiphoner employed a new and precise pitch notation. If this was the antiphoner that the extant Prologue introduced, it must have used the notational system described there: neumes on staff lines identified as to pitch by the color yellow for C and red for F and also by the letter name of the pitch placed at the beginning of these lines.[15]

In the letter we also learn that Guido was driven away from Pomposa by the envy of his brothers after he had devised a method that permitted learning new chants easily. Word of his success and that of the new Antiphoner reached Pope John, who invited him to Rome. Since John XIX died in January 1033, and Guido wrote of becoming ill from the summer heat during his

10. The two best sources for his biography were written independently and contemporaneously and, therefore, disagree on many points: J. Smits van Waesberghe, *De musico-paedagogico et theoretico Guidone Aretino* (Florence, 1953), and H. Oesch, *Guido von Arezzo* (Bern, 1954). Oesch added an appendix in which he reconciled his own views with those of van Waesberghe, pp. 118–23.

11. See van Waesberghe, *De musico-paedagogico*, p. 13, and bibliography cited there.

12. Quoted ibid., p. 30.

13. "Guido of Pomposa" in *New Catholic Encyclopedia* (New York, 1967) 6 : 842–43. According to *Biblioteca sanctorum* (Rome, 1966) 6: 510–12, Guido was elected Abbot in 998. He died in 1046.

14. *GS* 2 : 44a.

15. See van Waesberghe, "The Musical Notation of Guido of Arezzo," *Musica disciplina* 5 (1951) : 15–53.

sojourn,[16] the visit must have occurred no later than the summer of 1032. The Antiphoner, therefore, must have been at least begun in Pomposa, though it was probably not finished there, because in his letter Guido speaks of showing it to Abbot Guido of Pomposa only after his trip to Rome.[17] Impressed with our Guido's achievement, the Abbot invited him to return to Pomposa and advised him to avoid the cities, where most bishops were accused of simony. It is believed that Guido eventually did settle in a Camaldulensian monastery near Arezzo. An earlier period of residence in Arezzo must have preceded the journey to Rome, since he was accompanied, according to his letter, by an Abbot Grunwald and Dom Peter, Provost of the Canons of the church of Arezzo.[18] At the end of the letter Guido mentions the prologues "both in prose and verse," to the Antiphoner and "our little book called *Micrologus*."[19]

From these facts and inferences and from internal evidence in the treatises an approximate chronology of Guido's works can be hypothesized. In *Micrologus* Guido twice mentions "our notation,"[20] but he never refers to a completed antiphoner, nor does he describe a new notation. The examples in manuscripts of *Micrologus* are given in letter notation, sometimes heighted, without neumes. Even in the twelfth-century manuscript from St. Evreux, in which the Guidonian staff notation is used for a troper and for the *Epistola*, the examples for *Micrologus* are in letters.[21] The weight attached in *Micrologus* to learning new chants with the help of the monochord (chap. 1), a method belittled as "childish" in the *Epistola*,[22] suggests that a period of development leading to the final form of both the staff notation and the Antiphoner, as well as the solmization device, occurred between *Micrologus* and the *Epistola*.[23]

As for the dates when these works were written and when the events of his life took place, they can be circumscribed within a decade. Since Theodaldus became bishop in 1023 and it was he who drew Guido to Arezzo, Guido's relocation there must have been after this date. Mention of the Cathedral of St. Donatus in *Micrologus* puts the completion of the treatise after 1026. The trip to Rome must have occurred near the end of Pope John's reign, or approximately in 1032. Thus the most likely date for *Micrologus* is 1026–28.[24] The Antiphoner and the prose and verse prologues to it must have been completed around 1030, and the *Epistola* around 1032.

16. *GS* 2 : 44a.
17. Ibid.
18. Ibid.
19. Ibid., 50b.
20. In the Prologue and in chap. 1.
21. Paris, Bibliothèque nationale, MS lat. 10508, fols. 135r–43r.
22. *GS* 2 : 44b.
23. Van Waesberghe in *De musico-paedagogico*, pp. 22–23, put forward a similar chronology. Oesch, *Guido*, p. 79, was of the opinion that the *Aliae regulae* was written in Pomposa before *Micrologus*.
24. Van Waesberghe dates it 1028–32 in *De musico-paedagogico*, p. 37. Oesch dates it 1025–26 in *Guido*, pp. 79, 119.

In all his writings Guido named only two authors or sources: Boethius[25] and "the book *Enchiridion*, which the most reverend Abbot Odo wrote most lucidly."[26] Until recently it has been thought that this *Enchiridion* was the *Dialogus* often attributed as early as the twelfth century to an Abbot Odo.[27] Recently Michel Huglo has argued that Guido was here referring to the *Musica enchiriadis* by its proper title and attributing it to an Odo, as it is in a number of early manuscripts, thinking perhaps it was the Odo who left a well-known tonary from the vicinity of Arezzo.[28] An Italian manuscript of the *Enchiriadis*, Florence, Biblioteca Medicea-Laurenziana, MS Ashburnham 1051, indeed bears an attribution to an Abbot Odo.[29] Early ascriptions of the *Dialogus* to an Odo, on the other hand, are all from southern Germany,[30] so it is not likely that Guido would have come across this attribution. Moreover, Huglo has shown that the *Dialogus* is not by anyone named Odo, particularly not Abbot Odo of Cluny, but by an anonymous author from near Milan.[31] The most persuasive argument for believing that Guido meant *Musica enchiriadis*, as Huglo has pointed out, is that Guido explicitly joined to his recommendation of Odo's *Enchiridion* the comment, "I did not follow his example in the signs for the notes,"[32] that is the daseian diastematic notation. Guido did, on the other hand, follow the example of the author of the *Dialogus* in using an alphabetical notation.

Nevertheless, of the two authors, it was to the Pseudo-Odo of the *Dialogus* that Guido owed the most.[33] It was from him that he derived the method of teaching singers unfamiliar music by means of the monochord (Pseudo-Odo, chap. 1; Guido, chap. 1) and the two-octave A–$\overset{\text{a}}{\text{a}}$ gamut extended down one note to gamma (Pseudo-Odo, chap. 2; Guido, chap. 2); to these Guido added the notes $\overset{\text{b}}{\text{b}}$ to $\overset{\text{d}}{\text{d}}$. The letters were applied by Pseudo-Odo to the texts of chants in musical examples as a kind of letter notation. This practice too was followed by Guido, though some manuscripts show a staff notation, which must be a later addition.

The first of the two monochord divisions presented by Guido (chap. 3) is also based on Pseudo-Odo (chap. 2); only the order of divisions was altered by our author, who derived b-flat with the quaternary divisions, while the

25. *Epistola*, *GS* 2: 50b, where Guido says he did not follow him because "his book is not useful to singers, only to philosophers," and *Micrologus*, chap. 20.

26. *Epistola*, *GS* 2: 50b.

27. *GS* 1: 251–64, translated in Strunk, *Source Readings*, pp. 103–16.

28. Michel Huglo, "L'auteur du 'Dialogue sur la musique' attribué à Odon," *Revue de musicologie* 55 (1969): 119–71.

29. *RISM* 2: 46.

30. Huglo, "L'auteur du 'Dialogue,'" pp. 127f.

31. Van Waesberghe has dated the *Enchiriadis* 920–24 in "La place exceptionelle de l'*Ars musica*," *Revue gregorienne* 32 (1952): p. 95.

32. ". . . cuius exemplum in solis figuris sonorum dimisi." See Huglo, "L'auteur du 'Dialogue,'" p. 131.

33. Some of these debts are enumerated in van Waesberghe, *De musico-paedagogico*, pp. 147f.

author of the *Dialogus* came to this quaternary division only after all the binary divisions needed for the octave replicates were completed. The inclusion of both square and soft b in the higher octave was also probably owed to Pseudo-Odo.

Guido followed the example of the *Dialogus* also in enumerating the intervals. Their language differs somewhat in that for Pseudo-Odo (chap. 5) the general terms for interval are *coniunctio vocum* (connection or conjunction of sounds) and *differentia*, whereas for Guido it is the more common *modus*, as in the title of chapter 4, "Quod sex modis sibi invicem voces iungantur," for he probably saw that the multiplicity of terms was confusing and avoided *differentia* because it had a special meaning in chant practice. Guido adopted Pseudo-Odo's *consonantia* for the class of interval that joins the notes of a melody, namely the tone, semitone, ditone, semiditone, diatessaron, and diapente.

Guido's theory of the modes is at least partially based on the *Dialogus*, which was a pioneering attempt to define modal differences. Like Pseudo-Odo (chaps. 6, 8), Guido (chap. 13) uses both the numbering one to eight and the Greek numbering protus to tetrardus. The insistence on the last note of a chant as a determinant of mode (Guido, chap. 11; Pseudo-Odo, chap. 8), the injunction to make beginnings and endings of phrases (*distinctiones*) harmonize with the final by relating to it through one of the six *consonantiae* (Guido, chap. 11), are other links with Pseudo-Odo (chap. 8).

Guido's inclusion of range as a factor in the determination of modality may also be attributable to the influence of the *Dialogus*, but Guido's recommendations are more liberal on several points. Whereas Pseudo-Odo does not allow a chant to descend to the fifth note below the final in plagal tritus, evidently because it forms a tritone with the final, Guido does not specifically prohibit it. Guido finds that the authentic tritus rarely goes below the final (John prohibits it[34]), while Pseudo-Odo does not note the exception. Guido permits a melody to rise to the ninth and tenth notes above the final, while Pseudo-Odo stops at the octave. Otherwise, the two authors agree on the ranges of the modes.

If Guido knew *Musica enchiriadis* at the time he wrote *Micrologus*, he shows little evidence of it. Guido's division of the gamut into an octave of *graves*, an octave of *acutae*, and an annexed tetrachord of *superacutae* does not reflect the scale of four disjunct tetrachords in the ascending pattern tone-semitone-tone unique to the *Enchiriadis* treatise, nor its four names for the tetrachords, *graves*, *finales*, *superiores*, and *excellentes*. Of these Guido adopts only the term *graves*, and that for an entire octave.

But the chapters on organum and diaphony (18–19) do reveal some dependence, for example the definition of diaphony:

34. Chap. 12.

Micrologus	*Enchiriadis*
Diaphonia vocum disiunctio sonat, quam nos organum vocamus, cum disiunctae ab invicem voces et concorditer dissonant et dissonanter concordant.[35]	Haec namque est, quam Diaphoniam cantilenam, vel assuete, organum, vocamus. Dicta autem Diaphonia, quod non uniformi canore constet, sed concentu concorditer dissono.[36]

Guido's elegant antithesis, literally, "notes disjoined from each other both concordantly dissonating and dissonantly concording," seems to have been inspired by the older author's "it consists not of uniform song [i.e. unison singing] but of a concordantly dissonant consensus."

The most important parallel between *Micrologus* and *Enchiriadis* are the instructions for improvising or writing organum. Guido (chap. 18) describes a method of singing diaphony in which the organal voice duplicates the chant at the "symphony" of a fourth below, as in *Enchiriadis* (chap. 13). The possibility of doubling the voices to create organum at the fifth, fourth, and octave is also true to the *Enchiriadis*. But no sooner has Guido marveled at the "sociability and hence smoothness" (literal for *societate ac ideo suavitate*[37]) with which these intervals blend, paraphrasing "the smooth mixture" (*suavis commixtio*) of the Enchiriadis text, than he rejects the procedure as "harsh" (*durus*), and declares a preference for his own "smoother" method, which is a combination of parallel fourths, oblique motion to avoid the tritone, and convergence (*occursus*) of the voices at a close. Aside from the element of the occursus, this method, however, is not unlike that of *Enchiriadis*, chapters 17 and 18.

Otherwise Guido's dependence on previous authors is negligible. Almost as an afterthought in the last chapter he introduces from Boethius the story of Pythagoras's discovery of the ratios of consonances by means of the hammers. The citation of the psychological cures through music effected by David and Asclepiades seem to be derived from Cassiodorus.[38]

These, briefly surveyed, are the links to previous authors. They serve to throw into relief Guido's vigorous independence and originality. Indeed, there have been few works in the history of theory that spring so bravely from the thought of one man. Guido took upon himself the project of articulating several aspects of melody and chant practice never before treated. This is not a place for an extensive commentary, but a few of Guido's major contributions in this book may be signaled.

Guido gave prominence to the principle of affinity, already recognized by Hucbald (119b), which makes possible the ending of a chant on a cofinal as well as final in the protus, deuterus, and tritus (chap. 8). His chapters 15 and 16 constitute the first theory of melody writing in the West. He draws upon

35. Chap. 18, *CSM* 4: 196–97.
36. Chap. 13, *GS* 1: 165b.
37. Chap. 18, *CSM* 4: 198.
38. *Institutiones* 5. 9. Trans. in Strunk, *Source Readings*, p. 92.

grammatical analogies, setting thereby an important precedent, in dividing a melody into progressively smaller subdivisions: distinctions, parts, neumes, and syllables. The comments in these chapters on proportional durations in chant and its rhythmic performance have given rise to varied interpretations and are the more precious because so rare in medieval literature.[39] The motus theory, as it is usually referred to (chap. 16), has also attracted a host of commentaries.[40] It marks the first steps in a theory of melodic direction and combinatoriality, too brief, unfortunately, and undeveloped.

The instructions for the mechanical composition of melody through pairing textual vowels and pitches (chap. 17) is perhaps more important for its implications and the elaborations it inspired than the fecundity of the method itself.[41] It implies that melodic composition was an ongoing and normal occupation of a musician and that then, as now, not everyone was blessed with the divine afflatus for melodic invention. A perplexing detail of the system is that the vowels *a e i o u* are assigned to an ascending series of pitches, when the progression from open to closed vowels would suggest rather a descending scale, at least if voice production in the eleventh century was anything like ours. But it must not have been.

Aside from modern commentaries on individual chapters or problems in Guido's treatise, given in the footnotes above, there are a number of general commentaries dating from as far back as the eleventh century. Much of John's treatise, in the present volume, is a commentary upon Guido. Aribo in his treatise, from around 1070, also contains reflections upon Guido.[42] Other early commentaries are anonymous. The principal ones have been gathered together in one volume by Joseph Smits van Waesberghe, *Expositiones in Micrologum Guidonis Aretini*.[43] These are *Liber argumentorum* and *Liber specierum*, both probably of Italian origin from between 1050 and 1100; *Metrologus*, probably of English thirteenth-century origin; and the *Commentarius anonymus* first edited by C. Vivell in 1917[44] and identified by van Waesberghe as by either a native of Liège or a Bavarian between about 1070

39. Concerning chapter 15 see Utto Kornmüller, "Etwas zum 15. Kapitel des Micrologus von Guido von Arezzo," *Kirchenmusikalisches Jahrbuch* 20 (1907): 116–21; Cölestin Vivell, "Handelt das 15 Kap. des Micrologus Guidos von Arezzo vom Gregorianischen Gesang," *Kirchenmusikalisches Jahrbuch* 21 (1908): 143–44; Richard Crocker, "*Musica Rhythmica* and *Musica Metrica* in Antique and Medieval Theory," *Journal of Music Theory* 2 (1958): 2–23, including a translation of this chapter; Jan W. A. Vollaerts, *Rhythmic Proportions in Early Medieval Ecclesiastical Chant* (Leiden, 1958), pp. 168–72, 177–94, including a translation of chap. 15, pp. 169–72; and J. Smits van Waesberghe, Introduction, *Aribonis De musica, CSM* 2 (Rome, 1951): xvi–xxiv.

40. Kornmüller, "Die Choralkompositionslehre vom 10. bis 13. Jahrhundert," *Monatshefte für Musikgeschichte* 4 (1872): 57–112, and the bibliography in n. 39, above.

41. See van Waesberghe, "Guido of Arezzo and Musical Improvisation," *Musica disciplina* 5 (1951): 55–63.

42. Van Waesberghe, *Aribonis*.

43. Amsterdam, 1957.

44. Cölestin Vivell, *Commentarius anonymus in Micrologum Guidonis Aretini* (Vienna, 1917).

and 1100. A more recent commentary is Hubert Wolking's dissertation, *Guidos "Micrologus de disciplina artis musicae" und seine Quellen.*[45]

The message of *Micrologus* is so rich in significance both for understanding the music of its time and for the beginnings of indigenous Western theory that the full meaning of its text has not been fathomed even after generations of commentary. It is hoped that this translation will invite the probing study that this treatise deserves. The serious student, it goes without saying, will want the Latin version close at hand, for even Warren Babb's assiduously faithful and lucid translation places an interpretation, which it must be, between reader and author.

45. Emsdetten, 1930.

GUIDO OF AREZZO, *MICROLOGUS*

Translated by Warren Babb
Edited by Claude V. Palisca

[80] Gone from school are the Muses; there may I hope to induce them,
Unknown yet to adults, to unveil their light to the young ones!
Ill will's indiscriminate rage let charity frustrate;
Dire indeed are the blights that else will ravage our planet,
Opening letters of these five lines will spell you the author.

[81] [GUIDO'S EPISTLE TO BISHOP THEODALDUS]

To the most kind father and most revered lord Theodaldus, most radiant with the light of godliness and of all wisdom and worthiest of priests and bishops, from Guido, the salutations of a servant and son—would that he were the least of your monks.

Though I desire at least a modicum of solitary life, Your Gracious Eminence wished to associate my littleness with yourself in the study of the Holy Word. Not that Your Excellency lacks many outstandingly [82] spiritual men, most plentifully fortified by the practice of the virtues and most abundantly distinguished by their pursuit of wisdom, who together with you instruct properly the people entrusted to you and apply themselves assiduously and fervently to meditation on holy things; but that you took pity on the helplessness of my insignificant mind and body, and sheltered and sustained me by the protection of your fatherly goodness; so that if by God's will anything useful should come of me, God will impute it to your merit.

Since it was a matter of usefulness to the church, your authority decreed that this way of training in the art of music—for which I am mindful that with God's help I have toiled not in vain—be published. Just as [83] you created by an exceedingly marvelous plan the church of St. Donatus, the bishop and martyr, over which you preside by the will of God and as his lawful vicar, so likewise by a most honorable and appropriate distinction you would make the ministers of that church cynosures for all churchmen throughout almost the whole world. In very truth it is sufficiently marvelous and desirable that even boys of your church should surpass in the practice of music the fully trained veterans of all other places; and the height of your honor and merit will be very greatly increased because, though subsequent to the early fathers, such great and distinguished renown for learning has come to this church through you.

[84] Therefore, since I neither would nor could go against your command, fitting as it is, I offer to your most sagacious and fatherly self the precepts of the science of music, explained, so far as I could, much more clearly and briefly than has been done by philosophers, neither in the same way, for the most part, nor following in the same tracks, but endeavoring only that it should help both the cause of the church and our little ones. The reason that this study has remained obscure up to now is that, being truly difficult, it has been explained in simpler terms by no one. How it came about that I first undertook this explanation, and with what profit and what effort, I shall set forth in a few words.

[85] Prologue

Since both my natural disposition and my emulation of good men made me eager to work for the general benefit, I undertook, among other things, to teach music to boys. Presently Divine Grace favored me, and some of them, trained by imitating the [steps of the mono]chord, with the practice of our notation, were within the space of a month singing so securely at first sight chants they had not seen or heard, that it was the greatest wonder to many people. But if someone cannot do that, I do not know with what face he can venture to call himself a musician or a singer.

[86] I was extremely sorry for our singers who, though they should persevere a hundred years in the study of singing, can never perform even the tiniest antiphon on their own—always learning, as the apostle says, and never arriving at knowledge of the truth.[1] Desiring therefore to set forth my own so useful method of study for the general benefit, I summarized as briefly as I could, out of the copious musical theorizing which with God's help I have at various times collected, certain things that I believed would help singers. But I judged those musical matters not worth mention which are of little benefit for singing, as well as any of the things that are said but cannot be understood —not [87] worrying about any who might turn livid with ill will so long as the training of others made progress.

Here ends the prologue. The chapters begin.[88]

Chapter

1. 2 Tim. 3:7.

Chapter 1

What one should do to prepare himself to study music

[91] Let him who seeks our training learn some chants copied in our notation, let him train his hand in the use of the monochord, [92] and let him frequently ponder these rules, until, having learned the effect and character of the notes, he can smoothly sing unfamiliar music as well as familiar. Since we learn the notes, which are the primary foundation of this art, more easily at the monochord, let us first see how science, imitating nature, has given them their separate places thereon.

Chapter 2

What the notes are, of what nature, and how many

[93] The notes on the monochord are these. First is placed Greek Γ, added by the moderns. There follow seven letters of the alphabet as the *graves* [low], and therefore written in larger letters, thus: A B C D E F G. [94] After these the same seven letters are repeated as the *acutae* [high], but they are indicated by smaller letters. Among them, between a and ♮ [i.e. b♮] we put another b which we make round, whereas we made the former one square, thus: a b ♮ c d e f g. We add by means of these same letters, but differently written, the tetrachord of the *superacutae* [above the *acutae*], in which we likewise have the two forms b and ♮, thus: aa bb ♮♮ cc dd. The *superacutae* are considered superfluous

by many, but we had rather have too much than too little. [95] So in all there are twenty-one, namely Γ A B C D E F G a b ♮ c d e f g $\overset{a}{a}$ $\overset{b}{b}$ $\overset{♮}{♮}$ $\overset{c}{c}$ $\overset{d}{d}$. Their location, which the learned either are silent about or confuse by excessive obscurity, is here explained briefly, yet fully enough even for boys.

Chapter 3

On the location of notes on the monochord

[96] After marking Γ at the beginning, divide the space beneath the string from there to the other end into nine parts, and at the end of the first ninth put the letter A, with which all the ancients began. [97] When you have likewise measured a ninth part [of the length] from A to the far end of the string, in the same way place the letter B. After this, going back to Γ, divide the string from there to the other end by four, and at the end of the first quarter you will find C. By a similar division into quarters, just as C was found from Γ, in the same way you will find successively D from A, E from B, F from C, G from D, a from E, and b-flat from F. The following notes [98] are all easily obtained one after the other as halfway points of notes similar in sound and the same in letter: so, halfway from B to the far end of the string, you put another ♮. Likewise C will point out another c, D will point out another d, E another e, F another f, G another g, and the rest of the notes in the same way. You could continue up or down thus ad infinitum, did not the precept of art restrain you by its authority. Of the many and various systems of dividing the monochord, I have given one, because when one's [99] attention is turned from many things to one, that one is grasped without trouble. It is particularly useful too, since it is both easily learned and, once learned, rarely forgotten.

Here follows another method of dividing the monochord, which is harder to memorize, but by it the monochord is more quickly divided. You make nine steps, that is [equal] segments, from Γ to the other end. The first step will end at A, the second will have no letter, the third will end at D, the fourth will be unlettered, the fifth will end at a, the sixth at d, the seventh at $\overset{a}{a}$, and the others will be unlettered. [100] Likewise, when you divide [the length] from A to the other end into nine parts, the first step will end at B, the second will be unlettered, the third will end at E, the fourth will be unlettered, the fifth will end at ♮, the sixth at e, the seventh at $\overset{♮}{♮}$, and the rest will be unlettered.[1] When you divide [the length] from Γ to the other end into quarters, the first step will end on C, the second on G, the third on g, the fourth at the end of the string. Of the four similar steps from C to the other end of the string, the first will end on F, the second on c, the third on $\overset{c}{c}$, the fourth at

1. As the *Commentarius anonymus* noted (Vivell ed., p. 10, van Waesberghe, *Expositiones*, p. 104), this monochord is incomplete, for Guido failed to derive $\overset{b}{b}$ and $\overset{d}{d}$ (the commentator said $\overset{b}{b}$ was missing, but he must have had a faulty text).

the end of the string. Of the quarter-length steps from F, the first will end on b-flat, the second on f.

[101] For laying out the notes on the monochord let these two systems of measurements suffice, [102] of which the former is the easiest to memorize, while the latter is the quickest to apply. Next, all the intervals arising out of the divisions [of the string] will be briefly set forth.

Chapter 4

That notes should be joined to each other by six intervals

[103] With the notes laid out in this way, sometimes a greater distance is noticed between one note and another, as between Γ and A and between A and B, and sometimes a lesser, as between B and C, and so forth.

The greater distance is called a tone, and the smaller a semitone, from *semis* [a half], that is, not a full tone.

[104] Between any note and the third from it there is sometimes a ditone, that is two tones, as from C to E, and sometimes a semiditone, which has only a tone and a semitone, as from D to F, and so forth. A diatessaron is formed when between two notes there are two tones and a semitone in any order, as from A to D and from B to E, and so forth. A diapente is a tone larger, and occurs whenever between notes there are three tones and one semitone, as from A [105] to E and from C to G, and so forth.

Thus you have six melodic intervals [*consonantiae*], namely, tone, semitone, ditone, semiditone, diatessaron, and diapente. In no chant is one note joined to another by any other intervals, going either up or down. Since [106] all melody [*harmonia*] is formed by so few formulas [*clausulae*], it is most helpful to commit them firmly to memory, and, until they are completely perceived and recognized in singing, never to stop practicing them, since when you hold these as keys, you can command skill in singing—intelligently, and therefore more easily.

Chapter 5

On the diapason and why there are only seven notes

[107] The diapason is the interval in which a diapente and a diatessaron are combined; for while from A to D is a diatessaron and from that same D to acute a is a diapente, from A to the other a is a diapason.

[108] Its property is to have the same letter on both ends, as from B to ♮, from C to c, from D to d, and so forth. Just as both sounds are notated by the same letter, so both are held and believed to be in all respects of the same nature and the most absolute likeness.

Just as when seven days have elapsed we repeat the same ones, so that we always name the first and eighth the same; so we always represent and name the first and eighth notes the same way, because we perceive that they sound together with a natural concord, [109] as D and d. For from each of them you descend by a tone, a semitone, and two tones, and ascend by a tone, a semitone, and two tones. Thus, in singing, if two or three or more singers, as may be feasible, begin and sing through the same antiphon, whichever it be, with the various notes separated by this interval, you will be amazed that you get the same notes at different pitches [*loci*] but with a minimal difference of sound, and that the same melody resounds in the *graves*, *acutae*, and *superacutae* as if a single thing, thus [110]:

Example 1

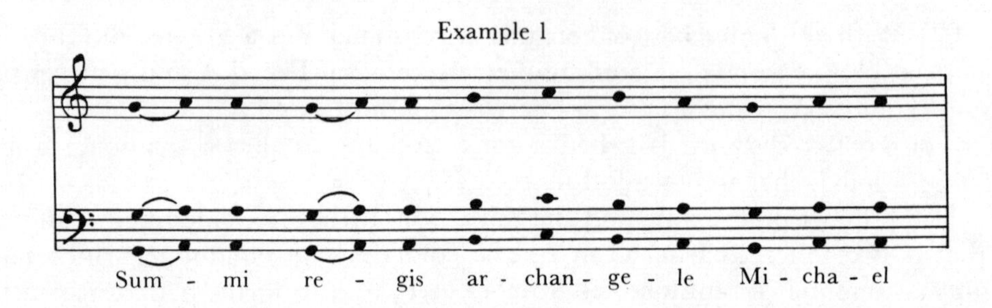

[111] Likewise if you should sing the same antiphon partly in a low and partly in a high register, or however else you transpose it at the interval of a diapason, that same unity of the notes [112] will be apparent. Therefore the poet spoke very rightly of "the seven different notes,"[1] because even if more occur it is not an addition of other ones, but a renewal and repetition of the same ones. For this reason we, like Boethius[2] and the musicians of old, indicate all musical sounds by seven letters. However some people nowadays [113] incautiously employ only four symbols. They indicate every fifth sound always by the same symbol, though it is true beyond a doubt that some notes disagree completely with those a fifth away, and that no note agrees perfectly with its fifth. For no note agrees perfectly with any other except its octave.

Chapter 6

Also on the divisions of the monochord and their meaning

[114] To compress many things about the division of the monochord into a few words: the diapason always moves in two steps to the other end of the string, the diapente in three, the diatessaron in four, and the tone in nine; and the more steps they have, the shorter the distance of these. But you can find no other divisions than these four.

[115] "Diapason" means "through all," either because it includes all the notes, or because citharas in antiquity had eight strings extending through a

1. ". . . septem discrımına vocum," Vergil, *Aeneid* 6. 646.

2. Guido may have had a copy annotated by a modern author, for Boethius did not limit himself to seven letters.

diapason. In this interval the lower note has two units of length; the upper, one, as A and a. "Diapente" derives from "five," for there are five notes in its span, as from D to a. Its lower note has three units of length; its upper, two.

"Diatessaron" derives from "four," both because it includes four notes and because its lower note has four units of length while its upper has three, as from D to G.

[116] You should remember that these three intervals are called "symphonies,"[1] that is, smooth unions of notes, because in the diapason the different notes sound as one and because the diapente and the diatessaron are the basis [*iura possident*] of diaphony, that is, organum,[2] and produce notes similar in every case.

The tone gets its name from *intonandus*, that is "to be sounded," and gives nine units of length to its lower note compared with eight to its higher. The semitone, however, the ditone, and the semiditone, although they connect notes in singing, get no dividing point.[3]

Chapter 7

On the affinities of notes through the four modes

[117] Since there are just seven notes—seeing that the others, as we have said, are repetitions—it suffices to explain the seven that are of different modes and different qualities. The first mode of notes arises when from a note one descends by a tone and [118] ascends by a tone, a semitone, and two tones, as from A and D. The second mode arises when from a note one descends by two tones and ascends by a semitone and two tones, as from B and E. The third is that in which one descends by a semitone and two tones but ascends by two tones, as from C and F. The fourth goes down by a tone but rises by two tones and a semitone, like G.[1]

Notice that they follow each other in order. Thus, the first [mode] on A, the second [119] on B, the third on C; and also the first on D, the second on E, the third on F, and the fourth on G. Notice too that these affinities of notes are made through the diatessaron and the diapente, for A is joined to D, and B to E, and C to F by the lower diatessaron, but by the upper diapente, [as in Fig. 1].

1. *Symphonia* is the standard term, from Cassiodorus (*Institutiones*. 2. 5. 7) up to Guido.

2. See below, chap. 18.

3. Since in Pythagorean tuning their ratios involve terms that are numerically large, for example 32:27 for the semiditone, 81:64 for the ditone, the number of string divisions required to produce them would be impractical on a monochord.

1. While the other modes have pairs of notes, the fourth, on G, lacks a pair, because it has no affinity, as proved in Fig. 1.

Figure 1

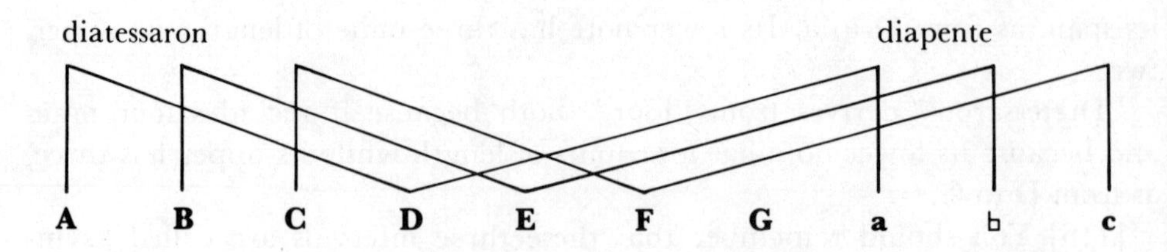

Chapter 8

On other affinities and on b and ♮

[122] Whatever other affinities there are, they are produced likewise by the diatessaron and the diapente. For since the diapason contains in itself a diatessaron plus a diapente and has the same letters on each end, there is always in the middle of its [123] length a letter which is so related to either end of the diapason that with whatever letter in the low register it gives a diatessaron, with that same one in the high register it makes a diapente, as is notated in the diagram above; and with whatever letter in the low register it made a diapente, with that same one in the upper register it will give a diatessaron, as A, E, a. Now a and E agree in that one descends from them by two tones and a semitone. Also, since G sounds with C and D by these same intervals, it has taken over the descent of the one and the ascent of the other; for C and G rise [124] similarly by two tones and a semitone, and D and G descend similarly by a tone and a semitone.

Moreover b-flat, which is less regular and which is called "added" or "soft," has a concord with F, and is added because F cannot make a concord with ♮ a fourth away, since it is a tritone distant. You should not join b and ♮ in the same neume.

We use b-flat mostly in that chant in which F or f [125] recurs rather extensively, either low or high. Here b-flat seems to create a certain confusion and transformation, so that G sounds as protus and a as deuterus, whereas b[-flat] itself sounds as tritus. Many therefore have never mentioned b[-flat], whereas the other ♮ has been acceptable to all. But if you wish not to have b-flat at all, alter the neumes in which it occurs, so that instead of F G a and b-flat you have G a ♮ c. If it is the kind of neume that, going up after D E F, [126] wants two tones and a semitone—which causes this b [-flat]—or going down after D E F wants two whole tones, then instead of D E F use a ♮ c, which are of the same mode and have the perfectly regular descents and ascents that were just mentioned. For it best avoids a sad confusion if one apportions such ascents and descents clear-sightedly between D E F and a ♮ c.

We have confined ourselves to just a few things about the similarities between notes, because insofar as similarity is sought out between different things, to this extent is lessened that diversity which [127] can prolong the labor of the confused mind, for organized material is always more easily grasped than unorganized.

All the modes and the "distinctions" of the modes are connected with these three notes [C, D, E]. Now I call "distinctions" what many call "differences." But the term "difference" is used because something distinguishes or [128] divides plagal modes from authentic; otherwise, it is misused. All other notes have some concordance with these three, either below or above; but no notes show themselves similar to other notes in both directions, except at the diapason. Anyone who seeks can find a representation of all this in the chart [Fig. 2] [129].

Figure 2

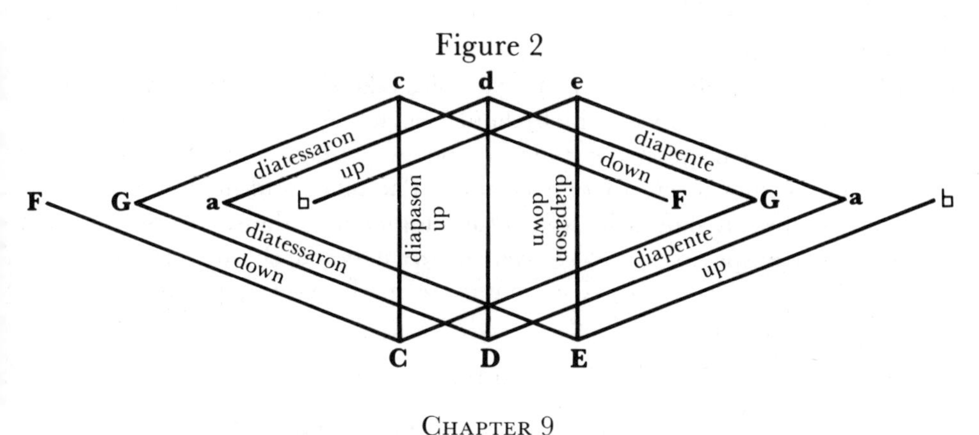

Chapter 9

Also on the resemblance of notes, which is perfect only at the diapason

[130] Insofar as the above-mentioned notes are alike—some in descent, some in ascent, some in both—they will make neumes sound alike. [131] Thus the knowledge of one makes another clear to you. As for those notes in which no resemblance is evident, or which are of different modes, no one of them will accept the neume or chant of another; or, if you force it to receive one, it will change its sound.

Thus if one should wish to begin on E or F, which are notes of other modes, an antiphon that should begin on D, one would soon tell by ear how great a change was taking place. But on D and a, which are of the same mode, we can most often begin or end the same piece. [132] I say "most often," and not "always," because likeness is not complete except at the octave.

For where there is a difference in the arrangement of the tones and semitones, there is bound to be one also in [the sound of] the neumes. And even among the notes just mentioned, which are assigned to the same mode, dissimilarities are found. For from D you can go down only one whole tone, but from a, two; and so also elsewhere.

Chapter 10

Also on the modes and on recognizing and correcting a wrong melody

[133] Here are [described] the four modes or tropes, which are improperly called "tones." They are so differentiated from one another by their inherent dissimilarity, that none of them will grant another a place in its domain, and any one of them either transforms a neume from another mode or never even admits it.

[134] False notes also creep in through inaccuracy in singing; sometimes performers deviate from well-tuned notes, lowering or raising them slightly, as is done by untrue human voices. Also, by ascending or descending more than is right for the prescribed interval, we pervert a neume of a certain mode into another mode or we begin at a place [in the scale] which does not admit [that] note.

[137] To make this clear by an example, take the communion *Diffusa est gratia*. Many put *propterea*, which should begin on F, a whole tone down, although there is not a whole tone just below F. As a result the end of this communion comes where there is no note. The place and mode where [138] each neume begins should be left to the judgment of the singer, so that if it needs to be transposed [*si motione opus est*], he may search out related [*affines*] notes. These modes or tropes we name, from the Greek, protus, deuterus, tritus, and tetrardus.

Chapter 11

What note should hold the chief place in a chant and why

[139] Though any chant is made up of all the notes and intervals, the note that ends it holds the chief place, for it sounds both longer and more lasting. The previous notes, as is evident to trained musicians only, [140] are so adjusted to the last one that in an amazing way they seem to draw a certain semblance of color from it.

The other notes should have a harmonious relationship with the note that ends a neume by means of the aforesaid six melodic intervals. The beginning of a chant and the end of all its phrases and even their beginnings need to cling close to the note that ends the chant. An exception is that when a chant ends on E it often [141] begins on c, which is a diapente plus a semitone away, as the antiphon:

Example 2

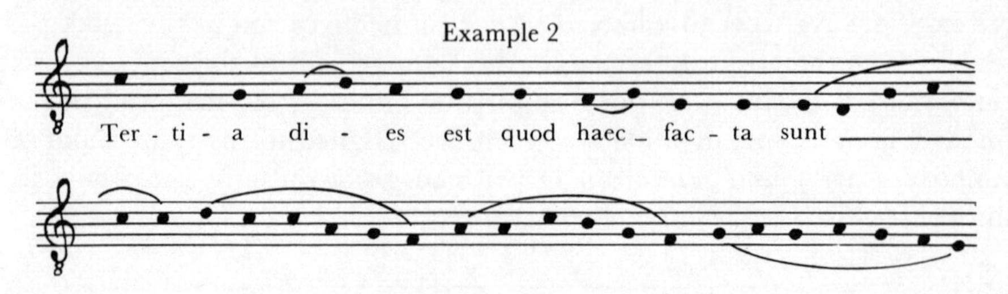

[144] Furthermore, when we hear someone sing, we do not know what mode his first note is in, since we do not know whether tones, semitones, or other intervals will follow. But when the chant has ended, we know clearly from the preceding notes the mode of the last one. For at the start of a chant you do not know what will follow, but at its end you realize what has gone before. Thus the last note is the one we are better aware of. So if you wish to add to your chant either a verse or a psalm or anything else, [145] you should adjust it most of all to the final note of the former, not go back and consider the first note or any of the others. This too we may add, that carefully composed chants end their phrases chiefly on the final note [of the chant].

It is no wonder that music bases its rules on the last note, since in the elements of language, too, we almost everywhere see the real force of the meaning in the final letters or syllables, in regard to cases, numbers, persons, and tenses. Therefore, since all praise, too, is sung at the end, we rightly say that every chant is subject to, and takes its rules from, that mode which it sounds last.

[146] In any chant it is right to go down [as far as] a fifth from the final note and up [as far as] an octave, though it often happens that, contrary to the rule, we go up to a ninth or tenth. Hence D E F G have been established as the final notes, because their location on the monochord fits in preeminently with the upward and downward progress just mentioned. For they have one tetrachord of the *graves* below and two of the *acutae* above.

Chapter 12

On the division of the four modes into eight

[147] Some chants in a certain mode, say the protus, with respect to their final notes are low and level, others high and raised. Therefore, when verses or psalms or whatever else, as we said, had to be fitted to their endings, although they continued in one and the same mode, [148] they could still not be adjusted to these different ranges. For what was added on, if it was low-pitched, did not go well with the high notes; but if it was high, it was at odds with the low notes. So the plan was that each mode should be divided into two, namely a high and a low, and, according to regulations assigned, high notes should go with high and low with low; and each high mode should be called authentic, that is original and principal, while the low mode should be called plagal, that is, collateral and lesser. For he who is said to stand at my side is lower [*minor*] than I; otherwise, if he were higher [*major*], I should be said rather to stand at his side.

Since therefore one says authentic protus [*autentus protus*] and plagal of the protus [*plagis proti*], and likewise with the rest, these modes, which naturally were four according to their notes, have been made [149] eight in chants. A mistaken usage transmitted by the Latins is to say first and second instead of authentic protus and the plagal of the protus, third and fourth instead of authentic deuterus and the plagal of the deuterus, fifth and sixth instead of authentic tritus and plagal of the tritus, and seventh and eighth instead of authentic tetrardus and plagal of the tetrardus.

Chapter 13

On the recognition of the eight modes by their height and depth

[150] Thus there are eight modes, as there are eight parts of speech[1] and eight kinds of beatitude;[2] and every melodic line, as it moves to and fro among these, is diversified by eight dissimilar qualities.[3] For ascertaining these modes in chants, certain neumes have been [151] composed,[4] so that we learn the mode of the chant from the way it fits these, just as we often discover from the way it fits the body which tunic is whose. For example,

Example 3

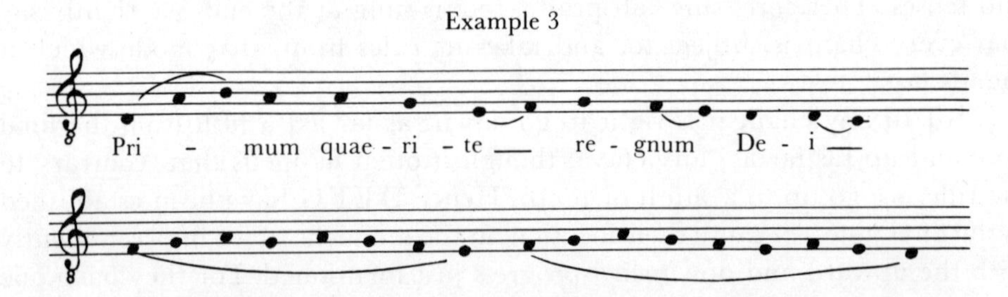

[154] as soon as we have seen that this neume [Example 3] accords with the end of an antiphon, there is no need to doubt that it is authentic protus; and similarly with the other modes. Most helpful for this are the verses of the responsories of nocturns, the psalms of the offices, and all the chants that are prescribed in the formulas of the modes.[5] It is a wonder if someone who does not know these understands any part of what is being said here. For there one can foresee on what notes of the particular modes chants less often or more often begin, and on what notes they do so least. Thus in plagal modes it is

1. Grammatically speaking, a word is either a noun, verb, pronoun, adjective, adverb, preposition, conjunction, or interjection.

2. The blessed qualities enumerated in the Sermon on the Mount, Matt. 5:3–11.

3. These must be the eight modes.

4. Guido refers here to either the *Noeane* formulas (see above pp. 6–8), or the Latin formulas of the modes, which begin with the melody "Primum quaerite regnum Dei" for the first mode, as in Berno, *Tonarius*, GS 2 : 79. See Antoine Auda, *Les modes et les tons de la musique*, pp. 176ff. and the references given in the Introduction to Hucbald, above, n. 14 to 18.

5. "... in modorum formulis"—here Guido may be referring once again to the series of melodic specimens for each mode that begins with "Primum quaerite regnum Dei" (see n. 4 above), or, as Huglo believes ("L'auteur du 'Dialogue,'" p. 166), to a tonary, since the term *tonarius* was not yet current in Italy, and possibly the tonary of Abbot Odo, the Prologue of which is in *GS* 1 : 248–249a, the tonary itself in *CS* 2 : 117–49. Compare the usage in Guido's *Epistola*, *GS* 2 : 48a: "Nota autem, quomodo modos dicimus eos, qui in formulis tonorum non proprie sed abusive nominantur toni, cum modi vel tropi proprie dicantur." And later on the same page: "Ideoque habes in formulis modorum duas formulas in unoquoque modo." See also the references in the translation of John, chap. 11, n. 7, p. 120.

least permissible to rise either in beginnings or endings of phrases [155] to the fifth degree [above the final], although one may very rarely rise to the fourth [degree]. In authentic modes, however, except the deuterus, it is most unsuitable to rise in these beginnings and endings of phrases to the sixth degree. Yet those of the plagal of the protus and the plagal of the tritus go as high as the third, and those of the plagal of the deuterus and the plagal of the tetrardus go as high as the fourth.

You should remember, furthermore, that authentic modes scarcely go more than one note below their finals, as is shown by the testimony of the chants generally used. From these it is evident that the authentic tritus does so very rarely because of the flaw of the semitone just beneath. [The authentic modes] go up an octave or ninth or even a [156] tenth. Plagal modes, however, go down and up a fifth. Yet the sixth above is also allowed by the authorities, as are the ninth and tenth in authentic modes. Moreover the plagals of the protus, deuterus, and tritus sometimes end by necessity on high a, ♮, and c respectively.

The above-mentioned rules are observed very particularly in antiphons and responsories, whose chants [157] should be based on the customary rules so that they will join well with psalms and verses. However, you will find a number of chants in which the low and the high are so intermingled that one cannot make out whether they should be assigned to authentic or plagal. Furthermore, in studying chants new to us, we are helped chiefly by juxtaposing the aforesaid neumes and appendages [*subiunctiones*], since from the way these fit we come to see the particular character of each note through the effect of the "tropes." "Trope" is the aspect of chant which is also called "mode," and we shall now discuss it.

Chapter 14

On the tropes and on the power of music

[158] Some men who are well trained in the particular characters and, so to say, the individual features of these tropes recognize them the instant they hear them, as one who is familiar with the different peoples, when many men are placed before him, can observe their appearance and say, "This is [159] a Greek, that one a Spaniard, this is a Latin, that one a German, and that other is a Frenchman." The diversity in the tropes so fits in with the diversity in people's minds that one man is attracted by the intermittent leaps of the authentic deuterus, another chooses the delightfulness of the plagal of the tritus, one is more pleased by the volubility of the authentic tetrardus, another esteems the sweetness of the plagal tetrardus, and so forth.

Nor is it any wonder if the hearing is charmed by a variety of sounds, since the sight rejoices in a variety of colors, the sense of smell is gratified by a variety of odors, and the palate delights in changing flavors. For thus through the windows of the body [160] the sweetness of apt things enters wondrously into the recesses of the heart. Hence it is that the well-being of both heart and body is lessened or increased, as it were, by particular tastes and smells and even by the sight of certain colors. So it is said that of old a certain madman was recalled from insanity by the music of the physician Asclepiades.[1] Also that another man was roused by the sound of the cithara to such lust that, in his madness, he sought to break into the bedchamber of a girl, but, when the cithara player quickly changed the mode, was brought to feel remorse for his libidinousness and to retreat abashed. [161] So, too, David soothed with the cithara the evil spirit of Saul and tamed the savage demon with the potent force and sweetness of this art.[2] Yet this effect is fully clear only to Divine Wisdom, thanks to which, indeed, we have gained some insight into obscure things. Since we have poured forth not a few words on the power of this art, let us now see what is requisite for shaping good melodic lines.

Chapter 15

On grateful melodic lines and composing them[1]

[162] Just as in verse there are letters and syllables, "parts" and feet and lines, so in music there are phthongi, that is, sounds, of which one, [163] two, or three are grouped in "syllables"; one or two of the latter make a neume, which is the "part" of music; and one or more "parts" make a "distinction," that is, a suitable place to breathe. Regarding these units it must be noted that every "part" should be written and performed connectedly, and a musical "syllable" even more so.

A "hold" [*tenor*]—that is, a pause on the last note—which is very small for a "syllable," [164] larger for a "part," and longest for a phrase [*distinctio*], is in these cases a sign of division. It is good to beat time to a song as though by metrical feet. Some notes have separating them from others a brief delay [*morula*] twice as long or twice as short, or a trembling [*tremula*], that is, a "hold" of varying length, which sometimes is shown to be long by a horizontal dash added to a letter. [165] Special care should be taken that neumes, whether made by repeating one note or joining two or more, be always arranged to correspond to each other either in the number of notes or in the relationship of the durations [*tenores*]. At some times let equal neumes be answered by equal; at others let "simple" neumes be answered by those two or three times [as long]; and at still others let neumes be juxtaposed with others three-halves or four-thirds [their size] [see Fig. 3].

1. This story about the Greek physician Asclepiades is told by Censorinus, *De/In die natali* 12; Martianus Capella, *Satyricon* 9; and Cassiodorus, *Inst.* 5. 9, from whom Guido probably got it.

2. 1 Sam. 16 : 23. This story too is told by Cassiodorus, *Inst.* 5. 9.

1. For a listing of some of the commentaries and translations of this chapter, see the Introduction to this treatise, n. 39.

Figure 3

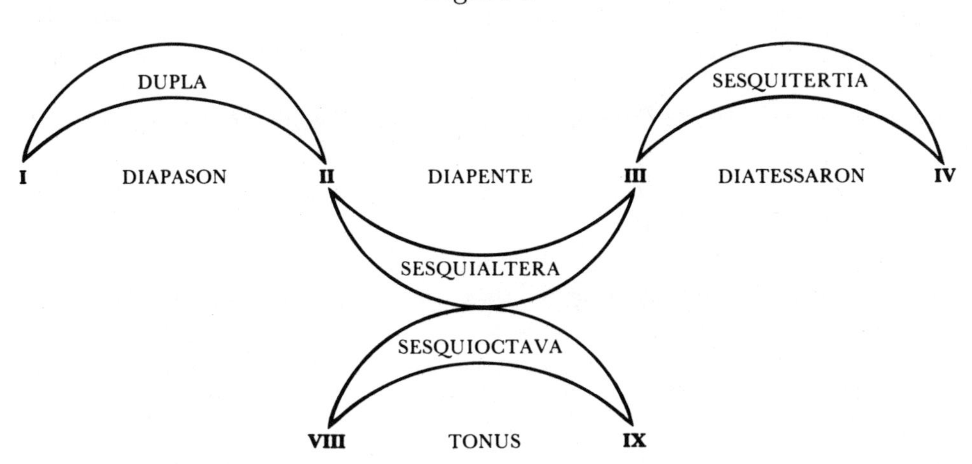

[167] Let the musician consider with which of these proportions [*divisiones*] he will construct the chant that is under way, as the versifier considers with which feet he will make the verse. However, the musician does not restrict himself by such stringency of rule, since in every way this art keeps transforming itself through a reasonable variety in the ordering of notes. Even though we often may not grasp this reasonableness, still that is thought to be reasonable which pleases a mind in which reason resides. Yet these and other such things are better demonstrated in speaking than can well be done in writing.

[168] The musician should also plan that the phrases be of the same length, like lines of verse, and be sometimes repeated, either the same or modified by some change, even though slight, and, if they are particularly beautiful, be duplicated, with their "parts" not too diverse; and let those occasional phrases that are the same be varied as to intervals [*per modos*], or, if they retain the same intervals, let them be heard transposed higher or lower.

Also a neume, turning back on itself, may return the same way it came and by the same steps.

[169] Also note that when a neume traverses a certain range or contour by leaping down from high notes, another neume may respond similarly in an opposite direction from low notes, as happens when we look for our likeness confronting us in a well.

Sometimes, too, let one syllable have one or more neumes, and at other times let one neume be divided among more than one syllable. [170] These—indeed all neumes—will be varied, in that in some places they will begin from the same note, in other places from a different one, according to the various qualities of low or high pitch.

Also let almost all phrases proceed to the principal note [of the mode], that is, the final, or some note related to it [*affinis*] if such be chosen instead of the final. Just as the same note may sometimes end all the neumes or the great majority of the phrases, sometimes, too, let it begin them, as can be found in Ambrosian [chant], if you are interested. [171] But there are, as it were, prose chants that follow these [practices] less, in which no care is taken as to whether some of the "parts" are longer and some shorter and whether the phrase endings [*distinctiones*] are found in indiscriminate locations in the manner of *prosae*.

I speak of chants as metrical because we often sing in such a way that we appear almost to scan verses by feet, as happens when we sing actual meters—in which one must take care lest neumes of two syllables persist excessively without an admixture of some of three or four syllables. For just as lyric [172] poets join now one kind of foot, now another, so composers reasonably juxtapose different and various neumes. Diversity is reasonable if it creates a measured variety of neumes and phrases, yet in such a way that neumes answer harmoniously to neumes and phrases to phrases, with always a certain resemblance. That is, let the likeness be incomplete, in the manner of the outstandingly lovely chant of St. Ambrose.

The parallel between verse and chant is no slight one, since neumes [173] correspond to feet and phrases to lines of verse. Thus one neume proceeds like a dactyl, another like a spondee, and a third in iambic manner; and you see a phrase now like a tetrameter, now like a pentameter, and again like a hexameter, and many other such parallels.

Let the subdivisions [*partes*] and phrases of both the neumes and the words end at the same time, [174] and do not let a long stay [*tenor*] on any short syllables or a short stay on long ones create an impropriety, though this will rarely demand attention.

Let the effect of the song express what is going on in the text, so that for sad things the neumes are grave, for serene ones they are cheerful, and for auspicious texts exultant, and so forth.

We often place an acute or grave accent above [the vowels in the text for] the notes, [175] because we often utter them with more or less stress, so much so that the repetition of the same note often seems to be a raising or lowering.

Towards the ends of phrases the notes should always be more widely spaced as they approach the breathing place, like a galloping horse, so that they arrive at the pause, as it were, weary and heavily. Spacing notes close together or widely apart, as befits, is a good way to indicate this effect [in writing].

At many points notes "liquesce," like the liquid letters, so that [176] the interval from one note to another is begun with a smooth glide and does not appear to have a stopping place en route. We put a dot like a blot beneath the liquescent note,[2] thus:

2. The liquescent clivis appears in *LU* 318 at the syllable "Ad":

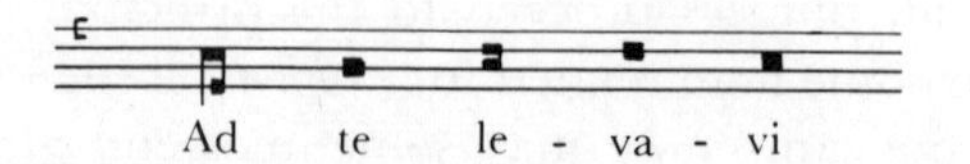

Example 4

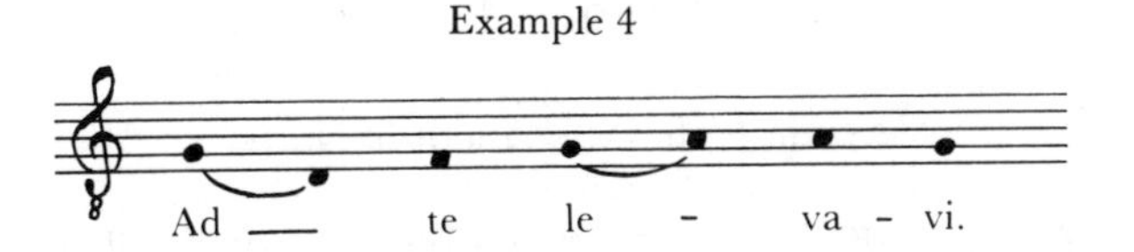

[177] If you wish to perform the note more fully and not make it liquesce, no harm is done; indeed, it is often more pleasing.

Do everything that we have said neither too rarely nor too unremittingly, but with taste.

Chapter 16

On the manifold variety of sounds and neumes

[178] It should not seem surprising that such an abundance of such different chants is created from so few notes—notes that are joined, as we said, by only six intervals either up or down. But from the letters, likewise few, not so very many syllables are made, [179] for the number of syllables can be estimated. Yet a boundless multitude of words [*partes*] has grown out of these syllables, and in verse how numerous are the kinds of meters from a few feet! One kind of meter, like the hexameter, is found varied in many ways. Let the grammarians investigate how this is done; let us, if we can, see in what ways we can make neumes that are different from each other.

Now melodic motion—which, we said, was made up of six intervals—consists of arsis and thesis, [180] that is, ascent and descent. Of this twofold motion, arsis and thesis, every neume is composed, except for repeated notes and single notes. Next, arsis and thesis are combined, either with themselves, as arsis to arsis and thesis to thesis, or each with the other, as arsis to thesis and thesis to arsis; and this combination is made now of like, now of unlike [elements].

Unlikeness arises if of the aforesaid melodic movements one has more [181] or fewer notes than the other, or closer together or farther apart. Furthermore, when a combination is made of either similar or dissimilar elements, one melodic figure [*motus*] will either be placed above another, that is, placed among higher notes; or placed below it; or placed beside, that is, so that the end of one and the beginning of the other are at the same pitch; or placed within, that is, so that one melodic figure is placed within the span of the other and is less low and less high; or mixed, that is, placed partly within and partly below or above or beside. Again, these [182] configurations can be classified according to various qualities: of lowness or height of pitch; of more or fewer notes; and of the intervals. The neumes, too, can be varied in all these ways, and occasionally the phrases.

We have appended a diagram of this topic, so that one can more easily get the picture of it [Fig. 4.]. [184]

Figure 4

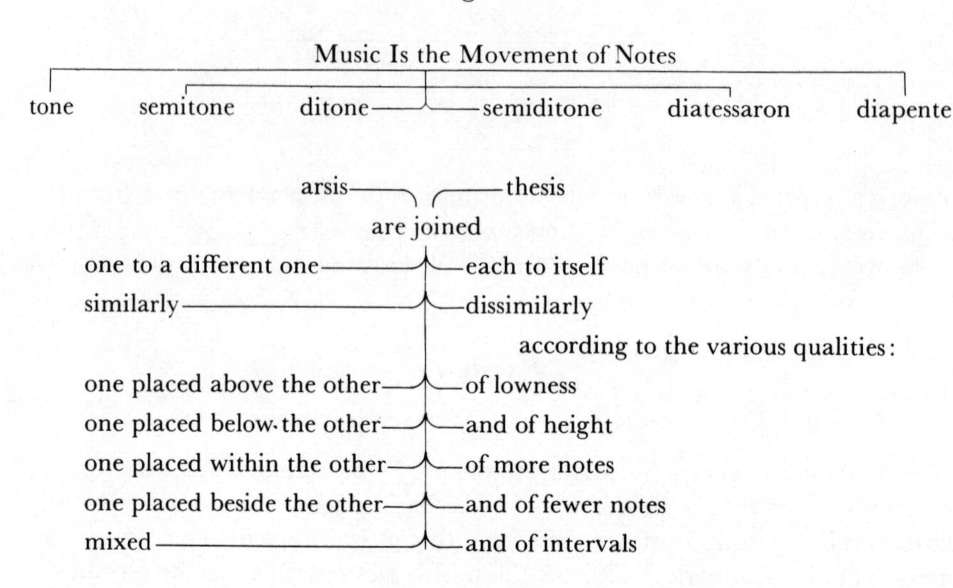

Chapter 17

That anything that is spoken can be made into music[1]

[186] Having briefly discussed the foregoing, we shall present to you another very simple matter, most profitable to consider though hitherto unheard of. While by it a basis [*causa*] for all [187] melodies will become perfectly clear, you will be able to retain for your use whatever you find appropriate and still reject whatever appears objectionable.

Consider, then, that just as everything that is spoken can be written, so everything that is written can be made into song. Thus, everything that is spoken can be sung, for writing is depicted by letters.

Not to draw out our method to great length, let us take from these letters only the five vowels. Without them, manifestly, no other letter or syllable [188] can sound, and it is for the most part due to them whenever an agreeable blending is found in the different units [*partes*]. Thus, in verse we often see such concordant and mutually congruous lines that you wonder, as it were, at a certain harmony of language. And if music be added to this, with a similar interrelationship, you will be doubly charmed by a twofold melody.

Let us take then these five vowels. Perhaps, since they bring such euphony to words, they will offer no less harmony to the neumes. Let them be placed

1. See the commentary in van Waesberghe, "Guido of Arezzo and Musical Improvisation," *Musica disciplina* 5 (1951): 55–63.

in succession beneath the letters of the monochord, and, since they are only five, let them be repeated until beneath each note its particular vowel is written [see Ex. 5].

Example 5

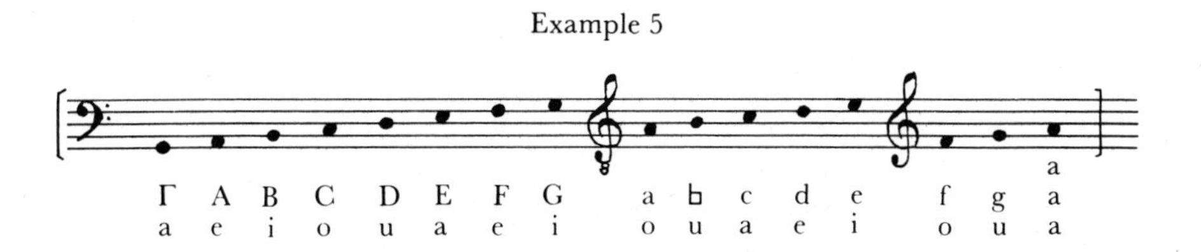

[189] Reflect about this arrangement. Since all speech is activated by these five letters, it should not be denied that five notes also may be set in motion among one another, as we have said. Since this is so, let us take any phrase, adding to its syllables those tones which are indicated by the vowels of these same syllables and sing them, as written beneath [Fig. 5, Ex. 6].

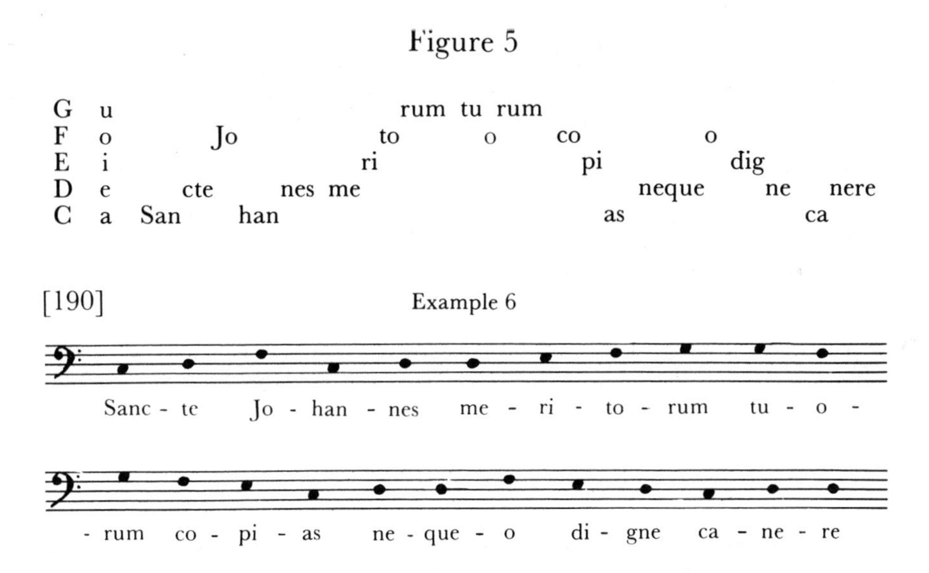

What has been done with this text can indubitably be done with any. By this system scarcely any tune [*symphonia*] would get less than five notes, and there would be no way to get beyond these five, as you may often wish. So that thus no onerous compulsion be laid on you and so that you can range about a little more freely, add another row of vowels beneath the first, but varied so that it begins from the third place of the earlier row, in this way [Ex. 7]. [191]

Example 7

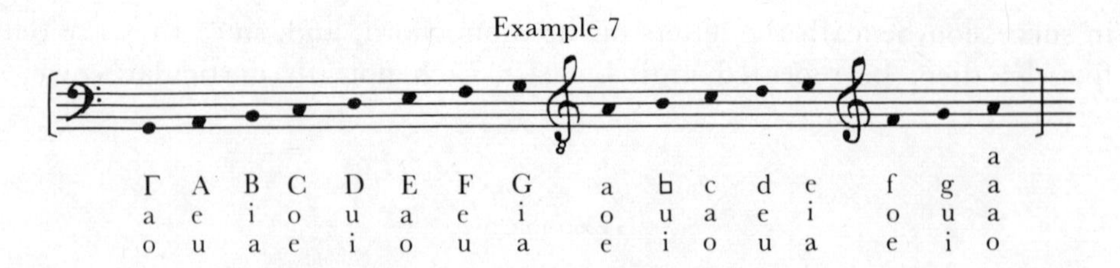

Here, with two vowels beneath each sound—the five vowels being present—since beneath each sound there is not just one vowel but a second also, you have sufficiently freer scope to proceed at will with more extended or more confined melodic movement. So now, with this arrangement, let us see what kind of musical setting [*symphonia*] for this verse its own vowels will provide [Ex. 8]. [192]

Example 8

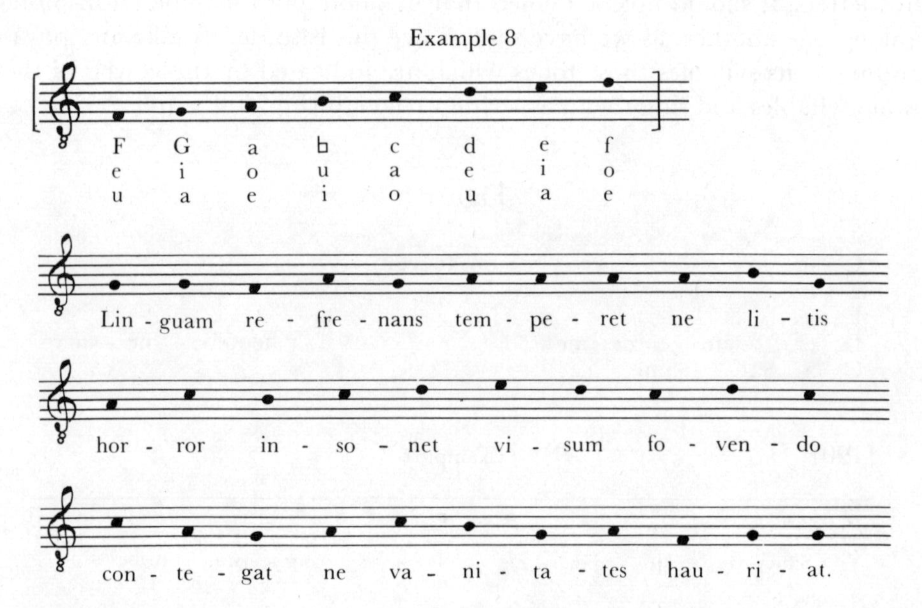

[193] Only in the last part did we abandon this system so that we could lead the melody back properly to its tetrardus. Since certain texts command a suitable vocal setting simply from their own vowels, there is no doubt that the vocal setting will be most suitable if, after practice in many such, you select from the numerous possibilities only the more effective and those that fit together better. If you then fill in gaps, space out the constricted places, draw together the overextended, and broaden the overcondensed, you will make a unified, [194] polished work. This, too, I wish you to know, that, in the manner of pure silver, all chant gains in color the more it is used, and whatever displeases at first, after being polished through use as by a file, is extolled; and, in accordance with the diversity of people and minds, what displeases one is cherished by another; and, anon, things that blend together delight this man,

whereas that one prefers variety; one seeks a homogeneity and blandness in keeping with his pleasure-loving mind; another, since he is serious-minded, is pleased by staider strains; while another, as if distracted, feeds on studied and [195] intricate contortions; and each proclaims that music as much the better sounding which suits the innate character of his own mind.

If you absorb all these things from our teachings with unremitting practice, you cannot remain ignorant. Certainly, such expositions must be employed as long as we know only a part, so that we may arrive at the fullness of knowledge. But since the brevity here aimed at demands that we not pursue these matters at length, although indeed there are many things worth garnering from them, let this suffice on setting words to music [*canendum*]. Now let us briefly examine the principles of diaphony.

Chapter 18

On diaphony, that is the principles of organum

[196] Diaphony sounds as a separateness of [simultaneous] sounds, which we also call organum, [197] in which notes distinct from each other make dissonance harmoniously and harmonize in their dissonance. Some practice diaphony in such a way that the fourth step down always accompanies the singer, as A with D; and if you double this organum by acute a , so that you have A D a, then A will sound a diatessaron with D and a diapason with a, whereas D will sound a diatessaron and a diapente with A and a respectively, and acute a with the lower two notes a diapente [198] and a diapason. These three intervals blend in organum congenially and smoothly just as it has been shown above that they caused a resemblance of notes. Hence they are called "symphonies," that is, compatible unions of notes, although the term symphony is also applied to all chant. Here is an example of this diaphony [Ex. 9].

Example 9

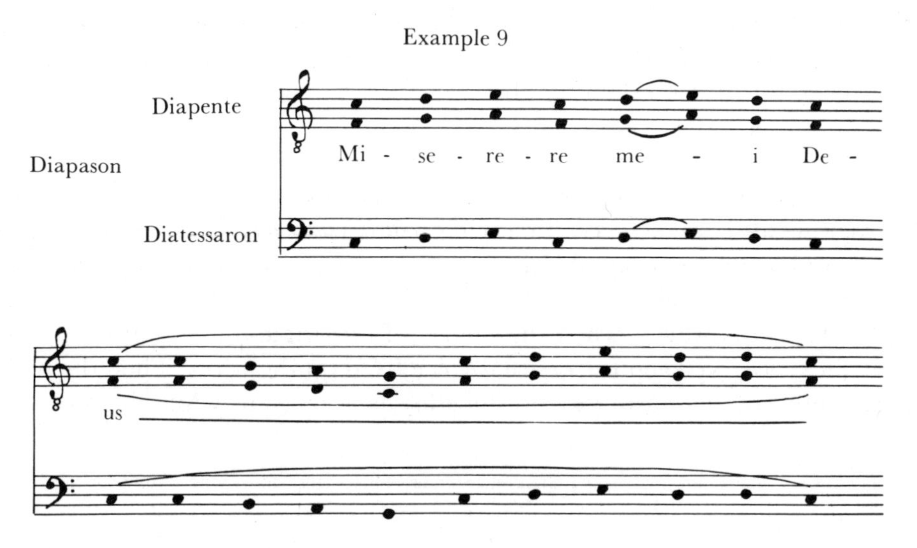

[201] You can both double the chant by an organal voice [*organum*] and the latter by its diapason as much as you like; for wherever there is the concord of the diapason, the aforementioned compatibility of the symphonies will not fail.

Since the doubling of notes has now been made sufficiently clear, let us explain the low voice added beneath the singer of the original line in the way that we employ. For the above manner of diaphony is hard [sounding] [*durus*], but ours is smooth [*mollis*]. In it we do not admit the semitone or the diapente, but we do allow the tone, the ditone, the semiditone, and the diatessaron; and of these the semiditone holds the lowest rank and the diatessaron [202] the chief one. With these four concords the diaphony accompanies the chant.

Of the tropes, some are serviceable, others more serviceable, and still others most serviceable. Those are serviceable that provide organum only at the diatessaron, with the notes a fourth from each other, like the deuterus on B and E; more serviceable are those that harmonize [*respondent*] not only with fourths but also with thirds and seconds,[1] by a tone and, though only rarely, a semiditone, like the protus on A and D. Most serviceable are those that make organum most frequently and more smoothly, namely, the tetrardus and tritus on C and F and G; for these harmonize at the distance of a tone, a ditone, and a diatessaron.

[203] The accompanying voice [*subsecutor*] should never descend below the tritus either when phrases end thereon or when the tritus is next below such an ending, unless the singer [*cantor* : singer of the original line] employs notes lower than that tritus. For the organal voice [*organum*] must never be taken below a tritus that is the lowest note [of the original voice] or that is situated next below this. But when [the original voice] employs notes lower than the tritus at a suitable place, the organal voice should also descend below it at the diatessaron; and as soon as that low region of the phrase is left so that [204] one does not expect it to recur, the accompanying voice should return to the place it previously had, so that it may remain on the final, if it has arrived there, or, if the final is above it, that the accompanying voice may proceed to it properly from nearby.

This convergence on the final [*occursus*] is preferably by a tone, less so by a ditone, and never by a semiditone. The occursus is scarcely made from a diatessaron, since a voice accompanying below [*succentus*] is more satisfactory in such a place; yet one should take care that this last does not happen at the final phrase-end of the piece.

[205] Often, however, when the singer [of the original line] employs notes below the tritus, we keep the organal voice fixed on the tritus. Then the main singer should not end a phrase on these lower notes, but, while the notes are

1. The usage "non solum quartis, sed tertiis et secundis" for fourths, thirds, and seconds is rare in this period.

moving quickly to and fro, go back up to the waiting tritus and avoid trouble for himself and the other part by making a phrase ending on higher notes.

When the cadential convergence [*occursus*] is made by a whole tone, there is a prolongation [*diutinus tenor*] of the final tone, so that it is accompanied partly from below and partly at the unison. In the case of a ditone this [prolongation] is still longer, so that often, when the accompanying voice is pitched, even though briefly, on the note in between [the ditone], [206] the occursus of a whole tone is not lacking. This is the close for the deuterus, because it takes place there harmoniously. If the cantus is not expected to descend beyond, to the tritus, it will then be useful for the organal voice to sound the protus [*proto vim organi occupare*], to accompany with the following [notes], and to converge properly on the ending via a whole tone.

Furthermore, the two voices must not be separated by more than a diatessaron; therefore, when the singer of the main part goes farther up, the accompanying part must ascend, as, for instance, C should accompany F; and D, G; and E, a; and so on.

Lastly, there is a diatessaron beneath each note except ♮-natural, so that in phrases where this appears, G will sound in the organal voice [*G vim organi possidebit*]. [207] When this happens, if the original chant either descends to F or ends a phrase on G, then F in the added voice accompanies G and a at suitable places; but if the original chant does not end on G, then F in the chant is not accompanied by F in the organal voice [*F cum cantu vim organi amittit*].

But when b-flat is used in the chant, F will be in the organal voice. Since therefore F and C [tritus] hold the chief place in diaphony to such a degree that they take precedence over the others as the most serviceable, we see that not undeservedly is the tritus beloved by Gregory more than the other notes. He assigns to it the beginnings of many melodies and most of [208] the repeated notes, so that often, if you take away the C's and F's of the tritus from his chant, it will seem that you have removed almost half of it.

The precepts of diaphony have now been given, and if you test them by the following examples, you will understand them perfectly.

Chapter 19

Testing this diaphony through examples

[209] We do not take the organal voice below the tritus if there is a close on it [here] or in the following notes. Here is a close on the tritus C:

Example 10

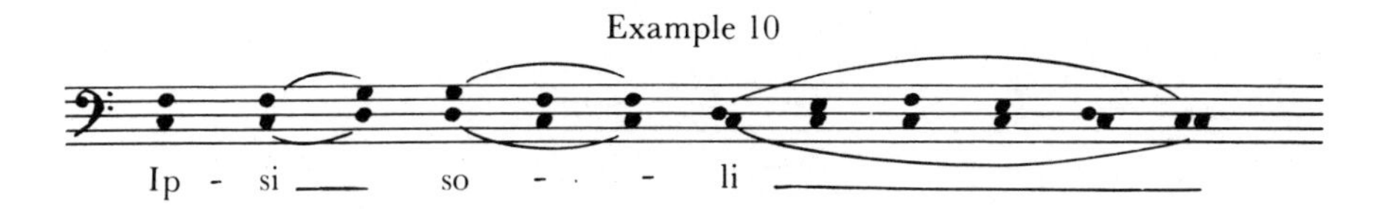

[210] Here is another phrase-ending on the tritus F, in which we accompany the chant at the diatessaron with the notes a fourth apart. At the end here an accompaniment a diatessaron below is more pleasing than an occursus.

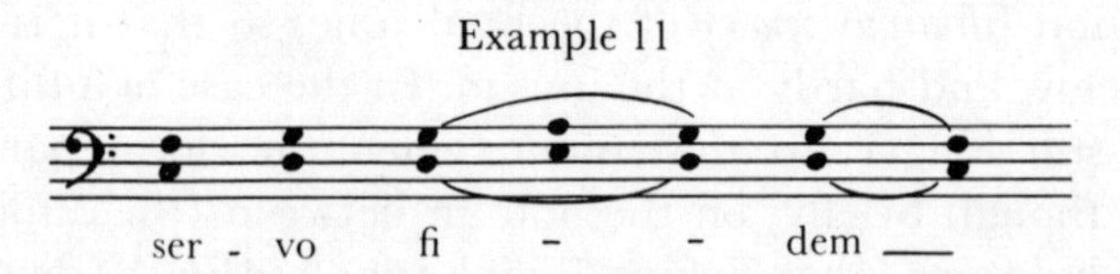

Here is another of the same mode:

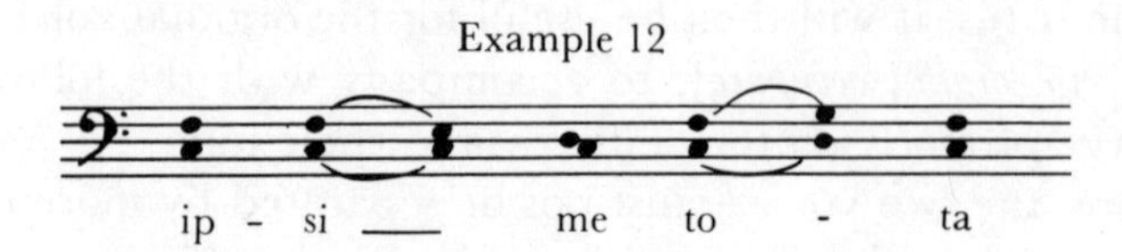

Here is another phrase in the protus D, in which an occursus of a tone appears at the end:

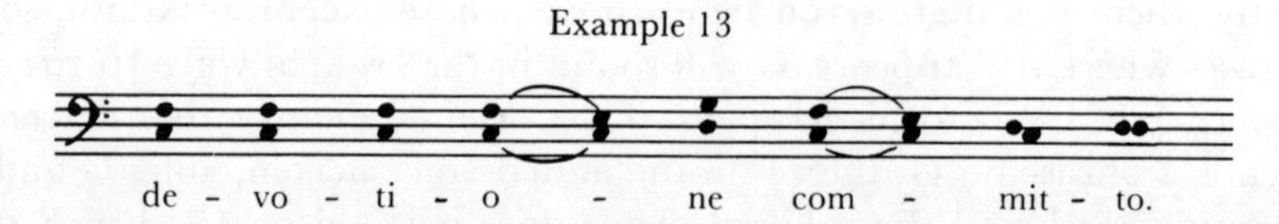

[211] Here are [examples of the] phrase-ending on the deuterus E, showing an occursus of a ditone, either simple [Ex. 14] or with intervening notes [*intermissae*] [Ex. 15]:

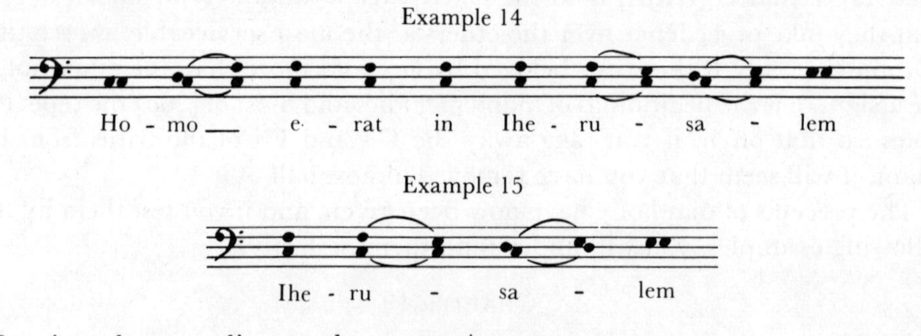

Here is a phrase-ending on the protus A:

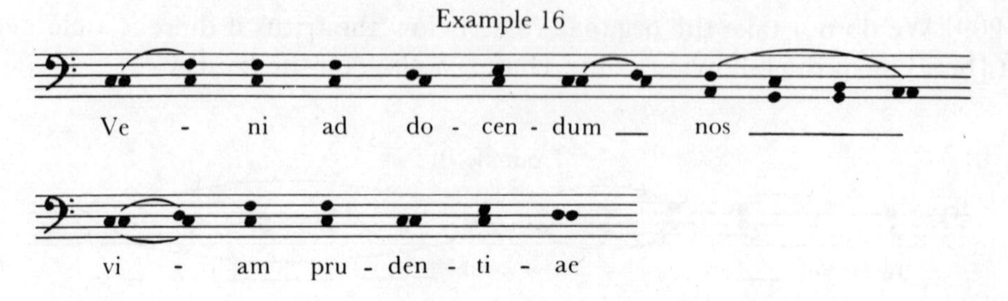

In this phrase-ending, notes below the tritus C, which [212] is next below the final D, are permitted, and after the low passage the earlier pitch [C] is resumed. Similarly in the following one, note how the organal voice rises, avoiding going below the main chant at the end of the final phrase.

Example 17

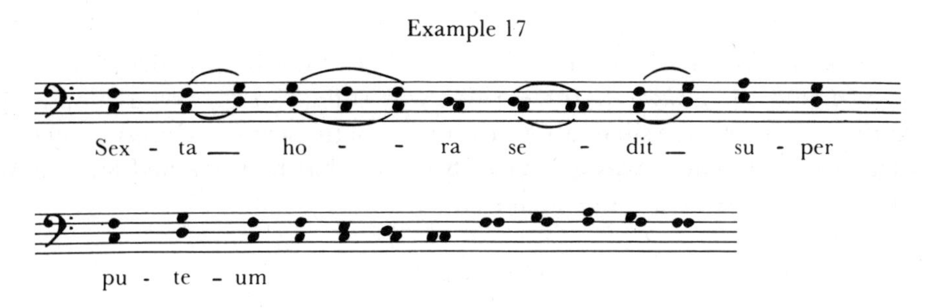

See how when the singer employs low notes we [may] keep the organal voice suspended on the tritus F:

Example 18

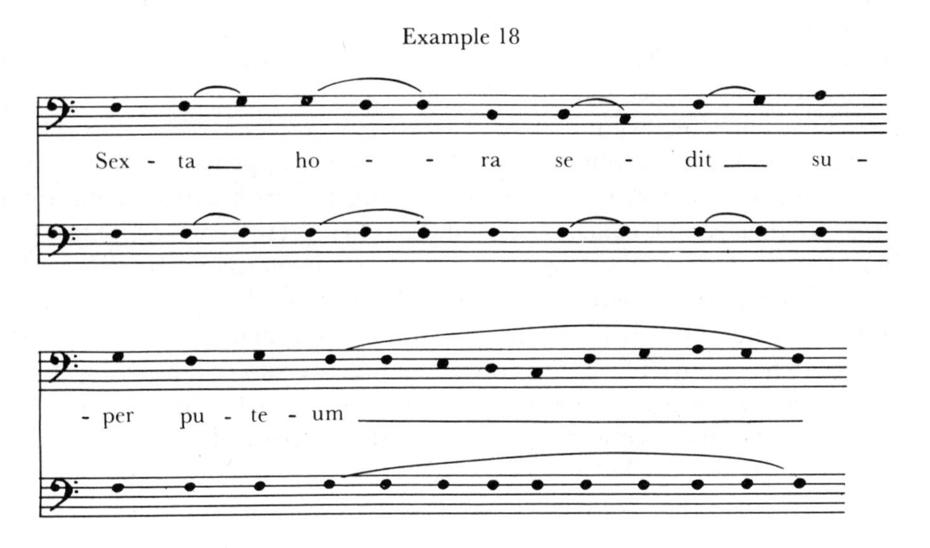

[213] See how toward the end F in the lower voice accompanies G and a in the chant:

Example 19

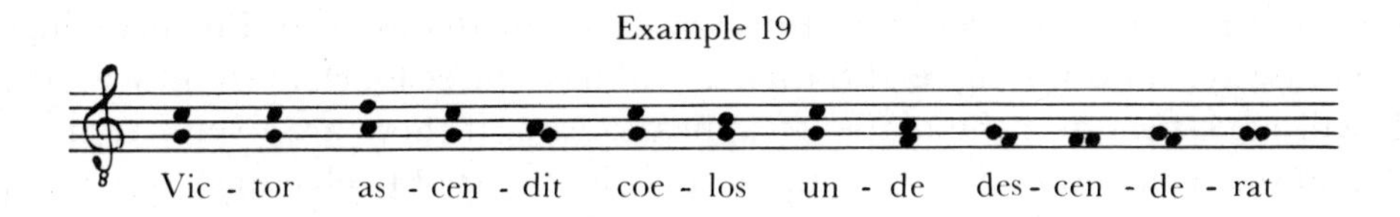

In the plagal tritus too you will find this practiced, so that b accompanies c and d, just as F accompanies G and a. Thus:

Example 20

[214] Take pains, then, and turn the foregoing to use by practice; for if you have a melody [*symphonia*], these rules will suffice to give you diaphony.

At the outset we were silent about the origin of the science of music, since we realized that the reader was a novice. But now that he is trained and knows more, we impart it to him in conclusion.

Chapter 20

How the nature of music was discovered from the sound of hammers

[228] In ancient times there were instruments that we are not clear about and also a multitude of singers who were, however, in the dark, for no man could by any train of thought reason out the differences between notes or a description of music. Nor could anyone ever [229] have learned anything certain about this science had not Divine Goodness of its own will at length arranged the following event.

When a certain great philosopher, Pythagoras, happened to be taking a walk, he came to a workshop in which five hammers were beating on one anvil. Amazed at their sweet concord, the philosopher drew near and, expecting at first that the basis of the variety of sound and its harmony [*modulatio*] lay in the differences of the hands of the workmen, he exchanged the hammers among them. But after this was done, its quality of sound [*vis*] followed each hammer. So he removed from the others one that was discordant and weighed the rest, and, in wondrous manner, by God's [230] will, they weighed the first with twelve, the second with nine, the third with eight, and the fourth with six, of I know not what units of weight.

Thus he learned that the science of music depended upon numerical ratios and comparisons; for there was precisely the interrelationship among the four hammers that there is among the four notes A, D, E, and a. For if A has twelve units and D nine, there being four groups of three divisions [on the monochord], A with its twelve units will have four groups of three; [231] and D with its nine, three groups of three. And thus you have the diatessaron. Further, since A has twelve units if E has eight, then A will have three fourfold steps, whereas E will have two, and the diapente appears. Also, if there are twelve units in A and six in the other a, the group of six is half that of twelve, just as acute a is obtained as the midpoint of the other A. Therefore the diapason is present. So from that same A to D gives the diatessaron, from A to E the diapente, and to the other a the diapason. Moreover, from D to E [232] sounds a tone, and from D to A and a, a diatessaron and a diapente respectively. And from E to D also provides a tone, and E to A and a, a diapente and a diatessaron respectively; whereas acute a sounds a diapason with A, a diapente with D, and a diatessaron with E. All these things the careful investigator will find in the aforementioned numbers.

[233] Beginning at this point, Boethius, the expositor of this science, has set forth the extensive, marvelous, and very difficult concordance of this science with numerical ratios.

What more? The renowned Pythagoras first arranged the monochord, ordering the notes by means of the aforesaid intervals. Since this monochord constitutes not a trivial but a diligently revealed knowledge of our art, it has pleased wise men in general. Up to this day our science has gradually increased and grown in strength, with that same Teacher bringing light to the darkness of human affairs whose supreme wisdom flourishes through all the ages. Amen.

[234] End of the Micrologus, that is, the short treatise on music.

JOHN

ON MUSIC

(*DE MUSICA*)

Vienna, Nationalbibliothek, MS Cpv. 51, fol. 62v, image supposedly of the author, appearing at the end of the table of contents of John's treatise (12th century).

INTRODUCTION

by Claude V. Palisca

The treatise of John is modeled on the millennial *Micrologus* of Guido. Written nearly a century later and across the Alps, John's manual was intended, like Guido's, to educate the boys of a cathedral or choir school in the singing of plainchant and to provide them with elementary precepts in melodic composition and in the improvisation of organum. A devout "servant of the servants of God," as he calls himself in the dedicatory letter, John articulates the concerns of a church musician at a time when most of the repertory of sacred chant was fixed, classified, and preserved.

The choirbooks of John's day were relatively uniform in their contents and readings, the culmination of the efforts of leading churchmen from Pope Gregory the Great on to realize conformity in the liturgy and its musical setting. By about 1100, when this treatise was written, there was no longer any obstacle to achieving uniformity of chant settings, because the notation, at least in terms of pitch, was capable of recording every melodic detail. The advances in notation spurred by Guido had made this possible. Whereas the author of the *Micrologus* was impelled by a crusading spirit, John obeyed the more modest call to consolidate the recent advances and to preserve the repertory at its best through enlightened performance. The severity and dogmatism of John's pronouncements reflect the pride he took in the great literature of Gregorian chant.

After years of debate, no fully convincing account of the identity of the author John has emerged. He survives only in this treatise; no other works by him can be drawn upon to fill out the picture we get of him here. To be able to tag him in the stream of medieval Johns with a second name or a place would be in itself advantageous; if, besides, we knew where he was educated, where he taught, what his main profession was, what rank he held in which monastic order, these facts would enable us better to judge the treatise in terms of its practical sphere of influence and resonance.

That the author's name is John rests on the secure evidence of a dedicatory letter from a Johannes to a Bishop or Abbot Fulgentius that appears before the treatise in the earliest manuscripts. Several manuscripts have in addition such words as "Here begins the music of John," or "Here begins the letter of

John to Fulgentius," and "Here ends the treatise of John on the art of music."[1]

Various hypotheses compete further to specify this identity. The traditional attribution, going back as far as the thirteenth century,[2] credits the treatise to a Johannes Cotto, whose name appeared on a number of manuscripts. But around 1260 Jerome of Moravia, who borrowed heavily from John, still called him simply Johannes.[3] English nationality was inferred by a number of writers as early as the twelfth century[4] from John's dedication of the treatise to a "Domino et patri suo venerabili Anglorum antistiti [or episcopo] Fulgentio" (To his venerable lord and father abbot [or bishop] Fulgentius, of the English). Already Charles Burney was troubled by the fact that he could find no record of a bishop or abbot Fulgentius in England in the twelfth century.[5] None has since emerged.[6] Another difficulty with the theory of English origin is that the treatise had practically no diffusion in the British Isles. The only documented copy in England in medieval times is perhaps represented by the entry "Musica Joh[ann]is et in eodem pars geometrice in principio" in the catalog of around 1491–97 of the Abbey of St. Augustine at Canterbury.[7]

The qualification "Anglorum" need not mean, of course, that Fulgentius resided in England, since he could have been of English origin and settled abroad, as not a few English ecclesiastics did. Similarly John could well have been other than English and still have dedicated his work to a native of England.

Edwin Flindell has proposed a solution of this sort.[8] He theorized that John worked under Anselm when he was Abbot of Bec in northern Normandy

1. The variant incipits and explicits are given in J. Smits van Waesberghe, ed., Johannis Affligemensis, *De musica cum tonario* (Rome: American Institute of Musicology, 1950), Corpus Scriptorum de Musica 1 (hereinafter *CSM* 1), pp. 43, 49, 162, and 200. Additions to the critical apparatus of *CSM* 1 are in van Waesberghe, "John of Affligem or John Cotton?" *Musica disciplina* 6 (1952): 146–53.

2. Ibid., p. 141.

3. Simon M. Cserba, ed., Hieronymus de Moravia, *Tractatus de musica* (Regensburg: Verlag Friedrich Pustet, 1935), pp. 11, 45, 46, etc.

4. The once anonymous chronicler from Melk whom Bernhard Bischoff recently identified as Wolfger von Prüfening, writing around 1170, said concerning a Johannes who may be our author: "John, musician, of English nationality, was a man of very subtle genius who also wrote an excellent little book on musical art" (Joannes musicus natione Anglicus, vir admodum subtilis ingenii fuit, qui et libellum praestantissimum de musica arte composuit): *De scriptoribus ecclesiasticis*, cap. 59, in Migne, *Patrologia cursus completus: Series latina*, 213: 982. See Bischoff, "Wolfger," in *Verfasserlexikon*, ed. Karl Langosch (Berlin, 1953), vol. 4, cols. 1051–56. I am indebted to Prof. Yves Chartier for this reference.

Another witness to our author's English nationality is the thirteenth-century writer of the *Tractatus correctorius*, who calls him "Joannes Anglicus" (*GS* 2: 53).

5. Charles Burney, *A General History of Music*, 2 vols. ed. Frank Mercer (1935; New York: Dover, 1957), 1: 507.

6. Pius Bonifacius Gams, *Series episcoporum ecclesiae catholicae* (Regensburg, 1873), does not list a single Fulgentius between 1000 and 1200 in Anglia or Hibernia (Ireland), nor for that matter in Batavia, Germania, Liège or Gallia (France).

7. Edwin F. Flindell, "Joh[ann]is Cottonis, corrigenda et addenda," *Musica disciplina* 23 (1969): 7.

8. Flindell, "Joh[ann]is Cottonis," *Musica disciplina* 20 (1966): 11–30.

between 1078 and 1093. In 1093 Anselm became Archbishop of Canterbury, and it would have been after this that John dedicated the treatise to him. In various letters Anselm was referred to as "episcopus Anglorum" but more frequently as "archiepiscopus Anglorum," appropriate appellations for the Primate of England. Flindell had to dispose, however, of the name Fulgentius, which occurs in the dative form, "Fulgentio," though in some manuscripts without a capital F. He interpreted this as a laudatory adjective or participle, "refulgent," rather than a bishop's name. The weakness of Flindell's thesis is that the evidence is overwhelmingly in favor of Fulgentius as a proper noun, not an adjective.[9] Flindell's other arguments in favor of a link to Bec, though interesting and ingenious, are not of the cogency to overcome this difficulty. He failed to find any record of a John Cotton or of a copy of the treatise at Bec. Still, he continued to call him Cotton and to regard him as an Englishman.

There is some support for the name Cotton in the manuscripts, but unfortunately none survives in which that name is inscribed by a hand earlier than thirteenth century. The manuscripts that have been said to contain the attribution to Cotton are:

1. The MS formerly in the Phillipps collection, now in the Library of Congress, ML 171 J 56, which begins: "Epistola johannis cottonis ad fulgentium episcopum anglorum," which inscription was apparently added by a thirteenth-century hand to the twelfth-century text below it.[10]
2. A MS once existing in Antwerp described in the catalog by A. Sanderus, *Bibliotheca belgica manuscripta* (Lille, 1641), p. 334, under the heading "Libri manuscripti latini Antverpiae in domo professa Societatis Jesu," as: "Johannis Cottonis ad Fulgentium Episcopum Anglorum, De Musica." Padre Martini had this reading of the MS verified for him by the Jesuit Giovanni Scotti.[11]
3. A MS once existing in Paris, which, according to Martin Gerbert, began: "Epistola Ioannis Cottonis ad Fulgentium episcopum Anglorum."[12] This could be the present Library of Congress copy.
4. A MS in Leipzig mentioned by Gerbert as naming Cottonius. This is a pure phantom. In the prefatory note to his edition of John's treatise Gerbert said: "I have applied myself in vain until now to investigate who this Ioannes might be who is given this surname in the Leipzig MS. . . ." This was obviously a slip, because in the introduction to the volume Gerbert stated ". . . in the catalog of the Pauline Library in Leipzig is written:

9. No adjective *fulgentius, -a, -um* is to be found in any of the standard classical or medieval Latin glossaries.

10. See van Waesberghe in *Musica disciplina* 6: 139–41.

11. See n. 14, below. Flindell, in *Musica disciplina* 20: 21, showed that this MS is not the Library of Congress copy.

12. *GS* 2: 230.

Ioannis pape musica ad Fulgentium Anglorum antistitem."[13] This reading is confirmed by Padre Martini's *Storia della musica*, published seventeen years before Gerbert's edition.[14]

The name Johannes Cotto does not by itself imply English origin. Cotto (genitive, Cottonis) could be a Latinization of the Italian Cotto, of the French Cotton, or German Kott, as well as English Cotton.

The identification of the author that has received the broadest consent, particularly among German scholars, is van Waesberghe's thesis that he was John of Affligem. He identified Fulgentius as the Abbot Fulgentius of the monastery of Affligem near Brussels from 1089 to 1120.[15] The identification is made more plausible by the circumstances that Fulgentius is not a common name and that his tenure as abbot coincides with the period when the book must have been written. Van Waesberghe maintained, further, that there is great affinity between John's treatise and others he has connected with the Liège region: those of Aribo,[16] Wolf's Anonymous,[17] the anonymous commentator on Guido's *Micrologus*,[18] and the anonymous author of *Quaestiones in musica*.[19] Waesberghe has also linked two who borrowed from John with the

13. Ibid., 2: 230: "Frustra hactenus, quis sit *IOANNES* iste, indagare studui, qui in Msc. Lips. COTTONIUS cognominatur . . . ." Ibid., 2: viii: ". . . in catalogo bibl. *Paulinae Lips.* scribitur: Ioannis *Papae musica ad* FULGENTIUM Anglorum *antistitem.*" This MS must be the present Leipzig, University Library 79, formerly in St. Mary's Cistercian Abbey in Altzelle, whose catalog of 1504 described the treatise as "Musica Johannis pape." See *CSM* 1: 10, n. 5.

14. Giovanni Battista Martini, *Storia della musica*, 3 vols. (Bologna: Lelio della Volpe, 1757–81), 1: 183, n. 62: "Due antichi Codici MSS. del medesimo Trattato di Musica trovansi, uno in Lipsia nella Biblioteca Paulina (*Repositor. Theolog. I series III. in fol. n. 10*), che nel Catalogo impresso viene attribuito a Papa Giovanni: *Johannis Papae Musica ad Fulgentium Anglorum Antistitem*, del quale tengo un' Esemplare intero esattissimo: e l'altro in Anversa nella celebre Casa Professa della Compagnia di Gesu, che nell'Indice de' Manoscritti ivi esistenti parimente stampato si attribuisce, e forse con piu ragione, a Giovanni Cottone: *Johannis Cottonis ad Fulgentium Episc. Anglorum de Musica;* ed avendomi il dottissimo, e gentilissimo P. Giovanni Scotti Segretario Generale della lodata sempre venerabile Compagnia favorito di far Collazionare col Codice d'Anversa quello di Lipsia, ho rilevato, contener l'uno, e l'altro l'istessissimo individuo Trattato, non di due diversi Autori, ma di un solo, che Giovanni appellavasi." The copy that Padre Martini said he owned may be that listed in Gaetano Gaspari, *Catalogo della biblioteca del Liceo Musicale di Bologna* (Bologna, 1890), 1: 205.

15. Van Waesberghe, "Some Music Treatises and Their Interrelation, A School of Liège (c. 1050–1200)?," *Musica disciplina* 3 (1949): 101–18. Also *CSM* 1: 22–23.

16. *Aribonis De Musica*, ed. J. S. van Waesberghe, *CSM* 2 (Rome: American Institute of Musicology, 1951).

17. Johannes Wolf, "Ein anonymer Musiktraktat des elften bis zwölften Jahrhunderts," *Vierteljahrsschrift für Musikwissenschaft* 9 (1893): 186–234.

18. *Commentarius anonymus in micrologum Guidonis Aretini*, ed. P. Cölestin Vivell (Vienna, 1917); ed. J. Smits van Waesberghe in *Expositiones in Micrologum Guidonis Aretini* (Amsterdam, 1957), pp. 93–172.

19. Ed. in Rudolph Steglich, *Die Quaestiones in musica: Ein Choraltraktat des zentralen Mittelalters und ihr mutmasslicher Verfasser Rudolf von St Trond.* (Leipzig, 1911). Van Waesberghe in *Muziekgeschiedenis der Middeleeuwen* (Tilburg, 1938), 1: 154–71 and 368–71 gives in parallel columns excerpts from the anonymous Commentarius on Guido beside corresponding texts of Aribo and John. These excerpts do not demonstrate any significant dependency by John on the anonymous commentator. The chant examples cited by the commentator are seldom concordant with those cited by John. As regards Aribo and Wolf's Anonymous, there are good grounds for believing they were Germans.

Liège school: the author of the ponderous *Speculum*, Jacques de Liège, and the anonymous author of the *Summa musicae*. He also pointed out that Jacques characterized John's treatment of the *differentiae* in the Tonary as "an older Liège tradition."[20]

These hypotheses, coincidences, and facts are not sufficiently documented to support the adoption of John of Afflighem as the name of the author. There remains also the qualification "anglorum," which does not square with what we know of Fulgentius of Afflighem.[21]

More profitable than to link up names and places is to try to locate the treatise geographically by internal and external evidence. Michel Huglo has contributed significantly to this approach.[22] Although he continues to call the author "Jean Cotton" and accepts as possible his affiliation with Afflighem because it is located in a "transitional region such as the diocese of Liège,"[23] the inferences Huglo draws from the tonary tend to locate John rather in the "East Zone" of his map of tonaries, the region of modern Switzerland. Huglo points to John's acquaintance with the notations practiced in this area, the interval notation of Hermannus Contractus (chap. 21) and the tonal letters of chapter 11, which Huglo shows were confined to the region immediately around St. Gall. Finally Huglo notes that John cited only one example of a response for each tone in the tonary (chap. 24), and the choice of versets situates the selected eight responses in the Germanic group rather than farther west in Europe. Moreover, the pains with which John explains the Romanic letters—the *litterae significativae* (chap. 21)—though disapprovingly, suggests that he was writing for students who might encounter them. And they were rarely to be encountered outside southern Germany and Metz. To these points should be added that the use of the Greek names Dorian, Phrygian, etc., was more characteristic of German authors than Italians or French.

Examination of the manuscript tradition points also to southern Germany and Switzerland. The determinable provenances of the earliest (12th-century) manuscripts are: Basel University; Abbey of St. Michelsberg near Bamberg (now Karlsruhe, Badische Landesbibliothek 505); the Cistercian Abbey at

20. *Musica disciplina* 3: 104; *CSM* 1: 27.

21. Van Waesberghe, anticipating this objection, pointed out that in one twelfth-century MS, Regina 1196 in the Vatican, *anglorum* is replaced by *angelorum* (of the angels). He maintained in *Musica disciplina* 3 (1949): 102, and in replying to Ellinwood reaffirmed in 6 (1952): 143, that the stroke or hook across the top of the "l" of *anglorum* indicated an abbreviation for *el*, transforming the word to *angelorum*. This hook, barely traceable in the illustration opposite p. 24 of *CSM* 1, is quite visible in *Musica disciplina* 3: 118. There are eight other similarly hooked letters elsewhere on the same page of the Vatican MS, all of them indicating abbreviations. On the other hand, it must be said that the hook of *anglorum* or *angelorum*, unlike others on that page, which are heavily inked, seems to have been part of what was rubbed out in the line above and then written over, so that this source too may indicate *anglorum*. Van Waesberghe has justified the otherwise inexplicable term *angelorum* before the title *antistiti* by the fact that in several documents the monks of Afflighem are referred to as angels; hence "abbot of the angels."

22. *Huglo*, pp. 299–301.

23. Ibid., p. 299.

Pforta and later St. Mary's Cistercian Abbey at Altzelle for the Leipzig, University Library MS 79; the Cistercian Abbey near Graz for the Rein Bibliothek, Zisterzienserstift, MS XXIV; and Heiligenkreuz, Stiftsbibliothek, MS 213.[24] The Washington MS has been affiliated with the Rhine-Meuse area through its neumatic notation.[25] The copying of the twelfth-century MS in Vienna has been located in Austria or southern Germany.[26] The manuscript diffusion would seem to point to southern Germany as the most likely site of John's activity.

The distribution of the chants that agree with John's examples or descriptions constitute another set of clues for locating the treatise. A number of the chants are found only, or in the most likely readings, in the Hartker Antiphonal.[27] This manuscript is not by itself transcribable, but it often is possible to decipher the notation through comparison with a version notated on staff lines. Among the uncommon chants mentioned or cited by John in the Hartker Antiphonal are (the location in the treatise is given in the index of chants): *A saeculo non est* (cf. Appendix, p. 189); *Caecus sedebat*, a respond that agrees with John's incipit; *Exivi a patre; Johannes quidam; Factus est dum tolleret; Philippe qui videt me; Quidam homo; Quid retribuam; Quod autem cecidit; Scio quod Jesum, Sepulto domino;* and *Tanto tempore*. Many of the uncommon chants and unfamiliar versions appear, therefore, to have been drawn by John from a repertory used in St. Gall. To these should be added the didactic chants of Hermannus, known only to a small circle.

24. See the list of MSS in *CSM* 1: 4–17. To this list should be added the Library of Congress copy, ML 171 J56; the Munich copy mentioned in *Huglo*, p. 300, n. 3: Univ. Library, MS 8° 375 (13th century); and Vatican Library, MS lat. 4357, listed in *RISM* 2: 95 (13th–14th century), which contains excerpts only. Lawrence Gushee recently pointed out that of the fourteen MSS of John from the twelfth through the fifteenth centuries, eleven are in German, Austrian, or Swiss libraries and raised the possibility that John was from a Germanic monastery: "Questions of Genre in Medieval Treatises on Music" in *Gattungen der Musik: Gedenkschrift Leo Schrade*, ed. Wulf Arlt, Ernst Lichtenhahn, and Hans Oesch (Bern and Munich, 1973), pp. 584–85.

25. Van Waesberghe in *Musica disciplina* 6 (1952): 146.

26. Hermann Julius Hermann, *Die deutschen romanischen Handschriften* ("Beschreibendes Verzeichnis der illuminierten Handschriften in Österreich," n. s. 2, vol. 8, pt. 2 of the entire series), p. 262, gave the following estimate on the basis of the illuminations: "Österreichische oder süddeutsche Arbeit vom Ende des XII. Jahrhunderts. Die Handschrift kam 1756 aus der alten Universitätsbibliothek in die Hofbibliothek." The presence of the treatises of Berno, anonymi concerning the measurement of organ pipes, Wilhelm of Hirsau, and fragments by Hermannus Contractus strengthen the likelihood of south German origin for this MS. H. J. Hermann accepted Johannes of Trèves as the author of the treatise, a possibility suggested by Gerbert in *GS* 2: viii. Gerbert cited Abbot Trithemius's praise in *Chronicon monasterii Hirsaugiensis* of a scholaster Johannes who took over the duties of Lambertus in 1047 at the monastery of St. Matthew in Trier (Trèves), "very learned in every kind of science, of singular erudition, particularly in music, who composed many chants and proses to the honor of almighty God and the saints, and sweetly decorated them with proper melody." Van Waesberghe rejected John of Trèves, because Trithemius estimated his death in 1065 or 1076 (*CSM* 1: 22, n.16). This John would probably merit further exploration as a candidate for the authorship of the treatise.

27. St. Gall, Stiftsbibliothek, MSS 390–91. Facs. ed. in *HA;* text only transcribed in Hesbert, *Corpus antiphonalium officii*, vol. 2 (1965).

Equally significant is John's mention (chap. 11) of the tonal letters a, e, i, o, u, H, y, and omega to designate the eight modes instead of by roman numerals or by the Greek ordinal numbers protus, deuterus, etc.[28] Huglo has shown that the mode letters were known only within the confines of the St. Gall area. This circumstance also points strongly to St. Gall as the place of origin of John's treatise.

Some of the writers whom John acknowledged by name also provide precious clues to his whereabouts. Those named are Boethius, Martianus [Capella], Odo, Guido, Berno, Hermannus [Contractus], Notker [Labeo? or Balbulus?].[29] Of these the presence of Berno, Notker, and Hermannus are suggestive of geographical limits for John's sphere of activity. The treatises of the other writers named were widely dispersed.

Berno's treatise was probably very rare in John's day outside Germany. Eleven of the thirteen eleventh-century manuscripts containing Berno's treatise and tonary surviving today are of German origin, while one copy is from north Italy and an incomplete one from Trier.[30] John, therefore, had the best chance of studying Berno's treatise and tonary in Germany, and particularly in the region between St. Gall and Bamberg.

Who might be the Notker acknowledged by John? Van Waesberghe suggested Hotger, the putative author of *Musica enchiriadis*.[31] Another possibility is Notker Labeo (950–1022), author of a brief treatise in Old High German concerning the modes, tetrachords, and the measurement of organ pipes.[32] But John does not reveal any dependence on this tract. On the other hand John's paragraph in chapter 21 concerning the Romanic letters (*litterae significativae*) that were added to the neumes in certain manuscripts may have been inspired by a letter about them that is attributed to Notker Balbulus (840–912). Ekkehard IV in *Casus Sancti Galli*, written between 1034 and 1053, maintained that the letter was written to clarify the signs in response to a query from a friend.[33] Indeed the letter opens in the St. Gall copy with a salutation from Notker to a Lamtbertus.[34] The identity of the author was probably not known outside St. Gall, for other early surviving copies are anonymous, one from the

28. A, e, i, o, u is also the order of the vowels used by both Guido (chap. 17) and John (chap. 20) for their mechanical method of composing melodies through the vowels of the texts.

29. All are cited in the dedicatory letter except for Hermannus, chap. 21.

30. *Huglo*, pp. 266–67.

31. *CSM* 1: 28; *Muziekgeschiedenis*, p. 364.

32. Ed. in *GS* 1: 96–102.

33. Quoted in Rombaut van Doren, *Étude sur l'influence musicale de l'Abbaye de Saint-Gall* (Louvain, 1925), p. 115, n. 1.

34. Facs. in *Paléographie musicale*, vol. 4 (1894), plates B and C; edited texts, pp. 10–11. Readings of other MSS in van Doren, *Étude sur l'influence*, pp. 105ff. Of the alphabetical letters listed by John in chap. 21 the following occur in Notker's epistle: c for *cito* and *clamitat*, l for *levare*, and s for *sursum*. Of the others mentioned by John, l for *leniter* and s for *similiter* appear in Einsiedeln, MS 121; see Anselm Schubiger, *Die Sängerschule St. Gallens* (Einsiedeln & New York, 1858), pp. 14–15. Another source through which the doctrine of the letters could have reached John is the Anonymous of Wolf, who paraphrased Notker, without, however, naming him: *Vierteljahrsschrift für Musikwissenschaft* 9: 204–05.

tenth century in Metz, and one from the eleventh century in Reichenau. Again the evidence points to the St. Gall area.

The treatise of Hermannus Contractus (1013–54) is the rarest of all those known to John; it must have been so also in his time. An eleventh-century codex now in Rochester is the oldest, and next to it is the twelfth-century copy of Vienna, Nationalbibliothek, MS Cpv. 51; these are the only extant early manuscripts that contain Hermann's treatise. Ellinwood has shown that the Rochester codex was probably written by Frutolf of Michelsberg (d. 1103) in the latter part of the eleventh century at the Michelsberg monastery in Bamberg.[35] Hermann, it should be recalled, was probably educated and spent most of his career in the monastery at Reichenau.[36]

To the treatises that John named must be added one he gave evidence of knowing. This is Aribo's *De musica*, which is dedicated to Bishop Ellenhard of Freising[37] (d. 1078) and was probably written in that Bavarian city between 1068 and 1078.[38] John borrowed the modal circles of chapter 12 from Aribo.[39]

On the basis of the distribution of treatises he knew, John can be located in the south German area between St. Gall and Bamberg. Indeed one may well counter van Waesberghe's Liège School with a South German School, for the treatises originating around St. Gall—Notker's letter in St. Gall itself, the works of Berno and Hermann in nearby Reichenau, and Aribo's in Freising—are closely linked with John's.

The promptness with which subsequent authors utilized an earlier author's doctrines is some indication of the route of dissemination. For John's treatise the picture is not at all clear. Among the early commentaries on John is an anonymous treatise of the twelfth century in London, British Museum, Egerton 2888, which appears to have some relation with the church of St. Maartensdijk in the island of Tholen in Zeeland.[40] Another is the anonymous of Coussemaker's second volume from St. Jacob's, Liège, formerly in Louvain Catholic University Library, which burned in August 1914.[41] Extensive quotations and paraphrases from John are in the Pseudo-Guido treatise known as *Tractatus correctorius* of the thirteenth century published by Gerbert from a manuscript in Munich.[42] A twelfth-century commentary on John in the Vatican Library,[43]

35. Leonard Ellinwood, ed., *Musica Hermanni Contracti* (Rochester, 1952), p. 2.

36. Hans Oesch, *Berno und Hermann von Reichenau als Musiktheoretiker* (Bern, 1961), p. 132.

37. *CSM* 2: 1.

38. Heinrich Hüschen, "Aribo," *Die Musik in Geschichte und Gegenwart*, vol. 1 (1949–51), cols. 610–12; Karl G. Fellerer, *Beiträge zur Musikgeschichte Freisings* (Freising, 1926), pp. 26ff. Van Waesberghe annexed him to the Liège group in *Musica disciplina* 3 (1949): 95–97.

39. *CSM* 2: 17–20, units 59–63.

40. The treatise is ed. in Marius Schneider, *Geschichte der Mehrstimmigkeit* (Berlin, 1936), 2: 106–18. See Van Waesberghe, *Muziekgeschiedenis* 1: 377.

41. Ibid., p. 377. *CS* 2: 484–98.

42. *GS* 2: 50–55. The MS is Clm. 18751, originating in Tegernsee around 1435–36.

43. Biblioteca apostolica vaticana, MS Pal. lat. 1346, fols. 7r–16v.

Pal. lat. 1346, fols. 7r–16v, shows by its verses concerning the tonary letters and its German neumes that it is from the St. Gall-Reichenau area.[44] More detailed studies of these sources may indicate a more consistent direction, but for the present we can detect a rather rapid diffusion through Germany, the Netherlands, and the Liège region for the earliest circle of commentators.

By the mid-thirteenth century John's treatise seems to have earned widespread renown, for, as we saw, it was liberally cited by Jerome of Moravia, who wrote in Paris.[45]

The date of 1100 for the drafting of John's treatise is very approximate. If the dedicatee was truly the Abbot Fulgentius of Affligheim who governed that abbey from 1089 to 1120, then the date of around 1100 has strong probability. However, if this hypothesis is discarded, the indicators are less precise. Aribo's treatise, completed before 1078, when its dedicatee Ellenhard died, gives us the early boundary date.

The earliest manuscripts containing the treatise are from the twelfth century. Among the oldest, Leipzig 79 belonged to the Cistercian Abbey at Pforta, founded in 1128; therefore it was probably not copied before that time. However it was copied before 1170, when it was donated to the cloister at Altzelle.[46] These chronological reference points are obviously too late to be of much value for establishing a date for John's *libellum*.

Unfortunately, the earliest treatises in which John is quoted, from the twelfth century, are anonymous and of uncertain date, and therefore of no help in fixing the time of John's writing.

The doctrine in John's treatise is not inconsistent with the date 1100. The organum described in chapter 23 resembles that of the manuscript Chartres 109 from the late eleventh century. The organal theory, characterized by improvised singing of the organal part, voice crossing, cadence at the unison or octave at the end of each word, preference for contrary motion, and the option of more than one note in the organal part against a note of the chant, places it between the doctrine of Guido and that of the Vatican, Milan, and Montpellier organum treatises,[47] all from France and of around 1100.

The closest that we can locate John in place and time, then, is that he probably wrote the treatise in the area between St. Gall and Bamberg around 1100.

The person who emerges from this treatise is first of all a teacher. He directs his efforts at the boys of a choir school—"we are addressing boys and those not yet mature"—and he is anxious lest he "tax the young and less learned" with mathematical complications (chap. 8).

44. See van Waesberghe, *Muziekgeschiedenis*, 1: 360, 380–81.

45. For reference to other works citing John, see van Waesberghe in *Musica disciplina* 3 (1949): 111–13.

46. Van Waesberghe, *Muziekgeschiedenis*, 1: 344, n. 18.

47. See Frieder Zaminer, *Der Vatikanische Organum-Traktat* (Tutzing, 1959), pp. 104–10; Hans H. Eggebrecht and Zaminer, *Ad organum faciendum: Lehrschriften der Mehrstimmigkeit in nachguidonischer Zeit* (Mainz, 1970).

The author is a practical man. Although he pays lip service to the principle that skill should be backed up by knowledge, he is more concerned that his choir learn to sing the repertory properly than that it assimilate the corpus of inherited theoretical thought. The author he is most fond of paraphrasing and quoting is Guido, who similarly disdained pure theory. But John displays more learning than Guido; he has obviously read widely in both classical and medieval literature. He cites, perhaps not always directly, Plato, Vergil, and Horace among the ancients, Donatus, Prudentius, Amalarius, Priscian, Isidore, Capella, and, of course, Boethius among the late Latin writers. He shows by his acceptance of fanciful and impossible etymologies of Greek-derived terms, such as *tonus*, *diaphonia*, and *lichanos*, that he was ignorant of Greek.

He is confident of his practical knowledge of the chant, for he ventures opinions about the incorrectness of certain contemporary and traditional versions. His views were obviously not shared by many, for the "incorrect" versions survive in greater number than his emended ones. He is quite conservative in admitting transpositions by means of B♭; he would rather have a chant end on the cofinal than to see accidentals introduced. On the other hand, he is an ardent advocate of fairly recent improvements of notation that permit definitive scribal recording of the repertory. He is also a zealous defender of the right of his contemporaries to compose new chants. Thus John fits the profile of the *musicus* that he drew, "a judge of music already created, an emender of faulty music, and an inventor of new" (chap. 2).

If John seems forward-looking in his defense of staff notation and of new chant composition, the most modern manifestation, polyphony, interests him but little. Probably because Guido included a chapter "concerning organum or diaphony," he feels bound to do the same, giving it a parallel title. The chapter (23) seems like an afterthought, for it interrupts the natural flow of the discourse from the subject of the *differentiae* in chapter 22 to the introduction to the tonary at the end of chapter 23. This chapter, indeed, contains the longest paraphrase of Guido of the entire book—a synopsis of Guido's theory of melodic motion. Its placement here rather than in chapters 18 or 19 on melodic composition underscores John's insistence on contrary motion in the organal voice, for making organum or diaphony is now an act of creating a new line, not merely paralleling a previously composed chant.

John, unlike Hucbald or Hermann, is no spinner of theoretical systems. This is just as well, for when he tries to be systematic, he blunders. The most glaring example of this is his division of the gamut into tetrachords in chapter 5. Although he eschews the term tetrachord in this chapter, he divides the gamut into four-note sets, and gives to each set a name borrowed from either Guido or Hermann:

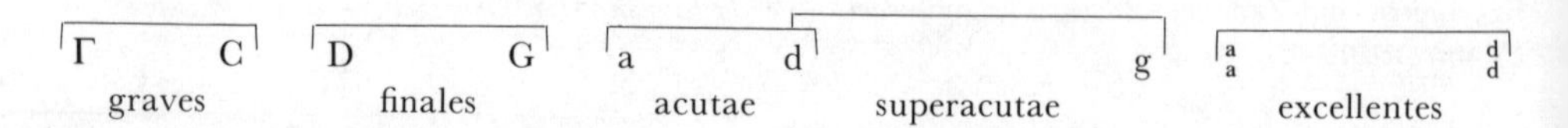

Having extended the scale down to gamma, one note lower than Hermann, John constructs a tetrachord gamma-C (tone-tone-semitone) to replace Hermann's A–D, thereby spoiling the consistency of the modular species, tone-semitone-tone, that was behind Hermann's system and that holds for John's upper tetrachords. What he needed was an added tone, a "proslambanomenos," gamma, to counterbalance Hermann's $\overset{a}{a}$, which for John is the beginning of a new disjunct tetrachord. (The chart in Fig. 1 compares the tetrachordal systems of the Greeks and earlier Latin authors and traces the conversion of the Greek to Latin names.)

It may be that his misunderstanding of the Greek tetrachords led to his unsystematic gamut, for in chapter 13 he finesses the etymology of proslambanomenos to signify "adopted for musical use from grammar," preferring this to the meaning "added," and makes it the first note of the lowest tetrachord A–D, thus disturbing the symmetry of a system which was based on the rising semitone-tone-tone pattern. Much of the chapter is spent rationalizing his misrepresentation of the Greek system:

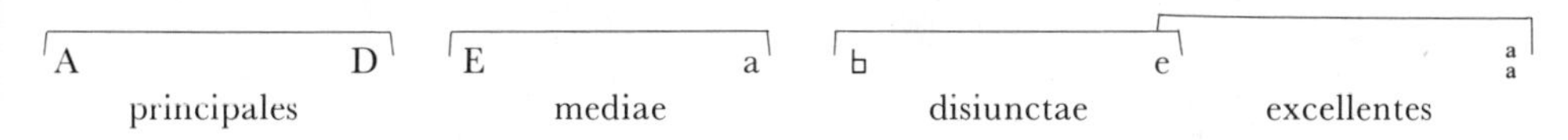

In all fairness it must be said that John lived at a time when there was a confusion of theoretical systems. The great virtue of this treatise is precisely its untheoretical nature, its undogmatic fidelity to the realities of musical practice. For example, when John comes to enumerating the species of fourths and fifths in chapter 8, although he patterns his triangular figures on Hermann,[48] he pragmatically begins numbering each species with an interval rising from C, which is ut in the "Guidonian" hand, rather than with D, the lowest note of the *finales* tetrachord. The everyday habits of the "Guidonian" hand and solmization prevail over considerations of theoretical consistency.

With no ax to grind, John gains credibility on a subject such as the modes, on which he is more illuminating than any other medieval writer. Modality is not determined solely by the last note of a chant, although judgment about the mode is deferred to the end (chap. 16). How often and how far it reaches below the final and how high and consistently it inhabits the notes in the fifth above the final and the fourth above that figure importantly in his criteria for classification. Further, there are two pitches besides the final to which John ascribes modal significance (chap. 11), the *tenor* or the tone on which the first syllable of the *saeculorum amen* falls, and the "Gloria,"[49] or the first tone of the intonation of the Lesser Doxology, "Gloria patri et filio et spiritu sancto, sicut erat in principio, et nunc et semper et in saecula [on the next syllable is reached

48. *GS* 2: 140b; Ellinwood ed., p. 48.

49. The note he calls "Gloria" agrees, except in mode 4, with the initial note of the psalm-tone intonation in the standard usage; see *LU*, pp. 112–17.

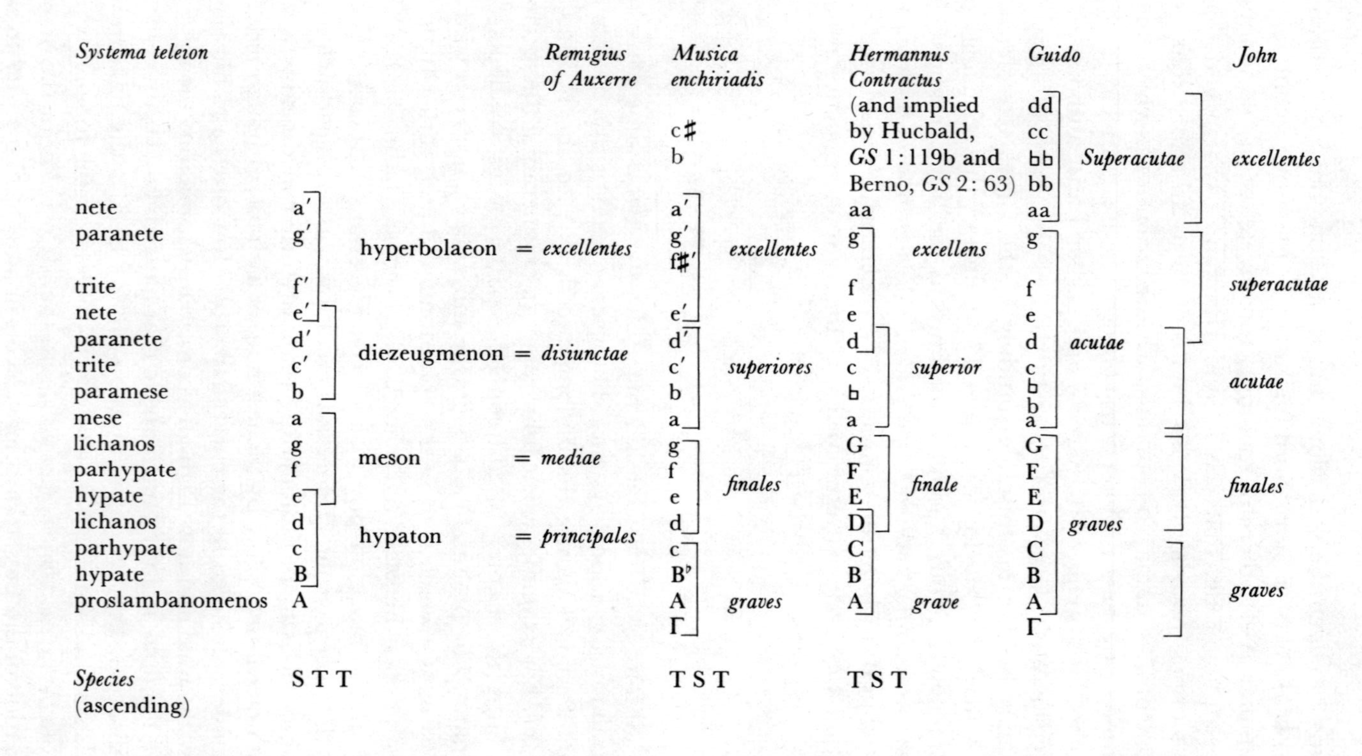

Systema teleion
Remigius of Auxerre
Musica enchiriadis
Hermannus Contractus (and implied by Hucbald, GS 1:119b and Berno, GS 2: 63)
Guido
John
nete a′
paranete g′
trite f′
nete e′
paranete d′
trite c′
paramese b
mese a
lichanos g
parhypate f
hypate e
lichanos d
parhypate c
hypate B
proslambanomenos A
hyperbolaeon = excellentes
diezeugmenon = disiunctae
meson = mediae
hypaton = principales
c♯
b
a′
g′
f♯′
e′
d′
c′
b
a
g
f
e
d
c
B♭
A
Γ
excellentes
superiores
finales
graves
aa
g
f
e
d
c
♮
a
G
F
E
D
C
B
A
excellens
superior
finale
grave
dd
cc
♮♮
bb
aa
g
f
e
d
c
♮
b
a
G
F
E
D
C
B
A
Γ
Superacutae
acutae
graves
excellentes
superacutae
acutae
finales
graves
Species (ascending)
S T T
T S T
T S T

Figure 1

the pitch of the *tenor*] saeculorum. Amen." He also dwells several times on the need for a melody to return to the final at a *distinctio* or pause that marks the end of a melodic phrase (chaps. 10, 19). There are certain notes, such as the third, fourth, or fifth above, or the tone below the final in authentic modes, as well as the final itself, which are appropriate for the beginning of chants or main sections of them (chap. 12). The modes were living categories to John, not just convenient pigeonholes for classifying chant: "The modes have individual qualities of sound, differing from each other, so that they prompt spontaneous recognition . . . ." (chap. 16). He even ascribed ethical and emotional values to them.

John ventured even more deeply than Guido into the realm of esthetics. Song has the power to move people to action, to soothe and uplift. Like the poet or comedian, the composer should suit his manner to the subject and audience. A melody must express the meaning of its text. John's many applications of grammatical precepts, as in his system of analyzing the phraesology of chant (chap. 10) and his advice to revert to the final when the sense of the words demands a pause (chap. 19), are further evidence of his sensitivity to the needs of communication. Similarly, composers should avoid the cloying repetition grammarians call *homoiophthongon*; on the other hand, musical repetition can be turned to advantage, as to round out a chant (chap. 18).

John was the first to come to terms with the transition from an ambiguous notation of relative pitch height to a notation that, if it did not assume absolute pitch, dwelt in a gamut that prescribed the precise placement of tones and semitones. Staff notation forced scribes to make decisions as to the intonation of a melody made earlier by the leader of a choir. Melodies sung by custom at whatever pitch was comfortable for the voice now had to be fitted into a scale that provided semitones in only certain configurations, requiring a B♭ and even E♭ to locate some melodies in a comfortable range. Was it better to emend the melody, insert a flat, or transpose it to end on the kindred final? This kindred final (*affinis*), now called cofinal, is an alternative for at least some of the modes—a, b, c, for the finals D, E, F—but G had no *affinis*. John preferred the solution of the kindred final where it was available, but he was conscious that many scribes and singers did not. Another question reopened by the choices that now had to be made was whether certain chants belonged to the authentic or plagal forms of a mode. John's discussion from these points of view of a large number of specific chants, many of which can still be identified, plunges us into the privy shoptalk of seasoned choirleaders.

Thanks to its informal character, John's treatise thus affords passing glimpses into the workaday habits of eleventh-century musicians. John tells us, for example, that the English, French, and Germans used the syllables ut, re, mi, etc., while the Italians preferred others (chap. 1). The remark, lifted by the author of the *Summa musicae*[50] and by Jacques de Liège,[51] has occasioned much comment. Riemann reacted with disbelief to the possibility that the Italians used syllables other than the ut-series,[52] but five of the oldest manuscripts of Guido's *Epistola* to the monk Michael set a second hymn text to the melody of *Ut queant laxis*, giving the syllables Tri, Pro, De, Nos, Te, Ad: *Tri*num et unum *Pro* nobis miseris *De*um precemur, *Nos* puris mentibus *Te* obsecramus *Ad* preces intende Domine nostras.[53] In another revealing hint, John advises his pupils to use the joints of the hand rather than the monochord to find the notes of a melody (chap. 1), an early testimony to the applications of the so-called Guidonian hand, not mentioned in any of Guido's writings, for finding the intervals in singing and composing. Such precious sidelights abound in John's *libellum*.

If John's theoretical lapses and his unschooled etymologies may have earned the epithet "ineptus liber" that Heinrich Glarean wrote in the margin of his copy,[54] it remains the most readable and comprehensible of the medieval introductions to the chant repertory. It deserves a critical reading by anyone interested in the music of its time or the history of theory.

50. *GS* 3: 203.

51. *CS* 2: 281; also in *CSM* 3, ed. Roger Bragard, vol. 6 (American Institute of Musicology, 1973), Bk. 6, cap. 62, p. 165.

52. Hugo Riemann, *History of Music Theory: Books I and II*, trans. Raymond H. Haggh (Lincoln, Neb., 1962), p. 201.

53. See my article "Guido" in *The New Grove's Dictionary of Music and Musicians* (forthcoming); van Waesberghe, *De musico-paedagogico et theoretico Guidone Aretino* (Florence, 1953), p. 101; and Hans Oesch, *Guido von Arezzo* (Bern, 1954), pp. 67–69.

54. Quoted in *Huglo*, p. 300, n. 3, from Munich, University Library MS 8° 375.

JOHN, ON MUSIC (*DE MUSICA*)

Translated by Warren Babb
Edited by Claude V. Palisca

Letter of John to Fulgentius

[44] To his venerable lord and father, Fulgentius, abbot of angels[1], a man who has his name from actual fact, since he is weighty in judgment and refulgent with holiness, John, the servant of the servants of God, wishes whatever a son wishes for his father and a servant for his master.

When you saw that I was exploring many and diverse studies, yet devoting particular pains to one art, namely music, you began to call me to account about that art, urging that I endeavor to give forth some tiny spark from my small talent for the instruction and enlightenment of those less learned. When I shrank from this with doubts and misgivings, since I considered myself by no means fit to accomplish it, you battered at my ears with repeated exhortations and, teacher of truth and lover of charity that you are, you kept dropping into my ear that little verse: "Concealed wisdom and hidden treasure—what use is either?" When I replied to this that my mind was dull and feeble, you cut me off with this rejoinder: "What are you saying, my son; what, indeed, are you talking about? Did I not learn, if I remember rightly, that you have read the musical treatises of Boethius[2] and Guido[3] and also Berno?[4] [45] Have I not learned through many, many tests just

1. All the MSS read "anglorum" or "of the English" except one, which van Waesberghe reads as "angelorum" or "of the angels"; his reading has been challenged but not, in the opinion of the translator, refuted. See the Introduction to this treatise.

2. Anicius Manlius Torquatus Severinus Boethius, *De institutione musica libri quinque*, ed. Gottfred Friedlein (Leipzig, 1867). An English translation of this treatise will appear as vol. 4 of the present series.

3. John would have known all of the extant works of Guido, namely the *Micrologus*, the prologue to the Antiphonary, and the *Epistola de ignoto cantu* to the monk Michael. Some of the surviving namuscripts containing these works dating from John's period were available in his area, namely Karlsruhe 504 of around 1100 from St. Michelsberg near Bamberg (see *CSM* 4: 25), Munich, MS lat. 14523, probably from Regensburg of the 10th century (ibid., p. 37), and Munich, Bayerische Staatsbibliothek, MS Clm 14965a, from St. Emmeran's Abbey in Regensburg of the eleventh century (see *CSM* 2: vi–vii).

4. Berno of Reichenau (d. 1048) is credited with several musical treatises. See Hans Oesch, *Berno und Hermann von Reichenau als Musiktheoretiker* (Bern, 1961), pp. 43ff. St. Gall, Stiftsbibliothek, MS 898, from the eleventh century, contains his *De consona tonorum diversitate*, ed. *GS* 2: 114–17 a prologue to a tonary (*GS* 2: 62–79), which is probably the work John was alluding to, and a tonary (*GS* 2: 79–91), concerning which see *Huglo*, pp. 264–78.

what is the scope of your ability, so that no one knows better or more indubitably than I what your shoulders can bear and what not? Assuredly, you defend yourself against me by no good or admissible reasoning, and if you were willing to consider all this more rightly, you would have no ground for refusing to follow me and my counsels. For, not to speak of Martianus,[5] Odo,[6] or Notker[7]—whose books, as being by the soundest men in this field, you said you had carefully perused—you could, if only you wished, cull sufficiently fit and useful rules for your readers from the opuscules of the men first mentioned. Moreover, I advise that you give up forthwith your one excuse, since, as St. Gregory says, "Love reinforces those powers which inexperience disclaims."

Overcome by these words, and, to be more outspoken, overborne by so mighty a command, I at once set boldly about the undertaking you had enjoined upon me. I preferred to undergo the scorn of the more circumspect and acute, rather than to incur your displeasure if I declined to comply.

I admit that I have used an elementary style. Moreover, whatever [46] seemed more useful or needful I gathered compendiously from the essays of others, adding light now and then from my own small flame. I decided also to divide my little book into various chapters, so that if the reader were seeking more eagerly for one thing than another, he would be able to find it more quickly and easily by the chapter headings.

I commend to your kindness this work which I began at your urging and have finished with God's aid, so that it may be tested by you and corrected by you and by your prestige be protected from the poisonous fangs of the scornful.

[*End of the preface. Beginning of the chapters*]

[47] [*Index of the chapters*]

5. Martianus Capella (4th–5th century), author of *De nuptiis Philologiae et Mercurii*, ed. Adolf Dick (Leipzig, 1925).

6. The Odo named here and in chap. 12 (see n. 3) as recommended by Guido is not the author of the *Dialogus* (*GS* 2: 252–64), according to Huglo, "L'auteur du 'Dialogue sur la musique' attribué à Odon," *Revue de musicologie* 55 (1969): 131ff. Huglo believes that when Guido recommended that the student "read also the book Enchiridion, that the Most Reverend Abbot Oddo most distinctly composed, whose example I departed from only in the figures of the sounds (librum quoque Enchiridion, quem Reverentissimus Oddo Abbas luculentissime composuit, perlegat, cuius exemplum in solis figuris sonorum dimisi)" (GS 2: 50b), Guido meant the *Musica enchiriadis*, which in some MSS is attributed to an Abbot Odo. It is possible, but unlikely, that John here referred to the Italian Abbot Odo, whose Prologue (*GS* 1: 248–49) and Tonary are transmitted in about twenty manuscripts (see *Huglo*, pp. 182ff.).

7. This is probably Notker Balbulus; see Introduction, p. 93 and n. 33 and n. 34.

Here end the chapter headings.

[49] Here begins John's treatise on the art of music.

Chapter 1

How one should prepare oneself for the study of music

First we enjoin him who wishes to prepare himself for training in music that he zealously master the letters of the monochord and the syllables written above them and not leave off this task before he has them by memory. But we shall postpone speaking of the letters just now, so as to deal with them more conveniently and fully later on. Now, however, let us say something about the syllables.

There are six syllables that we adopt for use in music. They are different, however, among different people. The English, French, and Germans use these: ut, re, mi, fa, sol, and la. But the Italians have others, and those who wish to learn them may arrange to do so with these people.[1]

It is said that the syllables we use are taken from the hymn that begins: *Ut queant laxis / Resonare fibris / Mira gestorum /*. [50] This may easily be seen thus: *Ut queant laxis*, here we have *ut; resonare fibris*, here is *re; mira gestorum*, there is *mi; famuli tuorum*, there is *fa; solve polluti*, this is *sol; labii reatum*,[2] here we have *la*.

So let him who strives for knowledge of music learn to sing a few songs with these syllables until he knows fully and clearly their ascents and descents and their many varieties of intervals. Also, let him diligently accustom himself to measuring off his melody on the joints of his hand,[3] so that presently he can use his hand instead of the monochord whenever he likes, and by it test, correct, or compose a song. After he has repeated these things for some time, just as we have directed, and has thoroughly memorized them, he will have an easier, unperplexed road to music.

Chapter 2

Of what use it is to understand music, and what the difference is between a musician and a singer

[51] It now seems fitting that we touch briefly on what practical benefit the knowledge of music brings. The more useful someone discovers music to be, the more he will devote himself to that art.

Music is one of the seven arts called liberal—and a natural one, as are the others. Thus we sometimes see jongleurs and actors who are absolutely illiterate compose pleasant-sounding songs. But just as grammar, dialectic, and the other arts would be considered vague and chaotic if they were not committed to writing and made clear by precepts, so it is with music.

One should know that this art is to be deemed by no means the lowest of the arts, especially since it is most necessary to clerics and is useful and delightful to anyone practicing it. [52] For whoever devotes unremitting labor to it, and perseveres without pausing or wearying, can gain from it this reward, that he will know how to judge the quality of song—whether it is refined or commonplace, true or false—and how to correct the faulty and compose the new. The knowledge of music, then, is no small ground for praise, is of no slight use, and is no mean achievement, since it makes him

1. In five of the oldest manuscripts of Guido's *Epistola*, dating from the eleventh and twelfth centuries, the set of syllables *Tri-Pro-De-Nos-Te-Ad*, sometimes with the *Ut queant laxis* melody, sometimes with a different one, are given as an alternate solmization system. See van Waesberghe, *De musico-paedagogico et theoretico Guidone Aretino*, p. 101 and above, pp. 99f.

2. Beginning of eighth-century hymn in Sapphic meter to St. John the Baptist, the text of which is almost certainly by Paulus Diaconus.

3. I.e. according to the so-called "Guidonian" hand.

who knows it a judge of music already created, an emender of faulty music, and an inventor of new.

Nor, it seems, should we omit that the musician and the singer differ not a little from one another. Whereas the musician always proceeds correctly and by calculation, the singer holds the right road intermittently, merely through habit. To whom then should I better compare the singer than to a drunken man who does indeed get home but does not in the least know by what path he returns. Yet even a millwheel sometimes gives forth a distinct pitch in its creaking, though itself unaware of what it is doing, since it is an inanimate thing. As Guido well says in his *Micrologus:*[1]

> From the musician to the singer how immense the distance is; [53]
> The latter's voice, the former's mind will show what music's nature is;
> But he who does, he knows not what, a beast by definition is. Et cetera.

Chapter 3

How it comes to be called music, and by whom and how it was discovered

[54] It is called music, as some would have it, from *musa* [bagpipe], which is a certain musical instrument proper and pleasant enough in sound. But let us consider by what reasoning and what authority music derives its name from *musa*. *Musa*, as we said, is a certain instrument far surpassing all other musical instruments, inasmuch as it contains in itself the powers and methods of them all. For it is blown into by human breath like a pipe, it is regulated by the hand like the fiddle, and it is animated by a bellows like organs. Hence *musa* derives from the Greek *μέση—mese*, that is, "central," for just as divers paths converge at some central point, so too do manifold instruments meet together in the *musa*. Therefore, the name "music" was not unfittingly taken from its main exponent.

[55] But some say that music got its name from *Musae* [the Muses], because among the ancients they were considered perfect in this art, and skill in making music was sought from them; and so the Muses were thought to be named *ἀπὸ τοῦ μῶσθαι*,[1] that is, "from seeking." Others suppose that music is so called as a modification of *modusica* [i.e. *modus*-like], from *modulatio*,[2]

1. Lines 1–3 of Guido's *Regulae rhythmicae* (*GS* 2: 25); not in the *Micrologus*.

1. *απο ϑυ μυσω* of John's text is a corruption, doubtless via Isidore's *Etymologies* 3. 15. 1, and Cassiodorus, *Institutiones* (*GS* 1: 15), of Plato's *ἀπὸ τοῦ μῶσϑαι* (*Cratylus*, 406A). Plato did not mean very seriously such derivations as this of "music" and "Muses" from the Muses' "search" for wisdom.

2. *Modulatio:* in classical Latin, "a regular or rhythmical measure, hence singing and playing melody"; in St. Augustine, *De musica*, 1. 2. 3, "skill in movement" (*peritia movendi*), apparently (ibid.) from a philologically incorrect relation of *mŏdus* (a measure) with *mōtus* (motion); in 1. 2. 2 Augustine says that *modulari* and *modulatio* are used only in relation to singing and dancing and equates these two with music—though he also suggests that all things well done or well made are so through music in a broader sense.

others as if it were a modification of *moysica*, from water,[3] which is called *moys*. Others think it is named "music" as a modification of *mundica*, from the singing of the *mundus*, that is, of the heavens. If anyone has better knowledge concerning the appellation of music, we by no means begrudge him it, since, as Paul says, the Holy Ghost apportions to individuals as he wishes.[4]

Moses relates that Tubal[5] was the inventor of this art. Others believe that Linus [56] the Theban discovered it, others Amphion, others Orpheus. But the Greeks, to whom, as Horace says,[6] the Muse made the gift of polished speech, would have us think otherwise on this matter.

They maintain that a certain Samian philosopher, Pythagoras by name, was the inventor of this art. He was, as they say, a man most renowned for wisdom, most invincible in eloquence, and by nature most intelligent. He is reported to have found the basis of music by a very subtle line of research. As he was walking along one day he passed a workshop and heard therein, as was usual, diverse sounds from the hammers. After he had listened there rather carefully for some time and was more and more entranced by the various sounds, he realized, since he had great understanding, that here lay hidden the basis of the science of music. Without delay he entered the workshop and began to weigh the hammers quite carefully, and bit by bit tracked down expertly the seven different notes as well as the intervals they make, with which we shall deal more fully further on. Thus, that eminent man was the first in Greece to investigate, write about, and teach music, theretofore formless and uncomprehended. His knowledge was presently communicated to the Latins by Boethius and by others who understood Greek.

Chapter 4

How many means there are for making musical sound

[57] One should also know that there are two kinds of means for making all sounds, namely, natural and artificial. "Natural" is either of the universe or of men. Now "universal," according to the philosophers, is the blend of diverse sounds from the spinning of the heavenly spheres, which is harmony in the strict sense. The natural human means I call those hollow places in the throat which we call the windpipes. For they are naturally suited to take in or give forth air, so that a natural sound is created. For this reason some also are accustomed to liken them to commerce, as did Prudentius in the *Psychomachia:* ". . . the broken commerce of the blocked throat constricts her wicked

3. *Moysica:* Exod. 2:10. See Noel Swerdlow, "Musica dicitur a moys, quod est aqua," *Journal of the American Musicological Society* 20 (1967): 3–9.

4. 1 Cor. 12:11.

5. Tubal: properly Jubal (Gen. 4:21–22).

6. Horace, *Ars poetica*, 323–24.

breath."[1] On the other hand, the artificial means is whatever is fitted for producing sound, not by nature, but by handicraft.

Furthermore, some natural sound is discrete, some indiscrete. That is discrete which has musical intervals [*consonantiae*] within it; that is indiscrete in which no musical interval can be distinguished, [58] as in human laughter or groaning, and in the barking of dogs or the roaring of lions. You can similarly consider artificial sound as discrete or indiscrete. That reed pipe by which small birds are deceived, or a jar with parchment drawn over its top, with which boys so often play, give an indiscrete sound. On the sambuca,[2] on stringed instruments, on carillons, and on organs a variety of musical intervals is well and clearly distinguished.

Therefore music in no way admits of that sound which we have said to be indiscrete. Only discrete sound, which is technically called *phthongus* [tone] pertains to music. For music is nothing other than the fit progression of tones. We assert this especially against the ignorant men who stupidly deem that any sound whatever is music, that we may check their error.

This too should be added, that although there are three genera of melodic music—the enharmonic, the diatonic, and the chromatic—the first has been rejected as too difficult and the third as too soft, while the second one has remained in use.

Chapter 5

On the number of musical letters and on distinguishing them

[59] Having thus touched lightly on these preliminaries, let us now begin to discuss the notes of the monochord, and first let us speak about their number. The oldest authorities placed not more than fifteen letters on the monochord, beginning, that is, with A[1] and ending with $\overset{a}{a}$. For Γ was not yet added, nor was the b which we call *molle* [soft] or *rotundum* [round], but which by some is called by the Greek name *synemmenon*, that is, "connected."

Contemplating all things more precisely and wisely—and since, as Priscian says,[2] the younger men are, the keener are they sighted—the moderns saw that those notes did not suffice for representing all melodies and, for want of letters, were sometimes defective [in representing] chant in the plagal protus. Therefore they put Γ in the first place. [60] Whoever wishes can see this easily in the following antiphon [Ex. 1].

1. *Psychomachia*, lines 33–34 after the introduction.

2. *Sambuca:* either a triangular, four-stringed instrument of high, shrill tone, Greek σαμβύκη, from Syrian *sabkâ;* or a pipe of elder wood (Latin *sambucus*, elder).

1. The medieval system of letter-notation will be used in this translation, i.e.: Γ (the second G below middle C), A, B (natural), C, D, E, F, G, a, b (i.e. b-flat), ♮ (i.e. b-natural), (middle) c, d, e, f, g, $\overset{a}{a}$, $\overset{b}{b}$, $\overset{♮}{♮}$, $\overset{c}{c}$, $\overset{d}{d}$, $\overset{e}{e}$.

2. Priscian, *Institutiones grammaticae*, proem.

Example 1

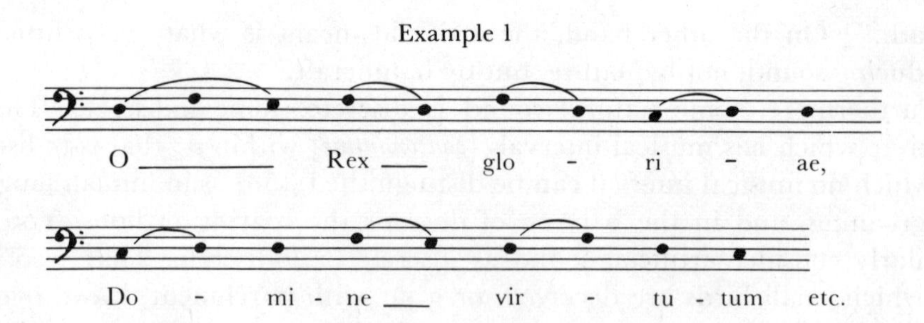

For *Spiritum veritatis*,[3] which should begin with capital A and go down, would have nowhere to descend to if Γ were not appended. They also added b *rotundum*, since they saw it was now and then necessary in plainchant, and they bestowed on it the following name, so that it was also called b *molle* because of its softness and sweetness of sound. With these two added, the letters are seventeen in number. But Guido, the Master, whom we consider the greatest in our field since Boethius, set up twenty-one notes in his musical system, so that no deficiency might ever find its way into plainchant.

[61] Let us now look at the difference between them. First let the reader observe carefully that all the letters on the monochord are different in appearance. For instance, Γ differs in appearance from capital G, likewise capital A from small a, likewise B from ♮, C from c, D from d, E from e, F from f, G from g, also small a from doubled $\overset{a}{a}$, similarly b from $\overset{b}{b}$, ♮ from $\overset{\natural}{\natural}$, c from $\overset{c}{c}$, and d from $\overset{d}{d}$. They are also varied by means of the spaces and lines. Whereas Γ is placed on a line, G will be on a space. Likewise, whereas capital A is on a space, small a will be on a line, and thus it is with the others.

Moreover it should be noted of b *molle* and ♮ *quadratum* that they differ both in appearance and in the syllables written above them. True, they occupy the same place, whether on a space or on a line, but they are told apart in this way, that in whatever neume b-flat sounds, the symbol b is to be placed above by the scribe.

All the letters of the monochord have yet another difference by which they are told apart, namely this: that from Γ to C they are called *graves* [low] on account of the lowness of their sound; [62] from D to G they are called *finales* because a chant in any of the modes is ended on one of them; from small a to d they are called *acutae* [sharp, high] because of the high sound they give; and from d to g they are called *superacutae* because in height of tone they exceed the *acutae*. Likewise from $\overset{a}{a}$ to $\overset{d}{d}$ they are named *excellentes* because in thinness of sound they excel even the *superacutae*.

In addition to this they are given by some men yet other identification by

3. *O Rex gloriae* does not require gamma in the versions transmitted by the MSS of John's treatise. Its continuation, *Spiritum veritatis*, does illustrate John's point. Transcribed from *AM* 512.

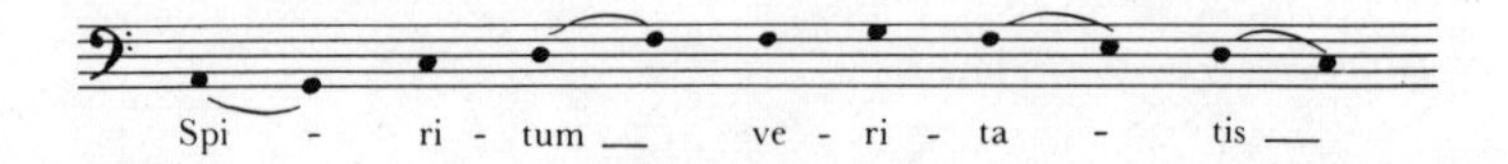

means of Greek words, which we omit for the present, as they do not seem to give much help to the less learned. All these distinctions of letters are made so that we can more easily distinguish which note is which, since each has different characteristics. Now enough has been said about the number and difference of the letters. Next let us look at the measurement of the monochord.

Chapter 6

How the monochord should be measured off

[63] There are many different ways of measuring off the monochord. To expound all of them would bore rather than benefit the reader. So, aiming at compendiousness, we have arranged to include, out of the many, that one which seemed easier and quicker, with our rules.

First, placing Γ wherever you wish on the left side of the monochord, measure off nine equal parts from here to the [right] end. After measuring these equally, note carefully that the first part will end on A, the second will be blank, the third end on D, the fourth will be blank, the fifth end on a, the sixth on d, the seventh on aa, and the rest will be blank.

Likewise, with nine parts divided equally from A to the [right] end, the first part will end on B, the second will be blank, the third end on E, the fourth will be blank, the fifth end on ♮ *quadratum*, the sixth on e, the seventh on ♮♮ *duplicatum*, and the others will be blank.

Moreover, when you have divided four parts equally from Γ to the right end, the first part will end on C, the second on G, the third on g, and the fourth at the end [64] of the string. Similarly, when you have measured four parts equally from C to the [right] end, the first will end on F, the second on c, the third on cc, and the fourth ends the string. But from F to the [right] end, the first of four parts will end on b *molle*, the second on f, and the rest will be blank. And when four parts are made from d to the [right] end, the first will end on g, which has already been located, the second on dd, and the rest will be blank. Also when four parts are apportioned from f to the [right] end, the first will end on bb *rotundum duplicatum*, the rest will be blank.

By this same division, namely, that made by four parts, he who is willing to be careful can quite accurately measure off the whole monochord. Four equal parts are made from any note to the [right] end of the monochord, of which three comprise a diatessaron, then a diapente, and then a diapason, whereas the last is at the end. For example, when four parts are measured off from Γ to the [right] end, the first will end on C, which is a diatessaron away, the second on G, which is a diapente farther, the third on g, which is a diapason farther, and the fourth is at the end. In the same way too you can find the rest.[1]

1. This inadequate account of a second way of mensuration can be made good from the early-12th-century *Quaestiones in musica* (Rudolf Steglich [Leipzig, 1911], p. 90) thus: Divide the length of string sounding Γ into quarters to get C, G, and g; likewise that of C to get F, c, and cc; likewise of F to get b and f. Divide G's length into thirds to get d and dd; go *out* a fourth such third from G to get D. Divide D's

Chapter 7

How the monochord came to be named and for what it is useful

[65] After learning the measurement of the monochord, one should consider how the monochord came to be named and what use it serves. It gets the name of monochord from "one string," which is all it has. For *monos* in Greek means "one" or "only," and thus a monk is so called, because he ought to be alone and single. Thus the monochord is named from the one string, just as *decachordum* from "ten strings" and *octochordum* from "eight strings." Moreover, this instrument is very useful, as on it one may verify chanting when one is uncertain whether it is correct or incorrect. It should also be used by boys or youths who aspire to musicianship, so that with the sound itself as guide, they can more easily make contact with that which they wish to learn. Add thereto that it is most efficacious against the recalcitrance of certain silly fellows. For there are indeed a great many clerics and monks who neither understand this discipline nor wish to understand it, and, what is worse, who avoid and abhor those that do.

[66] If, as sometimes happens, a musician takes them to task about a chant which they perform either inaccurately or crudely, they get angry and make a shameless uproar and are unwilling to admit the truth, but defend their error with the greatest effort. Reluctantly, but in the cause of uprooting nonsense, I declare that I should rate them, not unjustly, as less comprehending than the blind.

For the blind man seeks from without that which he has not in himself, namely, the guidance of a man or a staff, and thus he takes heed lest he fall into a pit.

Whereas such worthless folk, whom the Greeks aptly call *energumenos* [ἐνεϱγούμενος or ἐνεϱγουμένους, possessed of the Devil], neither see by themselves, nor are they eager to advance under the guidance of those who do. As we said, the monochord serves to silence their wrong-headedness, so that those who will not trust the words of a musician are refuted by the testimony of the sound itself.

Chapter 8

How many are the intervals [modi] from which melody is put together

[67] Among other things, one ought to know that there are just nine intervals from which melody is put together: the unison, semitone, whole tone, ditone, semiditone, diatessaron, diapente, semitone-plus-diapente, and whole-tone-plus-diapente. Six of these are called "consonances," either because in singing they sound together—at the same time—more often than the others; or, more likely, because they sound together in the sense that they are related

---

length into thirds to get a and $\overset{a}{a}$; go out a fourth such third from D to get A. Divide A's length into thirds to get E and e; divide E's into thirds to get ♮ and $\overset{♮}{♮}$; and go out a fourth such third from E to get B. Divide b into halves to get $\overset{b}{b}$.

among themselves, being generated from those ratios called sesquioctava [8: 9], sesquitertia [3: 4], sesquialtera [2: 3], and dupla [1: 2]. [68] Since a discussion of such matters would tax the young and less learned, and since we are addressing boys and those not yet mature, we leave this topic to the acumen of the arithmeticians.

Figure 1

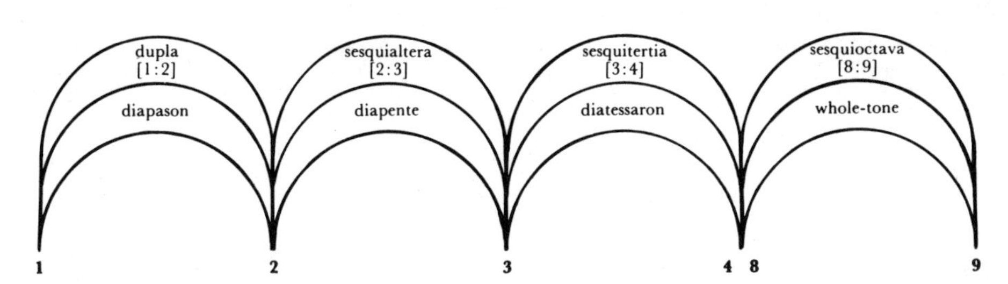

Now unison means *unus sonus* [one sound], because, since there is only one pitch, it is reiterated with no interval. Whole tone [*tonus*] is named after *tonando*, for *tonare* means "to sound mightily," and a whole tone has a strong sound in comparison with a semitone. But more likely this term is taken from the Greeks, for where they say *τόνος* [*tonos*] we say *tonus*, changing *o* to *u*. Thus, *κάλαμος* [*kalamos*] *calamus*, *ὕμνος* [*hymnos*] *hymnus*.

The semitone, called *limma* by Plato,[1] is [69] named "semitone" because it is not a full tone but an imperfect one, not, as some ignorant people say, because it is exactly half of a whole tone. Thus Vergil speaks of *semiviri Phryges*[2]—that is, incomplete Phrygian men—because they garb themselves like women.

The ditone is so named by the Greeks because it contains two whole tones; the semiditone, because it is an incomplete ditone. The semiditone is of two species, one with a whole tone beneath a semitone, the other with a semitone beneath a whole tone.

Diatessaron means "four," so it begins at one note and skips over to the fourth; it contains a ditone and a semitone, as from Γ to C. Moreover there are three species of diatessaron: ut–fa, re–sol, and mi–la.

Diapente means "five" in Latin since it begins on one note and skips to the fifth; it contains a diatessaron and a whole tone. There are four species:

1. *Limma:* cf. Isidore, *Rhythmimachia* (excerpt, *GS* 1: 25b); Chalcidius, *Platonis Timaeus commentatore Chalcidio*, chap. 45 (ed. J. Wrobel [Leipzig, 1876], p. 112); Macrobius, *Commentary on the Dream of Scipio*, transl. W. H. Stahl (New York, 1952), bk. 2, chap. 1, p. 189; Censorinus, *De/In die natali*, chap. 10; Theo[n] Smyrnaeus, *Expositio* (ed. Ed. Hiller [Leipzig, 1878], p. 67); Plutarch, *Concerning the Procreation of the Soul in the Timaeus* (from) *Moralia*, secs. 17–18 (ed. G. Bernardakis [Leipzig, 1895], 6, 194ff.; transl. J. Philips, ed. W. W. Goodwin [Boston, 1870], 2, 345–47). These refer to 36AB of Plato's *Timaeus*, where the demiurge, filling in 4/3 ratios with two 9/8 ratios each, leaves remainders of 256/243. Plato does not use the word *λεῖμμα* (*leimma*, "remainder," John's *limma*) for these.

2. Vergil, *Aeneid* 12. 99.

the first between C and G, the second between D and a, the third between E and b-natural, and the fourth between F and c using the inferior syllables.[3]

The two intervals that remain, the semitone-plus-diapente and the whole-tone-plus-diapente, are called "intervals."[4] You should note that when you say "semitone-plus-diapente," you refer to one thing, but when you say "semitone [70] and diapente," you refer to two; similarly when speaking of the whole-tone-plus-diapente. But these two intervals are rarely found in singing. For easy comprehension of the ascending and descending forms of all these intervals that we have spoken of, you should study the following diagram [Fig. 2].[5]

Figure 2

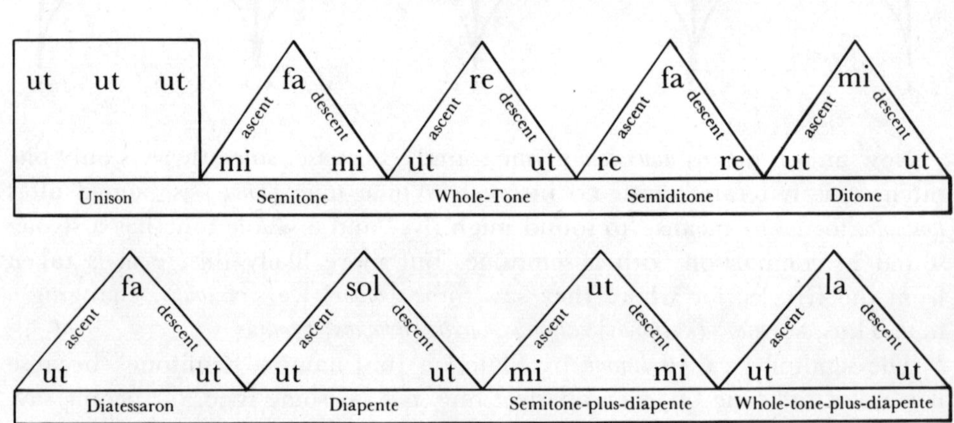

Whoever wishes to get to know specimens of all these intervals in chant, let him learn the song *Ter terni sunt modi quibus omnis cantilena contexitur* etc.[6] [71] This is so helpful toward distinguishing all the various intervals in singing that it makes a very easy introduction to music even for boys. Likewise, this one: *Ter tria iunctorum sunt intervalla sonorum.*[7]

3. The "inferior"—i.e. less preferable—syllables are *fa sol re mi fa* (i. e. mutating from the natural to the hard hexachord), which give b-natural and put the semitone on top, whereas *ut re mi fa sol* give b-flat and thus equal the species C–G.

4. "Intervals" (*intervalla*), both to emphasize their greater size and to distinguish them from the preceding "six consonances," which are those of Guido's *Micrologus*, chap. 4 (*CSM* 4: 105).

5. The form, if not the content, of this diagram is based on Hermannus Contractus, *Musica*, *GS* 2: 140; Ellinwood ed. (Rochester, 1952), p. 48.

6. The didactic song for teaching intervals, "Thrice three are the ways in which all song is composed," is attributed to Hermannus; but H. Oesch has suggested, in *Berno und Hermann*, p. 139, that this song may have been modeled by someone else on Hermann's *Ter tria iunctorum.* It is printed in *GS* 2: 152–53; Cölestin Vivell, ed., *Frutolfi breviarium de musica et tonarius* (Vienna, 1919), p. 72; Hieronymus de Moravia, *Tractatus de Musica*, ed. Simon M. Cserba (Regensburg, 1935), p. 62; and Arnold Schering, *Geschichte der Musik in Beispielen* (Leipzig, 1931), p. 4.

7. A didactic song, also for learning intervals, attributed to Hermann, printed in *GS* 2: 150–52, and Vivell, ed., *Frutolfi breviarium*, p. 69.

Chapter 9

How many different notes there are, and on the diapason

[72] Above, when we were dealing with the notes of the monochord, we left one topic undiscussed, namely, why after seven letters the same ones are repeated. This we now wish to disclose. Seven letters are employed because there are just that number of different tones. After seven have been employed, the same ones are repeated, because, whereas the seven tones have sounds different from each other, the eighth agrees with the first. This a most illustrious investigator of the arts very rightly bore in mind when he said: "He accompanies their measures by the seven different tones."[1] Hence, just as all time proceeds through seven days—for as soon as seven are past, the same ones are repeated—so music progresses through just seven varieties of tones.

Note, then, that the same notes are repeated—yet not entirely the same, since not the same in shape. Γ has one shape, capital G another, and that same [73] capital G a different one than small g; and likewise with the others. Accordingly, just as the eighth note is the same as the first—though not entirely—so, naturally enough, the eighth tone, combined with the first, is

Example 2

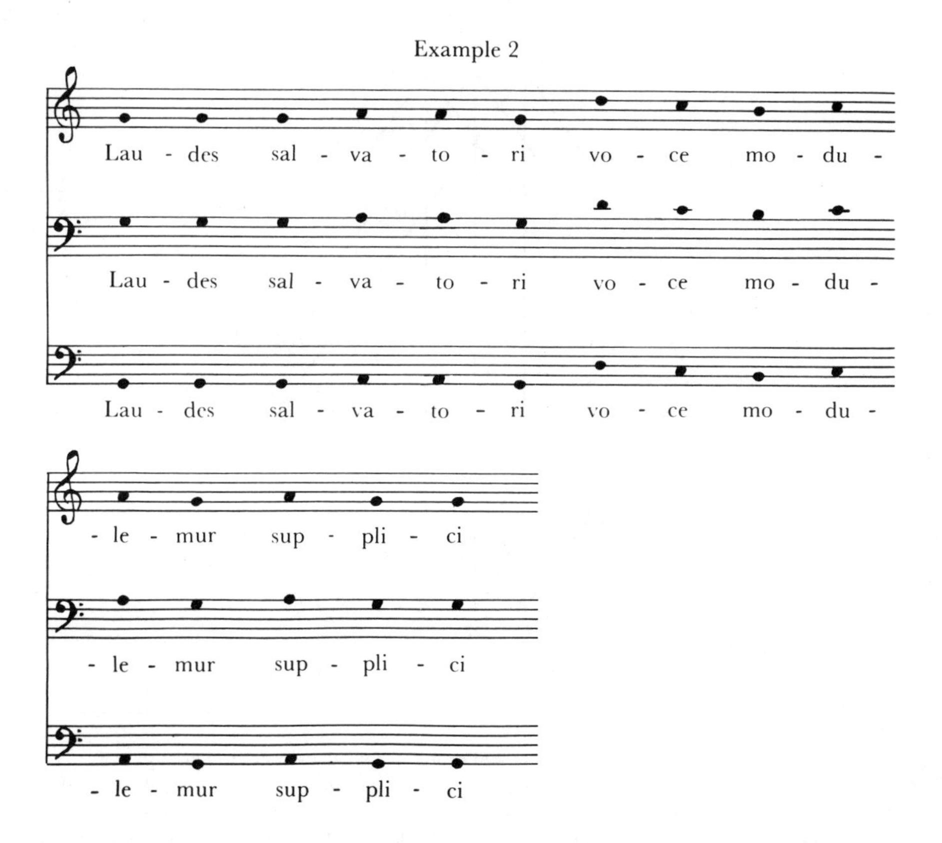

1. Vergil, *Aeneid* 6. 646.

identical in concordance of sound—yet not entirely, because the latter is low, the former high. But this method of singing is found very rarely in the customary chanting.[2]

The diapason is named for a Greek word, which means "from all," and it has this name either because it encloses within itself all the intervals, or because, beginning from one tone, it leaps to the eighth and thus contains within itself all the different tones, which are seven. It is very easy to test what a pleasant and seemly concord the diapason makes, if two or three sing at once in such a way that one uses a *grave* tone, the second an *acute*, and the third an *excellent*, as shown [Ex. 2].[3]

[74] Some indeed call the diapason a "consonance," either because of its ratio, or because it makes a melody consonant "at the unison and the octave," or even because it consists of consonances. For a diatessaron and a diapente make a diapason, inasmuch as between the first and the eighth tone there is either a diatessaron below and a diapente above, or the reverse, as between C and c, D and d, or E and e. This you can examine in the chart [Fig. 3].[4]

Figure 3

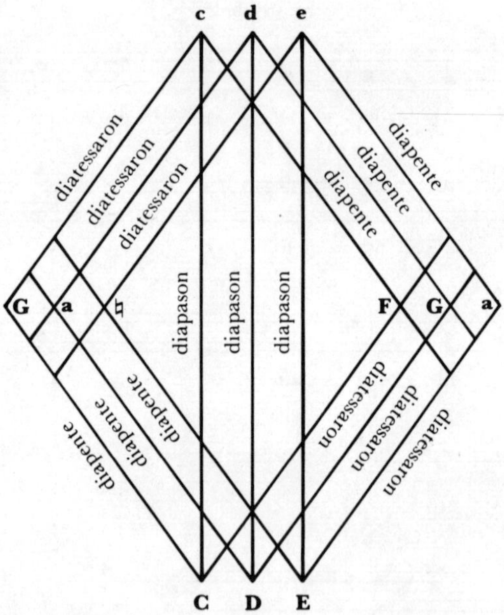

2. This sentence seems to be misplaced and should probably follow and refer to Ex. 2, p. 113.

3. "Let us sing praises to the Saviour with suppliant voice." Beginning of a sequence ascribed by Ekkehard IV to Notker Balbulus. See Index of Chants.

4. Compare this diagram with that in Guido, *Micrologus*, chap. 8 (Fig. 2 in the translation above).

Chapter 10

On the modes, which we improperly call "tones"

[76] One should know, furthermore, that the modes—which, as Guido declares,[1] we call "tones" improperly—are eight, in imitation, clearly, of the eight parts of speech. It seems fitting that, just as everything that is spoken is comprised within the eight parts of speech, so everything that is sung be regulated by the eight modes.

Whereas they are now eight, they were formerly only four, perhaps like the four seasons. Just as long periods of time are diversified by the four seasons, so all chant is discriminated according to the four modes. To these four modes the Psalmist seems to allude when he says: "Sing praises to God, sing praises; sing praises unto our King, sing praises."[2]

Let us for a while ignore why there are now eight, whereas formerly there were only four, and give the reason why they are called "modes" or "tropes." [77] They are called "modes" from *moderando* [controlling] or *modulando* [measuring off], obviously because through them chant is "moderated," that is, controlled, or "modulated," that is, composed. Anyone with a knowledge of music who concerns himself with composing a regular chant will first make up his mind as to what tone he will have it conform to. We said "having a knowledge of music" because even if one unversed in the subject does what he does correctly, still, because he does it unwittingly, he is little esteemed, especially since both actors and precentors of dancing choruses for the most part sing agreeably, which is granted to them not by art but by nature.

They are called "tropes" from a suitable turning back,[3] for however the chant may be diversified in the middle, it is always led fittingly back to the final by means of the tropes, that is, tones. But what we term "modes" or "tropes" the Greeks call *phthongoi*[4] [*φϑογγοί* : voices, cries, sounds].

One should know also that to Guido it seems unsuitable and a misuse that we call them "tones."[5] Yet, if we consider the point more carefully, that term will seem not wholly misapplied. For the Romans, from dearth of vocabulary, very frequently lack technical terms, [78] and thus they are now and then driven perforce to lay hold on and appropriate for themselves words belonging elsewhere—what the Greeks call κατάχρησις [*catachresis*].[6] So, while the Romans of old called only a certain interval in music a "tone,"

1. Chap. 10.
2. Vulg. Ps. 46 : 7; AV Ps. 47 : 6.
3. *Tropus* is from Greek *τρόπος* (*tropus*), "a turn, way."
4. *φθογγός* has no such meaning in classical Greek.
5. Guido, *Micrologus*, chap. 10.
6. According to the *Oxford Companion to Classical Literature*, comp. and ed. P. Harvey (Oxford, 1937), Quintilian extends *catachresis*, customarily "the misuse of a term," to "the adaptation, where a term is wanting, of the term nearest to the meaning."

presently the grammarians usurped the term and began to call the accents of words or the vocal inflexions at the ends of phrases "tones."[7] Again, the Roman singers, reflecting that there is no small resemblance between chant and the accents of prose speech and the "modes" of psalmody, sanctioned that this term be common to both practices.

Just as "tones," that is, "accents," are divided into three kinds—namely, grave, circumflex, and acute—so, too, three varieties are distinguished in chant. For chant ranges now among the *graves*, as in the offertory *In omnem terram*, now around the *finales*, as though it were engaged in a kind of circumflexion, as in the antiphon *Benedicat nos dominus deus noster*; [79] and now it is borne among the *acutae* as though dancing, as in the antiphon *Veterem hominem*.

Or, very likely, the modes are called "tones" from a resemblance to the tones that Donatus calls *distinctiones*.[8] For just as in prose three kinds of *distinctiones* are recognized, which can also be called "pauses"—namely, the colon, that is, "member"; the comma or *incisio*;[9] and the period, *clausula* or *circuitus*[10]—so also it is in chant. In prose, where one makes a pause in reading aloud, this is called a colon; when the sentence is divided by an appropriate punctuation mark, it is called a comma; when the sentence is brought to an end, it is a period. For example, "Now in the fifteenth year of the reign of Tiberius Caesar,"[11]—here and at all such points there is a colon. Later, where it continues "Annas and Caiaphas being the high priests," a comma follows; but at the end of the verse, after "the son of Zacharias in the wilderness," there is a period.

Likewise, when a chant makes a pause by dwelling on the fourth or fifth note above the final, there is a colon; when in mid-course it returns to the final, there is a comma; when it arrives at the final at the end, there is a period. So in the following antiphon:[12] "Peter therefore" colon "was kept in prison" comma "but a prayer was made" colon "for him without ceasing" comma "of the church [80] unto God" period. In this way it can be seen that not entirely without justification are the modes called "tones," and not inappropriately do they receive the nomenclature of the punctuation marks or the accents, whose varieties they copy.

7. The vocal inflections at the ends of phrases: *distinctiones*. Actually the use of *tonus* for "verbal accent" goes back to the 1st century B.C., whereas its meaning of "whole tone," used by Boethius, does not appear in Lewis & Short's (*Classical*) *Latin Dictionary*.

8. Aelius Donatus, author of *Ars grammatica*, 4th century A.D.

9. John consistently exchanges the meanings that *colon* and *comma* have in both ancient and modern usage, as well as in that of Isidore, *Etymologies* 1. 20. 1–2. Perhaps his anomalous usage was suggested simply by the word order in Berno's "*diastema* or *systema*, i.e. *cola* [*sic*] and *comma*," *GS* 2: 73b, lines 12–13, or by Donatus, *Ars grammatica* bk. 1, segm. 6: "In reading, a complete 'sentence' [or thought] is called a 'period,' whose parts are *cola* and *commata*."

10. According to Lewis and Short's *Latin Dictionary*, Cicero and Quintilian use *clausula* to mean "a close, especially of a period in rhetoric" and *circuitus* as a translation of Greek *περίοδος* to mean "a period."

11. Luke 3:1–2.

12. Acts 12:5. Cf. Index of Chants, *Petrus autem servabatur*.

What the grammarians call "colon," "comma," and "period" in prose, this in chant certain musicians call *diastema*, *systema*, and *teleusis*. Now *diastema* means an "ornament apart,"[13] which occurs when the chant makes a suitable pause, not on the final, but elsewhere; *systema* indicates an "ornament connected,"[14] whenever a suitable pause in the melody comes on the final; and *teleusis* is the end of the chant.[15]

That there are now eight modes, whereas formerly there were but four, is clearly to be explained as follows: those who first wrote about music, after reflecting carefully—insofar as their innate ability then enabled them—on the nature of tones, classified all varieties of composition among four modes, so that there are reckoned to be just four finals. The moderns, however, scrutinizing more closely the findings of their predecessors, concluded that the organization of the modes was confused and inconsistent.

They saw that a chant in the same mode would in one case begin among the low notes and roam amongst them and in another case commence among the high notes and dwell for the most part there. So, wishing to avoid this discrepancy, they divided each mode into two, [81] in such a way that any mode in singing that frequents the high notes is called "authentic," that is, "original" or "principal"; whereas one that spends more time among the low notes is called a *plagis* or "plagal" mode, that is, collateral or subordinate.

They are distinguished thus: the authentic protus is called by Latin singers the first "tone," the plagal protus the second, the authentic deuterus the third, the plagal deuterus the fourth, the authentic tritus the fifth, the plagal tritus the sixth, the authentic tetrardus the seventh, and the plagal tetrardus the eighth.

Now protus means "first," deuterus "second," tritus "third," and tetrardus "fourth." And *autentus* in Greek means "authoritative," for they call authority αὐθεντία [*authentia*]. *Plagis* can be explained as "partial" or "collateral," for we say "in that *plaga* [region]," that is, "on that flank" or "on that side."

The Greeks designate the *phthongoi*—that is, tones—by the names of peoples. Thus, 1 Dorian, 2 Hypodorian; 3 Phrygian, 4 Hypophrygian; 5 Lydian, 6 Hypolydian; 7 Mixolydian, 8 Hypomixolydian.

Chapter 11

On the tenors of the modes and their finals

[82] Just as there are eight tones, so too there are eight tenors for them. *Tenor* derives from *teneo*, just as *nitor* from *niteo* and *splendor* from *splendeo*. And in music we call "tenor" the place where the first syllable of the *saeculorum amen* of any mode begins. For, like the keys to locks, they control melodies, and

13. I.e. apart from the final. *Diastema* is Greek διάστημα, "an interval."

14. I.e. connected with the final. *Systema* is Greek σύστημα, "a system, a system of intervals, a scale."

15. *Teleusis* would be τελευσις, "a completion," not occurring in classical Greek.

they give us a way to identify [*ad cognoscendum*] chant. Guido, however, calls the delay on a final note a "tenor."[1]

Note, moreover, that just as the endings of the eight modes are disposed among four notes, which are therefore called "finals," so, too, four notes are assigned for the eight tenors, that is, the most often used notes of the tones [*aptitudines*]—but in a different way. The ending of the two forms [*tropoi*] [authentic and plagal] of a mode always gravitates to a single note, and in another pair, likewise, to one other note, and so with the rest. With tenors, however, that is not so, for sometimes just one and sometimes three [modes] are assigned [*considerantur*] a single note. Thus the tenor of the second tone is on F; of the first, fourth, and sixth on a; [83] of the third, fifth, and eighth on c, and of the seventh on d. Not inconsistently do the tenors of the second and seventh modes assume unique places, since the second mode goes down a fourth, to the lowest point, and the seventh goes up beyond any others.

The proper finals of the tones, as we said above, are these four: D, E, F, and G; and D is the final of the first and second, E of the third and fourth, F of the fifth and sixth, and G of the seventh and eighth. We say proper, because chants now and then usurp other finals too. How and why this occurs we shall, God willing, adequately set forth further on.

Now it should be known that the whole quality of chant turns on the finals. Wherever a chant begins and however it is diversified, it is always to be assigned to that mode on whose final it ends. So with the respond *Praeparate corda vestra:* although it clearly has the range of the protus, it is rightly attributed to the deuterus because it ends on the final E.[2] Likewise, [84] the respond *Factum est silentium*, although it begins like the responds of the seventh mode, such as *Missus est Gabriel*, *Lapides torrentis*, and *Ductus est Jesus*, still the ending assigns it to the first.[3]

Musicians of judgment have not unreasonably decided to base the decision as to modes on the endings, since in business affairs a singleminded regard for the outcome distinguishes the wise from the heedless, as Boethius attests, who says: "Forethought measures the outcome of things."[4] Therefore, just as things are done with a view to their outcome, so the composition of chants is

1. *Micrologus*, chap. 15 (*CSM* 4: 163).
2. All surviving versions end on D.
3. Musical examples given below (transcribed from *AS* 552 and *AS* 10).

4. Boethius, *De consolatione philosophae*, Loeb ed. (London and New York, 1918), Bk. 2, prose 1, line 47: *rerum exitus prudentia metitur*. Trans. "I. T." (1609): "Wisdom pondereth the event of things." (*Prudentia*, "good sense," derives from *providentia*, "foresight, foreknowledge.")

not inappropriately oriented [*tendit*] toward their endings. From this comes today's popular adage: "All praise is sung at the end."[5]

Something has now been said about the tenors and the finals of the modes. Nothing hinders our also informing the reader as to where the *Gloria* of any tone should begin. The *Gloria* of the second tone, then, begin on C of the *graves*; of the fourth [tone], on E of the *finales*; of the first, fifth, and sixth, on F; of the third and eighth, on G; and of the seventh, on c of the *acutae*. Now, below, let us add examples of the tenors, the [85] finals, and the *Glorias* of

Example 3

5. E.g. in Guido, *Micrologus*, chap. 11 (*CSM* 4: 145).

6. Van Waesberghe's reading, which gives the note ♮ on *Glo*, conflicts with the statement above that the Gloria of the seventh tone should begin "on c of the *acutae*." We have therefore adopted the reading of the MSS Basel, University Library, F. IX. 36 (12th century), and Rome, Biblioteca Vaticana, MS Regin. 1196 (12th century).

the tones, one by one, and first let us illustrate the *Gloria* and the *saeculorum amen* throughout [Ex. 3].

[86] In giving examples of the finals we thought it proper, for more fully showing how to get to know the modes, that we put down here some little chants which we may call "models" or "formulas of the modes." These are:[7]

7. For the texts of the first seven of these chants cf. Matt. 6:33; Matt. 22:39; Luke 24:21; Matt. 14:25; Matt. 25:1–2, 10; John 4:6; Rev. 1:4. For more such formulas of the modes (which were meant to show the scales and some characteristic melodic turns of the modes—cf. Guido, *Micrologus*, chap. 13), dating from the 10th to the 14th centuries, see (1) the *Commemoratio brevis de tonis et psalmis modulandis* (*GS* 1: 229, or transcribed on pp. 171–77 of Antoine Auda, *Les modes et les tons de la musique* [Brussels, 1930]; (2) the *De modorum formulis* (*CS* 2: 81–82, 88, 91, 94, 97, 99, 102, 107) "apparently not by Guido" (van Waesberghe, *De musico et paedagogico*, p. 143); (3) E. Rohloff, ed., *Der Musiktraktat des Johannes de Grocheo* (Leipzig, 1943), pp. 63–64; (4) W. H. Frere "Modes," in *Grove's Dictionary of Music and Musicians*, 3rd ed. (1927–28), 3: 481; 5th ed. (1954), 5: 802; (5) F. X. Mathias, *Der Strassburger Chronist Koenigshofen als Choralist* (Graz, 1903), pp. 48–51; (6) Auda, *Les modes*, pp. 176–77; (7) Dom J. Pothier, *Les mélodies grégoriennes* (Solesmes, 1881), pp. 289–90; (8) *Huglo*, pp. 234–35.

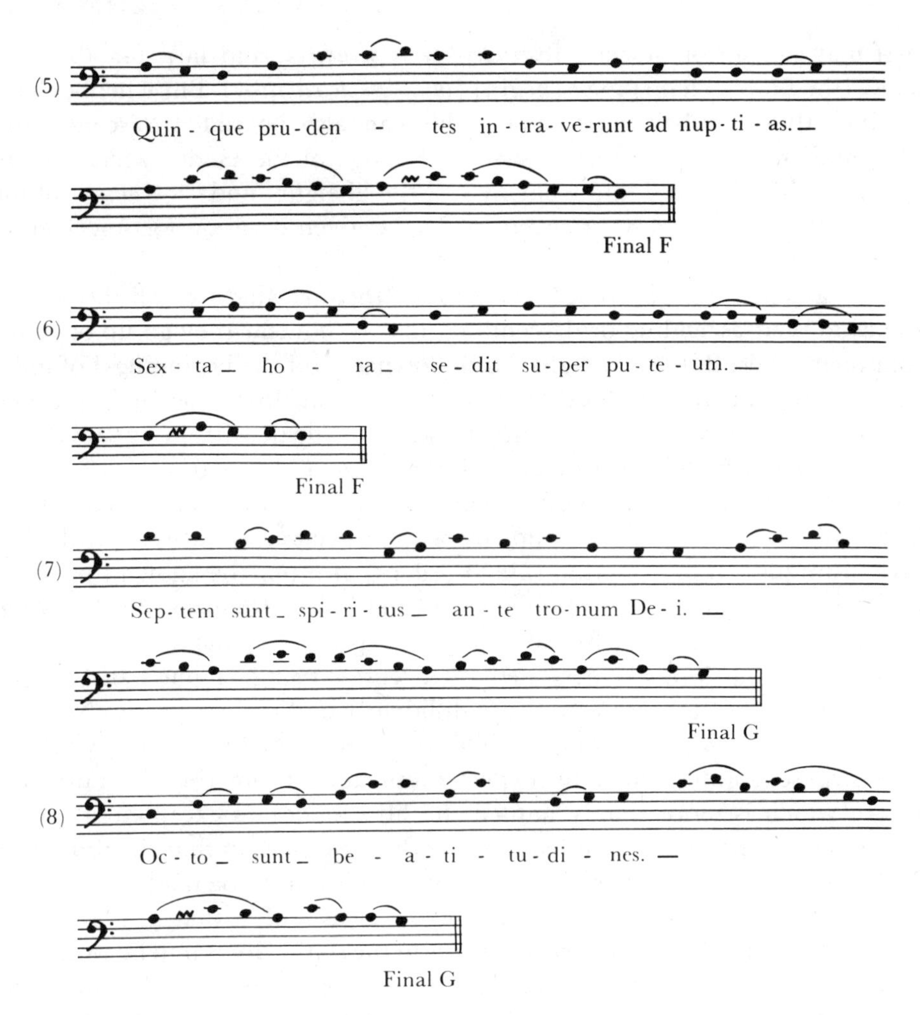

[90] One should also know that by some the *phthongi*—that is, the tones—are designated by vowels, and the *differentiae* of the tones—which some wrongly call *diffinitiones* [differing endings]—by consonants, in this way: a denotes the first tone, e the second, i the third, o the fourth, u the fifth, Greek H the sixth, y the seventh, and ω the eighth. And b indicates the first *differentia* of any tone, c the second, d the third, g the fourth, and so on, with the mute consonants in alphabetical order.

After this useful exposition of these points, it is now time that we give the rules for the regular or permissible ranges of all the modes.

Chapter 12

On the regular ranges [cursus] *of the modes and their permissible extension*

[91] Since we are about to speak of the ranges of the modes, we should first explain what we call their "ranges." We call "ranges" of the modes, or tones, the law according to which they are limited by a precise rule as to how far

each may ascend or descend [*ascendere vel descendere*], and how far above or below [the final a chant] may [begin] [*intendere ac remittere*]. But when a chant [begins] above or below [its final], this can also be called "ascent" and "descent," so we must distinguish in the range of the modes what we call "ascent" and "descent" and what we call the "height" and "lowness" [of the beginnings], lest the inexperienced reader be given occasion for uncertainty on any point.

The "ascent" and "descent" of the tones, then, is what we call the precise rule as to their ascending or descending, that is, how far they go up or down from their finals. But the "height" and "lowness" [of the beginnings] of tones [is what] we call that regulation as to the intervals from the final at which each mode ought to begin. So, with these points dealt with in advance as is necessary, let us discuss, as we planned, the range of the modes.

[92] All the authentic modes regularly ascend an octave—that is, a diapason—above their finals, and, by way of license, a ninth or tenth. We have distinguished license from rule in order that it may be known that those notes that are granted by license are very rarely to be resorted to. For what anyone has by regulation, he has as his due, as it were, and so he can use it more freely; but what is possessed by license—being at one's disposal as though by grace—is to be used more diffidently and circumspectly. Now the authentic modes descend from the final to the next note, where I have found some license granted them by expert musicians.[1] From this the authentic tritus—which is more simply named the fifth mode—is excepted. Here no descent below the final is granted, for no other reason than that the drawback of the semitone does not permit an acceptable descent to be made.

All the plagal modes, however, ascend as far as a fifth, that is, a diapente, from the final, and by way of license they add the sixth. Nor is it to be wondered at that the plagal modes have a smaller allowance going up than the authentic, because the plagal should always dwell among the lower notes and very rarely ascend a fifth from the final. Odo, too, who was highly versed in this subject and is highly recommended by Guido at the end of his treatise,[2] assigns to the authentic mode any chant that ascends to, and repeats three or four times, the fifth above the final.[3] Thus, although the antiphon *Ecce tu pulchra es* descends into the range of the second tone, nevertheless, since it quite often iterates the fifth above the final, it is assigned to the first tone. [93] So too the respond *Deus omnium exauditor est*, since it moves more often

1. Throughout this chapter and in the chart of chap. 19 John grants the next note below the final in authentic modes as regular, whereas some other experts do so as a license.

2. Last sentence of Guido's *Epistola GS* 2: 50.

3. See introductory Letter, n. 6, concerning the identity of Odo. None of the works that have been attributed to Odo contains the theory referred to here, not *Musica enchiriadis*, *Scolica enchiriadis*, the tonary of the Italian Abbot Odo, nor the *Dialogus*. H. Oesch in *Guido von Arezzo* (Berne, 1954), p. 102, n. 1, suggested that this theory may have been in the lost final section of the *Musica* attributed to Odo in *GS* 1: 265–84. But the attributions to Odo probably postdate John's treatise.

among the higher notes, even though at *unctione* it descends to capital A, still it is assigned to the first tone; this is done so that honor may be reserved for the foremost.[4] For a lord or master holds power not only over his own, but even over that which belongs to his subject. For a subject, however, it should suffice if he is permitted to use humbly the things granted him by his master; by no means should he rashly strive for the things that belong to his superior. If, therefore, the plagal modes ought very rarely to attain the fifth above, how much more rarely, then, the sixth!

On the other hand, all the plagal modes descend a fourth, that is, a diatessaron, or even a fifth from the final by rule. But I have observed that descent by license is nowhere allowed in either authentic or plagal modes. Yet one should know that certain musicians not unreasonably calculate the regular range of the modes (which are eight) as just one octave each. According to them almost all the modes claim by way of license a single note below the final, which we have previously assigned them as regular.

4. Transcribed from *LA* 267.

Figure 4

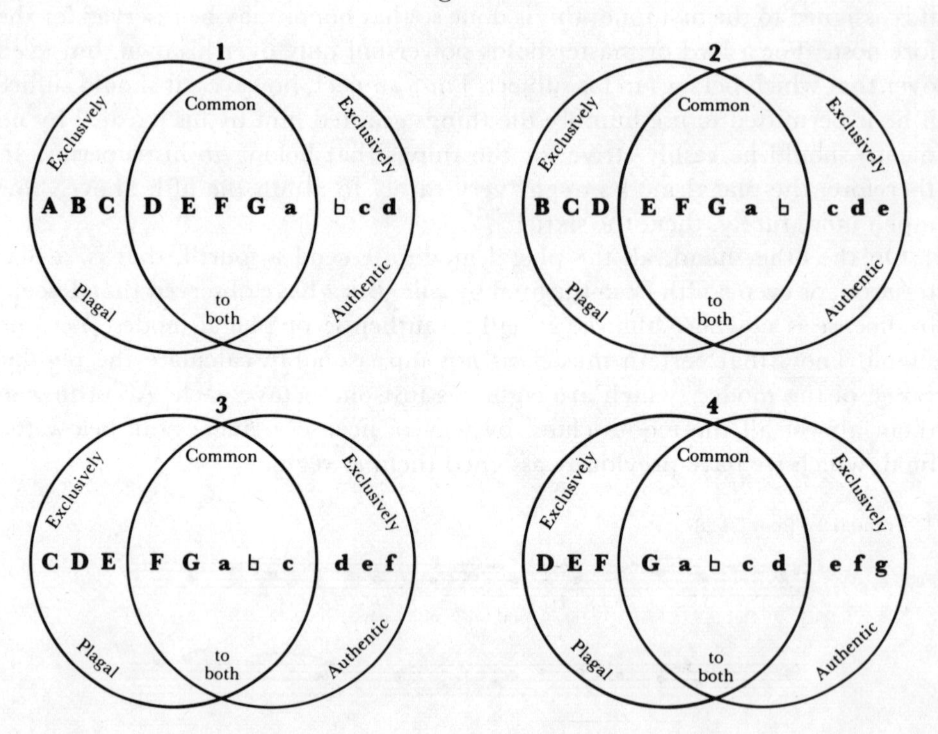

Inasmuch as the eight tones extend through the same number of octaves in such a way that the tones always group in twos, like master and pupil, [94] their octaves are interlinked, so that one can easily observe in them which notes are exclusively plagal, which authentic, and which common to both. The diagram of eight circles that we give [Fig. 4] makes this perfectly clear if closely studied.[5]

It seems we should also show how our statement is to be taken that authentic modes go up an octave and plagal a fifth, so that, as we declared above, we may in this little work make the path clear for boys. [95] That tones are said to ascend an octave or fifth is to be understood thus: that they ascend that high in the sense that they have the potential for doing so. For neither does every chant in an authentic mode reach up an octave, nor every plagal melody a fifth, as is shown in the antiphon of the first tone *In tuo adventu* and in the antiphon of the second tone *Consolamini, consolamini*.

This is to be noted about the height and lowness [of the beginnings] in the modes: in all authentic modes it is permitted to pitch the first note a fifth above the final or to lower it to the note that is next below the final. But if [an opening note] is permissible at the fifth [above], how much more, then, at the fourth or third? Only the authentic deuterus—that is, the third mode—

5. These diagrams modify those in Aribo, *De musica*, *CSM* 2: 18–20.

contravenes this law, for it very often pitches its first note a sixth above [its final], as in the antiphon *Tertia dies est.*

But in certain plagal modes it is permitted to pitch the first note—and even the "hemitones"—a fourth above and occasionally a fifth below [the final]. Now we call "hemitones" the beginning notes [96] that are set off by rests in the middle of chants, in the same way in which we use "tones" with more than one meaning, for "hemitones" properly mean "semitones."

It is, moreover, to be noted that although the foregoing law and fixed rule is laid down for the ranges of the tones, many modern composers who care only about how to tickle the ears very often jumble them up and make a mongrel chant by giving one melody the range of two tones, as is seen in the song *Ter terni sunt modi.*[6] In chants of this kind, which are so loosely and indiscriminately composed, it is left to the judgment of the singer to fit the chant to that mode with which its beginning best agrees.

Chapter 13

Exposition of the Greek names of the notes

[97] Since in an uninterrupted treatment of the modes it is boring always to name the notes themselves, we thought it would be pleasant to explain the terms for them given by the Greeks, so that whenever desirable we may substitute these for the letter names.[1] We made mention of these words in the discussion in the fifth chapter, but we then deferred speaking of them, so as not to disturb the raw and untrained mind of the novice reader by a sudden obscurity. So that what follows may be better understood, we must interpose something about the tetrachords of the ancient musicians.

Musicians of antiquity arranged four tetrachords on the monochord. The first was from A to D, and this they called the tetrachord of the *principales* [foremost, primary], since those notes were placed *in principio* [at the beginning]; the second was from E to a, and this they called that of the *mediae* [middle], since through these "media" or mediators chants might go back and forth between the low notes and the high. The third tetrachord was from ♮ natural to e, and this they called that of the *disjunctae* [disjunct] since they saw that these were not joined to [98], but different from, the preceding, both in notation and in sharpness of pitch. The fourth was from this same e up to double $\overset{a}{a}$, and this they named that of the *excellentes* [surpassing, overtopping], since they saw that these surpassed all others in thinness of sound.

So the names that we are about to explain were given to the musical tones by those who admitted neither Γ nor the three notes that we put after double $\overset{a}{a}$. The first A is called by Greek musicians *proslambanomenos*, that is, "added" or

6. See chap. 8, n. 6.

1. Literally, "for the notes themselves."

"adopted," since it was adopted for musical use from grammar, for which it was first invented; or else it is called "added" because the earliest musicians placed not it but B at the beginning, presumably so that the arrangement of the notes might commence with the smallest interval, namely, the semitone, which is between B and C. So, too, this B is called *hypate hypaton*, that is, *principalis principalium* [the first of the foremost], because, of course, for the earliest musicians it was the first of the *principales*, that is, of the *graves* [low].

This is the opinion of some, but a shrewd listener can object that the argument that we have added about the semitone is not clinching. If the earliest musicians had wished the arrangement of the tones to begin with a semitone, they could have located that just as well between A and B as between B and C. Therefore, it is better that we say that A was placed first on the monochord for the former reason [that is, because proslambanomenos means "adopted" from grammar].

Then again one can ask in objection why B [99] should be called the *principalis principalium* when A should rather be so named, since A is the first of the *graves*. To this we rejoin that B is called the *principalis principalium*, not because it is the first of them in succession, but because it is the first of the *principales* to make a different sound. For A, being situated at the beginning of the monochord, produces no change of sound.

C is called *parhypate hypaton*—that is, "next to foremost of the foremost"—because it is next to B. D is called *lichanos hypaton*, that is, "the fingerlike of the foremost"; and it is called "fingerlike" as "serving to distinguish," because it marks off—that is, divides—the *principales* from the *mediae*.

E is called *hypate meson*, that is, "the foremost of the *mediae*"; F, *parhypate meson*, that is, "the next-to-foremost of the *mediae*"; G, the *lichanos meson*, that is, "the fingerlike of the *mediae*," and it has this name because this very one among the *mediae* marks off the upper-case letters from the lower-case ones.

There follows a, which is called *mese*, namely "mean"—that is, between capital A and double $\substack{a\\a}$; for among the earlier musicians no note was repeated thrice but that one. ♮-natural is entitled *paramese*, that is, "next to the mean," namely a.

Next in order is c, which is called *trite diezeugmenon*, that is, "the third of the disjunct," a name which it has from the system of numbering of the notes placed above it. Since d is after c and e after d, if you call e the first and d the second, c will be the third. [100] Our calling c "the third of the disjunct" amounts to the same as if we said "one of the three notes that are called disjunct." After this comes d, which is called *paranete diezeugmenon*, that is, next-to-last of the disjunct, because it is beside e, which is called *nete diezeugmenon*; *nete* means "last" and *diezeugmenon* means "of the disjunct."

There follows f, which is called *trite hyperbolaeon*, that is, "third of the *excellentes*," about which name the same holds true that we said about c. After f is placed g, which is called *paranete hyperbolaeon*, that is, "next-to-last of the *excellentes*," because it is next to $\overset{a}{a}$, which is called *nete hyperbolaeon*, that is, "last of the *excellentes*."

So that what we have been saying may be clearer, we have appended the tetrachords of the ancient musicians with the words for the notes written above.

Figure 5

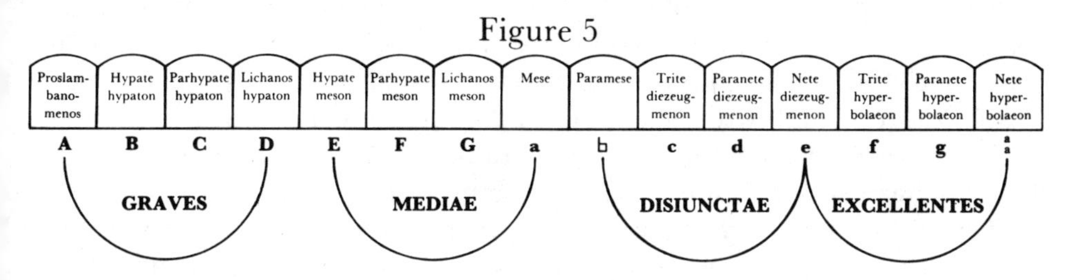

Chapter 14

What is to be done with chant that is defective with respect to the proper range

[101] Now that we have explained the word names for the notes, we must discuss the chants that are defective with respect to the proper range and therefore appropriate for themselves the finals of other modes. Such irregularity in chants is in some cases excusable, but in others, not at all. This comes about from the fault of singers and is very often of undeniable antiquity. The modes in which such a mixing-up of the chants turns out bearably are these: the protus, deuterus, and tritus. Musicians overlook infraction of the rule in these because they have kindred notes.

We call those notes "kindred" [*affines*] which agree in descent and ascent. For example, D, the final of the protus, concords with high a, since from both notes one descends by a whole tone and ascends by a whole tone and a semitone. E, too, the final of the deuterus, has a kinship with ♮-natural, since the descent and ascent from them is similar. And F, too, the final of the tritus, agrees with high c in descent and ascent.

There is no real kinship [102] in descent or ascent unless both—or at least the ascent—are identical. Since the final of the tetrardus has no kinship of this nature, its absence is not permitted. For whoever cannot get a deputy must perform his duties properly himself. So if any deviation transpires at any time in a chant in the tetrardus, we say that it arises from the ignorance of singers and must be corrected by the skill of musicians. In chant in the previously mentioned modes—that is, the protus, deuterus, and tritus—on the other hand, the kindred notes are substituted for the finals without incompatibility whenever need be.

To throw a clearer light on what we have said we add examples of each. The antiphon *Gaudendum est nobis*, although it is in the protus, cannot be sung in its natural location because in certain places it demands, according to some, a whole tone below parhypate hypaton, that is, low C, which is not there. Yet if begun on the mese, that is, a, it proceeds to this same a at the end without going astray. Thus too the antiphon *Magnum hereditatis mysterium*.[1]

Some people who wish to avoid this [transposition] [103] place between A and B a Greek S,[2] which they call *synemmenon* [conjoined], that is, "adjunct," so that they may have a whole tone below C. Nevertheless they cannot corroborate this by any authority. Guido, who was concerned precisely that no notes should be wanting on the monochord, would undoubtedly have intercalated this one had it seemed to him necessary. Having added those notes that can be judged superfluous so that nothing would be lacking, he would all the more have added this note if he had found it necessary.

There is yet another fact that disproves their contention, namely, that a chant very frequently demands a whole tone not only below parhypate hypaton [C] but also below parhypate meson [F]; and by this requirement we are forced to migrate to the higher notes, as in the communion *Aufer a me* and the antiphon *Germinavit*. A chant of the deuterus too may be defective with respect to its proper range, as in the antiphon *Tu Domine universorum*. Sometimes, too, a chant in the tritus cannot be sung in its natural position,

1. Transcribed from *AM* 275.

2. A Greek S: σ, Σ, or C.

as, for instance, the communion *De fructu operum tuorum.*[3] Whoever sings all these around the notes kindred to the regular finals will arrive at the end without going astray.

Chapter 15

How the ignorance of fools often corrupts the chant

[104] We are not sure whether the fact that these and other such chants cannot be sung in the range proper [to their modes] results from the fault of the singers or whether they were thus issued by their composers in the first

3. Transcribed from *GS* 155.

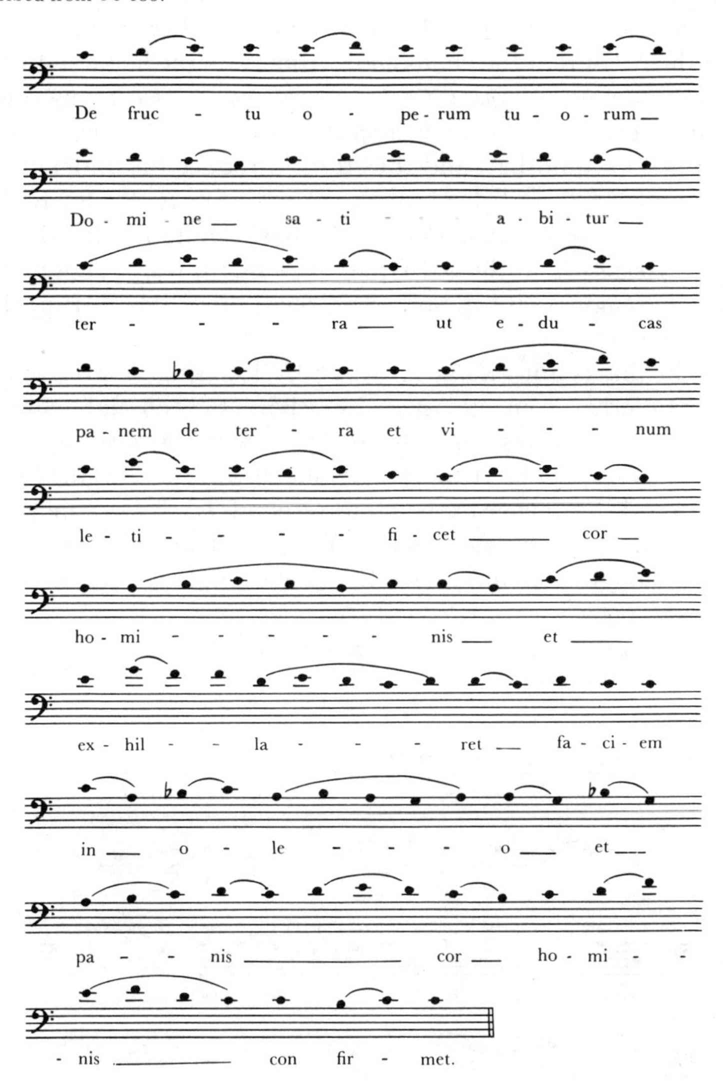

place. On the other hand, we do know most assuredly that a chant is oftentimes distorted by the ignorance of men, so that we could now enumerate many corrupted ones. These were really not produced by the composers originally in the way that they are now sung in churches, but wrong pitches, by men who followed the promptings of their own minds, have distorted what was composed correctly and perpetuated what was distorted in an incorrigible tradition, so that by now the worst usage is clung to as authentic.

Thus, raw singers, weighed down by weariness in singing, have sometimes lowered what should be kept up; and very often, impelled by high spirits, they have raised unlawfully what should have been sung lower down. This is seen in the gradual *Qui sedes domine*; *super Cherubim*, which should begin on the paranete diezeugmenon [d], they habitually begin on the mese [a], [105] with the result that the chant ends wrongly on the lichanos hypaton [D].

In the communion *Principes persecuti sunt me*, too, a great many singers make no small mistake. They begin *Concupivit*, which should begin on the trite diezeugmenon [c], on b-flat, and thus they introduce the anomalous interval between E and b-flat and displace the chant from its lawful range. Some, likewise, perform the gradual *Probasti Domine* unsuitably, for they begin its verse *Igne me examinasti* on the parhypate meson [F], which should commence on the trite diezeugmenon [c], and, thus, they completely disrupt the regular course of the chant.

Whereas in this chant one goes wrong by lowering what should be kept high, in certain others some go astray by striving to keep high what should be pitched low, as in the respond *Ductus est Jesus in desertum*. Whereas *Dic ut lapides* should begin on the trite diezeugmenon [c], they begin it on the trite hyperbolaeon [f]. Moreover in the [106] respond *Terribilis est* many go wrong at the point where *et porta coeli* comes. They suddenly raise this, leaping up to the *acutae*, though it should rather be sung around the final D.[1]

1. Available versions of *Qui sedes domine*, *Principes persecuti sunt me*, *Probasti domine*, and *Ductus est Jesus in desertum* show no trace of the errors John mentions. The version of *Terribilis est* in *LR* 235, however, does "leap up to the *acutae*" at *et porta coeli*:

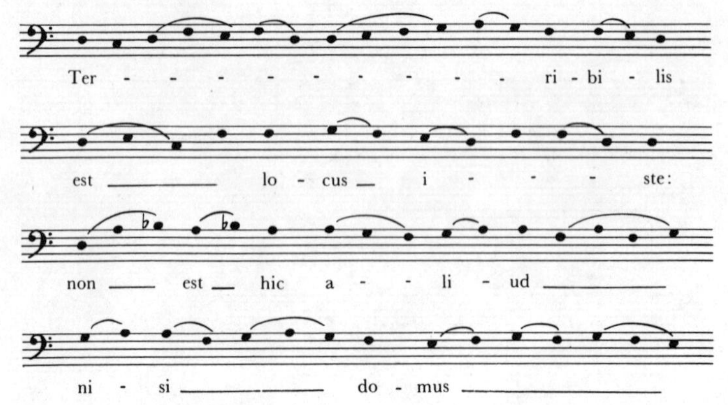

Uneducated singers very often go wrong in judging the tones from similar beginnings of chants. For example, many assign the antiphon *Iste puer* to the plagal deuterus, because at the beginning it agrees with the antiphon *In odore*. Yet *Iste puer* is in the authentic protus and *In odore* in the plagal deuterus.[2] Similarly, although the antiphons *Ipse praeibit* and *Dirupisti domine* are Mixolydian, certain people wrongly assign them to the Hypophrygian on the ground that they seem to agree with certain antiphons of the Hypophrygian, as for instance *Ipse praeibit* with the antiphon *Rorate coeli*, and *Dirupisti domine* with the antiphon *Da mercedem domine*, etc. Likewise, although the antiphons [107]

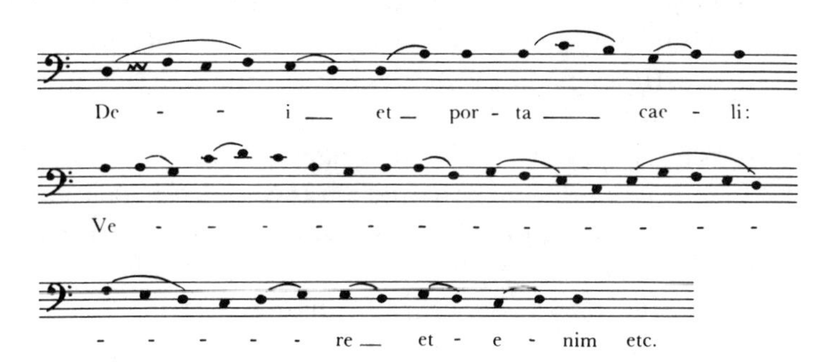

2. *In odorem* is classified as plagal deuterus because of the half-step a–b♭ near the end; *Iste puer*, lacking this half step above the cofinal a, is authentic protus, though in the transposed version (c) *LU* classifies it mode 4. Sources: (a) *WA* 323; (b) *LU* 1496; (c) *LU* 1233.

Malos male perdet and *Qui odit animam suam* and *Novit dominus* are Hypomixolydian, and their smaller and larger phrase units testify to this very clearly (as is manifest from the ending), yet by some they are assigned to the Phrygian, because at the beginning they agree with the antiphons *Domine spes sanctorum* and *Tu Bethlehem*.[3] Likewise the antiphons *Ascendente Jesu*, *Benedicta sit*, and *Gloriosi*, although they are Hypomixolydian, are by some fitted into the Phrygian. Yet *Gloriosi* seems to fit better into the Hypolydian.

Not only are some people misled by like beginnings, but they deflect certain chants from their rightful course by singing wrong notes, as for instance the antiphons *Quid retribuam*, *Cum inducerent*, and *Cum audisset Job*. Although these are Dorian and should begin unobtrusively, [108] these people elevate them to the high range with a sharply raised voice, so that at the beginning they agree with the following: *Qui de terra est* and *Quando natus es*. The beginnings are not to be wondered at, since they [the singers] distort even the endings of chants and by false singing displace them from their proper location, as in the antiphon *Petrus autem*. Although this has the range of the protus, and its smaller and larger phrase units plainly show this, some make it end, cacophonously enough, on the hypate meson [E], singing thus:

Example 5

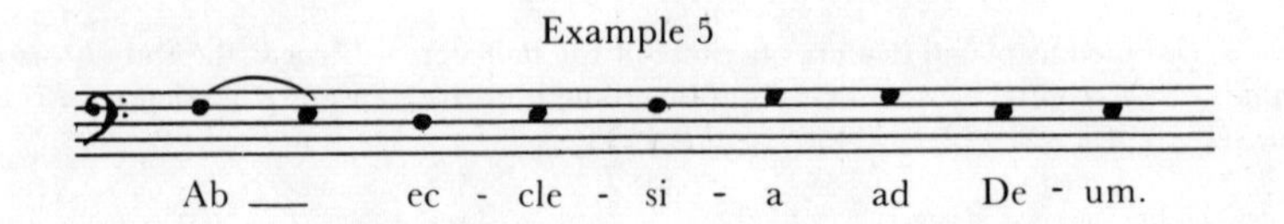

3. Two different versions of *Malos male perdet* survive, one in mode 8, one in mode 3. It is the version in mode 3, however, whose incipit agrees with those of *Domine spes sanctorum* and *Tu Bethlehem*. Sources: (a) *AM* 359; (b) *LU* 1088; (c) *WA* 395.

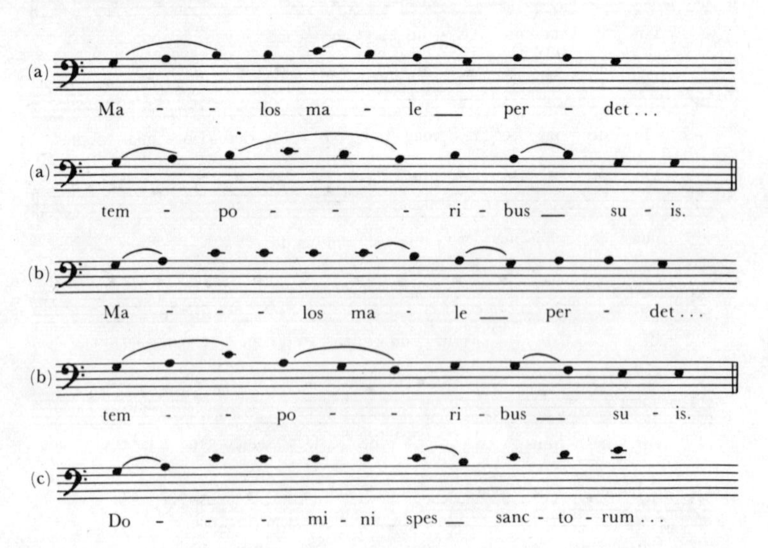

It should, rather, be sung in this way:

Example 6

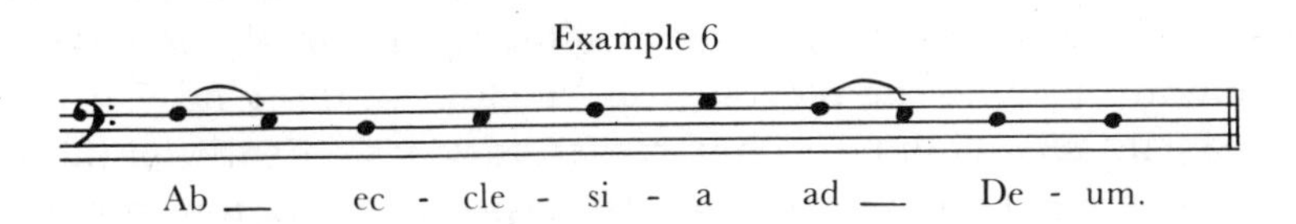

Chapter 16

How different people are pleased by different modes

[109] It has already been shown by many examples how the modes are differentiated and how they are corrupted by incompetent singers. Yet it should be added concerning their nature that different men are attracted by different modes. Just as not everyone's palate is attracted by the same food, but one man enjoys more pungent dishes, while another prefers milder ones, so assuredly not everyone's ears are pleased by the sound of the same mode.

Some are pleased by the slow and ceremonious peregrinations of the first, some are taken by the hoarse profundity of the second, some are delighted by the austere and almost haughty prancing of the third, some are attracted by the ingratiating sound of the fourth, some are stirred by the well-bred high spirits and the sudden fall to the final in the fifth, some are melted by the tearful voice of the sixth, some like to hear the spectacular leaps of the seventh, and some favor the staid and almost matronly strains of the eighth.

Therefore, in composing chants, the duly circumspect musician [110] should plan to use in the most fitting way that mode by which he sees those are most attracted whom he wishes his chant to please. Nor should it seem surprising to anyone that we say different men are attracted by different things, for by nature itself men are so endowed that not everyone's senses cherish the same desire. Thus, it often happens that while to one man what is being sung appears most delightful, by another it is pronounced ill-sounding and utterly formless. Indeed I myself remember singing a number of chants for some people, and what one praised to the heights another disliked profoundly.

The modes have individual qualities of sound, differing from each other, so that they prompt spontaneous recognition by an attentive musician or even by a practiced singer. Just as someone who has studied the manners and appearances of various peoples distinguishes expertly the nationality of any man he sees, noting, for instance, that this one is a Greek and this one a German, but that one a Spaniard and that one a Frenchman; so it is no wonder that a musician, when he hears any music, recognizes at once what tone it is in—and not simply by label, though the sound may deceive in some cases.

Sometimes a chant uses the range of some tone, not only at the beginning but even in [111] the middle, which it nevertheless contradicts at the end. This is shown in the respond *Gaude Maria Virgo*, which, although it adheres to the authentic deuterus both at the beginning and in the middle, still at the end commits itself to the plagal tritus.[1] Chants of this kind warn one not to leap to conclusions about tones, but, rather, to wait prudently for the ending, on which all judgment of chant depends. If one proclaims the tone prematurely, the ending may refute his words and make him regret not having kept silent.

Besides this, one should consider that chants in certain modes appear at times to resemble each other so closely that the singer can scarcely, if at all, make out which tone he had better class them with. This is likely to be the case in the authentic tritus and tetrardus, and in their plagal forms as well, as you can examine in the antiphons *Gloriosi principes* and *Pro nobis Gallus*. These match the Hypolydian as well as the Hypomixolydian, so that you could not easily make out which one they should rather be assigned to. Likewise, the respond [112] *Genti peccatrici* seems to match the Lydian as well as the Mixolydian. Consequently its verse is by some men sung as shown [Ex. 7].

Example 7

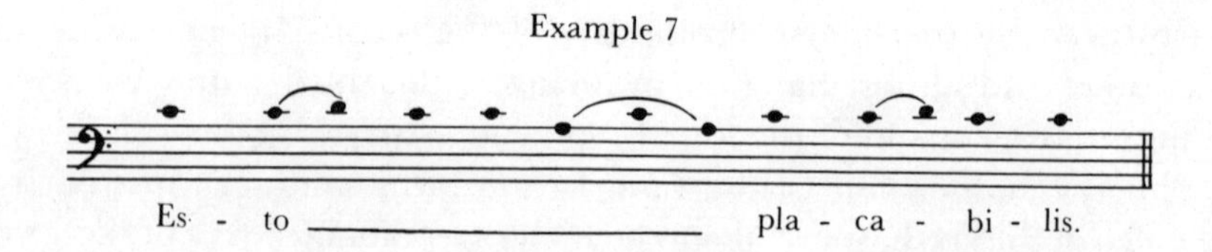

but by most people it is as shown [Ex. 8].

Example 8

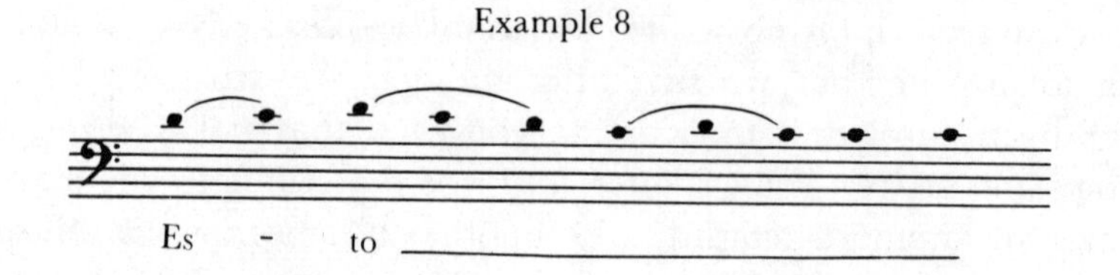

Some put the introit *Deus in loco* in the Lydian mode and some in the Mixolydian; my verdict is to follow those who assign both these chants to the Lydian.

Unless I am mistaken the Greeks had in mind this kind of similarity of sounds [*consonantiam*] in the modes just mentioned when they bestowed on them names hardly differentiated, indeed almost the same. Among the other modes, you will find no such resemblance, except that a chant of the protus sometimes makes an opportune pause on the hypate meson [E], which is the

1. The version in *AM* 1195, although it conforms to the plagal tritus ending on the cofinal, in the first part of the chant does not fit John's description.

final of the deuterus, as in the *Alleluia Juravit dominus* and in the communion *Principes persecuti sunt.*[2]

Furthermore, there are some chants whose resemblance is so close that according to [113] different endings they can be linked with congruity to different tones—such as the antiphons *Et respicientes* and *Lupus rapit.* The former gravitates to the plagal tetrardus and the latter to the plagal tritus if they are sung as follows:

Example 9

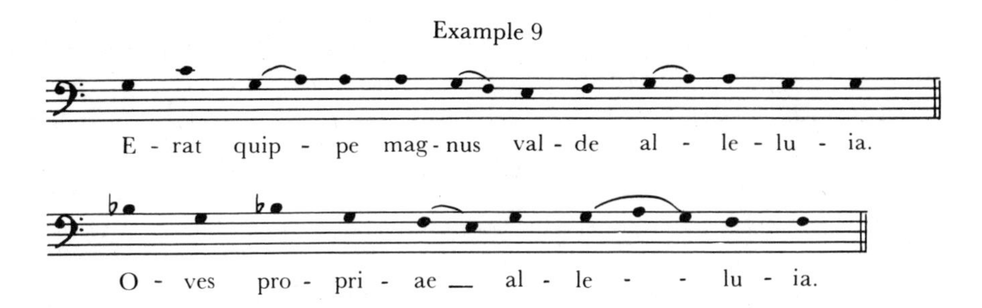

But they will both be Phrygian if they are performed thus:

Example 10

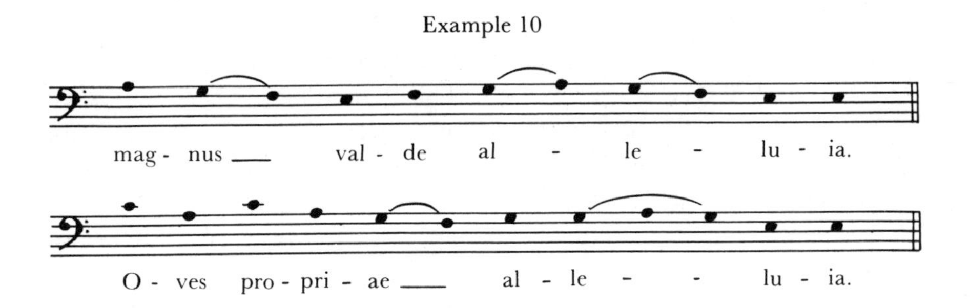

2. Source: *LU* 1238.

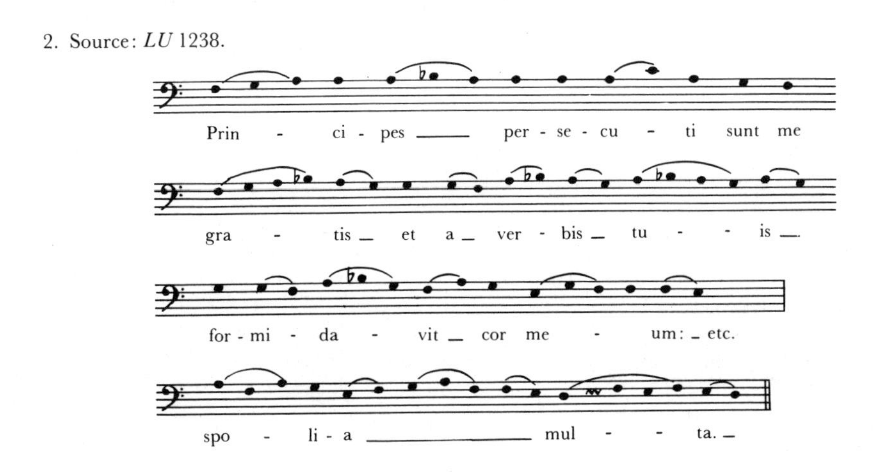

Chapter 17

On the power of music and who first used it in the Roman church

[114] It should not pass unmentioned that chant has great power of stirring the souls of its hearers, in that it delights the ears, uplifts the mind, arouses fighters to warfare, revives the prostrate and despairing, strengthens wayfarers, disarms bandits, assuages the wrathful, gladdens the sorrowful and distressed, pacifies those at strife, dispels idle thoughts, and allays the frenzy of the demented.

Thus one reads of King Saul in the Book of Kings that when possessed by an evil spirit, he was soothed by David's singing to the harp, but when David stopped he was as tormented as ever.[1] Likewise, a certain madman is said to have been freed from insanity by the singing of the physician Asclepiades.[2] It is also recounted of Pythagoras that he recalled a certain licentious youth from his disordered passion by the ordered quality of music [*musica modulatione*].[3]

Music has different powers according to the different modes. Thus, you can by one kind of singing rouse someone to lustfulness and by another kind bring the same man as quickly as possible to repentance and recall him to himself. Guido recounts the demonstration of this in the case of the aforementioned youth.[4]

[115] Since music has such power to affect men's minds, its use in the Holy Church is deservedly approved. The first use of music in the Roman church was made by St. Ignatius the Martyr and also by St. Ambrose, bishop of Milan. After them the most blessed Pope Gregory composed chant with the assistance and at the dictation, it is said, of the Holy Ghost, and he gave the Roman church the chant by which the Divine Service is celebrated throughout the year.

In the Old Testament we have no slight authority that God should be praised by singing. For we read in the Book of Exodus that when Pharaoh was drowned, Moses and with him the sons of Israel sang a song to the Lord.[5] The Psalmist too, being far from ignorant of this art, sang praises to the Lord on the instrument of ten strings, which is a musical instrument, and urges us to make music together, saying: "Sing unto the Lord a new song, and his

1. Vulg. 1 Regum 16:14–23; AV 1 Sam. 16:14–23.

2. This story stems back through Guido, *Micrologus*, chap. 14; Isidore, *Etym.* 4. 13. 3; Cassiodorus, *Inst.* 5. 9 (*GS* 1: 18b–19a); Martianus Capella, *De nuptiis*, bk. 9, par. 926; and Censorinus *De/In die natali*, chap. 12.

3. Guido (*Micrologus*, chap. 14) does not name Pythagoras in this tale, but Boethius does (*De musica*, Bk. I, chap. 1, p. 185 in the G. Friedlein ed.). The simpler of Boethius's two versions is quoted by both him and St. Augustine (*Contra Julianum Pelaqium*, bk. 5, chap. 5, sec. 23) as from Cicero, *Liber de suis consiliis* (see his Fragments).

4. Guido, *Micrologus*, chap. 14.

5. Exod. 15.

praise in the congregation of the saints."[6] He wished us to use not only natural sound in the praise of the Lord, for he said, urging that the Lord be praised also with man-made instruments of musical art: "Praise the Lord with the sound of the trumpet, with the psaltery and harp, with the timbrel and dance, and with stringed and wind instruments."[7] Since we find such great authority for this practice in the Old Testament, since such pious men have ordained it in the Church, [116] and since, lastly, its power is effective, as we have said, in stirring men's minds, what sane man would object to this art? Who would not zealously embrace it with all his heart?

In truth, not only because the holy men mentioned created chants for the services of the Holy Church, but also because certain other composers of chants have arisen not long before our time, I do not see what forbids us to fashion chant likewise. Even if new compositions are now not needed for the Church, still we can exercise our talents in putting to music the rhythms and threnodic verses of the poets. Now since we both seek and grant permission[8] to compose, it seems fitting that we next give precepts for composing chant.

Chapter 18

Precepts for composing chant

[117] The first precept we give is that the chant be varied according to the meaning of the words. We showed earlier what mode in singing suits what material when we said that different people are pleased by different modes. We showed that some are suitable for courtly ceremony, some for frivolity, and some even for grief. Just as anyone eager for a poet's fame must take pains to match the action by the words and not to say things incongruous with the circumstances of the man he is writing about, so the composer eager for praise must strive to compose his chant so aptly that it seems to express what the words say.

If you intend to compose a song at the request of young people, let it be youthful and playful, but if of old folk, let it be slow and staid. Just as [118] a writer of comedies, if he gives the characteristics of a youth to an old man or of a wastrel to a miser, is exposed to such scorn as Plautus and Dossenus are introduced by Flaccus to receive;[1] so a composer can be censured if he employs for sad subject-matter a dancing mode, or a mournful mode for joyful words. Therefore the musician must see to it that the chant is so regulated that for inauspicious texts it is pitched low and for propitious ones it is pitched high. Yet we do not go so far as to direct that this must always be done, but when it is, we say that it is to the good.

6. Ps. 149:1.

7. Ps. 150:3–4.

8. Echoing Horace, *Ars poetica* 11, as pointed out by Prof. Paul Pascal of the Classics Dept. of the University of Washington.

1. See Horace, *Epistles* 2. 1. 170–76.

We have some examples of what we have just said. For instance, the antiphons for the resurrection of our Lord seem to reflect jubilation in their very sound, like these: *Sedit angelus*, *Cum rex gloriae*, and *Christus resurgens*. The antiphon *Rex autem David*, on the other hand, seems to express grief not only in words but even in sound. By even the earliest composers, lamentations are most often sung in the Hypolydian, because this has a doleful sound.

This too we enjoin upon the composer eager for praise: that he not abuse one neume by unduly harping on it, but that the composer of chants devote as much effort to avoiding the fault that is called by musicians ὁμοιόφθογγον [*homoiophthongon*], that is, similarity of sound, as the experienced poet expends toil to escape the defect that the Greeks call ὁμοιόπτωτον [*homoioptoton*], that is [119], identity of case endings. But let the grammarians—and the rhetoricians, too—watch out for the latter fault.

We, however, shall give an instance of the former, which we say should be avoided by musicians, in the respond *Ecce odor filii mei*, where at *Crescere te faciat deus meus* there is an objectionable reiteration of one melodic figure.[2] Similarly in the tract *Qui habitat*, at the place where *et refugium deus meus* comes, the unremitting repetition of one podatus is bad.[3] But we do not find fault if now and then some appropriate melodic figures are repeated just once, as at

2. The passage from *Ecce odor* is transcribed here from *AS* 161.

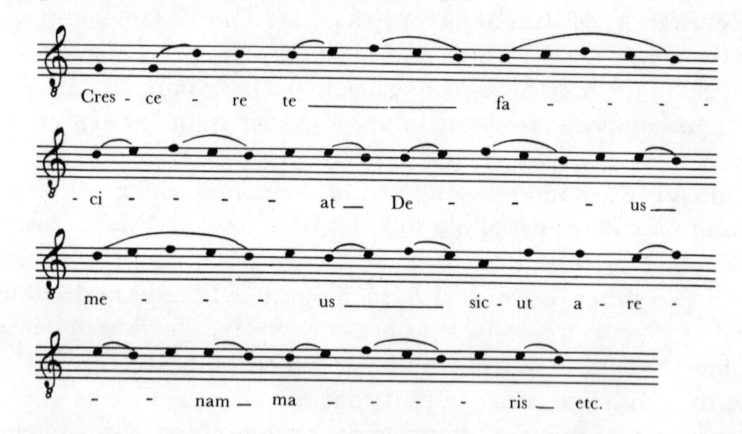

3. The passage from *Qui habitat* is transcribed here from *LU* 533.

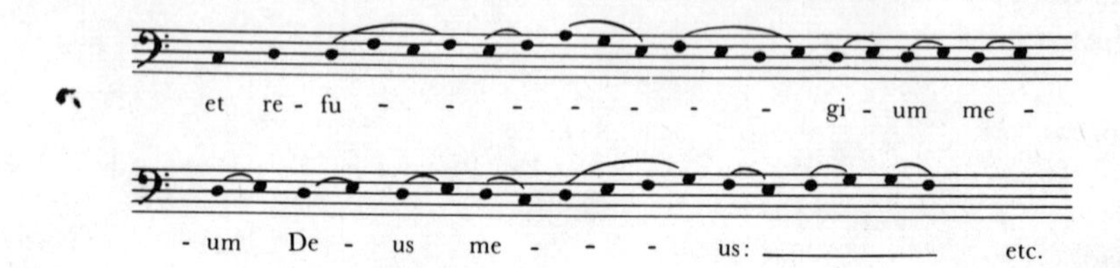

the end of the respond *Qui cum audissent* at *laudantes clementiam*, and also at the end of the respond *Sint lumbi vestri* at *a nuptiis*.[4]

And one should know that it is commendable in the authentic modes to prolong the chant slightly near the end, whereas in the plagal it is fitting to hasten the chant at the ending.

Chapter 19

What is the best plan for ordering melody

[120] The best plan for ordering melody is this: for the chant to have a pause on its final where the sense of the words calls for a punctuation mark. This you can see in the antiphon *Cum esset desponsata*.[1] Whoever composed the

4. The excerpt from *Sint lumbi vestri* is transcribed from *LR* 202.

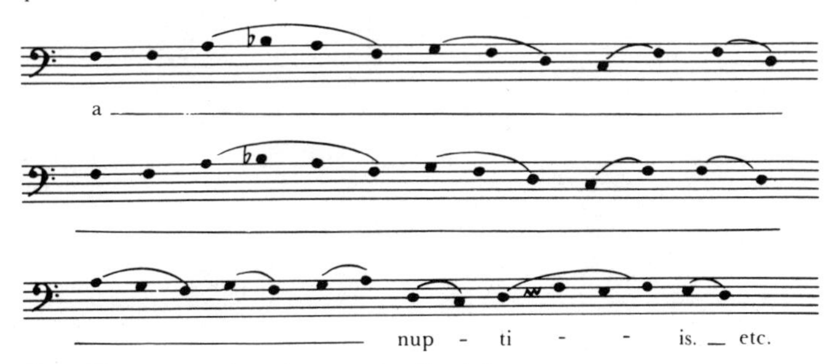

1. Source: *AS* 44. The punctuation of the text is editorial.

versicles beginning *Homo quidam erat dives valde*, however, did not heed this precept well, for this versicle never touches on its final at a proper point for punctuation.[2]

Moreover, it contributes not least to the euphony if in plagal chants one takes heed that they repeat the final often and hover around it, and very rarely make a rest on the fourth [scale degree], and by no means on the fifth. If they should ever touch on the fifth, let them quickly turn back, as though touching on it in haste and almost trepidation, as in the antiphon *Ait Petrus*.[3]

2. Source: *Stäblein*, p. 487, no. 1014.

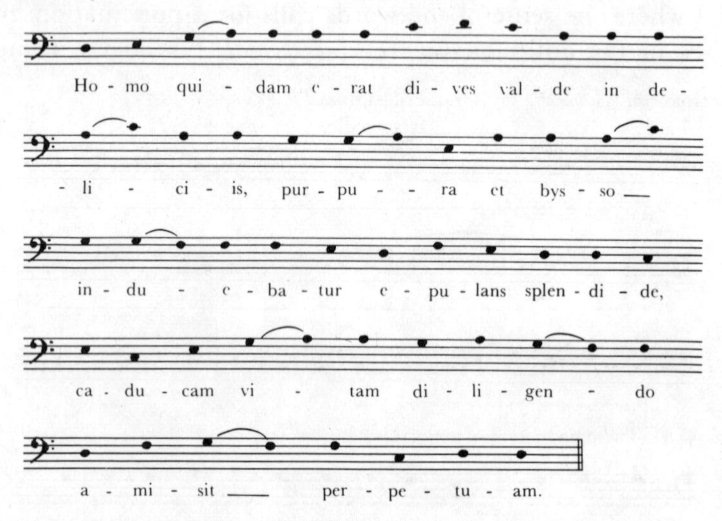

3. Source: *AS* 441.

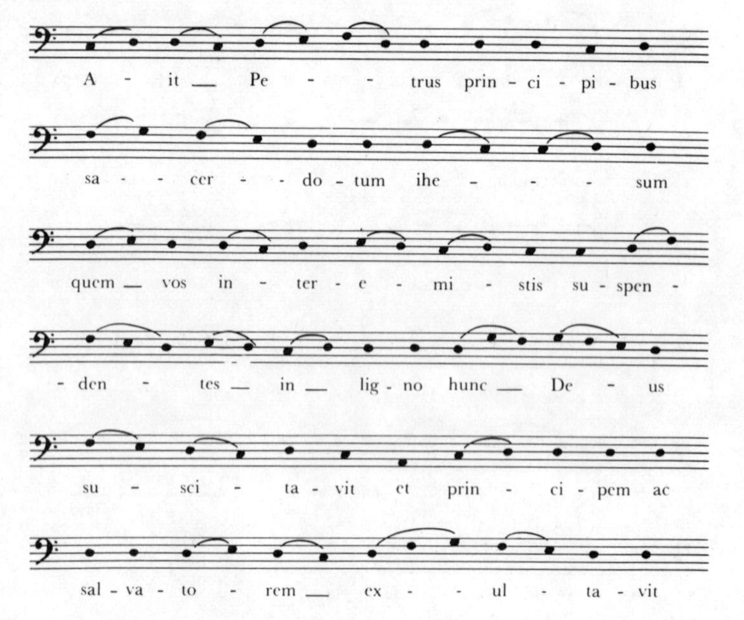

For chants in the authentic modes, however, care should be taken that they circulate mostly among the high notes, and after they have paused two or three times on the fifth from the final, they should revisit the final, and again betake themselves hastily to the higher notes; for just as it is the nature of plagal chants to move chiefly among the low notes, so it is of the authentic [121] to move chiefly among the high ones. You have an example of this precept in the antiphon *Muneribus datis*.[4]

It should also be noted concerning the diapente that in a plagal melody one never leaps that interval from the final to the higher notes, whereas a diatessaron occurs freely, up or down. But a chant of the fourth mode falls [from] and rises [to the final] by a diapente more suitably than by a diatessaron. And no wonder, since the music of the authentic form of this mode rises to or falls [from] the sixth [scale degree] more often and better than the fifth. Note also that, while it is beautiful in chants in authentic modes for them frequently to fall [to] or rise from the final by a fifth, in the third mode this is rather awkward,

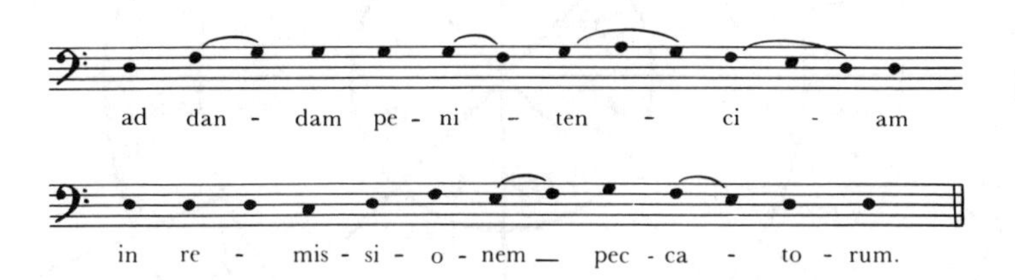

4. Source: *AS* 358. The segmentation is editorial.

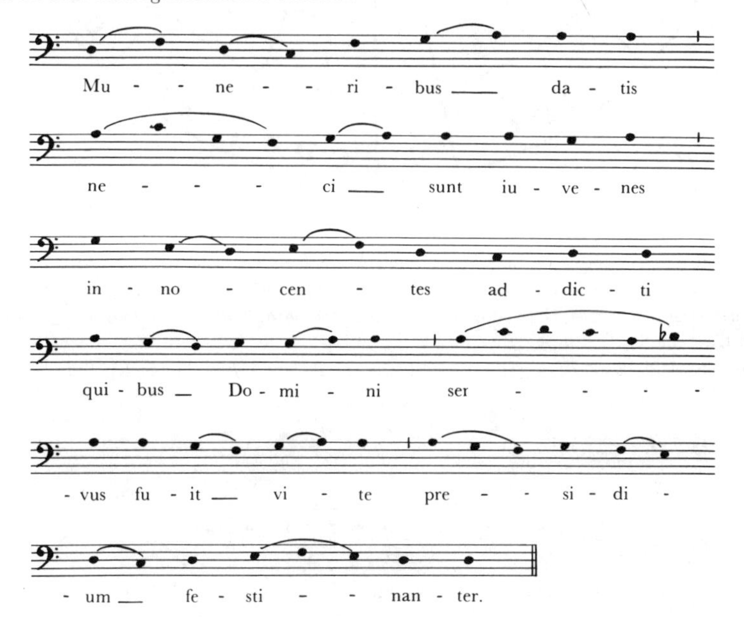

but in the fifth [mode] it is most appropriate.[5] In the latter it is also attractive if the chant often rises from the final by a ditone, then a semiditone, as is shown in the antiphon *Paganorum*.[6]

Moreover, we give briefly this precept concerning both classes of modes: that a plagal chant should very rarely reach a note a fifth below or above the

Figure 6

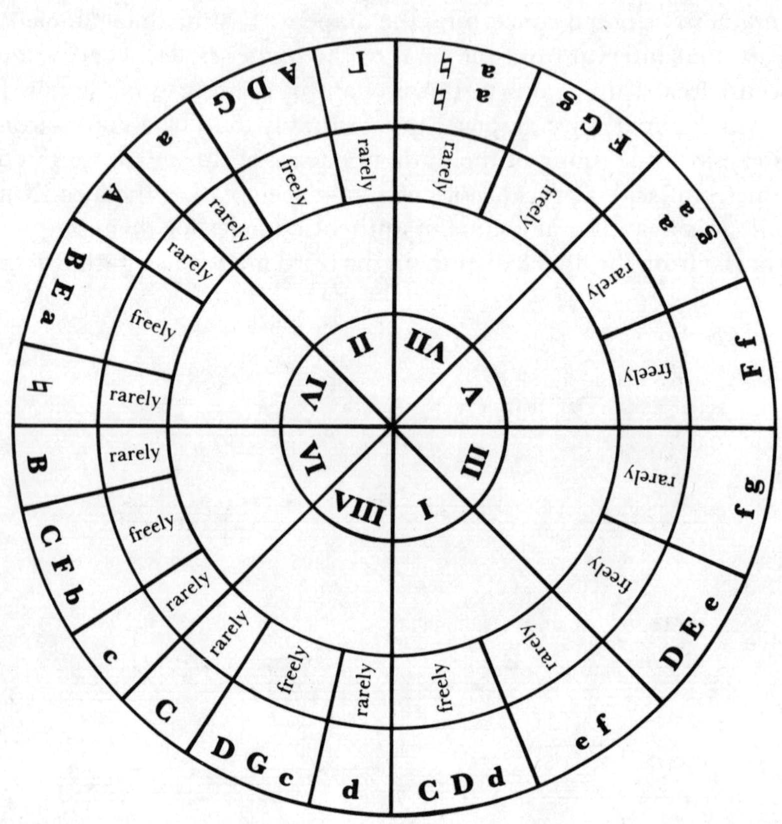

5. Throughout this paragraph John uses different words for rising and falling: *saliat; supra et infra fiat; cadit et resurgit; intendatur et remittatur* (despite the special meaning of these terms in chap. 12 of "beginning"); *deponi et elevari; surgat; contingat.* He is also careless about including both *ad* (to) and *ab* (from) in his grammatical construction. For example, the phrase beginning "while it is beautiful" needs to be corrected somewhat as follows: *pulchrum sit eos a[d] final[em] crebro per diapente deponi et [a finali] elevari.*

6. Source: *AR* 626.

final—below because of its being too deep, above because of its being too resonant, lest the chant be attributed to an authentic mode.

Yet a chant in an authentic mode, except for the fifth, may descend to the next note below the final; and both the fifth and the other authentic modes may validly go up an octave, but may very rarely reach the ninth or tenth—as this chart instructs you most lucidly. [See Fig. 6.]

[123] One should observe moreover that these two consonances, the diatessaron and the diapente, give the greatest pleasure in chant if they are disposed suitably in their places; for they make a beautiful sound if sometimes after descending one ascends immediately to the same notes, as can be seen in the *Alleluia Vox exultationis*.[7] Yet the fourth makes a much sweeter melody—and especially in the authentic deuterus—if now and then it is repeated with various notes three or four times, or even more than that, [124] as at the end of the antiphon *O gloriosum lumen*, which appears in this way to one who regards it rightly.

Example 11

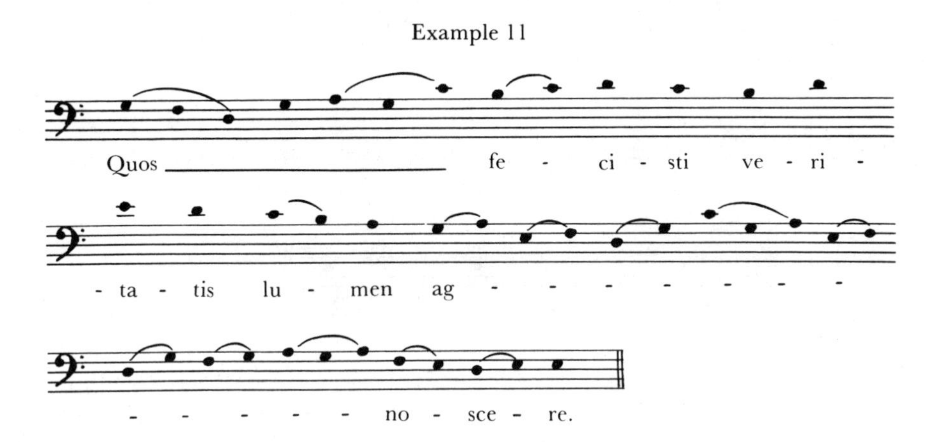

It is beautiful too if, by whatever notes a neume descends, it at once ascends by the same ones, as here:

7. Source: *GS* 215.

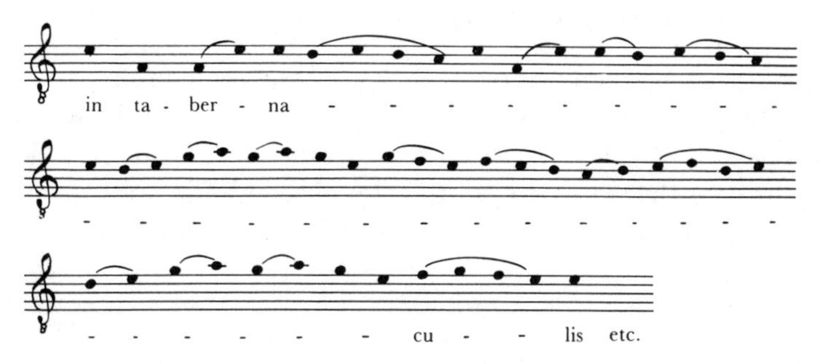

Example 12

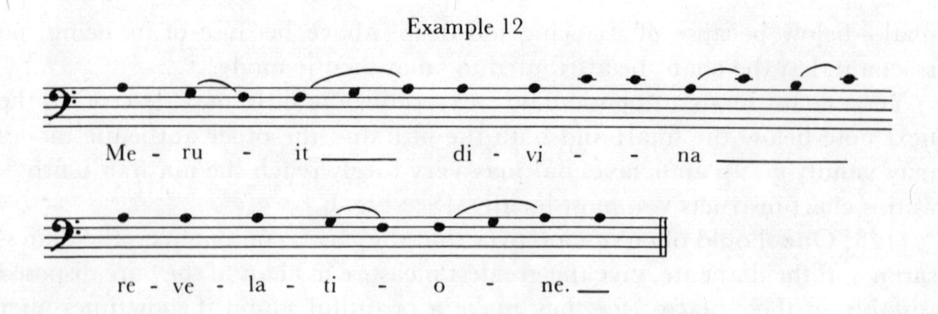

[125] The sound in a chant is likewise excellent if the diatessaron is occasionally varied in that a semiditone or ditone now precedes and now follows it, as is illustrated in this example:

Example 13

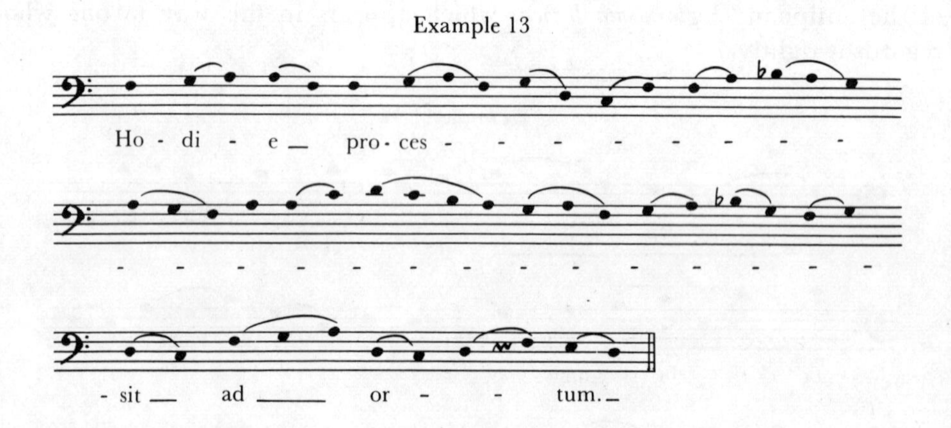

[126] There are also many other excellent ways of ordering melody, all of which we need not explain, lest we bring weariness rather than learning to our readers. Musicians call chants of this kind "studied" [*accurati*] since care is taken with their composition. They also call them "metrical" by analogy, since they are measured off by definite laws in the manner of verses—as are, for example, the Ambrosian.[8]

Chapter 20

How chants can be composed by means of their vowels

[127] Here we shall show yet another method of composition—beautiful indeed, but not used before Guido.[1] First decide for yourself which tone you wish to compose a chant in, then place on your writing tablets five notes with the same number of vowels written in order above them, and proceed to chant systematically as the vowels of the individual syllables guide you, thus:

8. These closing remarks, particularly the reference to "metrical" chants, are illuminated by reference to Guido, chap. 15.

1. *Micrologus*, chap. 17, which is paraphrased here.

Figure 7

a e i o u
DEFGa

u	a													tu	a	u
o	G						so								G	o
i	F		ri			ri		lis			li				F	i
e	E				ve					ter		be			E	e
a	D	Ma		a					Ma				ra		D	a

u	a		sup												a	u
o	G	os								o		o			G	o
i	F			pli		in			ti			ti			F	i
e	E				ces		ces							ne	E	e
a	D							san			ra				D	a

[128] Also a specimen of another mode according to the same method:

Figure 8

u	c													tus			sus			u	c
o	♮														nos	tros				o	♮
i	a				tis			i		ti			mi					ci		i	a
e	G		cer			tes	De				ne	ge							pe	e	G
a	F	Sa		an					Mar											a	F

u	c			dul												bus		u	c
o	♮																	o	♮
i	a		in			ti		im					gi		ti			i	a
e	G	et			gen				pe		semper						te	e	G
a	F						am			tra		fla		tan				a	F

Since this method of composition that we have given appears too rigid, we shall instruct you as to how you can provide yourself with a freer and more flexible way of composing. Put down six or eight notes in order, or even more if you desire, and next to them write the vowels twice, [129] so that you give each note two successive vowels, thus:

i	o	u	a	e	i	o	u
F	G	a	b	c	d	e	f
o	u	a	e	i	o	u	a

Example 14

[130] See to it that the arrangement of vowels that we have presented does not lead you to suppose that they must always be arranged thus. Just as painters and poets are free to undertake whatever they wish, so, of course, anyone composing thus according to the vowels has an equal right to arrange them to his liking in the first place. Also, just as the former must see to it that they complete whatever they have begun, so the latter must take care to maintain to the end the arrangement they began with. For instance, although in the preceding chant I assigned *o* and *i* to the parhypate meson [F], you can place there *e* and *i*, or *a* and *o*, or *a* and *u*, or whatever you wish, provided that you adhere to the plan you have begun with. That this may be clearer, we add as an example a melody based on another arrangement.[2]

e i o u a e i o
C D E F G a b c
i o u a e i o u

Example 15

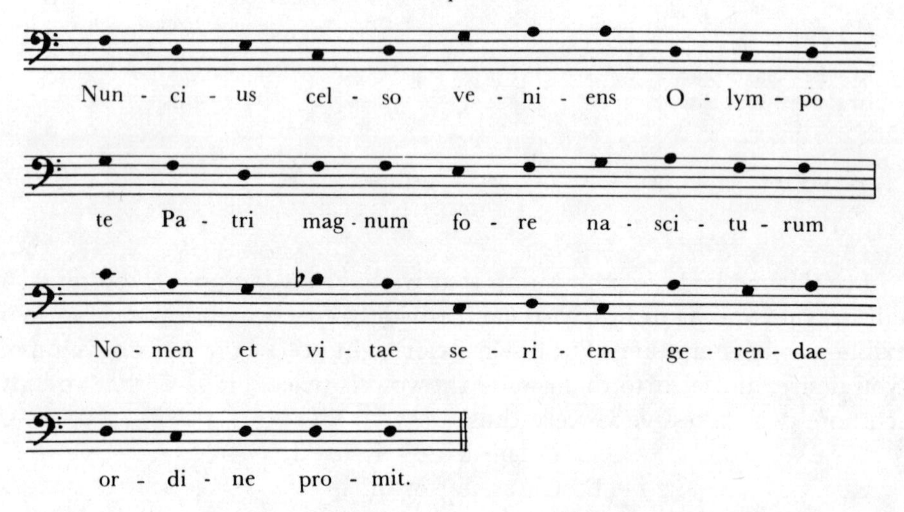

[132] The vowels could be arranged in such fashion in even triple or quadruple rows, unless the resulting excessive mixture impeded the composer. Since chant may be composed from the vowels of its text, as has been shown, and since it is clear that whatever is spoken is based on vowels, Guido was quite right in saying that whatever is spoken may be translated into chant.

Chapter 21

Of what use the neumes are that Guido invented

[133] Lest perhaps it disturb the reader that in the first chapter we charged him to practice singing from musical neumes but have deferred dealing with

2. The text is the second stanza of *Ut queant laxis*. See chap. 1, n. 2.

them as yet, let him note that we did not do this without reason. Unless he first knew how to sing from music, he would be utterly unable to understand the examples adduced for various reasons here and there. There was no need to explain right off why neumes of this kind were invented by Guido, for their justification and usefulness could be sufficiently perceived from what has been dealt with already.

Since in the ordinary neumes the intervals cannot be ascertained, and the chants that are learned from them cannot be securely committed to memory, many inaccuracies creep into them. These Guidonian neumes, on the other hand, indicate all the intervals unambiguously. Not only do they completely obviate error, but, once learned perfectly, they will not allow one to forget how to chant from them. Who, then, would not see their great usefulness?

[134] It can easily be seen how neumes without lines promote error rather than knowledge in the case of virgae, clives, and podati, since they are all placed on one level and no degree of ascent or descent is indicated by them. The result is that everyone makes such neumes go up or down as he himself pleases, and where you sound a semiditone or a diatessaron, another might make a ditone or a diapente at the same place, and if a third person were present, he might disagree with you both.

For one says, "Master Trudo taught me this way"; another rejoins, "But I learned thus from Master Albinus"; and to this a third remarks, "Master Solomon certainly sings far differently." Not to delay you with lengthy circumlocutions, rarely do three men agree about one chant, far less a thousand. Naturally, since everyone prefers his own teacher, there arise as many variations in chanting as there are teachers in the world.

That you may plainly see that chant in unregulated neumes is often corrupted through ignorance, let the antiphon *Collegerunt* be an illustration for you. A great many people make the clivis during the first and the next-to-last syllables [of *Collegerunt*] descend more than is right, that is, making a diapente and beginning the following neume a whole step lower.[1] It is undisputed that from Γ to the lichanos hypaton [D] [135] is a diapente, and that below Γ no note exists, and, furthermore, that no plagal chant ought to go a sixth below its final. Some, too, garble the music of this antiphon in another place by beginning *concilium* on the note with which they end *Pharisei* and commencing the antepenult of the same word lower than they end its first syllable. But he who prefers to submit to the truth of a rule rather than to [136] cling stubbornly to a debased usage ought to sing that chant in this manner:

1. The neumatic notation of the beginning of the example, as printed in *CSM* 1: 136, follows:

Example 16

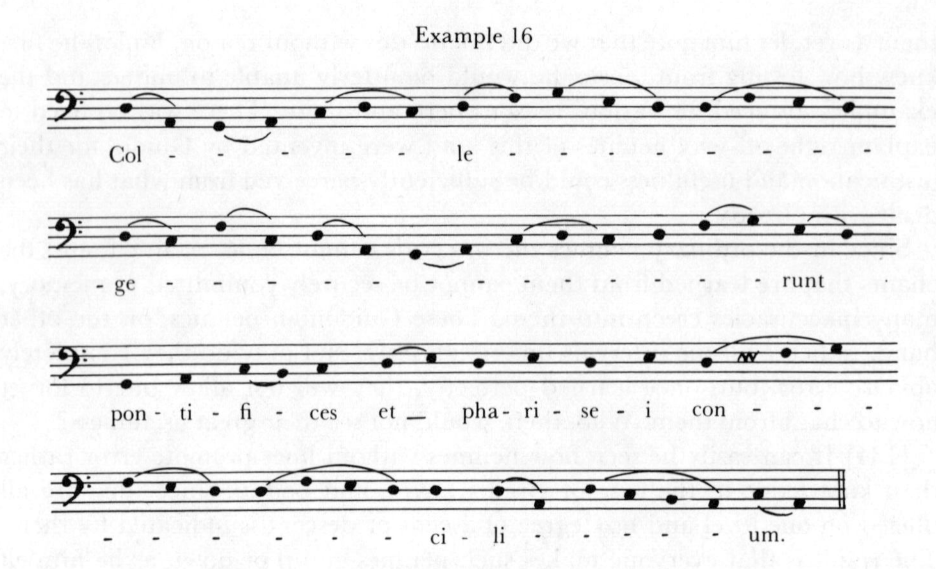

[137] In the communion *Beatus servus* too an error is easily made by performing a single podatus unsuitably. Some correct it thus: they make *Dominus* fall from the trite diezeugmenon [c] to the mese [a], and they begin *invenerit* on the parhypate meson [F] and *super omnia* on the lichanos meson [G]. Others so emend it that they begin *invenerit* as is the custom, but after beginning its penult on the mese [a] they end it on the lichanos meson [G]. Beginning its final syllable on the hypate meson [E], they make it end on the parhypate meson [F]. Then they correct *super omnia* in the same way as do the former. Yet to me it seems an easier correction if the last syllable of *invenerit* is sung to a unison on the lichanos meson [G], as pleases both Guarinus and Stephanus, who are musically discriminating.[2]

2. The "single podatus" on "rit" of *invenerit* (a) would require a half step where there is none in the gamut. Some amend the chant as in (b), others as in (c). John agrees with Guarinus and Stephanus in accepting the version of (d), which is based on *LU* 1203, where it is transposed up a fourth. Guarinus and Stephanus have not been identified.

If anyone protests that semitones are missing at certain points, we rejoin that semitones may not be necessary where it seems to him that they are. Singers from ineptitude often make, among other corruptions of the chant, semitones where they should not be made and now and then omit them where they should not be omitted.

It is obvious that men with harsh and intractable voices avoid semitones as much as possible, while those who have flexible voices relish them greatly—[138] so much so that they sometimes produce them even where they should not be made, as can be seen in many antiphons of the fourth tone, such as *Custodiebant*, *Ex Egypto*, and *Sion renovaberis*. Some go similarly astray in the respond *Conclusit vias meas*, sounding semitones where they are not in place, for example at the words *inimicus insidiator*. A great many bungle the same respond at the end by beginning *animae meae*, which should begin on the mese

[a], on the nete diezeugmenon [e].[3] But we shall discuss chants corrupted by neumes without lines more fully in the next chapter.

Some are in the habit of eking out these neumes by certain marks, by which it is clear that they do not enlighten the singer but ensnare him doubly in error. While there is no certainty in neumes,[4] letters written above them offer no less ambiguity, chiefly because many words of various meanings begin with the same letters, and hence one does not know what [139] they mean. Even if some specific meaning is assigned to each, not all uncertainty is eliminated thereby, since the singer remains uncertain of the interval of ascent or descent. Thus *c* begins various words, such as *cito* [swiftly], *caute* [carefully], and *clamose* [loud]; likewise *l*, such as *leva* [lift up], *leniter* [gently], *lascive* [playfully], *lugubriter* [mournfully]; in the same way *s*, for example *sursum* [on high], *suaviter* [smoothly], *subito* [suddenly], *sustenta* [sustain], *similiter* [similarly], etc.[5]

We can briefly state about musical neumes with lines that these musical neumes lead the singer by a path so true and so easy that even if he wished to he could not go astray. Anyone at all—whether grownup or child—once he has learned four "histories"[6] or the same number of offices by means of the neumes from his precentor, will be able to learn the whole antiphonary and gradual without a teacher.

Unlined neumes, however, as we have shown, cause doubt and error. Even after a singer has by means of them learned from his master the whole Gradual, except for a single office, indeed a single communion, they cannot be of sufficient avail to him that he will know by himself how to sing that one remaining communion. It is clear, therefore, that he who clings to these unlined neumes is a lover of error and falsehood, but he who sticks to musical neumes wishes to hold to the path of certainty and truth.

3. *Animae meae* does not begin on a or e in any surviving source. The passage, *inimicus insidiator*, in the Sarum Antiphoner seems to be the result of emendation to produce John's unwanted semitones on the natural notes (*AS* 204):

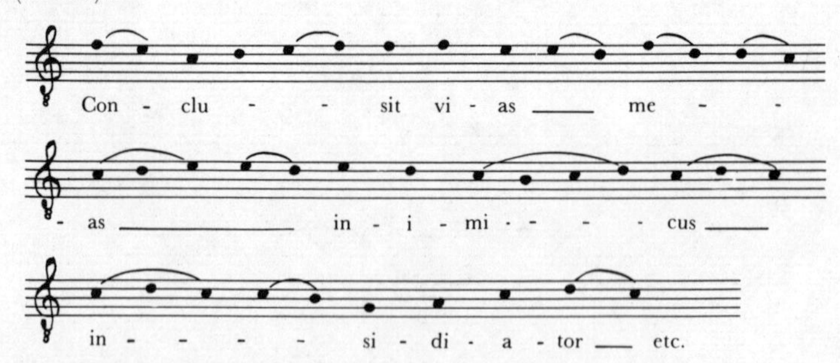

4. That is, no certainty in reading staffless neumes.

5. Some of these letters are found in Notker's epistle, others in a manuscript in Einsiedeln. See Introduction, n. 34.

6. "Histories," i.e., responds connected in early times with narrative lessons (Utto Kornmüller, [abridged translation of] "Der Traktat des Johannes Cottonius über Musik," *Kirchenmusikalisches Jahrbuch* 12 [1888]: p. 19n.).

[140] One should know moreover that music is notated by three methods. One, which was used by musicians of old, is by letters arranged on the monochord.

The second method is by the designation of the intervals, a species of symbol that Hermannus Contractus[7] is said to have invented. It works in this way. E indicates that the pitches are equal. S denotes the semitone. τ represents the whole tone. τ combined with S signifies the semiditone thus: $\overset{S}{\tau}$. Double τ announces the ditone, so: $\overset{\tau}{\tau}$. Capital D proclaims the diatessaron. Δ represents the diapente, and if you add an S to it, it denotes the semitone-plus-diapente by this symbol: $\overset{S}{\Delta}$; while if you add τ, it indicates the whole-tone-plus-diapente in this manner: $\overset{\tau}{\Delta}$; but if you wish to designate the diapason, combine Δ and capital D thus: $\overset{D}{\Delta}$. Furthermore, each one of these signs without a dot signifies ascent, but with a dot,[8] descent. All these are quite fully exhibited by the melody composed, it is said, by Hermann himself, *E voces unisonas aequat* etc., except that it does not make an ascent of an octave.

The third method of notation was invented by Guido. This is by means of virgae, clives, quilismata, puncta, podati, and other such [141] signs, located in the proper ranks, which a sign placed in the margin makes very explicit. Whoever wishes to be quickly and successfully initiated into the singing of music written by this method should know that there are three tasks he must labor at. The first task is that one scrupulously consider which and how many syllables have been assigned to each note. Next he must take no less pains to notice precisely which notes have been placed on lines and which in spaces.

The third concern in singing is that the various arrangements of the notes may lead the singer astray, which can easily be avoided if one keeps very carefully in mind that every F[9] is represented by red and every C[10] by yellow. The colors are disposed in five places according to the five semitones. But some, if the color is lacking, place a dot at the beginning of the line in place of the red.

We urge such great attention to these two notes, namely F and C—or rather the colors by which they are indicated—because by them the other notes are regulated, and if they are moved from their places the others are moved correspondingly. But if these neumes lack colors or letters, they are like a well without a rope.

7. It is remarkable that John should have known of this notation, which was short-lived and geographically confined. His knowledge of it is one of the strongest evidences that John worked near Reichenau. The notation is described in *Cantilena de IX intervallis*, the text of which with an English translation is given in Ellinwood, *Musica Hermanni Contracti*, p. 9. Aside from MSS containing Hermann's didactic songs, such as Rochester, Sibley Music Library, MS 14 (Accession no. 149667), and Vienna, Nationalbibliothek, MSS 2502 and 51, it is found only in the *Frutolfi breviarum*, Munich, MS 14965, and Paris, Bibliothèque nationale, MS lat. 1121.

8. A dot beneath it.

9. I.e., every F-line.

10. I.e., every C-line.

Chapter 22

On rejecting corrupt usage and on the extra differentiae *of some modes*

[142] We wish now to consider certain chants that have long since been corrupted by unlined neumes and to urge strongly that the corrupted usage be cast out which has debased either these or any other chants whatsoever and has been preserved to this day. Since it is established that the one Lord is pleased by one faith, one baptism, and complete unanimity of morals, who would not believe that he also is offended by the manifold disagreement of singers, who wrangle, not reluctantly or unwittingly, but willfully? Therefore it has not befitted us, who by God's favor have come to know the right way of singing, to tolerate error; nor should we be greatly concerned if certain foolish singers, stubborn in their faults, do not give way to the truth, so long as we can bring it about that some of sound judgment forgo their errors and freely reform. Yet we have used such great moderation in the correction of chants that revision, being infrequent, will not weary the reader, and that in emendation they will not depart far from the accustomed usage.

One must of course realize that whatever is sung wrongly goes wrong either at the beginning or in the middle or at the end. Thus chant [143] is sometimes corrupted at the beginning in that it either does not begin on the right note or, beginning on the right note, it is taken too far down or up by the undisciplined voice of the singer.

In the middle, too, or at the end, chant is very often spoiled by the unsuitable sound of some ascent or descent; we give below specimens of each. Different singers begin the respond *Ego pro te rogavi* in different places—some on the hypate meson [E], some on the lichanos meson [G], and some on the mese [a]. Realizing partway through that something is amiss, they blame the chant for being wrong and strive to emend it. Yet if it takes its start on the paramese [♮], it runs regularly and without a hitch to its final. Thus:

Example 17

E - go ___ pro te ___ ro - ga - - -

- vi ___ Pe - - - - tre. ___ etc.

℣ Ca - - ro ___ et san - guis.

[144] Error crops up likewise in the middle of a chant, as in the respond *Bethlehem civitas*, which ought to be emended in two places, that is, so that the last syllable of *dominator* begins on the parhypate meson [F], and *in terra* starts on the paranete diezeugmenon [d], in this way:

Example 18

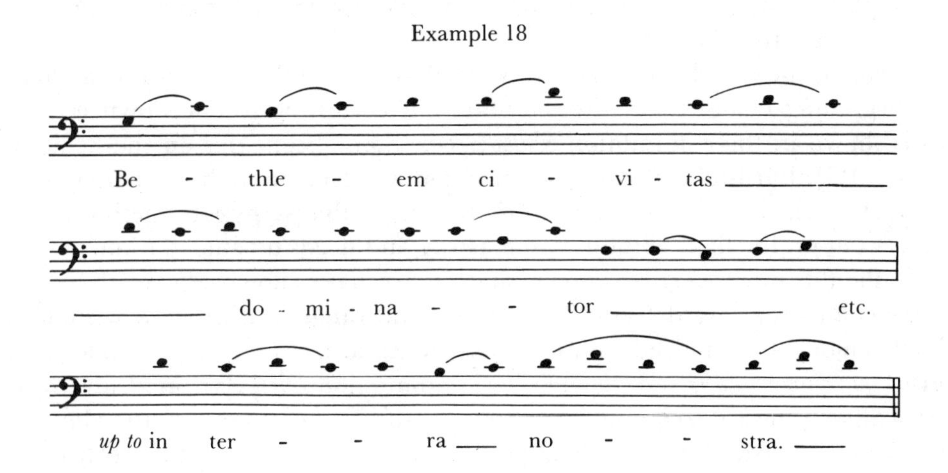

[145] At the end of chants, too, errors are made by some, as in the respond *Mane surgens Jacob*. Although this is assuredly in the fourth tone, some inexperienced singers end it on the lichanos meson [G], and they even incongruously add to it a verse in the fourth tone, whereas it should rather be sung in this way:

Example 19

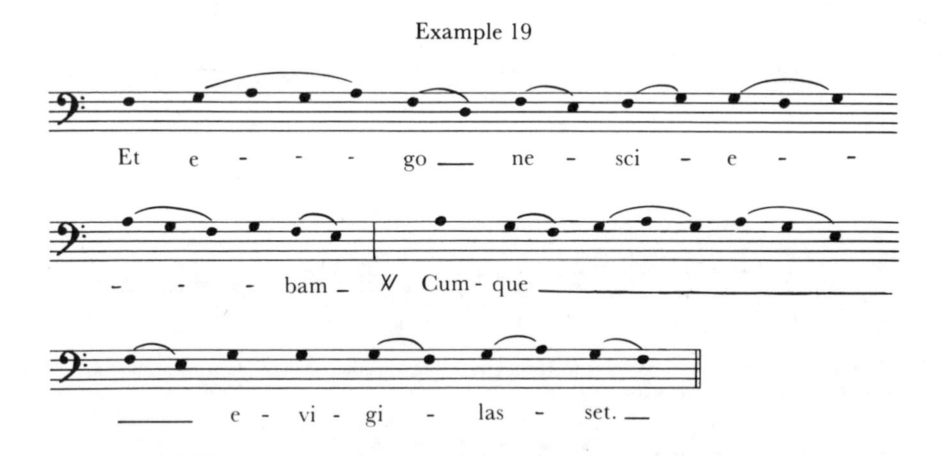

[146] Some indeed end the antiphon *Pater manifestavi* on the lichanos hypaton [D] and assign it to the Dorian, although it is Hypolydian. This error is easily

avoided by those who sing *Alleluia* to a unison on the parhypate meson [F].[1]

Likewise, a great many untrained performers err in the antiphon *Simile est regnum coelorum decem virginibus* by [147] ending it on the parhypate hypaton [C], not wishing to sing *alleluia*, as though it were a great crime if an alleluia were performed after Pentecost with an antiphon or other chants. The same error places those in the wrong who end the offertory *Posuisti domine* on the mese [a] and omit the alleluia.

It should be noted, too, that, as we said above, one often corrupts a chant by beginning it, not on a suitable note, but according to one's own notion, as is shown in the communion *Scapulis suis*. Some begin this on the lichanos meson [G], but finding that it suffers from a defect, they think it should be corrected. If, on the other hand, it is begun on the parhypate meson [F], it comes out on the final without going astray and needs no emendation.

It should, moreover, be known that, as we have shown above, there are some chants that are defective in their natural range, but proceed without a hitch among the kindred notes [*affines*], like the introit *Exaudi domine vocem meam qua clamavi ad te, alleluia* etc.[2] The communion *Dicit Andreas* also is to be sung among the kindred notes, according to those who assign it to the Hypolydian, but according to those who [148] attribute it to the plagal tetrardus it goes well in its natural range.

There are, too, some chants that can be sung neither in their natural range nor among the kindred notes. For such we give this advice, that they be

1. Two different versions of the antiphon survive: (a) *LU* 844, and (b) *WA* 146.

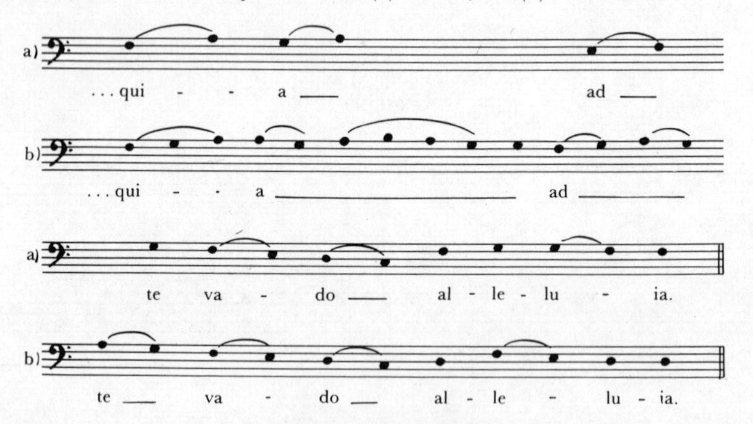

2. The opening half step is the problem. If sung in mode 1, rather than as shown transposed, it would require an $E^{\flat}$ on the third note. Source: *LU* 854.

emended within their natural range. If, however, they are much disordered and can be emended more easily in the kindred range, let them be rearranged there, as for example this offertory [*In die solemnitatis*]:[3]

Example 20

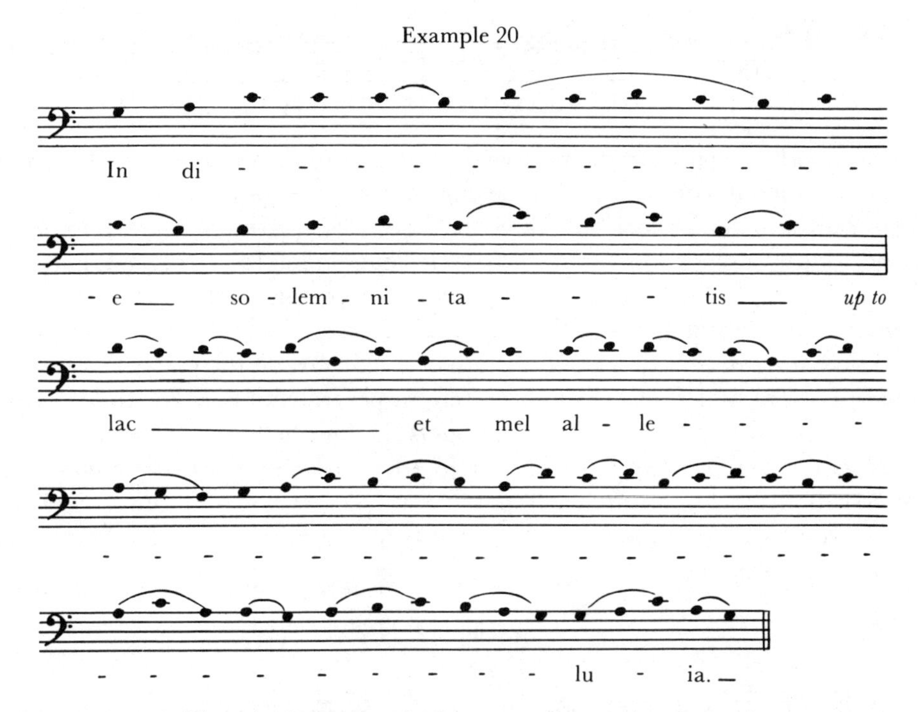

The respond *Hic qui advenit* should be so arranged that it begins on the mese [a], and that *habens* starts at the same pitch and ends on the [149] paranete diezeugmenon [d]. But in the respond *Viri impii*, too, care should be taken that at *et rei facti sunt* it be emended thus:

Example 21

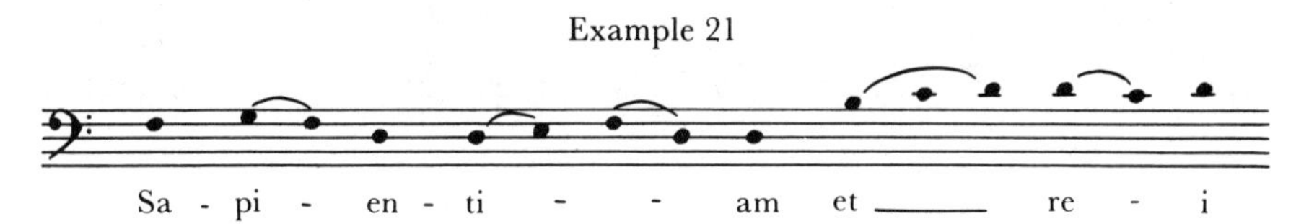

3. As John's example ends on the natural final rather than the cofinal, it must represent an unemended version. Modern chant books, e.g. *LU* 798, classify the melody in mode 1 and it ends on D. It is considerably emended, as in the opening:

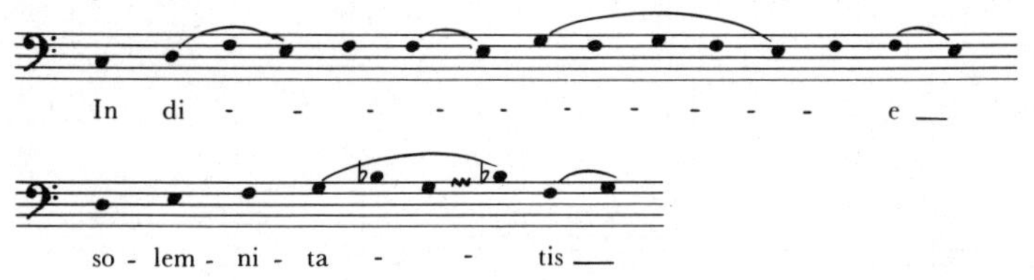

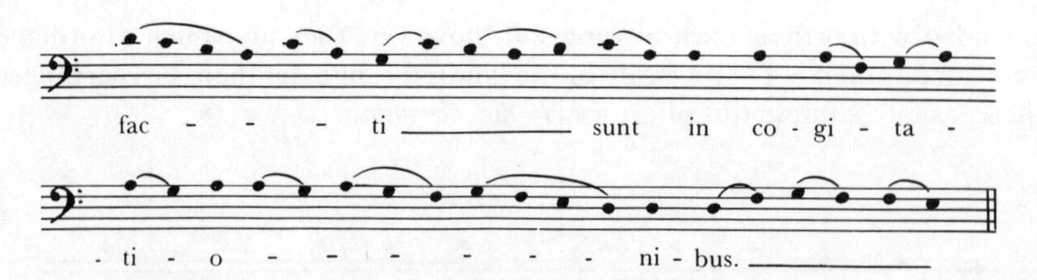

The respond *Domine ne in ira* also needs emendation in the middle. [150] For *Miserere*, which in corrupted usage begins on the lichanos hypaton [D], should begin on the lichanos meson [G]. Some, too, corrupt the respond *Egregie dei martyr*, for they do not end *dei* on the trite diezeugmenon [c] and do not perform *Ecce* unobtrusively. In the respond *Aegypte noli flere*, also, an error is made by some, who raise *flere* beyond the mese [a]. In the gradual *Ad dominum*, too, some do wrong in that they do not begin *dum tribularer* on the parhypate meson [F]. In the gradual *Esto mihi in deum*, too, some are confused, for they do not begin *protectorem* on the lichanos meson [G]. Bear in mind too that in the offertory *Confirma hoc deus*, *Confirma* should not be taken up above the mese [a], but *deus* should begin on the parhypate meson [F]. In the offertory *Oravi deum meum* as well, emendation is needed in two places, namely, at the beginning and at *super*, as is shown here:

Example 22

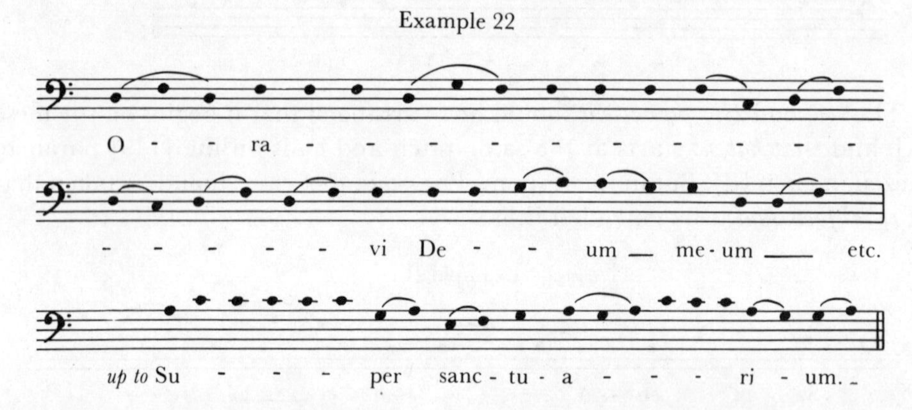

[151] In the communion *Cantabo domino* whoever does not begin *Qui bona* on the parhypate hypaton [C] sings wrongly. Furthermore the communion *Potum meum* is sung more correctly if *cum fletu* and *et ego* begin on [152] the parhypate hypaton [C]. And the communion *Domus mea* should begin thus:[4]

Example 23

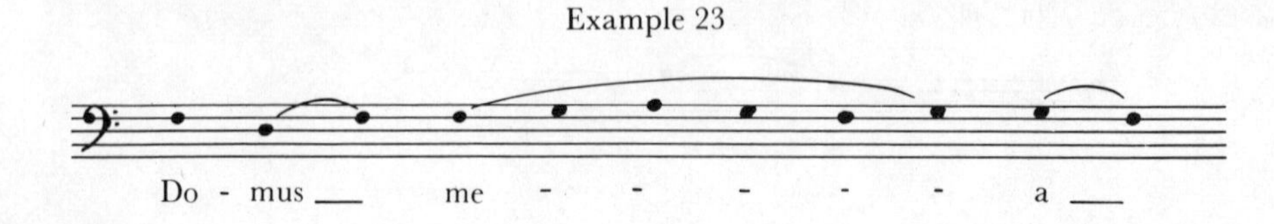

But let it suffice for the present that these very few chants are corrected. Further on we shall emend in the Tonary some others that may also come to mind.

[153] Now, however, before we come to give examples of the modes, their extra *differentiae* must be discussed. Since the term *differentia* is used in many ways, we must first make clear what it is we call the "*differentiae* of the modes." In the various tones, when certain neumes are with reason permitted for the *saeculorum amen*, we term them *differentiae*.

It should be known that of the *differentiae* which are classed under the various tones, some are fitting and necessary, others fitting but not necessary, and still others neither fitting nor necessary—or rather, they simply are not *differentiae*! We call those *differentiae* fitting and necessary which the customary repertory of singers contains as established by composers of old. Those are termed fitting but not necessary which are added by reason—not of necessity, but simply of decoration—as is evident, for example, in the antiphon *O beatum pontificem*. Although this should have the second *differentia* of the authentic protus, a great many singers, ignoring this, fit it to a *differentia* as follows:

Example 24

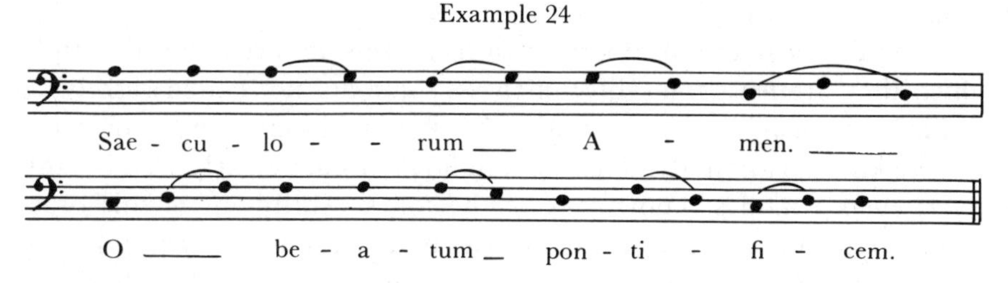

4. The first three notes were probably sung F–E♭–F, which John emended to F–D–F, while other compilers transposed the offending phrase up a step, for example (a) Munich, Bayerische Staatsbibliothek, MS 2599 (in the text of this treatise), (b) *LU* 1253.

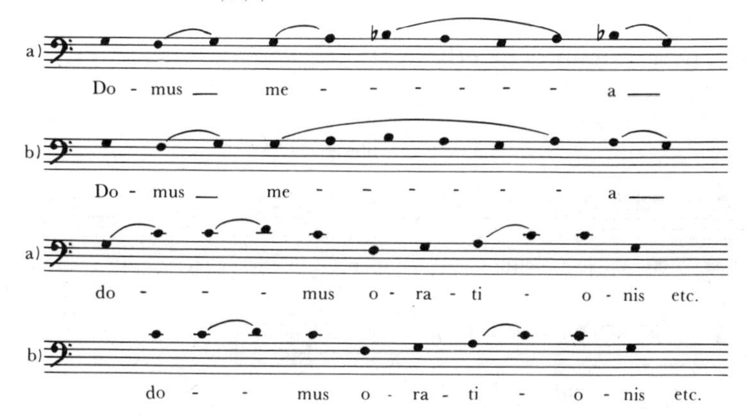

[154] Those are neither fitting nor necessary which are suited, not to the correct tenor of the mode, but to the fancy of the singers, like this one:

Example 25

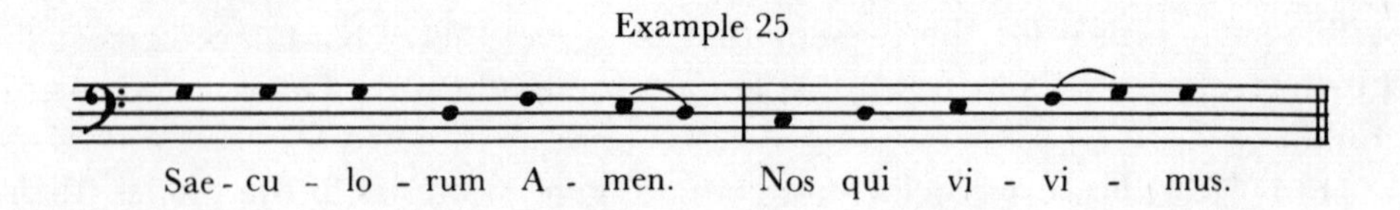

As for these "*differentiae*"—and some maintain that they are *differentiae*—I say, not that they are unnecessary, but simply that they are not *differentiae*. That is, [they arise] when a single *saeculorum amen*, no part of which is logically diversified, is prefixed to many chants having diverse beginnings.

Again, some quite pointlessly make two *differentiae* for the antiphons *Tecum principium* and *Biduo vivens*, although they are properly of the first tone. If the [155] different beginnings of chants determined the number of *differentiae*, there would be many more *differentiae* in the Hypolydian, Mixolydian, and Hypomixolydian than there now are.

All this will become sufficiently clear in our Tonary. But we wish the reader to realize that we shall deal only with those *differentiae* that we have pronounced both fitting and necessary; the others, since we deem them superfluous, we shall omit.

Nor should it be overlooked that most transgressions are in ferial antiphons, in which they are least tolerable; of these, some are not ended rightly, some are led into [*reguntur*] by incongruous *differentiae*, and some are performed with both these kinds of anomaly. These manifold errors are clearly seen by anyone who has even a modest knowledge of the tones. Antiphons of this type are corrupted by rustic and uneducated clerics as a result of their careless reading of ordinary neumes, as is seen in the antiphon *Facti sumus*. This has been so distorted that it can in no wise be sung to the monochord with the *saeculorum amen* that is customarily joined to it, one or the other proving inadequate. So that this corruption may be more clearly seen, we add below the said antiphon notated in unlined neumes together with the *saeculorum amen:*

Example 26

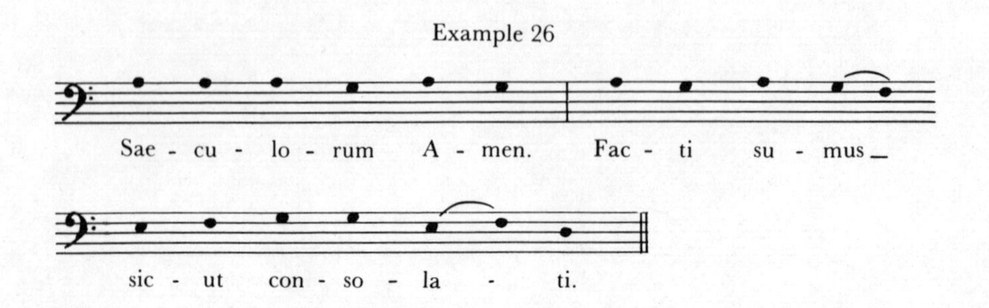

[156] But most assuredly it is authentic tritus and should end on the parhypate meson [F].[5]

Other antiphons too that are corrupted in this manner can be emended by a sufficiently easy change—if only, as Berno says, a corrupt usage could in any way be expunged from the mouths of singers.

Chapter 23
On diaphony, that is, organum

[157] We now wish to discuss diaphony briefly and succinctly, so as to satisfy the reader's eagerness about this subject as well, as much as we can. Diaphony is the sounding of different but harmonious notes, which is carried on by at least two singers, so that while one holds to the original [*rectam*] melody, another may range aptly among other tones, and at each breathing point both may come together on the same note or at the octave. This method of singing is popularly called "organum," because the human voice sounding tones different but compatible shows a resemblance to the instrument that is called the organ. Diaphony means "twofold sound" or "difference of sound."

Before we give rules for "organizing," we wish to mention a few things about melodic motion, as its consideration is appropriate to our discussion. Since organum is produced by consonances, and the disposition of these is varied according to the melodic motion, there is no doubt that the inclusion of the latter is advantageous at this point.

Melodic motion[1] is by arsis or thesis, that is, by ascent or descent. [158] Every neume except the single or repetitive ones is formed by the twofold motion of arsis and thesis. By a single neume we mean a virgula or punctum, and by a repetitive neume what Berno calls a distropha or a tristropha. Now arsis and thesis are sometimes combined with themselves, as arsis to arsis and thesis to thesis, and sometimes to each other, that is, arsis to thesis and thesis to arsis.

Furthermore, this combination is made partly from like motion, partly from unlike. The melodic figures in the aforesaid combinations are unlike whenever one has more or fewer notes than the other[2] or notes closer together or farther apart.

In a combination made of either like or unlike elements, one finds a melodic figure either placed above another,[3] that is, located among higher notes; or

5. None of the available sources end the chant on F; rather, on D, evidently preserving the "corrupt" version.

1. What follows in the next three paragraphs paraphrases Guido, *Micrologus*, chap. 16.

2. Or one might interpret thus: "traverses (*habet*) more . . . tones," i.e., that one interval contains more seconds than the other, whereas "closer together and farther apart" compares intervals containing the same number of seconds but of different quality, e.g., major with minor thirds. The continuation (*Micrologus*, chap. 16) of the passage from which John is quoting shows, I think, that Guido must have had in mind all three elements: number of notes per melodic figure (*motus*), number of seconds per interval, and quality of interval.

3. I.e., the preceding melodic figure.

placed below, that is, located among lower notes; or placed beside, whenever the beginning of the following figure is on the same note as was the end of the preceding; or placed within, when one figure is located within the preceding and is both less low and less high; or mixed, that is, placed partly within and partly below, or above, or beside. If I gave instances of all these, I should by an undue length irk rather than benefit the reader, especially since anyone who is an earnest student of chant can discern all this for himself.

[159] The same neumes vary in their movement according to the different qualities of the modes. We wish to add an example of this, so that not only may the student of organum profit from it, but whoever wishes to compose a new chant may have a model therein for forming melodic lines.

Example 27

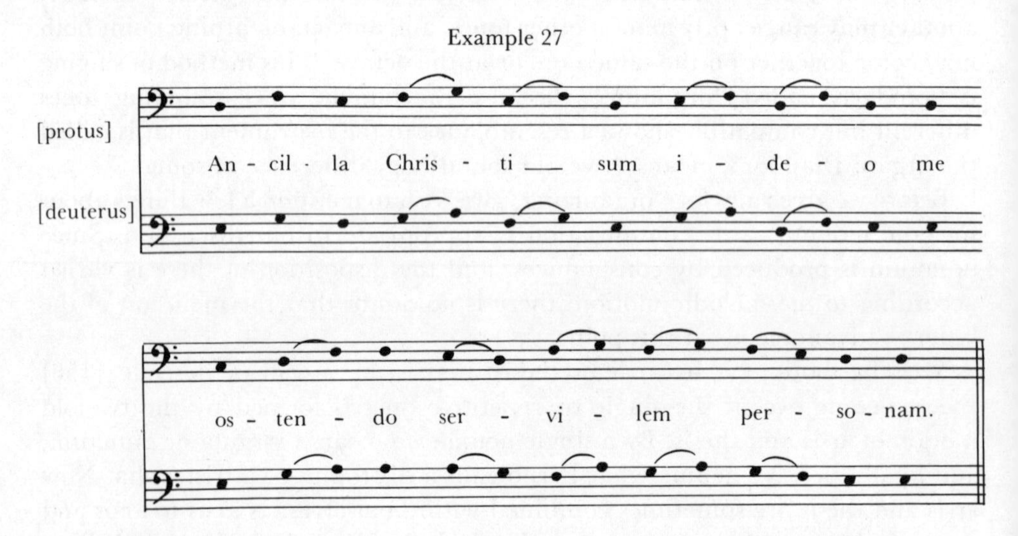

Now take note that if you sing a chant of the protus in the range of the deuterus with a similar arrangement of the notes,[4] you will see a very slight discrepancy. The same thing regularly occurs between the tritus and the tetrardus.

With this compendious parenthesis let us return to diaphony. Different musicians practice this differently. The simplest method for it is when the various melodic progressions are borne carefully in mind, [160] so that wherever there is an ascent in the original melody, there is at that point a descent in the organal part and vice versa. The performer of the organal part [*organizans*] must take care that if the original melody pauses on a low note, he makes a diapason with that singer on a high note, but if the original melody pauses on a high note, he makes a concord of a diapason on a low note, whereas he meets with a perfect unison a chant that makes pauses on or around the mese [a].

4. I.e., with the corresponding scale degrees of the deuterus. (Note that in the above example this is not always done.)

One should take heed, too, that the organum be so fashioned that by turns it arrives now at a unison, now at a diapason, but more often and more fitly at a unison. Although what we have said is clear to an attentive reader, still we wish as a kindness to offer a small example.

Example 28

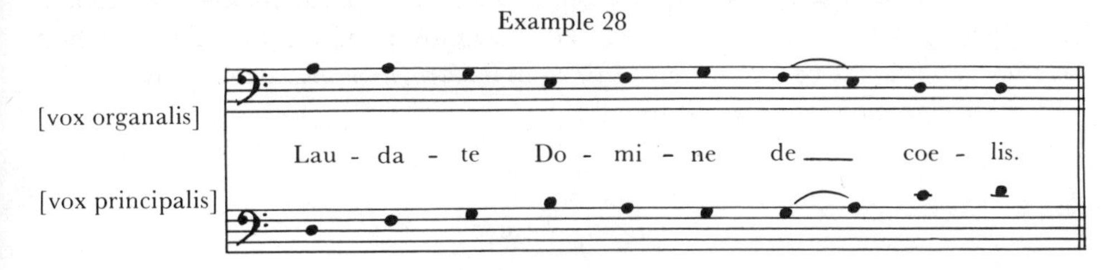

You should take note, too, that although I have set a syllabic [*simplex*] organum against syllabic motion, it is allowable for anyone making organum to double or triple the syllabic progressions[5] if he wishes, or [161] to build them up suitably in any way whatever. May this little that we have said about diaphony suffice.

[Preface to the Tonary]

As I am about to give examples of the modes in all respects, I do not wish to leave undiscussed the question some ask concerning the order of the *differentiae*. Some ask whether there is any plan to the order of the *differentiae*, that is, why they have the order they do. Now I find no reason for this but custom alone, nor have I discovered one written by any musician. As for some saying that they are arranged in the order of the antiphons in the antiphonary, even an idiot can see that is not so.

I have also made a point of not omitting this: that is seems to me that those who decreed that the principal *saeculorum amen*s of all modes end with a neume of one note did better than those who arranged them otherwise. For the former give the singer some assurance, the latter none at all.

Lest anyone think I am going to say anything about the etymology of the names of the items of the office, such as the responses and the antiphons, I decline right now to do so. For it is enough for me if I can cope fully with what I have planned. I direct whoever wishes to know these things to go to the book of Isidore that is entitled *Etymologies*[6] or to [162] the useful work of Amalarius.[7]

I also refuse to arrange my Tonary in Berno's way,[8] that is, to write down first the *nonannoeane* for each mode singly, or to include the *differentiae* that I censured

5. I.e., to have two or three or more notes per syllable, either in all parts or in one part against single notes in the other. This sentence has also been interpreted as referring to the doubling and tripling of the musical lines.

6. *Etym.* 6. 19, *De officiis.*

7. Amalarius, *De ecclesiasticis officiis* and *De ordine antiphonarii*, in J. P. Migne, *Patrologiae cursus completus: Series latina* (Paris, 1844–55), 105: 985ff. and 1243ff., and in J. M. Hanssens, *Amalarii episcopi opera omnia liturgica* (1948), vol. 2 (under the title *Liber officialis*) and vol. 3.

8. Berno of Reichenau, *Tonarius*, in *GS* 2: 79–91. See *Huglo*, pp. 274–76 for passages omitted by Gerbert.

above as superfluous, or to gather together all the antiphons associated with each *saeculorum amen*—the more so as prolixity is wearisome and a very few examples will suffice for the reader who has advanced thus far.

Yet I shall give compendious examples of all the chants of the office except for the little chants which above we termed "formulas of the modes." As I have already given them, there is no need to do so again. Having, then, first touched on these points, let us examine the principal *saeculorum amens* of all the modes and their *differentiae*, as was planned.

John's Tonary

Chapter 24

The first tone

[163] The principal *saeculorum amen* of the first tone leads into [*regit*] antiphons beginning on the lichanos hypaton [D], on the parhypate meson [F], or on the lichanos meson [G] thus:[1]

Example 29

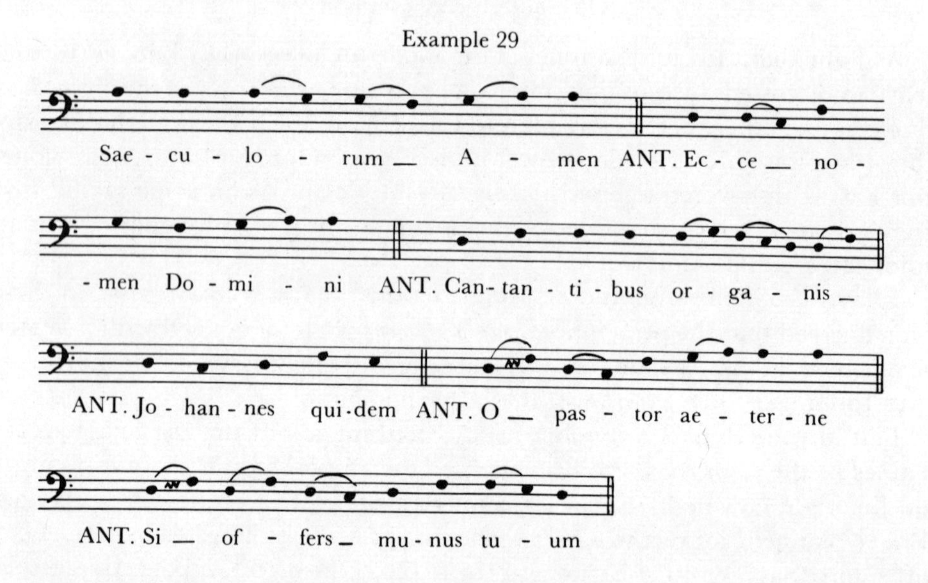

[164] Some prefer to assign the last two antiphons and those like them to the second *differentia* on account of the lengthening of the quilisma, but this classification is not to be followed.

1. The musical examples in the Tonary are those given in Leipzig, University Library, MS 79, early twelfth century, formerly in the Cistercian Abbey in Pforta and St. Mary's Cistercian Abbey in Altzelle. They are transcribed from *CSM* 1. Additional chant incipits occurring in Erfurt, MSS Amplon. 93 and Amplon. 94, both fourteenth century, are not included but may be found in *CSM* 1.

Example 30

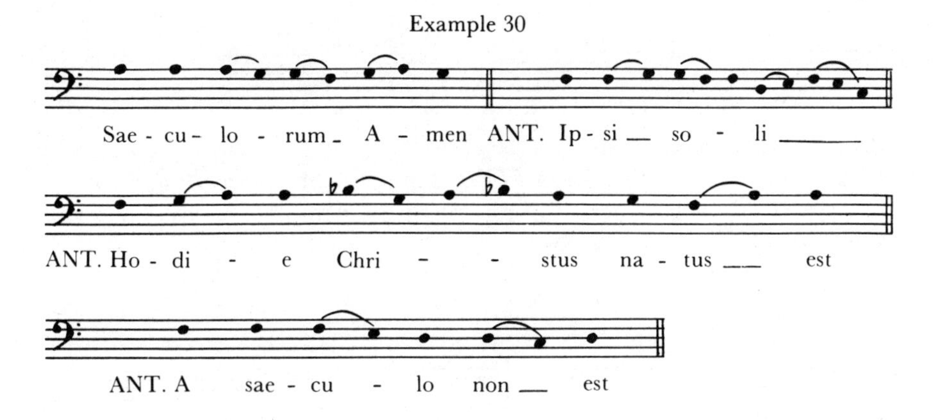

These last two antiphons fit well enough into the sixth mode if they are ended on its final.

Example 31

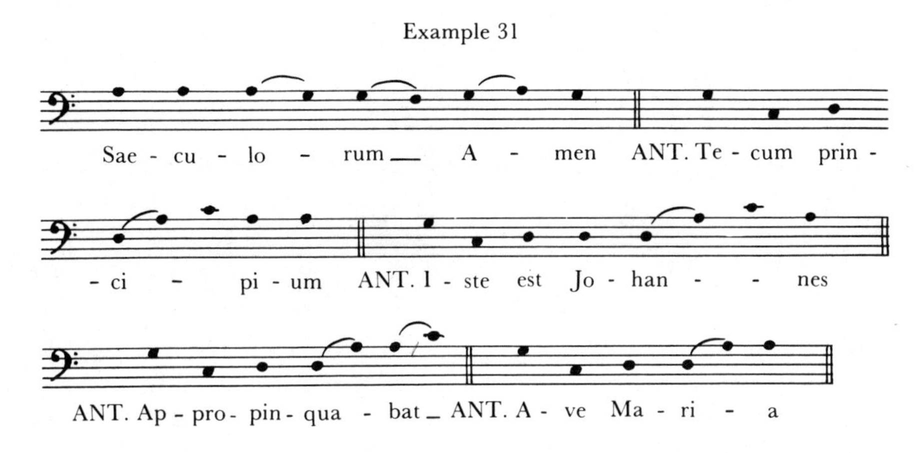

Some fit more *differentiae* to this mode, others fewer, as they like. But there are six that are in more frequent use and are not judged superfluous. The first of these fits [*recipit*] antiphons beginning on the lichanos hypaton [D] with an immediate fifth, or else beginning below the final and at once rising a fifth from the final, as is shown in these examples:

Example 32

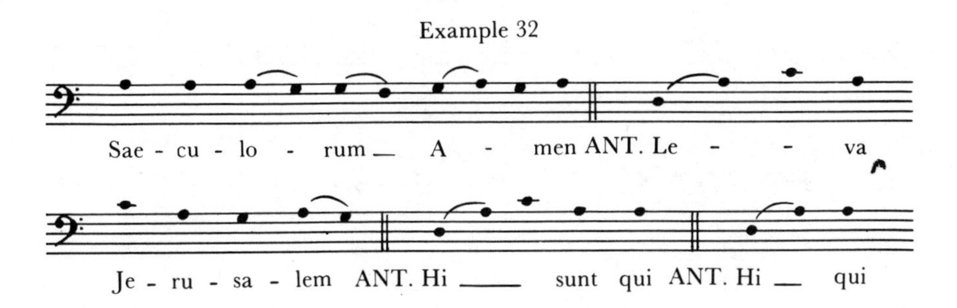

[165] [Also they fit the] antiphon *Mulieres* and the antiphon *Beatus iste*.

The second *differentia* fits antiphons beginning on the parhypate hypaton [C] without the fifth, such as these:

Example 33

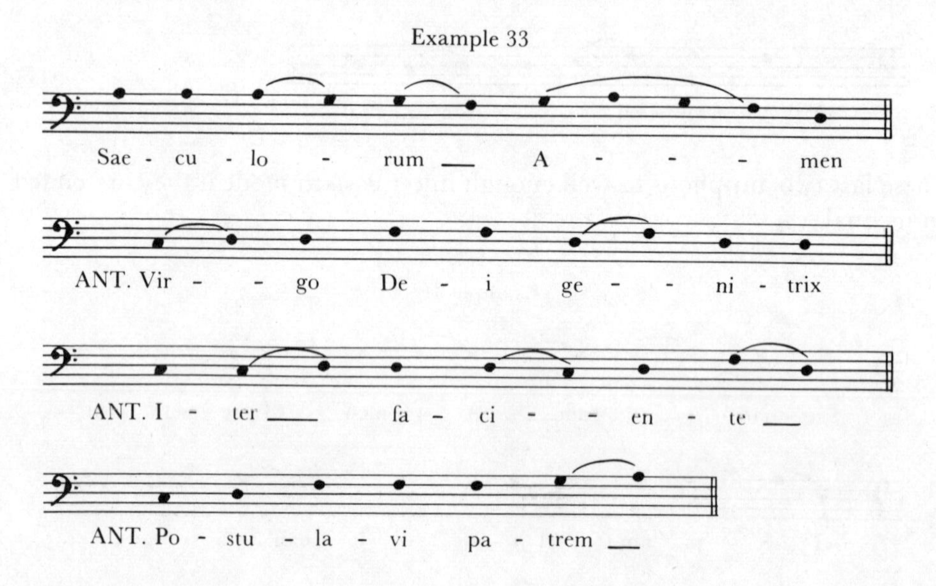

This last antiphon is sung by some stupid folk in the fourth tone.

The third *differentia* fits antiphons rising a ditone from the parhypate meson [F], then descending a whole tone and again ascending a whole tone, even if a unison intervenes. Examples:

Example 34

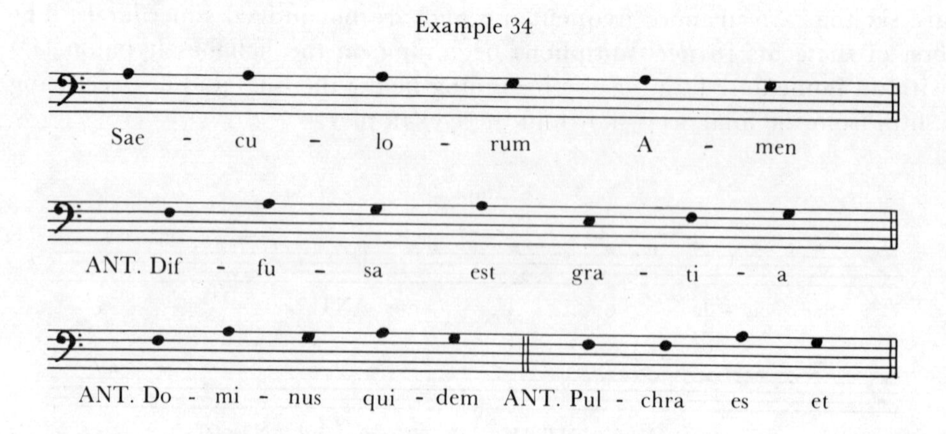

[166] The fourth *differentia* fits antiphons ascending stepwise from the parhypate meson [F] to the mese [a], like these:

Example 35

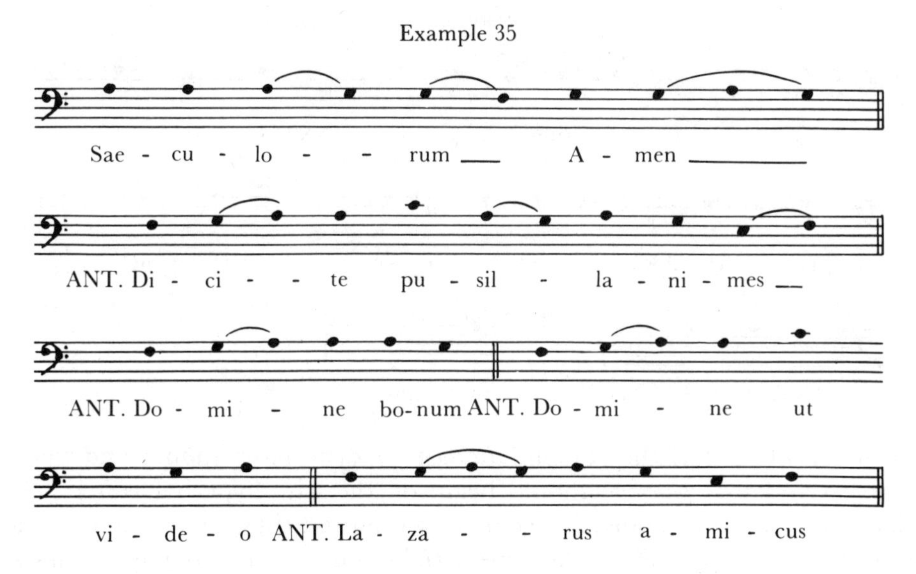

The fifth *differentia* fits antiphons descending stepwise from the parhypate meson [F] to the final, like these:

Example 36

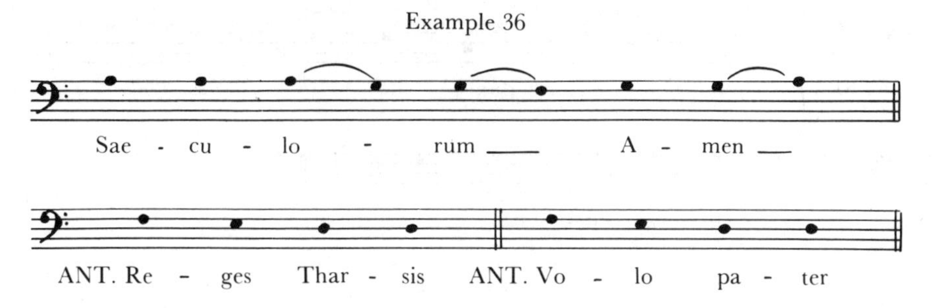

[167] The sixth *differentia* fits antiphons beginning on the mese [a]. The *saeculorum amen* of this *differentia* differs from that of the preceding one, according to Berno, in that the *saeculorum amen* of the preceding one has at the end a double [*connexum*] podatus, while that of the present, a single one. But this difference seems inadequate, for whoever cares to consider the point carefully will be able to see—as it is obvious—that not all syllables fit the sound of the double podatus, and that instead of the double podatus a torculum is the sound best [preceding the initial] syllables of a great many [antiphons],[2] whereby the fourth *differentia* becomes the same as the fifth. Therefore, one

2. Literally, "the torculum sounds in a great many syllables."

should rather follow those who end the *saeculorum amen* of the fifth *differentia* by a single podatus and that of the sixth by a virgula, thus:

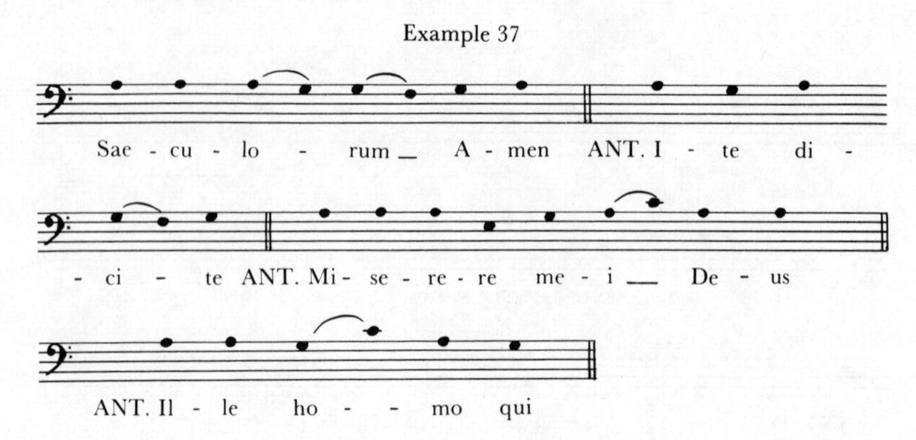

Berno considers that the respond *Factum est dum tolleret* should end on the mese [a] and that *pater mi* should begin on the trite hyperbolaeon [f]. But since it should be emended, it seems to me more fitting that it be emended to the natural final. This can be done if *Heliseus* is begun on the hypate meson [E], thus:[3]

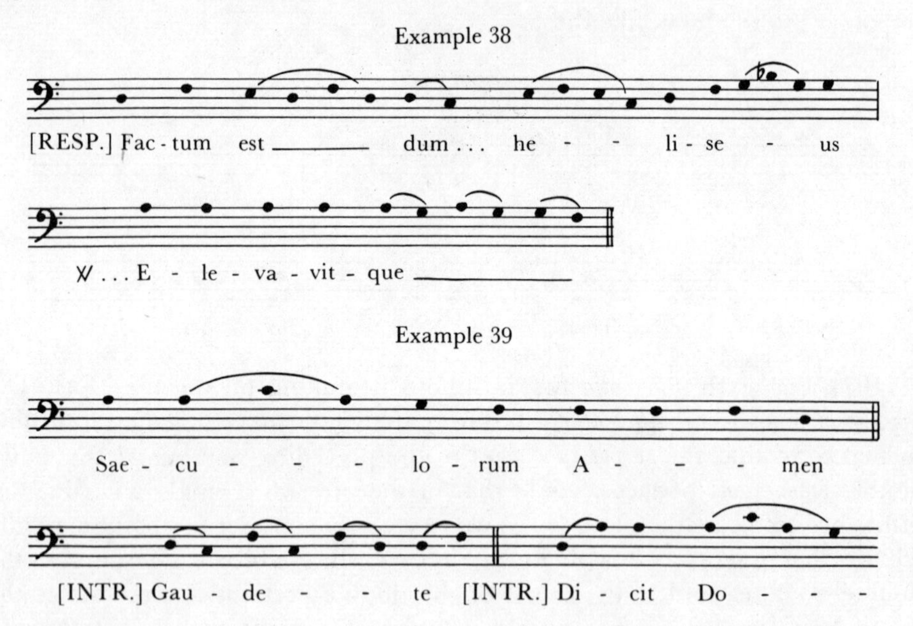

3. In *GS* 2: 74b, Berno says only that this respond begins regularly, ascends a tenth illegally, and ends on the cofinal, a, instead of its final, D. *LA* 272 and *WA* 167 begin *pater mi* on a—which suggests that Berno may have done so on e (if not on f, as John says)—and continue untransposed, ending on D, as John wishes. Since John speaks of beginning *Heliseus* on E (*LA* and *WA* begin on D—as do the musical examples in two out of three MSS of John's text), this may well be where Berno began transposing up a fifth.

[169] In this [*Christus resurgens*] some mistakenly sing a semitone on the first syllable of *moritur*, though it should rather be performed with a semiditone. And *ultra* too should end with a whole tone or a semiditone, not with a semitone. Some ignorant singers even end this alleluia with a semitone. Those who make the *Alleluia Nonne cor nostrum* end by a semitone and not by a semiditone are guilty of the same fault.

Example 41

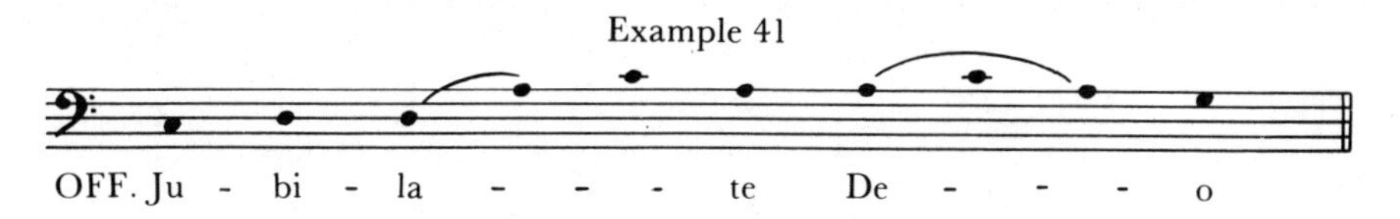

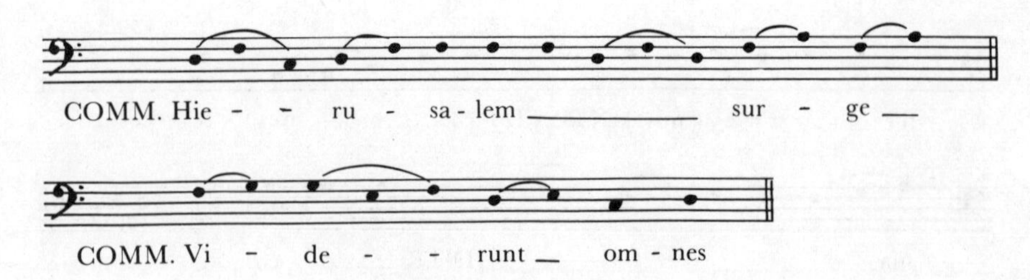

The second tone

Antiphons with diverse beginnings fit the second mode, such as these:

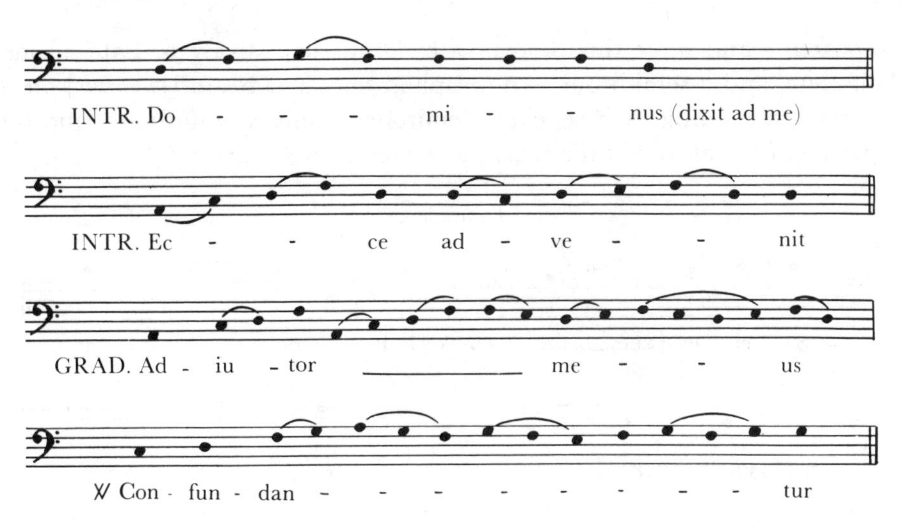

[170] This gradual [*Adiutor meus*], like almost all the others, disregards the lawful range.

Example 43

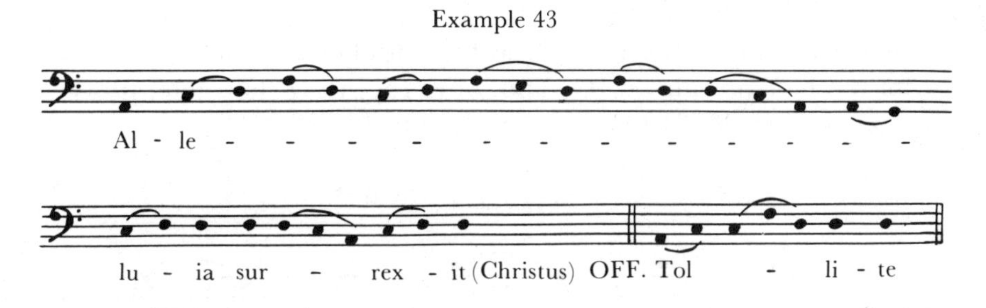

[171] This offertory [*Tollite*] is customarily sung wrongly at the end, whereas legitimately it should be sung thus:

Example 44

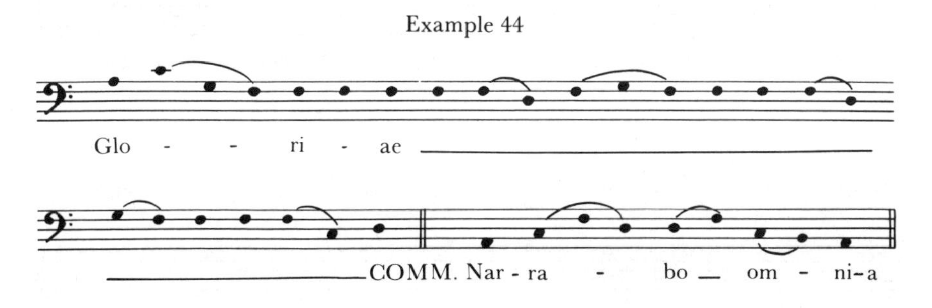

Chapter 25

The third tone

[172] The principal *saeculorum amen* of the third mode leads into antiphons descending a whole tone from the hypate meson [E]—even if the first note

is repeated—and after this descent ascending successively a diatessaron, a whole tone, and a semiditone. An antiphon may also begin [*invenitur*] on the same note, ascending by a repeated semitone, falling a semiditone, and then ascending in the aforesaid manner. Examples of these [are]:

Example 45

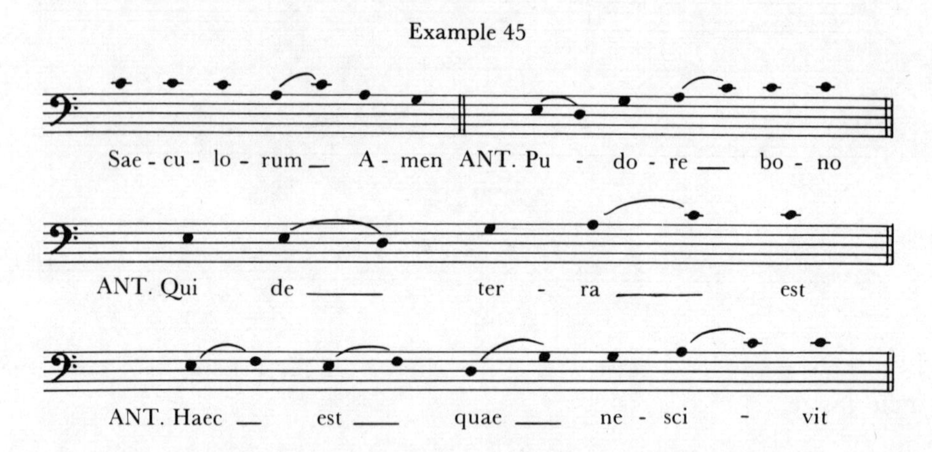

The first *differentia* of the third tone fits antiphons ascending by a whole tone from the lichanos meson [G] and, after repeating that note, proceeding a semiditone higher. [173] Examples of this [are]:

Example 46

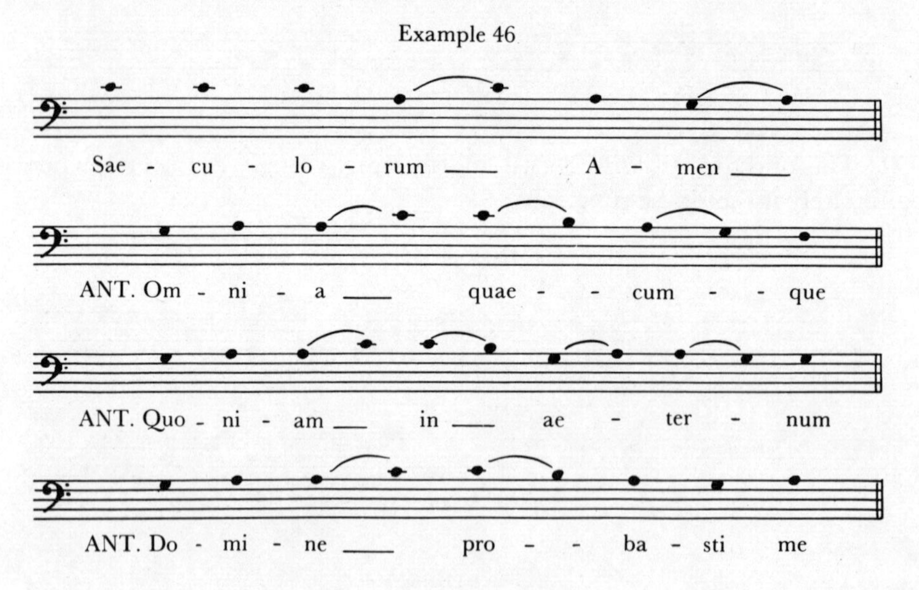

The second *differentia* fits antiphons beginning on the lichanos meson [G], some of which rise a whole tone and a semiditone; some, [after] rising a whole tone, descend a whole tone and rise a whole tone and a semiditone; and some rise a diatessaron and, immediately [after] descending a semitone and a whole tone, rise either by a whole tone and a semiditone or else by a diatessaron. Examples of these [are]:

Example 47

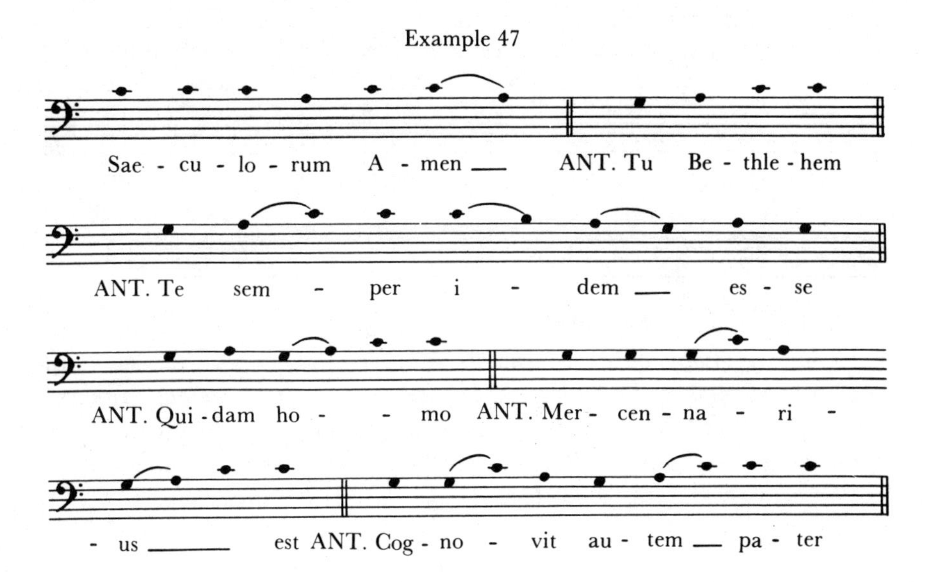

[174] The third *differentia* fits antiphons beginning on the lichanos meson [G] and leaping up a diatessaron, but not those that, like the ones just discussed, fall to the lichanos meson [G] or rise from it. Examples are:

Example 48

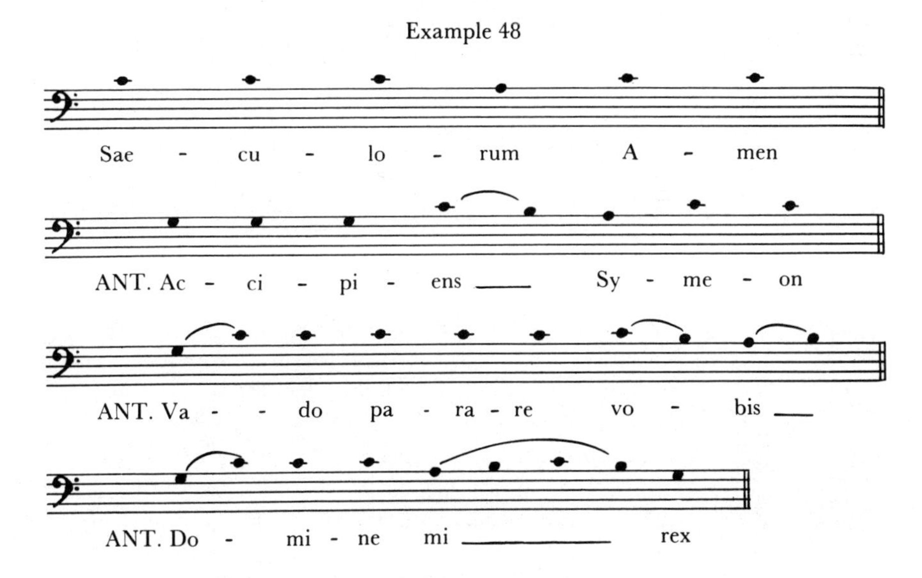

The fourth *differentia* fits antiphons beginning on the trite diezeugmenon [c] such as these:

Example 49

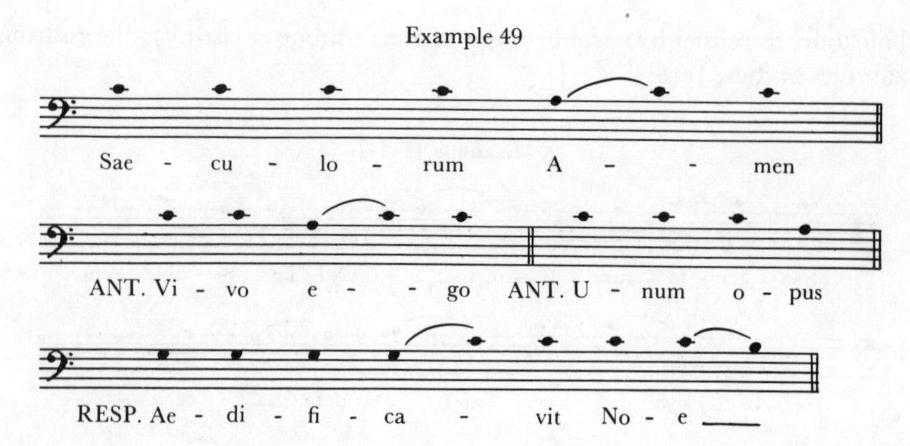

This respond [*Aedificavit*] is customarily sung wrongly in two places, namely, at the words *odoratus* and *crescite*; this is easily corrected if *odoratus* is begun on the lichanos meson [G] [175] and *crescite* on the mese [a]. But if this respond is begun irregularly on the parhypate hypaton [C], the customary practice at *odoratus* is not to be followed. *Crescite*, however, needs the said emendation.

Example 50

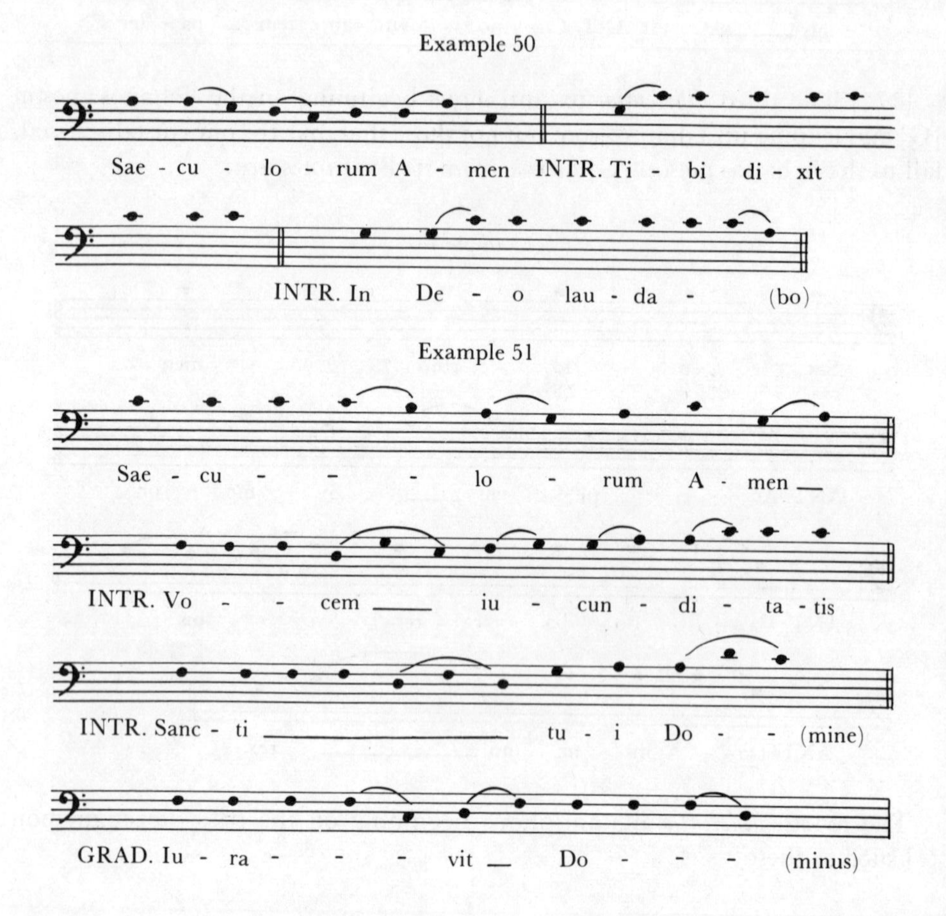

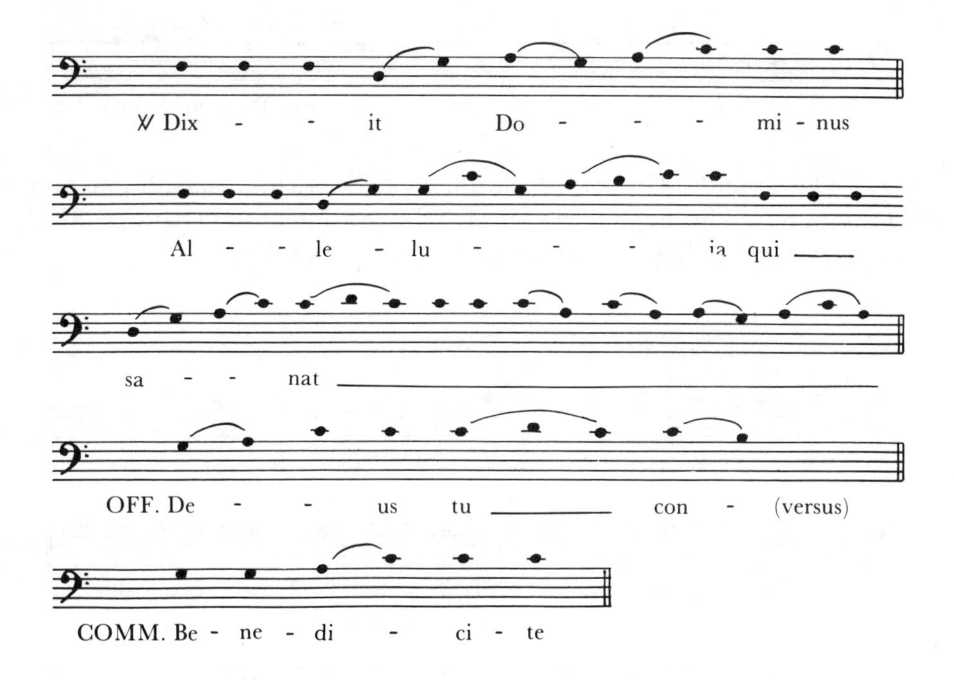

The fourth tone

[176] The special *saeculorum amen* for the fourth mode applies to antiphons that descend a whole tone from the hypate meson [E] and at once return, such as these:

Example 52

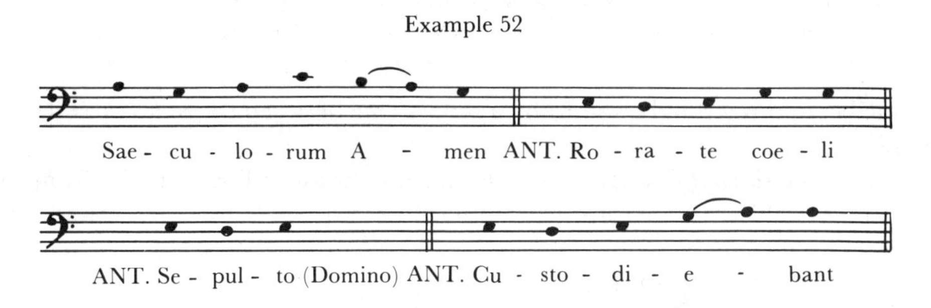

This tone has six *differentiae*, of which the first fits antiphons that begin on the lichanos hypaton [D] and rise a whole tone, a semiditone, and a whole tone, even if a unison intervenes. Examples of this:

Example 53

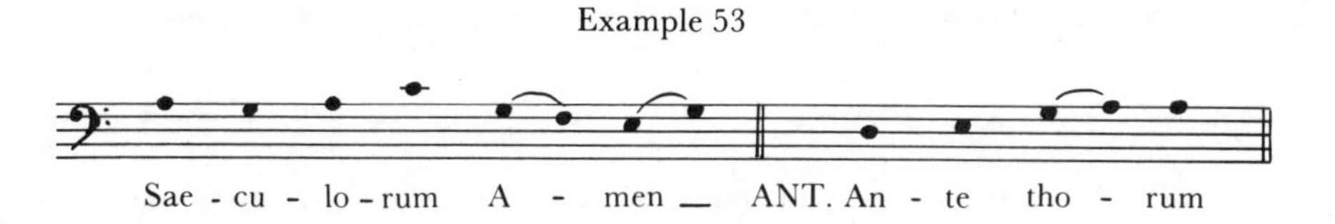

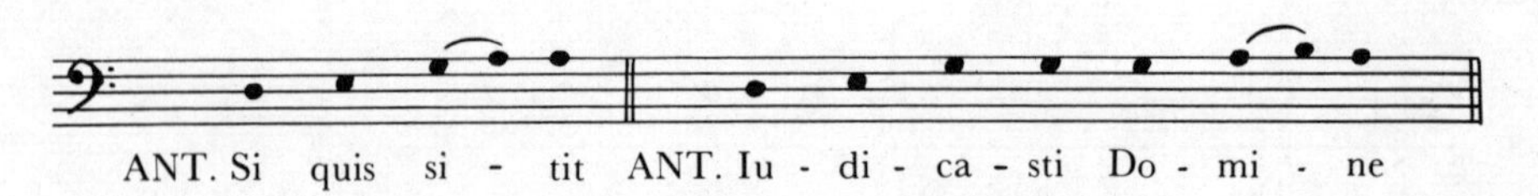

[177] The second *differentia* fits antiphons that ascend a semiditone and a whole tone from the hypate meson [E]. It also fits antiphons ascending a whole tone from the lichanos meson [G]. Examples of this:

Example 54

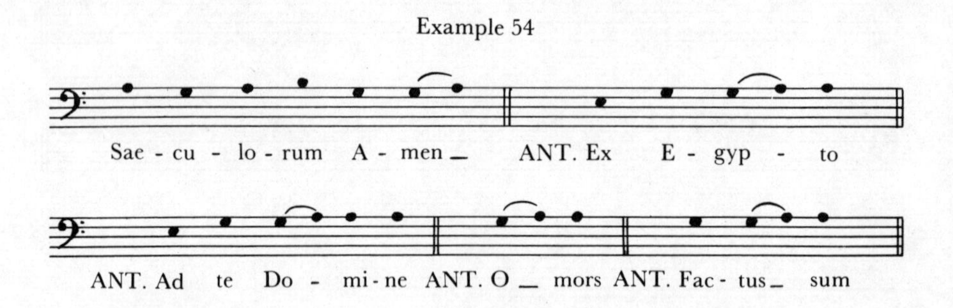

With this same *differentia* one also finds one antiphon beginning on the mese [a], namely this:

Example 55

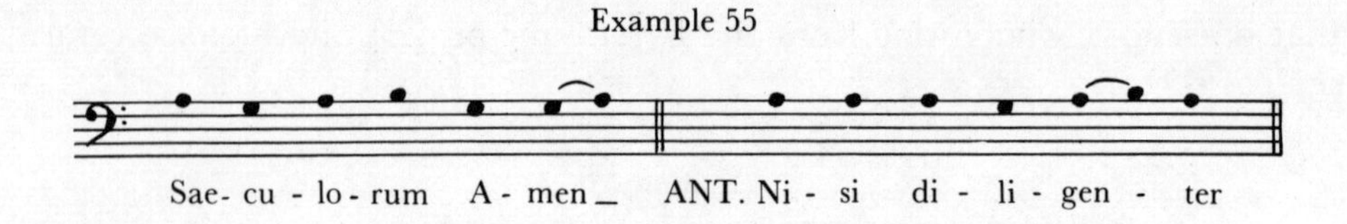

Some begin this wrongly, sounding a semiditone between the first two syllables of *diligenter*.

[178] The third *differentia* fits certain antiphons ascending stepwise from the hypate meson [E] to the third note, others that fall a semitone or a semiditone from the parhypate meson [F], and still others beginning on the lichanos meson [G]. Examples of these:

Example 56

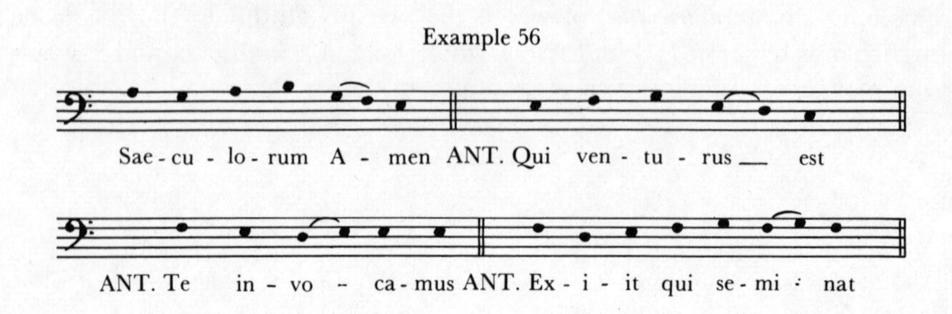

Some stupid men end the preceding antiphon on the parhypate hypaton [C].

Example 57

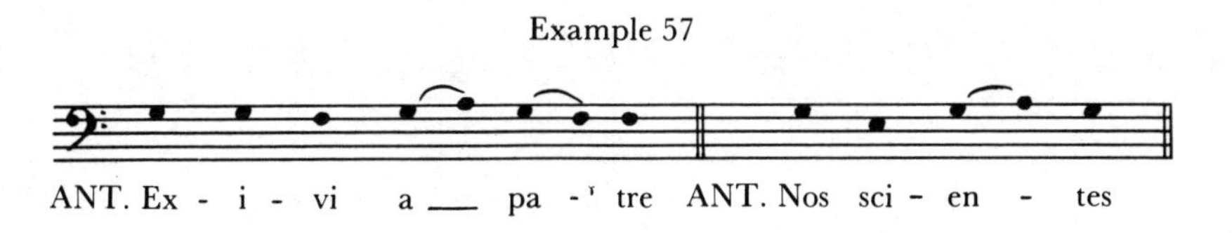

The fourth *differentia* fits antiphons rising a semiditone—or even ascending stepwise—from the lichanos hypaton [D], as is seen in these examples:

Example 58

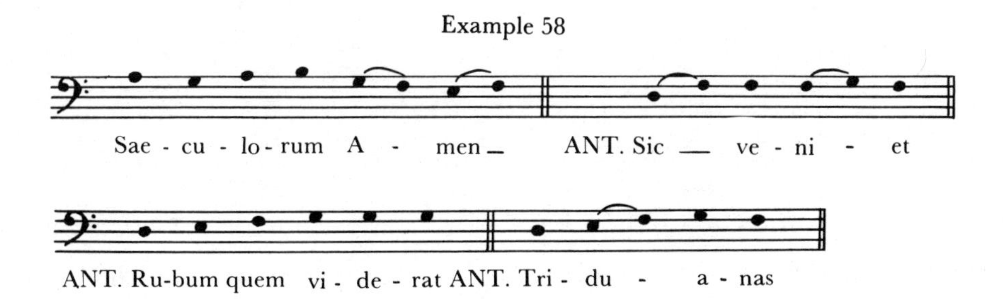

[179] The fifth *differentia* fits antiphons beginning on the parhypate hypaton [C], like these:

Example 59

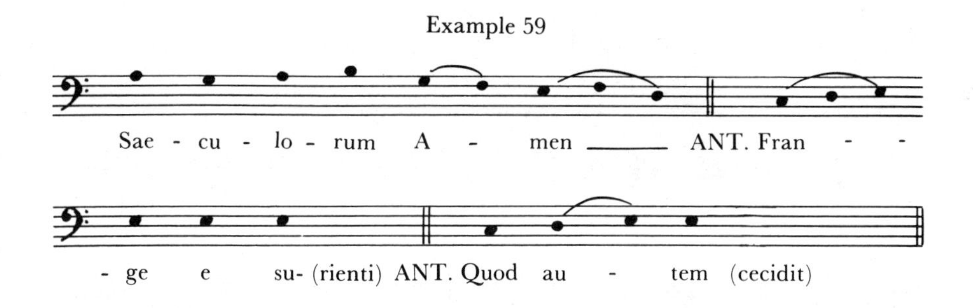

[Also] *Iste cognovit.*

[180] The sixth *differentia* fits ferial antiphons beginning on the hypate meson [E], like these:

Example 60

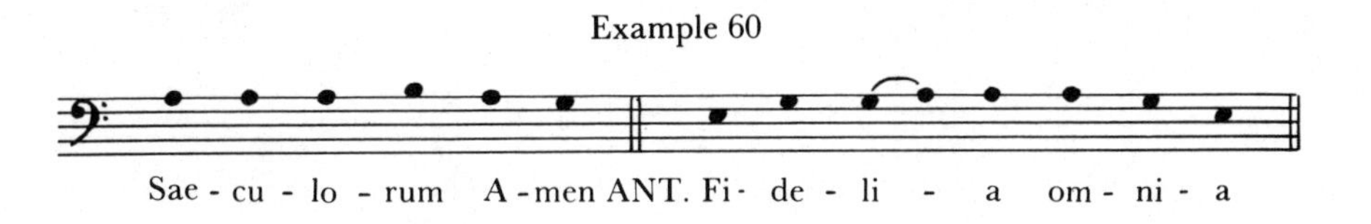

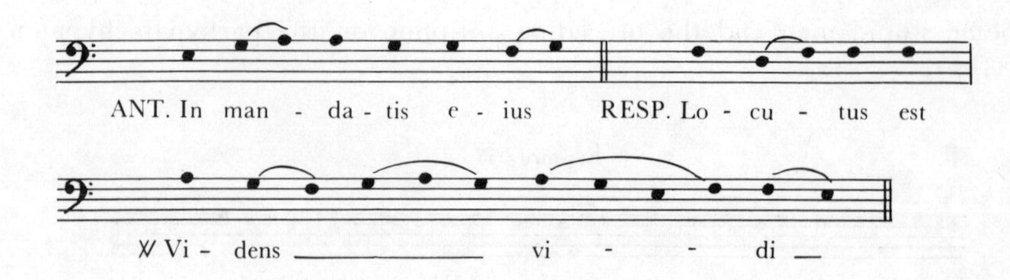

Example 61

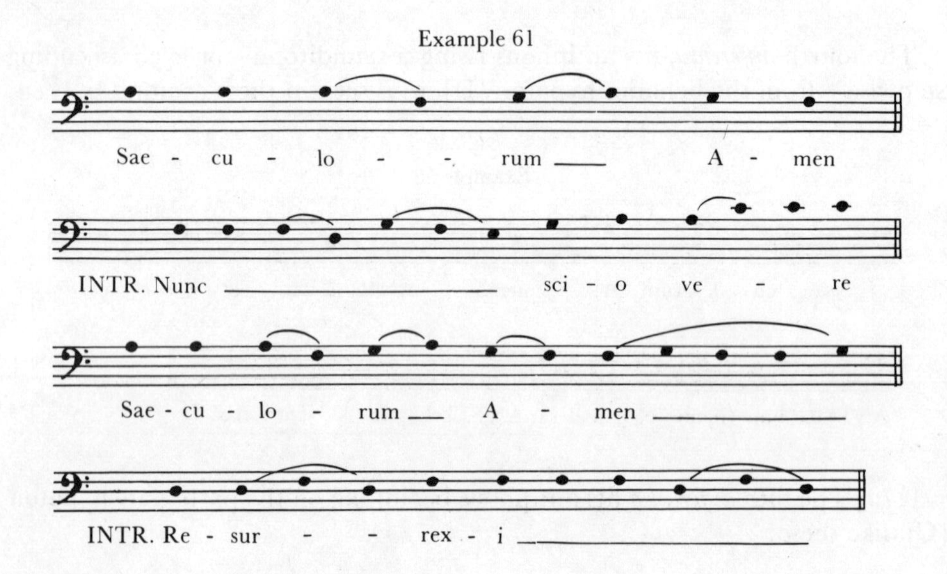

[181] I have not found a regular gradual of this tone.

Example 62

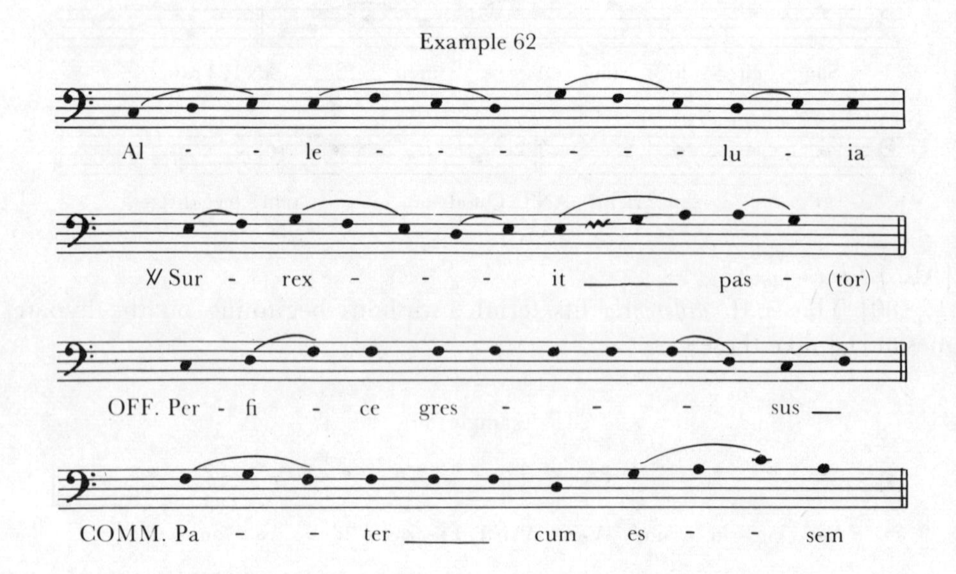

Chapter 26

The fifth tone

[182] The principal *saeculorum amen* of the fifth tone heads antiphons beginning on the mese [a] or the trite diezeugmenon [c], as do these:

Example 63

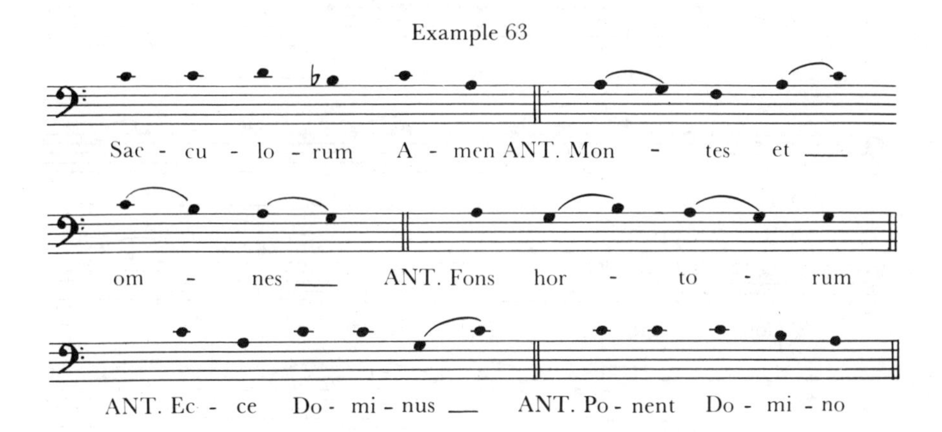

[183] This tone has a single *differentia*, which fits antiphons beginning on the parhypate meson [F], like these:

Example 64

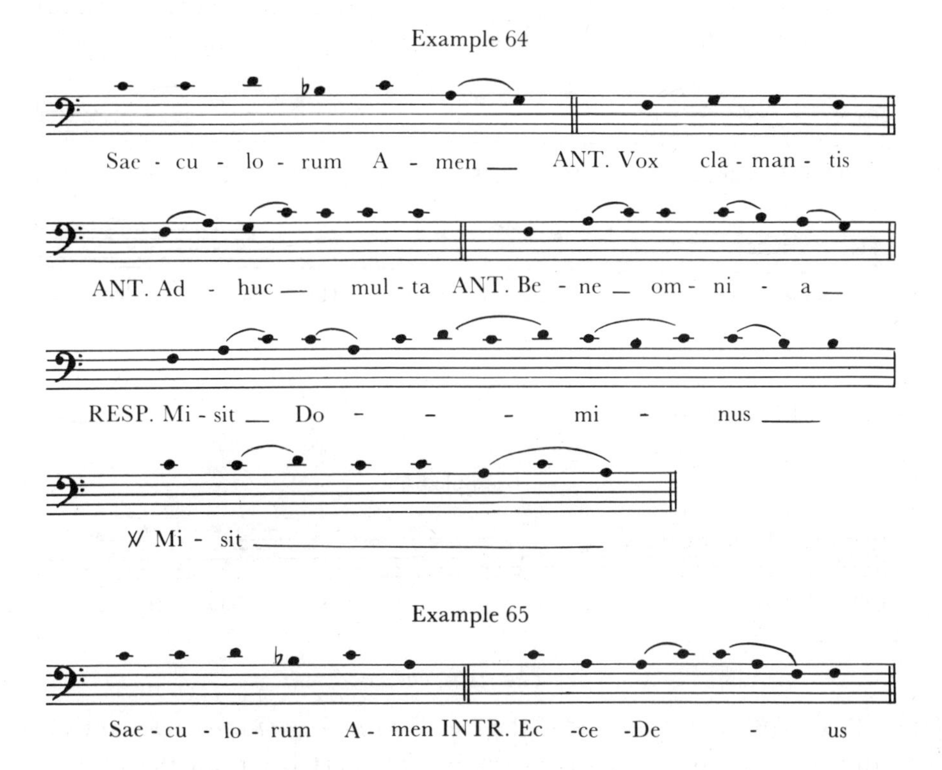

Example 66

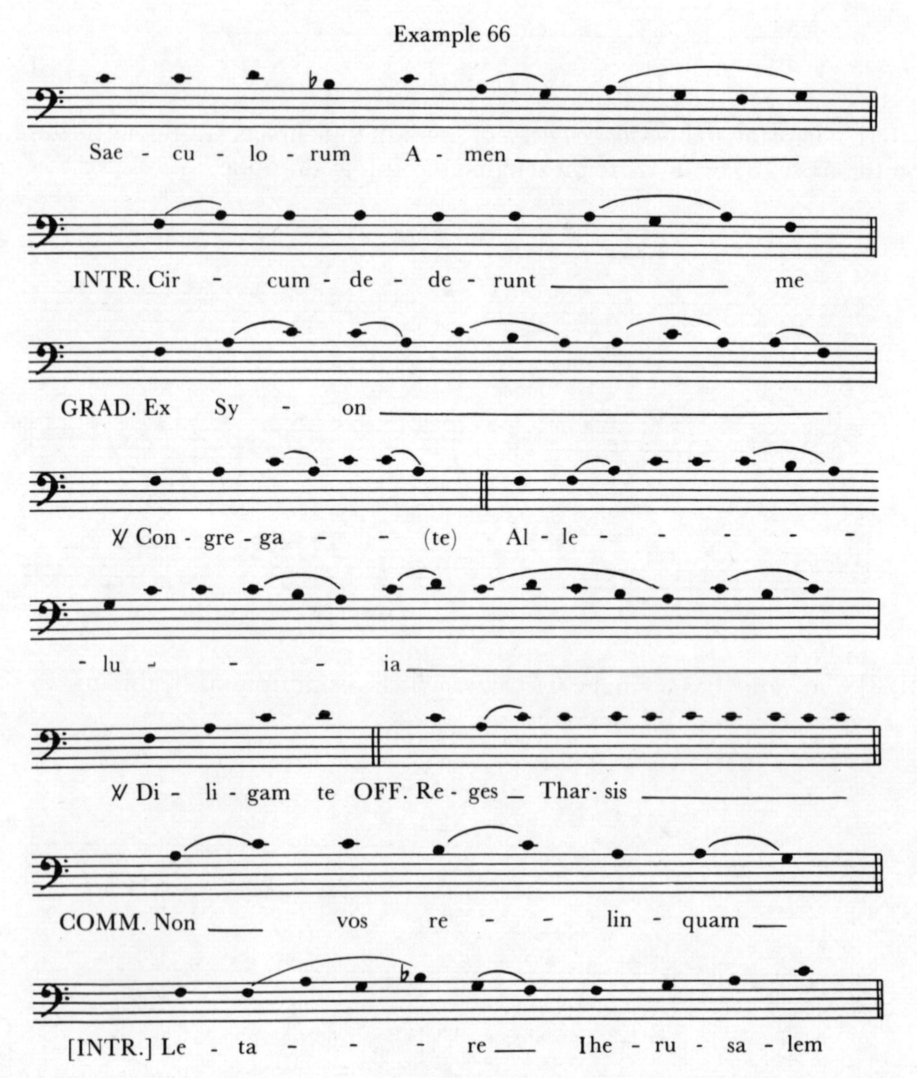

[184] The following communion, *Ultimo festivitatis die*, also is of the same tone, and its beginning according to usage sounds less bad. Therefore whoever wishes may begin it thus:

Example 67

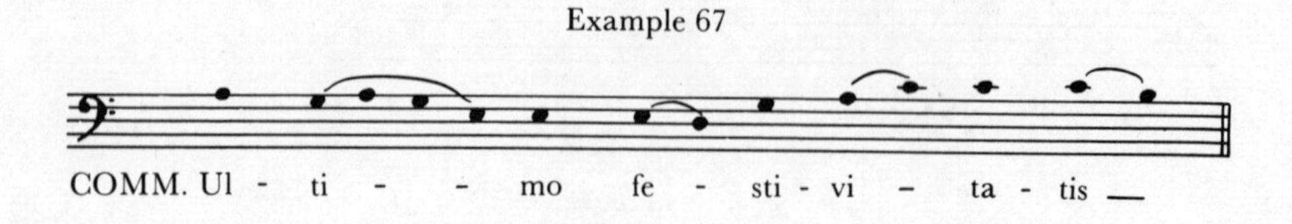

The sixth tone

[185] The sixth mode prefaces with [*regit sub*] one *saeculorum amen* antiphons with diverse beginnings, of which the greater part begin on the parhypate

meson [F], a few on the lichanos hypaton [D], and one on the lichanos meson [G]. Examples of this:

Example 68

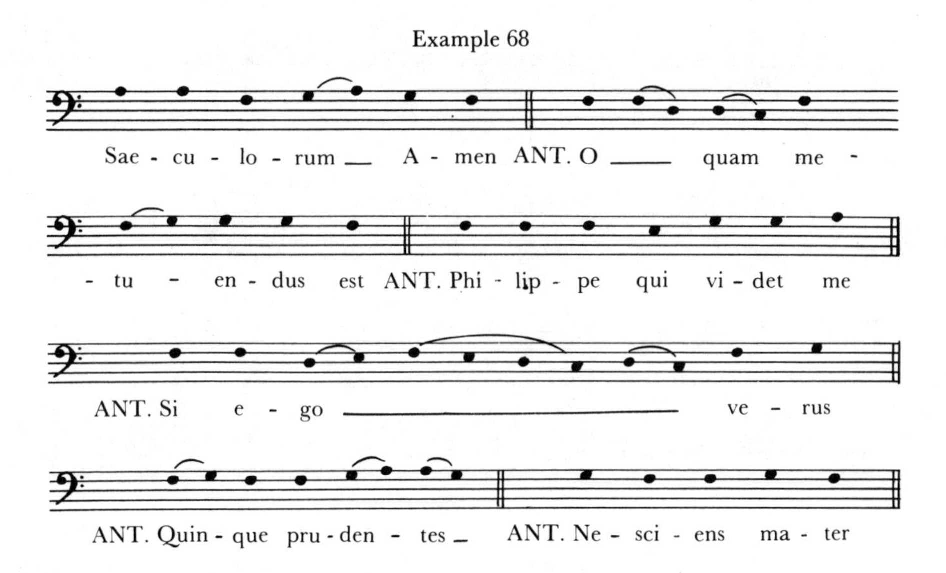

[186] Some, however, begin this last antiphon on its final with a unison. This mode has one *differentia*, as follows:

Example 69

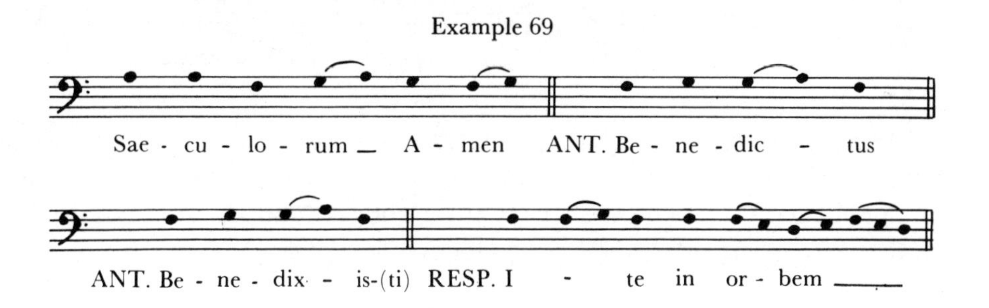

[187] We have placed this respond [*Ite in orbem*] among the kindred notes, since it is defective in its natural range.

Example 70

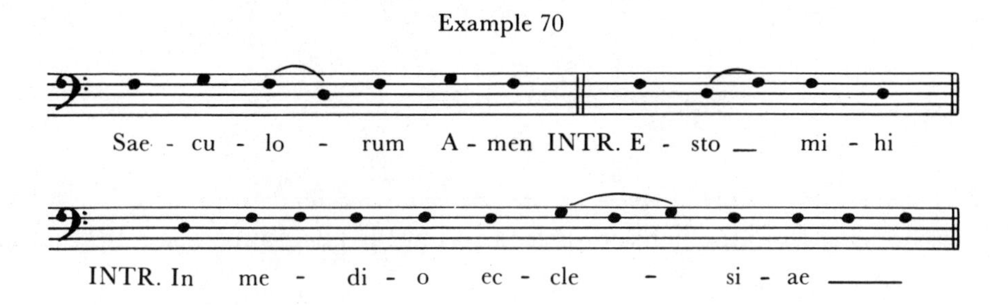

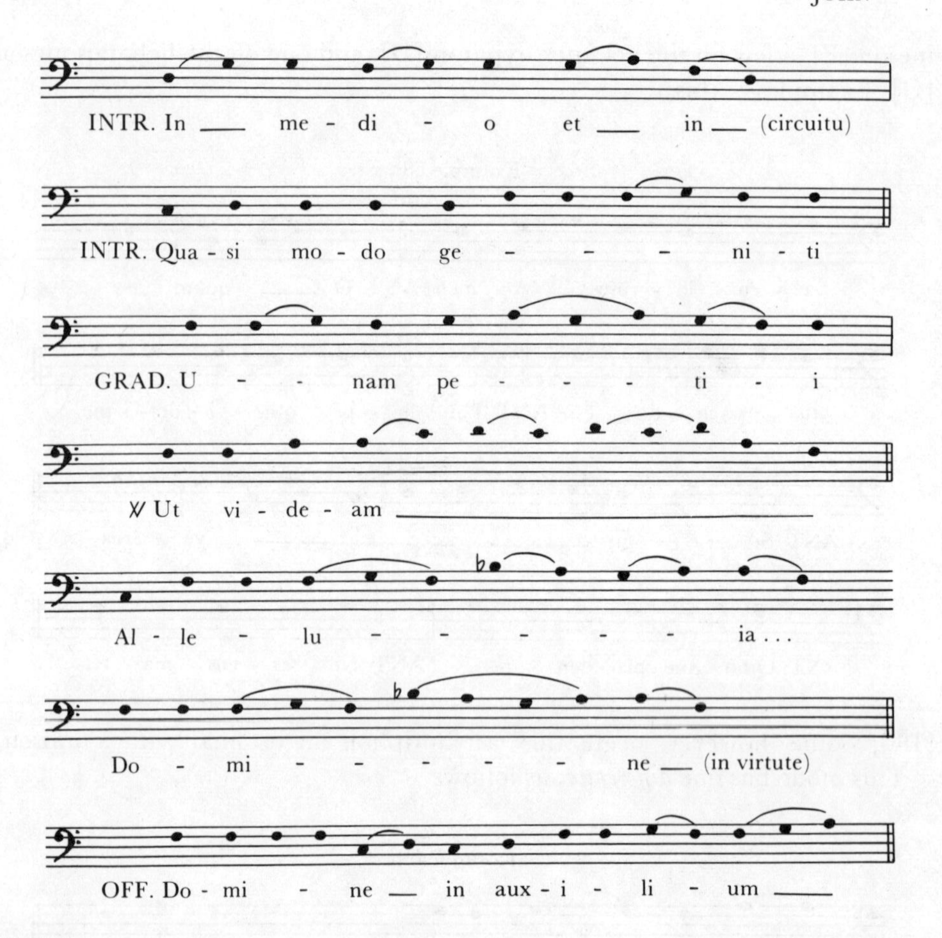

[188] Most performers end this offertory [*Domine in auxilium*] badly by avoiding the "heptaphone" that is at the end because it seems to them ill-sounding. Therefore in certain books they repeat at the end what occurs at the beginning of it. Likewise in the offertory *Dominus deus in*.

Example 71

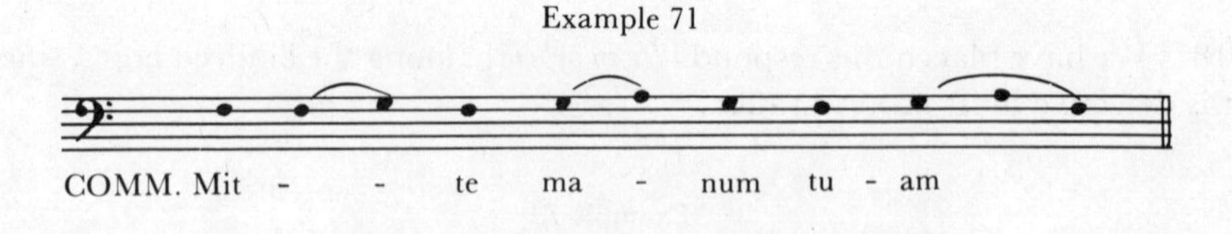

Chapter 27

The seventh tone

[189] The chief *saeculorum amen* of the seventh tone leads into antiphons that rise a diapente from the lichanos meson [G] at the beginning, a few beginning

on the trite diezeugmenon [c], and one on the mese [a]. Examples of these [are]:

Example 72

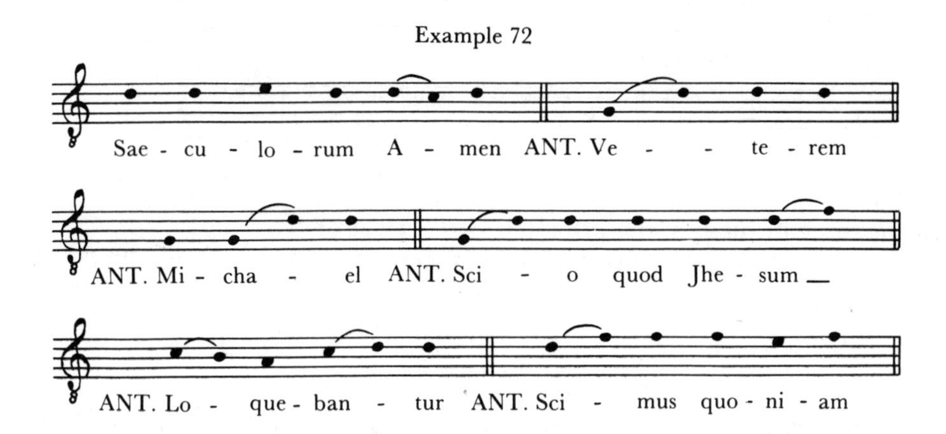

But some begin this last antiphon by a diapente from the final [G].

Example 73

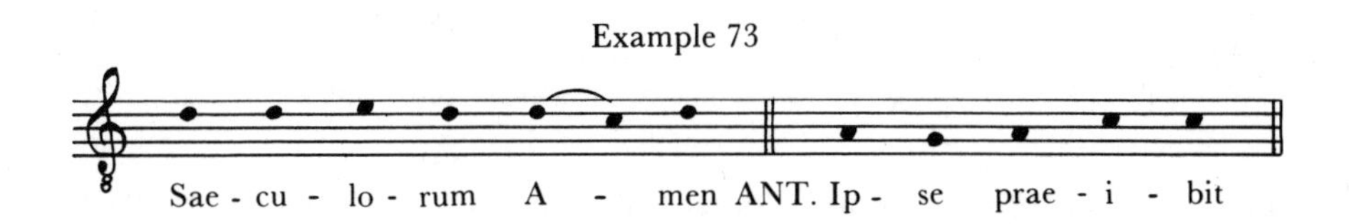

[190] This tone has four *differentiae*, the first of which fits antiphons rising from the lichanos meson [G] by a whole tone or a ditone or by a diatessaron, like these:

Example 74

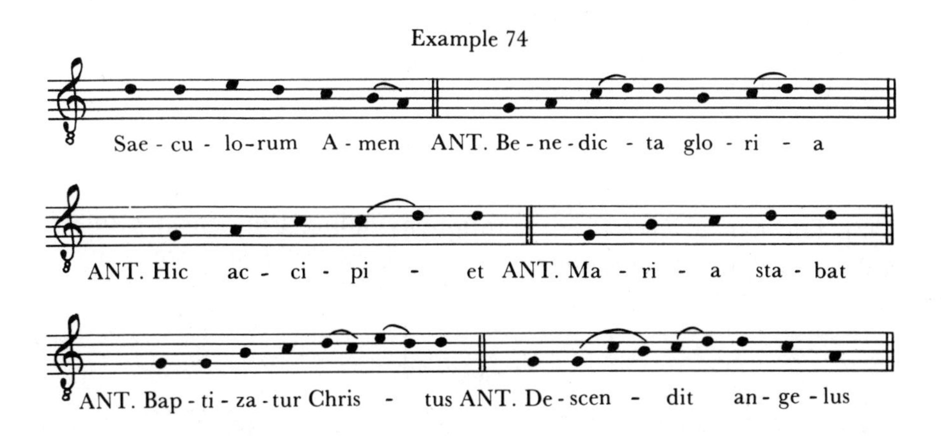

[191] Some assign to this *differentia* antiphons of this type:

Example 75

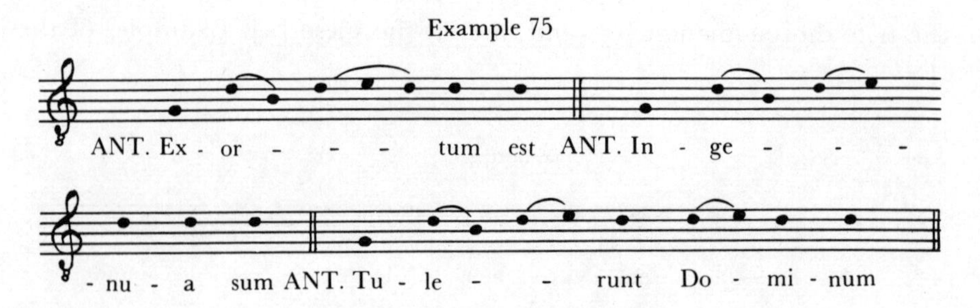

But many join these to the principal *saeculorum amen.*

The second *differentia* fits antiphons ascending stepwise from the *paramese* [♮], like these:

Example 76

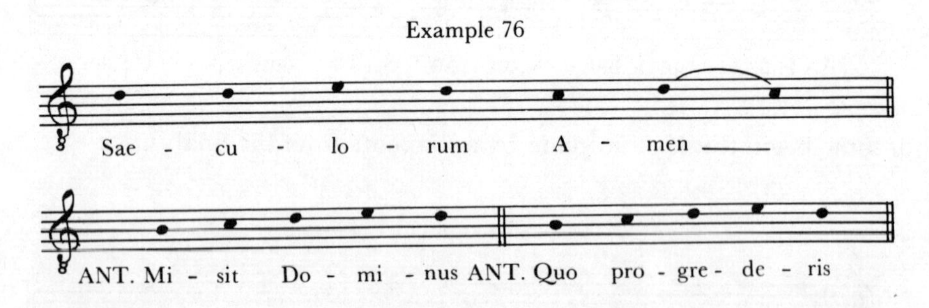

The third *differentia* fits antiphons falling a ditone from the *paramese* [♮], even if first there is a unison, like these:

Example 77

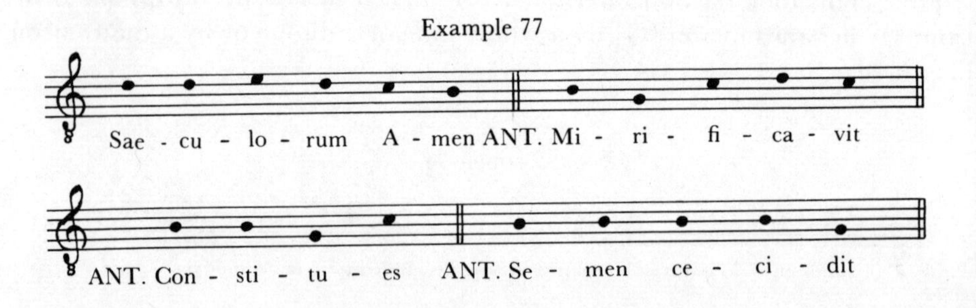

[192] The fourth *differentia* fits antiphons falling from the paranete diezeugmenon [d] by a semiditone or stepwise, even if first there is a unison, like these:

Example 78

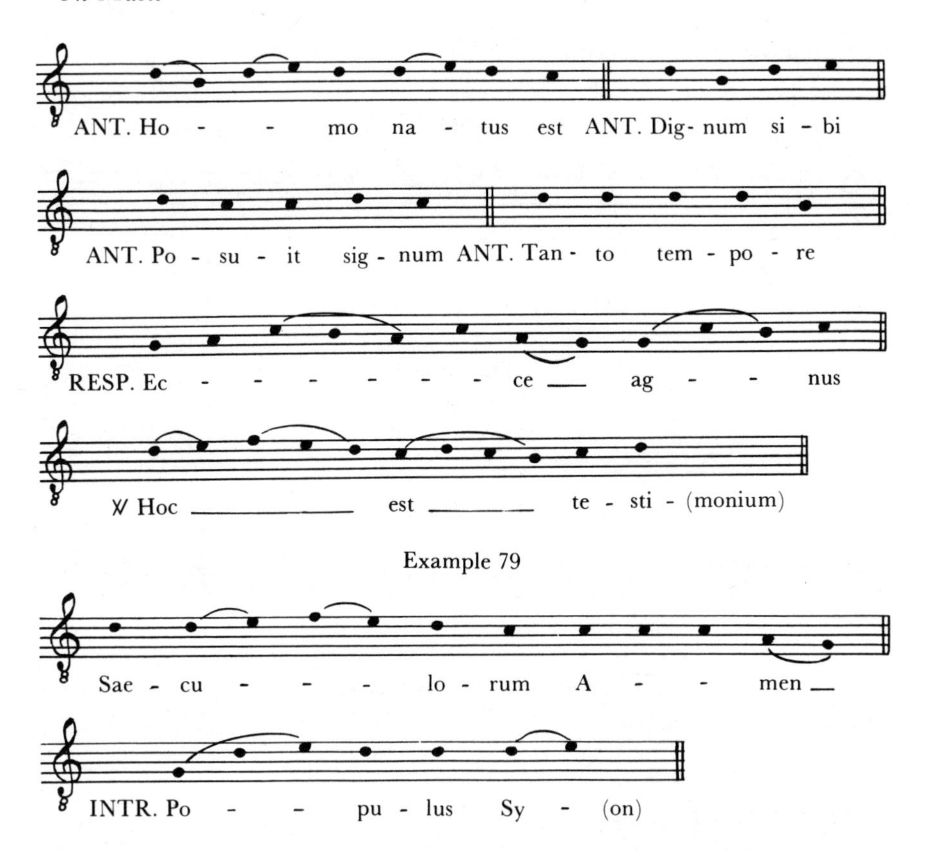

Example 79

[193] Begin *ad*[1] on the nete diezeugmenon [e], and lower *gentes* to G.

Example 80

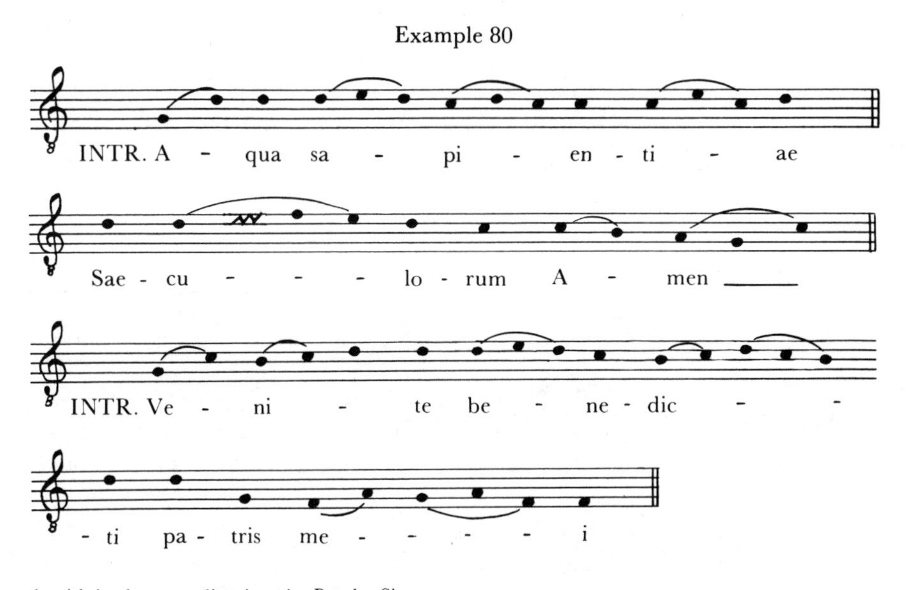

1. *Ad*: in the preceding introit, *Populus Sion*.

[194] But some do not trouble with this *differentia*.

Example 81

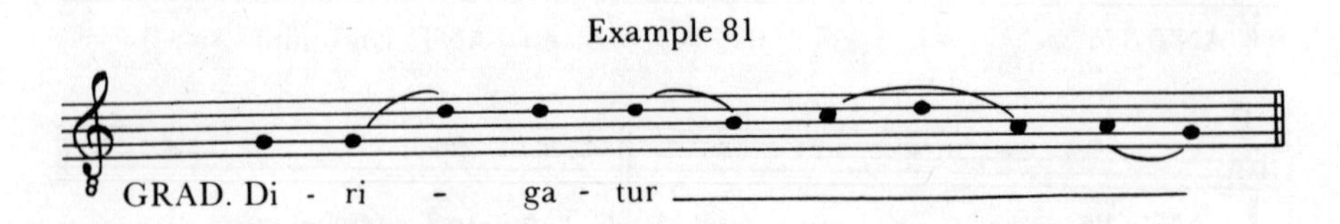

The verse of the preceding gradual should begin thus:

Example 82

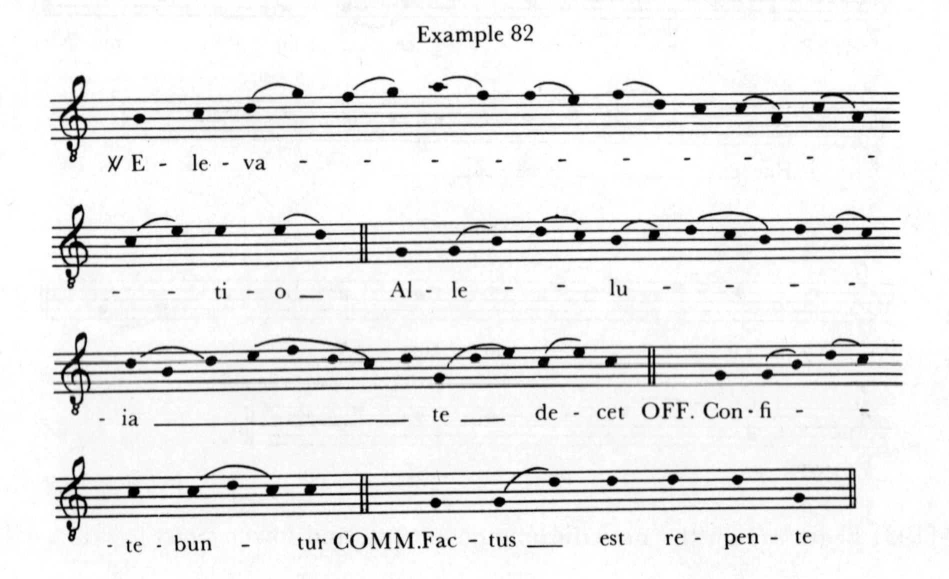

The eighth tone

[195] The principal *saeculorum amen* of the eighth mode leads into antiphons beginning, some on the lichanos meson [G], some on the *mese* [a], some on the lichanos hypaton [D], and some lower, like these:

Example 83

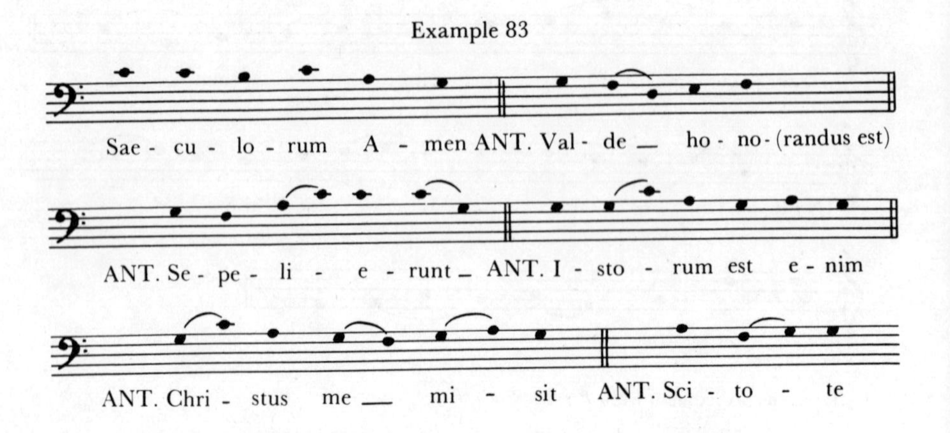

[197] This tone has three *differentiae*. The first fits antiphons beginning on the parhypate meson [F] or on the next note below it, like these:

Example 84

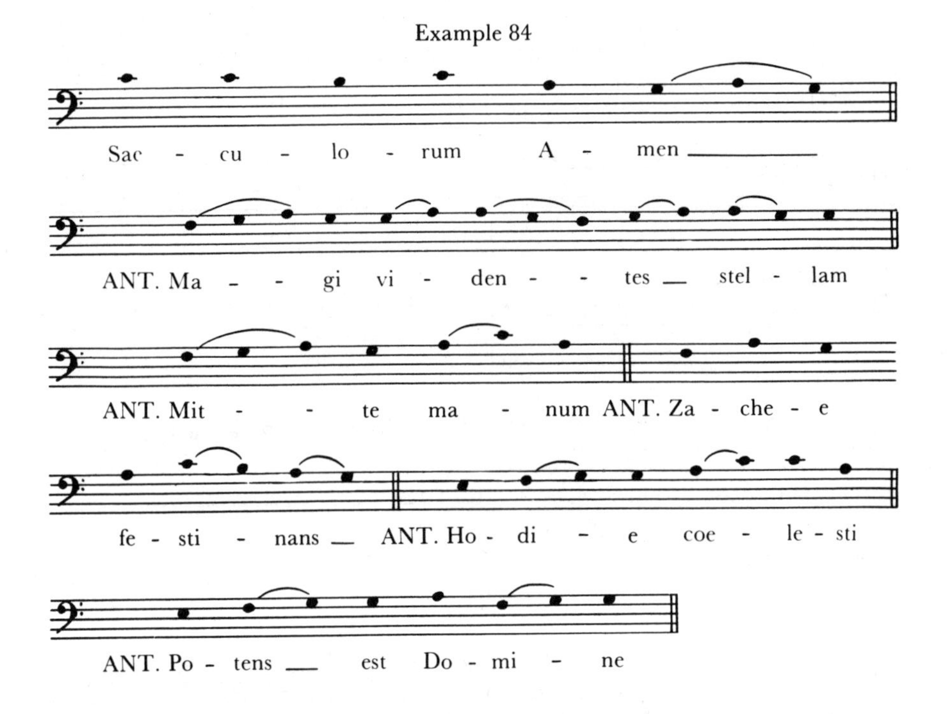

[198] The second *differentia* fits antiphons falling a semiditone from the trite diezeugmenon [c]. Examples [are]:

Example 85

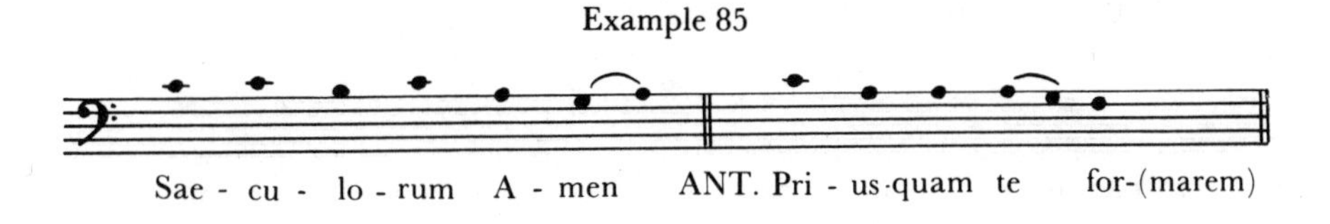

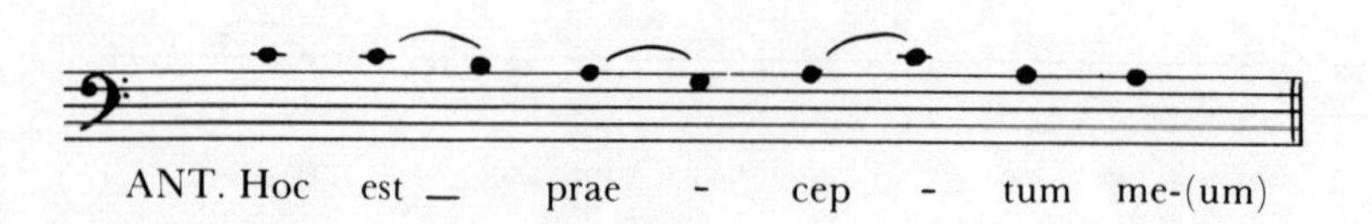

The third *differentia* fits antiphons beginning with a unison on the trite diezeugmenon [c], then ascending a whole tone, like these:

Example 86

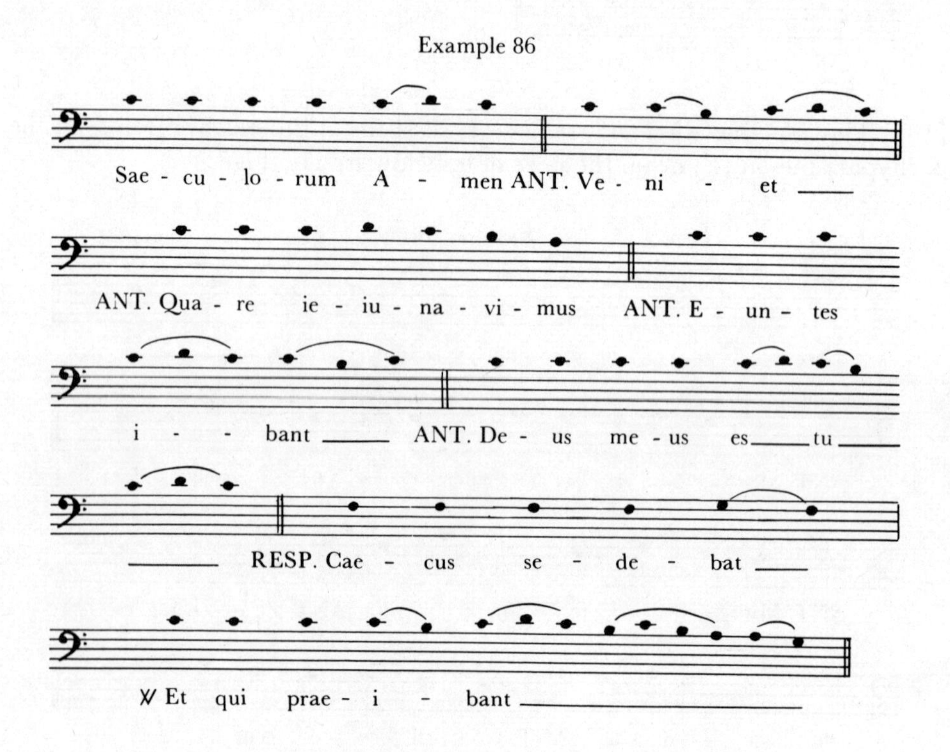

Example 87

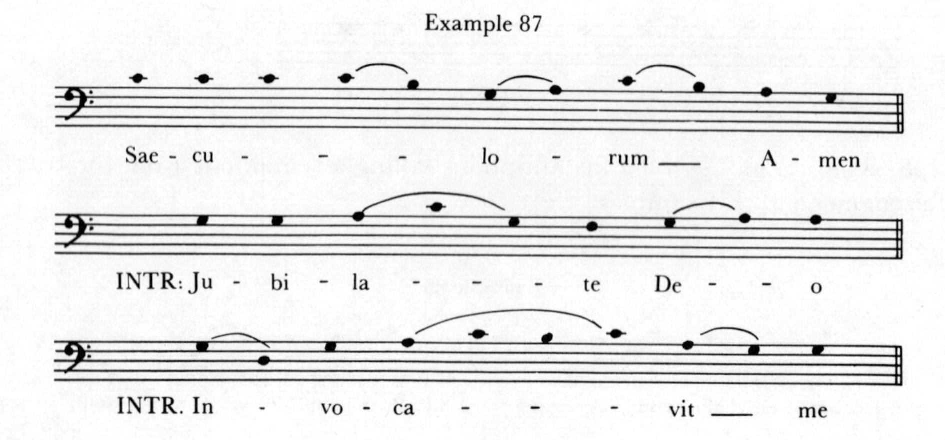

Example 88

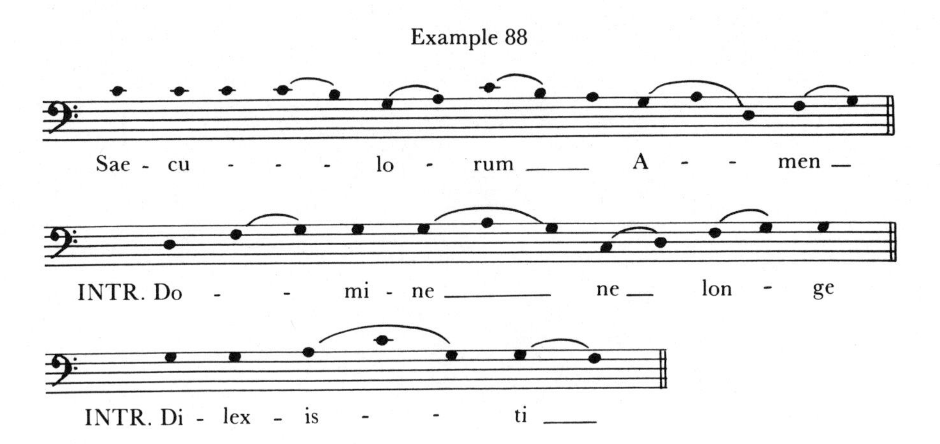

[199] The verse should begin on G, thus:[2]

Example 89

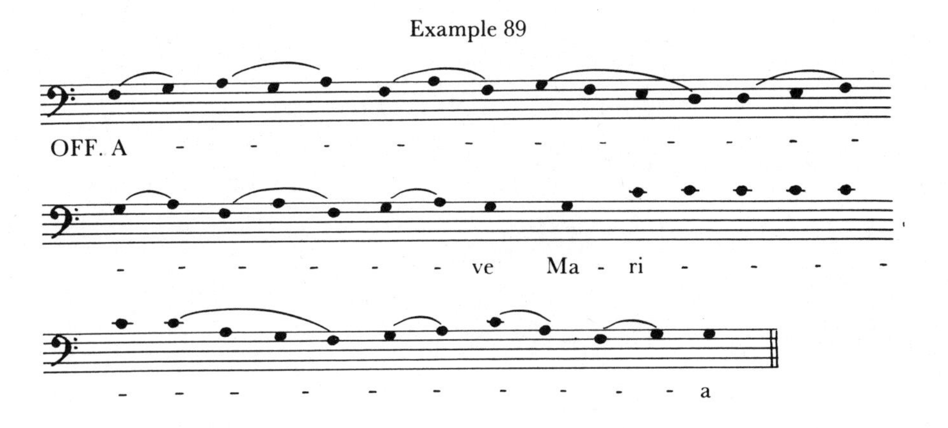

[200] Sing *fructus* thus:

Example 90

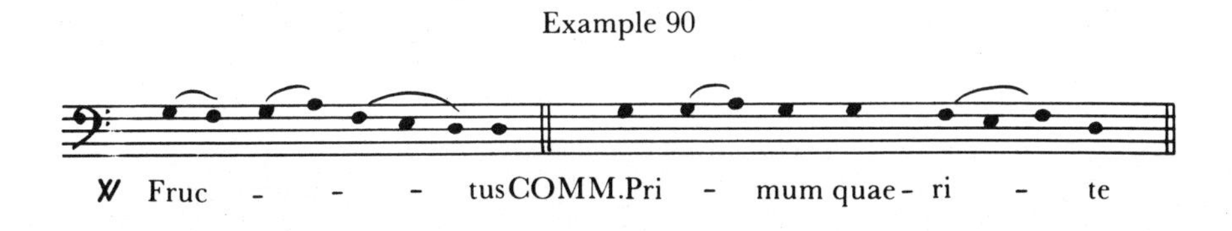

[FINIS]

2. John's musical illustration of the beginning of the verse (that of the preceding introit *Dilexisti*) has not survived.

CORRECTIONS AND EMENDATIONS FOR THE TEXT OF JOHANNIS AFFLIGEMENSIS, *DE MUSICA CUM TONARIO*

Ed. Jos. Smits van Waesberghe (Rome: American Institute of Musicology, 1950), *CSM* 1.

Page	*Unit or Line*	*For*	*Read*
7	21	Ahsburnham	Ashburnham
29	23	dissimles	dissimiles
45	9	Martiale	Martiano
54	5	MHCA	MÉCH
55	8	ΑΠΟ ΘΥ ΜΥCΩ	’ΑΠÒ ΤΟΥ̃ ΜΩ̃CΘΑΙ
	8*n*	Isid. Etym. III, 19.	Isid. Etym. III, xv, 1.
	11*n*	2 Cor.	1 Cor.
66	11	anergumenos	energumenos
68	4	erduditis	eruditis
70	19*n*	Breviarum	Breviarium
73	8	*see footnote 2 on p. 114*	
73	11	D C ♮ C A	D C B C A
79	22	clausura	clausula
82–83	8	sexti. In	sexti, in
83	10	secundi.	secundi,
85	⟨7⟩	Glo-	Glo-
86	⟨5⟩	in-tra ve-runt	in-tra-ve-runt
93	27	unam quam infra	unam notam infra
96	42	cursum, duorum	cursum duorum
118	15	*ὁμοιώπτωτον*	*ὁμοιόπτωτον*
133	4–5	subrepant. Hae	subrepant, hae
136	20	-ge- *3 puncta before* -runt	-ge- *14 puncta before* -runt *as in LU* (#780) 579
	ap. crit.	-ge- *under column headed* CDC	-ge- *under column headed* DCFC
137	24	meson, incipientes in	meson incipientes, in
139	15	commionem	communionem
140	53	Hic sit	Hic fit

147	27	etc., et	etc. Et
	27–28	asscribunt. Secundum	asscribunt, secundum
148	33	habens	*habens*
163	1–2	parhypatemeson. et	parhypatemeson et
164	6	emittuntur:	emittuntur.
166	15	*Disregard the errata-note on p. 207 of* CSM *1*	*The C-clefs as they are, on the top line, are right*
167	26	patet mi	*pater mi*
169	31	ultra	*ultra*
170	Stave 3	OFF. LAETENTUR	RESP. LAETENTUR
172	Stave 2	DF F	DG G
		Quae ne-	Quae ne-
173	7	levate deponuntur	levatae [tono] deponuntur
174	10–11	exilientes. Sed	exilientes, sed
	11	surgentes ut	surgentes,– ut
176	21	Sex habent	Sex habet
178	33	semiditonum, surgentes,	semiditonum surgentes,
180	Stave 3	ANT. VIDENS	℣. VIDENS
182	Stave 2	*Clef of* ANT. ECCE DOMINUS *on top line*	*Clef of* ANT. ECCE DOMINUS *on next-to-top line*
186	Stave 1	ANT. BENEDIXIT	ANT. BENEDIXISTI
	Stave 2	ANT. ITE IN ORBEM	RESP. ITE IN ORBEM
188	17	libris in	libris [quod] in
189	1	Septmi	Septimi
193	16	A.D.	*Ad*
		Gentes	*Gentes*
194	Stave 2	*C-clef on top line*	*C-clef on next-to-top line*
196	Stave 3	GRAD. CHRISTUS ME MISIT	ANT. CHRISTUS ME MISIT
	Stave 4	*First C-clef on top line*	*First C-clef on next-to-top line*
199	ap. crit.	*Precede* first *line by 31*	*Precede* second *line by 30*

To these, add the corrections listed on p. 173 of Smits van Waesberghe's edition of *Expositiones in Micrologum Guidonis Aretini* (Amsterdam, 1957) and on p. 153 of *Musica Disciplina* 6 (1952), Fasc. 4.

APPENDIX

Cited chants available only in Zagreb, University Library, MS MR 8

Transcribed by Alejandro E. Planchart

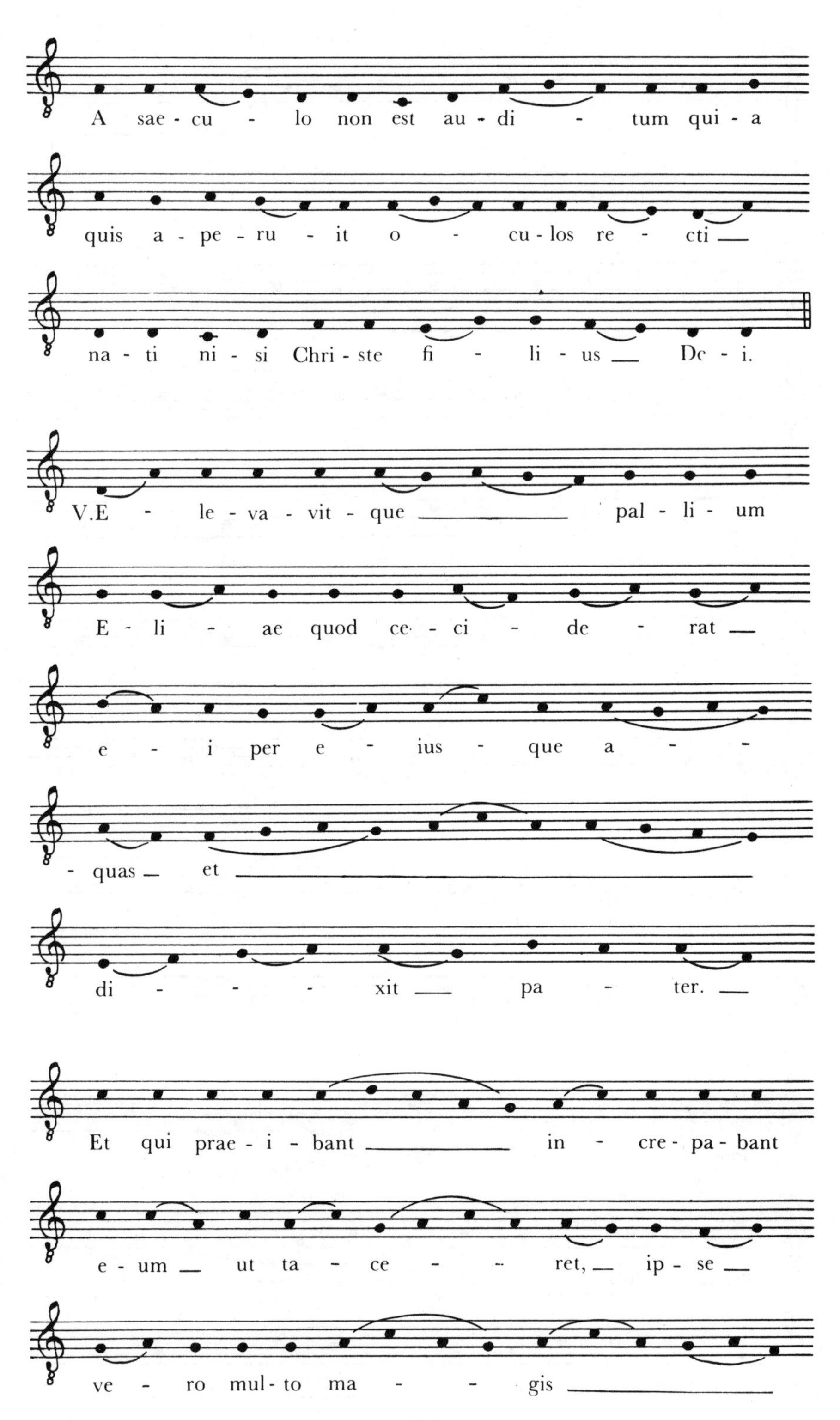
A sae - cu - lo non est au - di - tum qui - a
quis a - pe - ru - it o - cu - los re - cti
na - ti ni - si Chri - ste fi - li - us De - i.
V.E - le - va - vit - que pal - li - um
E - li - ae quod ce - ci - de - rat
e - i per e - ius - que a -
- quas et
di - - - xit pa - ter.
Et qui prae - i - bant in - cre - pa - bant
e - um ut ta - ce - - ret, ip - se
ve - ro mul - to ma - - gis

cla - ma - - - - - - - bat.
Hic qui ad - ve - - - -
- - nit al - - - mo scit
no - men e - ius ni - si
ip - - - - se so - - -
- lus vo - ca - tur
ver - bum Do - - mi - ni
et ha - - bes ve - stem
prae - cla - - - - ram et om - - -
- nes cho - - - ri an -
- ge - lo - - - rum in

al - - bis se - - cu - -
- un - - tur il - - lum.
Ho - mo qui - - dam fe - cit ce - nam
ma - gnam et vo - ca - vit mul - tos et
mis - - - sit ser - vum su - um ho - ra
ce - nae di - ce - re in - vi - ta - tis ut
ve - - ni - rent qui - a om - ni - a
pa - ra - ta sunt al - le - - lu - ia.
Lu - pus ra - pit et di - sper -
- sit o - ves, mer - cen - na - ri - -
- us fu - git, qui - - a mer - cen - na -

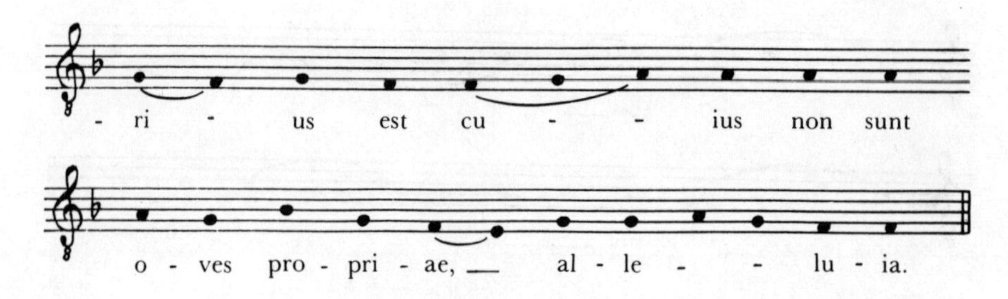
-ri - us est cu - - ius non sunt
o - ves pro - pri - ae, al - le - - lu - ia.

O glo - ri - o - sum lu - men om -
-ni - um ec - cle - - si - a - rum,
so - - - le splen - di di - us;
o ve - - re a - po - sto -
-li - cum si - dus al - - tis - si - mum,
san - cte Pau - le, qui ae - ter - ni re - gis
splen - do - rem te - ne - bris gen - ti - um
in - fu - di - sti, qui in ter - ra
po - - si - tus cae - lo - rum

se - cre - ta pe - ti - - sti, et quae
non li - cet ho - mi - - - ni
lo - qui per vi - di - sti;
il - luc sup - pli - ces tu - os post
hu - ius car - nis ter - - mi - - -
- num per - du - ce - re di - - -
- gna - - re quos
fe - ci - sti ve - ri - ta - tis lu - men
a - - - - - - - - - -
- - - - - - - - gno - sce - re.

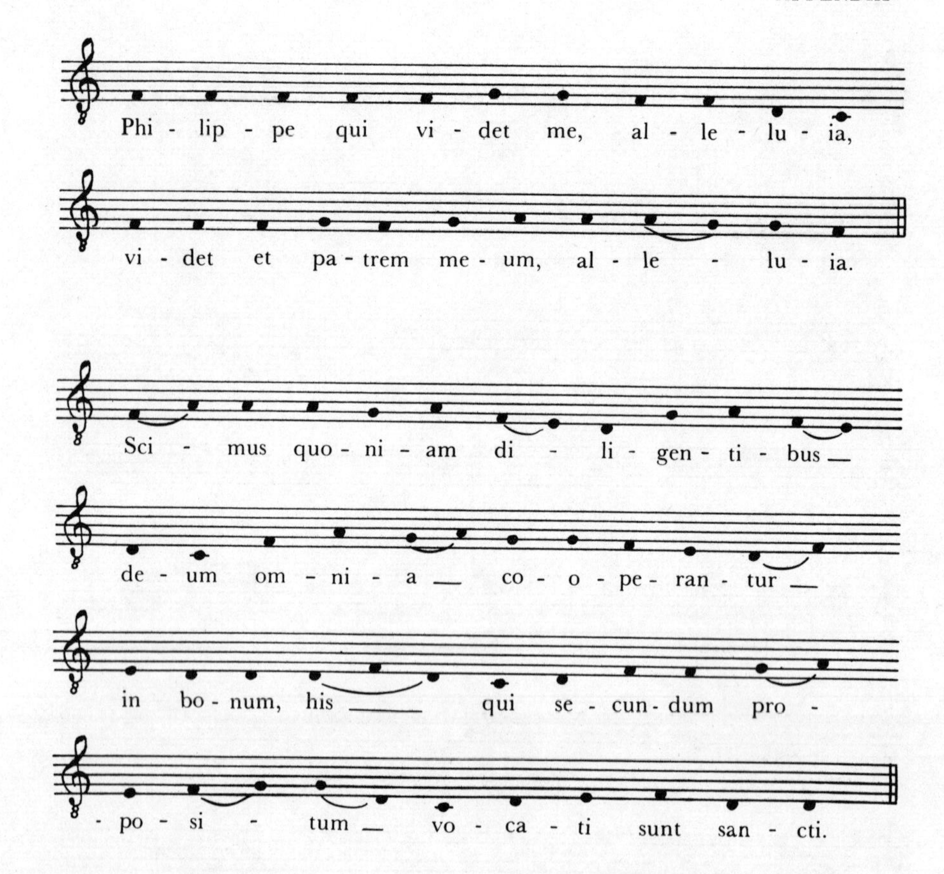
Phi - lip - pe qui vi - det me, al - le - lu - ia,
vi - det et pa - trem me - um, al - le - lu - ia.
Sci - mus quo - ni - am di - li - gen - ti - bus
de - um om - ni - a co - o - pe - ran - tur
in bo - num, his qui se - cun - dum pro -
- po - si - tum vo - ca - ti sunt san - cti.

Index of Chants

by Alejandro Enrique Planchart

In the following index, the chants cited in the treatises of Hucbald, Guido, and John are arranged alphabetically by first words of the text. The items of information given after the text incipit are the following: category of chant (antiphon, gradual, etc.; if the author did not mention the category this information is in brackets); the letter H, G, or J for Hucbald, Guido, or John; the page number in this book; a list of printed sources for the chant indicated in alphabetical order of sigla (a list of sigla and the sources they represent is found in the Abbreviations, p. xiii above); and the page in the source.

Whenever Guido or John cited a fragment from within a piece, both the incipit of the fragment and that of the whole piece are indexed.

Some of the cited chants do not survive in the available sources except in staffless, unheightened neumes. These sources (*CA* and *HA*) are listed in the index only for such pieces. A few melodies are available only in the manuscript *ZA*. Since it is not accessible to most readers, these melodies have been transcribed in the Appendix.

KEY TO INDEX

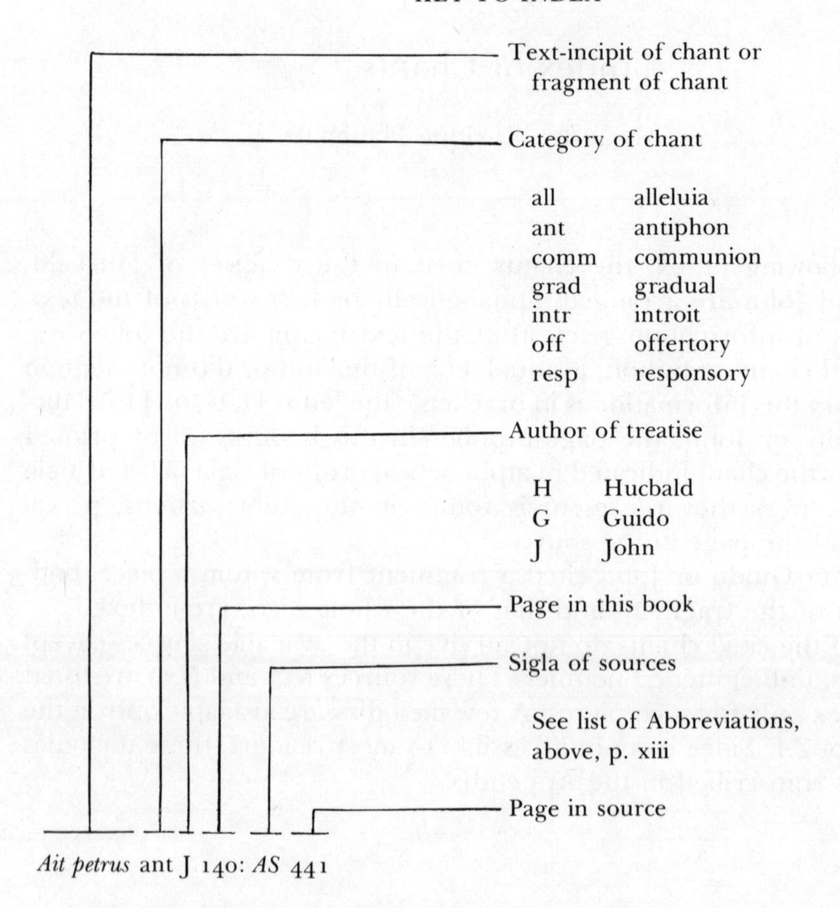
Text-incipit of chant or fragment of chant
Category of chant
all alleluia
ant antiphon
comm communion
grad gradual
intr introit
off offertory
resp responsory
Author of treatise
H Hucbald
G Guido
J John
Page in this book
Sigla of sources
See list of Abbreviations, above, p. xiii
Page in source
Ait petrus ant J 140: *AS* 441

General Index